1

The Circlet of Isis

Scroll of Isis, in holy rest,

Offers earthly delights to Tuat's blessed.

Fresh air from heaven and justice given

To Horus enemy, blood-lust driven

Bear you the Circlet of Isis

Possess the glory of the Divine Enchantress

Look to the Scorpion for healing wind

For plague and drought from Circlet rescind.

A Trial of Faith shall you pass with heart

For if you fail, shall ye be torn apart

By Shannon Nichola Stoner

Illustrated by Karl A. Nordman

2

3

The Circlet of Isis

By: Shannon Nichola Stoner

Prologue

"Azi, your mother loves you," Khepret said as her body began to quake. The child struggled against the man holding him in his arms. His cheeks flooded with tears at the sight of his condemned mother. The five-year-old boy watched with horror as General Gahiji raised his sword above his head. Azizi reached out his hands in a futile attempt to reach his doomed mother.

"OSIRIS, WATCH OVER MY SON!" Khepret raised her head, screaming into the sky.

"Mother!" Azizi screeched. The little boy watched in horror as the General's sword decapitated his mother. Azizi sobbed as her head and body fell to the ground. He watched in terror as mother's body fell motionless onto the sand. Azizi's heart raced as he struggled in the arms of his captor. His shrill, ear-piercing wail rose over the crowd as he kicked his legs.

"Mother! Mother!" the orphan boy's cries of terror echoed through the merchant quarter.

I opened my eyes as the old nightmare returned. My heart raced like a horse charging into battle. My sweat-covered hands tremble from this recurring nightmare which has haunted me for ten years. I leaned over and dipped my hand into the rising, cool Nile waters. My head rested on the ground as I caught my breath. In the night air, my black cloak wrapped tightly around me, shielding me from the cold, the predators of the night, and blending me into the shadows where I belong.

Akhet has arrived causing the Nile to overflow its banks. Thoth's Eye reflects off the rippling water's surface. The cool night air brushes across my cheeks as the reeds sway gently in the night. I will need to retreat to the oasis shortly as the water creeps closer to my feet.

I sat beside the bank and reached into my small cowhide bag. The bread I had borrowed from the baker was a good dinner. I must tell Nen-Re that he needs to purchase a better lock for his bakery. It is no longer a challenge to break into his establishment. A thief needs a good challenge to keep his skills sharp. Skills not practiced are as useless as a feather on the field of battle.

Inside the palace of Heliopolis, hovering over the city like a hungry jackal over a carcass, resides Pharaoh Runihura. He hunts for me, sending the *Nuu* and his soldiers. The rival gang of street thieves, the Seth Thief Clan, under the leadership of Kaphiri Seti, fight us for territory and dominance. Kaphiri wants to own all of *Iunu*'s riches and wants to eliminate my clan as competition. Kaphiri's clan has repeatedly denied responsibility. Who is stealing from Nen-Re?

Broken from my own thoughts, I hear someone approaching. With my lip curled in a snarl, I tense. My hand slowly rested upon the hilt of my dagger. My breath stalled as I waited to see if friend or foe would emerge from the reeds.

A figure emerged from the reeds and stepped into the moonlight. My body relaxed as I saw Kahla standing before me. With relief, my hand released the dagger's hilt. She sat beside me and caressed my cheek with a happy smile.

"It makes my heart happy to see you, Azizi Keket." Kahla leaned over and pressed her lips lightly against my own. My arms embraced her, pulling her closer towards me. I could smell her sweet fragrance which she applied to her skin before wandering the night.

Her fingers drifted down my shoulders to my bare chest as I kissed her honey-sweet lips.

She leaned her head against my right shoulder as we looked across the Nile. I moved my black cape to cover her beside me. "The reflection of the moon is beautiful tonight."

"Yes. It is pleasant."

Kahla and I have been friends since we were children. When she was not serving wine to the guests of the bordello, we would play together in the streets. When mother was finished servicing Mbizi's clients, she would take me home and we would return the next morning as the sun rose in the distance.

Mbizi's greed and ignorance know no boundaries. Mbizi has offered women too young to serve an old man's desires. I cannot help but be protective of the women there because I had seen what my mother had to endure. They were compassionate towards me, caring for me in during my mother's absence. I will not have another woman suffer as my mother. The people I love, the people I protect, are the people of the streets. Orphans, prostitutes, criminals, all are my companions.

Kahla nodded beside me. "Maysun told me that you would be here waiting for me."

I must remember to reward Maysun for delivering my message. "I will soon be returning home to the oasis. I wanted to see you and Amsi before I left."

The son of a Noble landowner, Amsi had visited me among the reeds before I fell asleep. He promised to keep watch until I drifted into slumber. Among those of Noble Blood, only Amsi Al-Sakhir Ibn Kaemwaset has earned my trust and fidelity. Besides Kahla, I would have none other stand beside me.

"Did you see one of Kaphiri's gang follow you here?"

Kahla shook her head. "Nobody followed me." She looked up at the twinkling stars with me. Her grip tightened as she held my hand. "Did you know the Pharaoh has raised the bounty on your head?"

I took Kahla's hand and kissed her palm. "The King of Thieves will not submit to the will of the Pharaoh," I said caressing her cheek tenderly, "I will send his *Ka* to the Hall of Judgment, even if it means I must die in the process."

"The Commoners need their king. If the King of Thieves is destroyed, they will have lost all hope of ending Sekhmet's reign." Kahla looked down sadly. I watched as a tear glistened in the light of the moon. "Thief Clan Osiris will be devastated without their leader. The children of the street will suffer." Kahla paused. "I don't know what I would do without you, either."

"Fear not," I whispered in her ear and kissed her cheek. Kahla turned her head to me and I pressed my lips against hers once again. Kahla wrapped her arms around me and laid on the ground. I rested on my arm as my free hand touched her warm, sweetly-scented skin.

"Mbizi would charge you for this," Kahla moaned as I lightly glided my hands against her breast.

I tilted my head to the side to watch her smile and look up at me. "How much will you charge me?" I asked as I leaned over to kiss her naked breast.

Kahla caressed my cheek as I looked down at her. "How could I charge the King of Thieves?" she asked with a smile. I kissed her warm skin as the reeds of the Nile banks swayed lightly around us. Kahla's breathing was slow and relaxed as she let my hands brush across her skin lightly. I hesitantly pulled away from kissing her neck. We entwined our fingers together as I looked into her eyes.

My brown eyes stared into hers, unable to look away. She smiled up at me and caressed my cheek. "You could have any girl in *Iunu*," she whispered to me. "Why do you choose to spend your time with me?"

"I don't want any girl in *Iunu*," I said, caressing her cheek tenderly. "I only want you."

I want you to know before you die, that you are to blame for your mother's death.

As I closed my eyes tightly, that voice filled with hatred and loathing returned to my mind. Pharaoh Runihura will pay for his cruelty. I will not allow Runihura to lay as much as a finger on Kahla.

Kahla's hands cupped my face. My eyes shot open as I saw her looking up at me with concern. "What is it, my king?"

I sat beside her. How can I tell Kahla that I still remember that morning in the merchant square? I do not wish to burden Kahla with my thoughts about my parents. Darwishi's Lesson #48 on becoming a Master Thief: Keep your weapon close in hand and your emotions at arm's length. Stone hearts weep no tears. "I have a headache."

Kahla sat beside me and put her arm around my shoulders. "You were thinking of her again, weren't you?"

"What makes you ask that?"

"I see your heart. I know you are bothered, my hero."

"I am no hero, Kahla," I said, lowering my head.

"You have saved your friend from the pharaoh's gallows. Following the pharaoh into the desert and into the battle at Edfû was very brave. You could have been killed."

"I am trying to prevent further bloodshed at the hands of the pharaoh."

A jackal howled in the night nearby, attracting our attention. I stood and offered my hand to Kahla with a smile. "Shall we return to *Iunu*?"

Kahla stood up hesitantly. Our parting foretold her return to her nightly errand of servicing men on the streets. However, that would not be the case tonight. I reached into my small money purse and removed one hundred dînars. Kahla looked up at me with surprise.

"Where did you find that money?"

"I accidentally brushed against some well-dressed snob in the market today. I pretended to be a blind man." I placed the money in Kahla's open hand. "Now you need not service tonight." I closed Kahla's fingers over the money and kissed her forehead.

Kahla smiled at me and shook her head. "I can't accept this money."

"Take it. You know how I hate seeing men put their hands on you." I reached up and touched her face lightly. "I love you."

Kahla stepped close to me and pressed her lips against mine. I wrapped my arms around her, the cape covering both of us under the moon's light. "I love you, too, Aziz."

"Allow me to return you to your home."

Kahla took my hand as we cautiously left the safety of the reeds. A light emanated from behind the slave home of the Al-Sakhir plantation. We cautiously crept towards the entrance to Heliopolis. Our ears were ready to hear the sound of approaching footsteps or soldier's armor. We passed between the two colossi statues of Runihura and stepped into the streets of *Iunu*, the merchant quarter. Torches illuminated the road as some people wandered the night.

Under my cloak, I kept a tight grip on the Pharaoh's golden dagger. "Keep an eye out for Ini-Herit. I know he wanders this road."

A dark figure stood at the end of the road and disappeared into an alley. My eyes narrowed. I could not recognize the figure from this distance. It had better not be Ini-Herit trespassing on my territory! Khalil plays with his toys around these streets at night when soldiers are scarce. The nine-year-old boy would be no match for Ini-Herit, a member of the rival Seth Thief Clan, who was almost twice his age and preferred to beat his victims to death.

"Did you see that, Kahla?"

"I didn't see anything."

A scream resonated from the alley ahead. I raced ahead, breaking my grip on Kahla's hand. It has to be Ini-Herit! Marid is also as tall as that figure! Marid's skills with a dagger were similar to my own. Kahla ran behind me as I readied myself for combat.

"Azizi, be careful!" Kahla screamed behind me.

I turned into the alley and found Khalil and Saqr on the ground. The dark figure I had seen in the streets was hovering over them, holding a loaf of bread. "Stop!"

"He took our bread!" Saqr cried.

"We saw him breaking into Nen-Re's shop!" Khalil exclaimed, clasping his ball to his chest.

I pulled the golden dagger from under my cloak and stood beside the boys, growling angrily at the thief. "You leave my friends alone! Who are you? Speak!" The figure remained silent and kept hidden in the shadows. "Speak, I command you! Are you a member of Kaphiri's gang? Talk to me!"

The figure dashed down the alley quickly. You are not going to get away with this that easy, stranger! He ran fast; His speed was faster than anyone in my gang. What manner of demon is he that his feet can carry him as fast as the wind? My prey turned the corner sharply. I ran from the alley and looked down the street. My chest rose and fell quickly. The thief had disappeared.

Saqr and Khalil ran beside me looking around for signs of the figure. Saqr wrapped his arms around my waist, shivering.

"Did he say anything to you, Saqr?"

Saqr shook his head. "He didn't say anything to either of us! We found him breaking into Nen-Re's bakery. He chased us when he saw us watching him."

"His words sounded strange, Azizi. He couldn't talk like we do," Khalil said.

You may have escaped me this time, stranger. The next time our paths cross, you may not be so lucky.

I

The Circlet of Isis

Pharaoh Runihura's metallic, golden eyes gazed into the distance with a menacing glare. *Where are you, Blessed Servant of Osiris? I will find you, boy. You cannot escape me. You cannot run forever!* The Pharaoh crossed his arms, determined to find his young nemesis. "I'll find him, Janani. When I find all of the ancient relics I need to become immortal, he will cower at my feet like a dog. He knows that

I already possess the Eye of Horus." Pharaoh Runihura turned his head towards Janani with an evil grin. His metal eyes blinked, the clinking sound making her swallow nervously. "Tell me, Janani, do they make me look powerful?"

Janani took a deep breath and took a step backward from her master. "Yes, my lord," she responded timidly.

Runihura chuckled as he saw her fear through his golden eyes. "This is only the beginning, my dear Janani. The Scroll of Thoth beckons me to find the other relics of legendary power. Once I obtain the Circlet of Isis, my wounds will heal at the hands of the goddess, Isis. Sickness cannot fester within my body. Nobody will be able to stop me, Janani. I am one step closer to achieving godhood on Earth."

Janani looked at the gourd of wine in her hands. "Yes, my lord," she said sadly.

Pharaoh Runihura looked down into the royal gardens where Hamadi, the royal gardener and soldier, was working the soil with his hands. Janani looked over the edge of the balcony and saw her forbidden lover. A two-year-old boy scurried to his father, carrying a hand shovel. Hamadi took the tool from his son. Janani smiled at her son with his father, who was teaching him how to work the ground. Runihura turned his head and saw the woman smile at her lover and son.

The Pharaoh turned and walked calmly towards the throne room. "Janani, follow me!"

Janani turned her head with a gasp and rushed towards the Pharaoh with the jug of wine. "I would not become so attached to Hamadi, my dear Janani." The Pharaoh grinned as his hand touched a large stone statue erected to glorify Sekhmet. "The lion goddess thirsts for his blood. Do not make me satiate her thirst this night."

"My deepest apologies, my lord!" Janani exclaimed quickly, bowing her head. "Please do not take Timin's father from him!"

Pharaoh Runihura glared at her menacingly. "For too long have you had eyes for Hamadi! I thought I had taught you a lesson that night when I put you in your place!" Runihura raised his voice loudly. "Perhaps you need a reminder of my power!"

Janani fell to her knees trembling before the Pharaoh. "My lord, please mercy! I did not mean to incur your wrath!" She kneeled before him on her hands and knees, the jug sitting beside her.

Pharaoh Runihura hovered above the woman, looking down at her with contempt. His fists clenched tightly as he growled low in his throat. "You should praise the gods that I am a patient, generous man."

Janani felt a drop of sweat course down her forehead and drip onto the marble floor. "Yes, my Great Pharaoh!"

Pharaoh Runihura turned slowly towards the altar to Sekhmet. Candles flickered as he walked calmly toward the altar decorated with fine white linen, candles of beeswax, a golden goblet, and a glistening new golden dagger. The Scroll of Thoth rested before the gold statue of Sekhmet, the goddess of destruction. "Bring me my mid-day meal."

Janani rose to her feet quickly and placed the jug of wine beside the Pharaoh's throne. The woman bowed her head and rushed from the room.

Pharaoh Runihura looked at the Scroll of Thoth and reached for the papyrus with calm hands. "I must find the Circlet of Isis. My enemies will not harm me and I shall become invincible! Immortality is within my grasp." Pharaoh Runihura opened the scroll and smiled with satisfaction as he read the powers given him by the golden Eyes of Horus.

The Eye of Horus shall the seeker obtain

For Uniting one's enemies and godly strength to gain

To harness the power of the almighty Heru

Search for the Scroll of Horus in his Glorious city of Edfû.

The Pharaoh grinned at the memory of commanding the army of Edfû to slaughter themselves. The golden goblet belonging to the High Priest of Horus from which he had drank the blood of the priest rested casually on his altar. Pharaoh Runihura licked his lips at the memory of tasting the priest's blood.

Pharaoh Runihura opened the Scroll of Thoth and read the passages. His golden eyes narrowed as he read the sacred script.

Scroll of Isis, in holy rest,

Offers earthly delights to Tuat's blessed.

Fresh air from heaven and justice given

To Horus enemy, blood-lust driven

Bear you the Circlet of Isis

Possess the glory of the Divine Enchantress

Look to the Scorpion for healing wind

For plague and drought from Circlet rescind.

A Trial of Faith shall you pass with heart

For if you fail, shall ye be torn apart

Pharaoh Runihura reread the passage and grunted with frustration. *Mistress Isis seems intent on dispensing justice upon my head, does she?   Does she intend to intimidate me?   The goddess Sekhmet will protect her loyal faithful.*

The Pharaoh touched the four scars falling down his left cheek.   His young nemesis could not flee forever from Sekhmet's wrath.   *I will never forgive you, Blessed Servant of Osiris! You will pay for your assault!   I will defame your body ten-fold as punishment!*   The

Pharaoh left the altar, walking towards his golden throne.   The Pharaoh climbed the three steps and sat slowly.

Runihura crossed his legs and leaned on his arm.   Looking outside of the arch, he could see the blue skies above Heliopolis.   His mind contemplated the scroll's passage. Scorpions were creatures of great destructive power. How could a Scorpion offer healing?   Runihura was distracted from the outside as Janani returned with his tray of fruit and dates.   Janani placed the tray beside the Pharaoh and kneeled before his throne.

"Eat a date, Janani," the Pharaoh said sternly.

Pharaoh Runihura consistently asked her to taste his food, fearing the same fate as he had given his father.   Janani swallowed and looked up at her king. "It is poison-free, my lord."

Runihura took a date in his hand and chewed it, watching Janani closely.   "Has the Al-Sakhir scribe returned with the tally for this month's production?"

Janani shook her head slowly. "No, my lord."

"I am a man of little tolerance for tardiness,"   Pharaoh Runihura took a handful of grapes and popped two into his mouth.   Janani watched as the juice from the grapes dripped from one corner of his mouth. His teeth dug into the fruit, grinding and ripping the fruit to shreds.

Kazemde, the royal physician, slowly entered the throne room with a reverent bow. "My Pharaoh," Kazemde said solemnly. "Master Hakim has fallen ill with fever, my lord. His skin glows a fiery red and his bed has become as the Nile, wet and damp."

Pharaoh Runihura took another grape casually and bit into it. He chewed slowly as he watched the physician remain bowed. "When did he fall ill?"

"Master Hakim had complained of stomach upset yester-morn. He summoned me to his bedchamber at dawn's light. His arm bears a red mark which resembles a burn by fire."

Runihura raised his eyebrow. "I would see this mark upon him."

"As you wish, your grace," Kazemde said, standing tall before the Pharaoh.

Pharaoh Runihura followed Kazemde from the throne room. Runihura entered the room as the other high priests gathered around him, praying to Rā to heal their sick superior. The priests kneeled before the Pharaoh and touched their foreheads to the ground in supplication.

Hakim turned his head to see the Pharaoh. "My Pharaoh, you grace me with your presence."

Runihura watched as his former tutor and conspirator lay in the bed, his body red and perspiring. "I hear you have taken ill, Hakim. What ailment ravages your body?"

"I cannot eat, my king. Weakness fills my body and it burns as fire."

Runihura glared down at the man who had helped him rise to power.
Runihura covered the man's hand with his own. "My doctor will save
your life, my teacher. I will spare no expense to have healing herbs
brought before you."

Hakim reached for the Pharaoh's arm. "The gods are angry,
Runihura. You and I have brought their fury onto our people."

"No, Hakim. We are their saviors. We have saved them from
themselves."

"You have angered Horus," Hakim whispered with a groan of pain.
"He wants his eyes returned to their sacred resting place."

Runihura pulled his arm from Hakim's grip. The Pharaoh's golden
eyes narrowed. "Never! The Eyes of Horus are destined to remain in
my possession! Delirium has clouded your mind and your judgment,
Hakim!"

Hakim closed his eyes as his head rested against the silk pillow.
Runihura watched as his tutor breathed heavily through wheezing
lungs. The Pharaoh turned to Kazemde. "What have you done for
him?"

Kazemde bowed his head before the king. "I have placed protective
amulets over his chest. I have sent Hamadi to bring me some

medicinal leaves to place into a tea for him as well as for a salve for his burning skin."

Pharaoh Runihura looked at Hakim and towards Kazemde. "I expect his full recovery, Kazemde. Do not disappointment me."

Kazemde nodded and swallowed nervously. "Yes, my great Pharaoh."

"You know what happens when I am displeased."

Kazemde bowed lower to hide his fearful countenance. "Yes, my lord! I shall not disappoint you! I will do everything within my power to ensure his survival."

Pharaoh Runihura watched Hakim whimper in the bed, his right hand trembling as it laid on his chest. Runihura placed a hand on Hakim's shoulder lightly. "May Sekhmet keep you safe."

Kazemde watched as the Pharaoh casually walked from the room. While the other priests chanted healing prayers, Kazemde removed a piece of papyrus from the table beside the patient. He took his reed and inkwell. He slowly began to write a prayer to remove the evil spirit festering in Hakim's body. "Oh Rā, God of Light and Health, inspire me," he prayed quietly as he began the sacred incantation.

II

The Hunt

Baruti looked towards the balcony of his master where his angry voice bellowed over the land.   Imani was scolding her husband for some infraction, but Baruti could not understand her complaint screamed in Noble Tongue.   Kaemwaset had reduced their daily rations since the harvest season was complete and he believed they required less sustenance.   The waters of the Nile would soon flood its banks and the slaves would no longer be harvesting.

Khentimentiu sat beside his father, sharpening a small hand axe with a stone.   The eight-year-old boy looked towards Baruti.   "They fight like Horus and Seth, father."

Baruti nodded. "And like the battle between Horus and his brother, that battle began long before you were born, my son."

Khentimentiu continued to sharpen the blade of the tool.   The boy looked up at his father with sad eyes. "Father, must I work in the home as Master Kaemwaset commands?"

Baruti's attention was taken from the axe that he was sharpening to look at his boy. "We must do as Master Kaemwaset commands, Khenti, or he will become angry. If it is his wish that you work the garden for Najam, then that is what you must do."

"I have worked the fields with you, father, since I was able to walk! I do not want to be separated from you!" Khentimentiu exclaimed, stamping his foot on the ground defiantly.   Baruti put his arm around his son calmly. "I know the master frightens you, my son. You will see your mother when she goes to Najam. She will be there."

"Why cannot Laila work the garden?"

Baruti bit his lip as he remembered that night. Nakia and him had found Kaemwaset raping Qamra in the stable. Kaemwaset was infuriated that Qamra had become pregnant and ordered Laila to work the fields to prevent his wife from knowing the girl's parentage. Imani had discovered her husband's infidelity and refused to share a bed with him.

"She must remain in the fields, son. I promise that if you need me, I will not be far away."

Khentimentiu dropped his tools and hugged his father. "I want to leave this place," the boy sniffled sadly. "I don't want to be a slave. I want to be like Master Amsi! He can leave the lands and go hunting and fishing! He doesn't have to work and he eats the best food!"

Baruti hugged his son and caressed the boy's side-lock of youth. "I know, my boy. One day we will be free and all of this will be behind us."

Nakia stepped from the slave home and into the morning sun. The young man stretched as he looked into the cloud-filled sky. Baruti watched the twin spread his arms, which fell to his side quickly.

"Good morning, Nakia."

Nakia turned his head and smiled slightly at Baruti. "Good Morning, Father Baruti," Nakia said quietly. The twin walked slowly towards the family home. Baruti removed his arm from Khentimentiu and he dropped his wooden pole on the ground. He ran towards the solitary twin. "Nakia! Wait!" Nakia continued to walk towards the house. "Kelile!" Baruti called.

Nakia stopped walking and stood still. His fists clenched tightly as he lowered his head. *My brother called me by my tribal name. It has been two years since his death. I miss him. My twin brother was all that I had after Pharaoh Atenhotep slaughtered our people. Nassar. Ulan…I want you back so much; My heart grieves and aches for you.*

Baruti ran in front of Nakia and put his hands on his friend's shoulders. "Anubis feasts with your brother, Nakia. He grieves no more. Nassar would not wish for you to mourn for him."

A tear fell down Nakia's dark cheek. "Kaemwaset killed my brother. His blood cries out for vengeance."

"Kaemwaset will pay for his crime, Nakia. When you and your twin are reunited in Osiris'Hall of Judgment, you will both watch Kaemwaset's soul be devoured by Ammut."

Nakia wiped his teary eyes. "That's not enough for me, Father Baruti."

Baruti looked into the young man's eyes and saw the same wild fire that burned in his brother's eyes. Nakia was the most non-combative of the twin brothers. Since Nakia had learned of Nassar's death,

Nakia's attitude had become one of rebellion. "Your brother's spirit burns within you. I see him in your eyes."

Nakia shoved Baruti's hands off his shoulder. "My brother is dead," he said with venom in his voice. "Excuse me, Father Baruti."

Baruti watched as the twin walked around him and entered the Al-Sakhir home. "Your brother is reborn in you, Kelile. Master Kaemwaset will pay for your brother's death. Anubis had told me that he is condemned to oblivion."

Nakia entered the family home and walked down the lavishly decorated hallway, covered in murals of Rā and protective spells. He stood before Amsi's bedroom door and sighed. *Master Amsi has always treated me with respect and friendship. Not once has he raised his hand in anger towards me. Since my brother and I arrived here as gifts for Master Kaemwaset, Baruti has always cared for us. He protected us and loved us as if we were his own children. I did not mean to become angry with him. He took two frightened, angry five-year-old twin boys from a different culture under his wing. He taught us the Egyptian Common tongue and Qamra taught us how to clean and care for our master. I shall apologize to him tonight for my anger.*

Nakia slowly opened Amsi's door and saw the Noble teen bathing in his tub. "Master Amsi, I apologize for my tardiness!"

The teenaged boy shrugged his shoulders as he reached for a cloth to dry himself. "I rose early for prayer. It is not you who is late."

Nakia took the towel in his hand and held it as Amsi stepped from the tub. "Let me help you, master."

Amsi took the towel from his slave's hands and pointed to a plate of food beside his bed. "Take some before my father arrives," Amsi said quickly.

"Thank you, Master Amsi," Nakia said, bowing his head.

The slave took a handful of raisins and shoved them into his mouth hungrily. Amsi watched in amazement as Nakia covered his lips to keep the raisins inside his mouth. "You must be hungry!" Nakia nodded as he turned his back to the door.
Amsi opened his chest of perfumes and body oils. "Which one shall I use today?"

Nakia finished chewing and swallowed the food. "Thank you, my master!"

"The next time, Nakia, don't eat so many at once. You can hurt yourself."

"Good morning, my boy!" Kaemwaset exclaimed as Amsi turned his head to the doorway.

Amsi stood up holding a bottle of perfumed oil and bowed his head. "Good morning, father!"

"Nakia, why are you just standing there like a lazy mule?"

Nakia bowed and kneeled before his master. "My master was selecting his oil, sir!"

Kaemwaset slowly stepped into the room. "Perform your duty to my son, Nakia, or I will make you join your brother sooner than you think!"

Amsi watched as Nakia removed the cloth from his body. The slave took a padded cushion and placed it under his knees. Nakia took the bottle from Amsi and poured some of the sweet-smelling oil onto his hand.

Kaemwaset watched as Nakia rubbed the oil on Amsi's legs. "My son, have you completed your studies for today?"

Amsi bowed his head. "Yes, father! I have begun to memorize the incantations from the sacred scriptures! I have been studying them diligently."

Nakia rubbed the oil onto Amsi's thighs, feeling his owner's eyes watching his every move. His hands trembled as he rubbed some oil on Amsi's thin stomach and his chest. His knees were grateful for the cushion he had placed below them.

"You will speak to the slaves and see that their tools are in working order for the season of *Peret*. When it comes time to plant, those tools must be in working order. I will not have my slaves lounging."

Amsi watched as Nakia's hands rubbed the oil over his chest. Nakia's large, brown eyes looked at him with fear knowing that Kaemwaset could strike him without warning. Had Amsi told his father of Nakia's lateness, his father's wrath would be terrible.

Had his father discovered that he had given Nakia some food, his wrath would be uncontrollable.

"Father, I have a request."

Kaemwaset slowly approached his son and stood beside the kneeling slave. Nakia swallowed nervously at his master's close proximity. He took Nakia's wrist and guided his hand along Amsi's chest. "Anoint my son's body properly, Nakia! I want my son's body protected from the harsh rays of Aten!"

"Yes, sir!" Nakia exclaimed as he continued to rub the oil onto Amsi's shoulders.

"Father, I am fifteen-years-old! I no longer need Nakia to rub oil onto my body!"

"Tell me your request, son," Kaemwaset said, ignoring his son's protest.

Amsi looked up at his father. "For the Festival of Hapi, I wish the slaves to have a day of rest."

Kaemwaset's eyes widened. "What?! A day of rest? Are you mad?"

Amsi looked up at his father. "Heliopolis will be offering tribute to Hapi and Isis! If the slaves do not give offerings to the River Nile, Hapi's waters will no longer rise and our crops will suffer."

Kaemwaset looked at his son suspiciously, his falcon eyes narrowing. Amsi had adopted his mother's lenient attitude towards the slaves, much to Kaemwaset's disappointment. His lands depended on the Nile for its bounty as well as the rays of the Aten. Without proper tribute, his lands and crops would suffer. Kaemwaset knew he would fall into disfavor with the pharaoh since his lands fed the living god and the palace court.

"Very well, my son. The slaves may have one day of rest, but no more." Kaemwaset placed his hand on Nakia's head. "This one must still be present to attend to your body. Qamra must also be here to attend to my body and that of her mistress."

Nakia shivered as he felt his master's talons dig into his scalp. Amsi heard Nakia whimper in fear. Kaemwaset chuckled as he felt his slave quiver under his hand.

Nakia's hands left Amsi's body as he bent over, resting his head on Amsi's leg.

Kaemwaset released Nakia and turned, walking out of the room.

Amsi touched Nakia's back, giving it a gentle rub. "Nakia, he is gone." Nakia's arms wrapped around himself as he trembled. "Nakia, it is alright." Amsi tilted Nakia's face upwards to look him in his teary eyes. "Don't cry, Nakia," Amsi said as he reached down and hugged the other teen. The slave returned the embrace, his body still shaking.

"Master Amsi, I fear him still after all these years."

"I know, Nakia.   I didn't know if he was going to snap my neck like he did…"

Amsi held Nakia closer and looked into the eyes of the slave.   "I would have stopped him if he tried," Amsi said.   "I wouldn't let him do that to my friend."

Nakia smiled slightly and lowered his head. "Master Amsi, I am not worthy of such a merciful owner."

Amsi pat Nakia on the back. "I suggest we go for a ride, Nakia.   A good excursion will help you and I need to practice my archery lessons."

Nakia's eyes brightened with a light that returned only when he was riding horses.   They offered him the freedom he craved while trapped within the Al-Sakhir lands.

Nakia smiled as he looked into the dark, brown eyes of his master. "I think I would enjoy that."

Amsi pat his slave on the arm reassuringly. "Get the horses ready, Nakia. Perhaps we will also ride to Azizi's oasis. With the flooding of the Nile banks, the reeds would not make a suitable hiding space during the day."

The slave grabbed a clean white linen skirt and tied the material around his master's hips. Nakia adorned Amsi's body with gold cuffs and a golden ankh. Golden bracelets and anklets were placed around his wrists and ankles. Nakia placed a golden ankh necklace around his master's neck and bowed before him. Amsi smiled at himself in a large, golden-framed mirror. Nakia watched as his master's jewelry glittered in the sunlight. Amsi slipped his feet into his reed sandals and followed Nakia to the stable.

Nakia lead his master to the stable where he prepared the horses for their excursion into the desert. Nakia fastened the reigns on Hamza and Naji. The slave pulled himself onto Hamza's back as the horse whinnied loudly and stamped his front hoof on the ground with excitement. Hamza would still only allow Nakia to ride him. Amsi had tried to ride the wild beast the year before and was quickly thrown onto the hay by the rearing stallion. Amsi's heels nudged Naji and the horse ran from the stable. Nakia gripped onto the reigns as Hamza darted from the stable. The horses passed the family gate and galloped into the desert.

Hamza raced beside Naji, his black mane flying in the wind. Nakia smiled as he felt the wind brush across his skin. His eyes peered down at the sand and saw many tracks leading from the city.

"A large number of people left Heliopolis not long ago, Master Amsi," Nakia said.

Amsi looked down at the sand and noticed the tracks left behind by horses. "My father hasn't mentioned any campaign that the pharaoh is fighting."

Nakia turned his head to Amsi. "Your father knows you are a friend of the very people he despises. Do you believe that he would tell you of the pharaoh's plans to achieve godhood?"

Amsi looked ahead into the heart of the desert. *My father has always borne hatred in his heart for our slaves. He took pride with his belief that he 'civilized' Nakia and Nassar. For long have I tried to make my father proud. I have excelled in my studies to please him.*

Azizi has asked me to train him in the art of reading the script of Noble Tongue. He says it will help him defeat the pharaoh. Noble Tongue is a protected secret among the Nobility. It is strictly forbidden to teach commoners how to read Noble Tongue. Should my father or the pharaoh discover that I have taught the King of Thieves how to read the script, I would suffer a very harsh sentence.

I want to join Azizi in his exploits, exploring caverns of the desert. Azizi cares not for formal study. He has taught me some Common

Tongue so that I may talk to the street children under his protection. I
bring them raisins and dates as a treat when I visit Azizi in the dark
alleys of Iunu. The young children are excited when I come with small
gifts for them.

"Amsi, are you unwell?" Nakia asked as he looked at his pensive
master. Nakia put a hand on Amsi's shoulder.

Amsi raised his head with a sigh. "You are right, Nakia. My father
would not tell me of the pharaoh's plans because he knows that I am
friends with Azizi."

"To be the friend of the most notorious criminal in Heliopolis is a
dangerous affair, my lord," Nakia said.

"Is he really a criminal, Kelile Ngangi?" Amsi asked. "He steals from
the pockets of the rich, but he doesn't always the money for himself.
He fought against the entire army of the pharaoh to save his friend from
death. How can these be the actions of a criminal?"

Nakia gripped Hamza's reigns tightly as the horse made a sudden
gallop forward without Nakia's cajoling. "He defies the Will of the
pharaoh and General Gahiji. In the eyes of the Nobility, that makes
him a criminal. That also makes you a criminal, too, Master Amsi."

Amsi narrowed his eyes at the desert before them. He silently peered
ahead, knowing that Nakia was right. Azizi was a defiant child, but
could Amsi blame him? Azizi had told him of General Gahiji

beheading his mother and looking into her lifeless eyes. Amsi had wondered how Azizi could live with that memory.

"Master Amsi, look ahead!" Nakia exclaimed in alarm.

Amsi lifted his head and saw a body laying on the sand face-down. Golden bracelets glimmered on the person's wrists. Fine, white linen decorated the motionless body. Amsi saw long, black hair spreading onto the sand.

"It's a woman!"

Nakia and Amsi arrived beside the body. Amsi ran to the body and turned the body onto its back. Lifeless eyes stared towards the sky as her mouth screamed silently towards him. Her lips were colored red and her eyes were lined with black ochre.

Nakia looked at the woman's flesh where a black dart stuck into her neck. Nakia kneeled beside the woman and removed the dart from her cold flesh. He looked at the black dart closely, keeping his fingers from the sharp point. "This is what killed her. It's tipped with poison. Our tribe used these in battle."

"Are you saying someone of your tribe did this? I thought you and your brother were the only survivors."

Nakia nodded and stared at the deadly dart with wonder. His heart leapt into his throat, hoping another Enzi had survived the massacre that claimed his village, warrior father, and his mother. "Maybe I'm not alone.   Perhaps I am not the sole survivor of my tribe. The *Nuu* also use these darts in their hunting of desert game."

Amsi looked down at the dead woman. "Are you suggesting this girl was hunted like game?"

Nakia raised his head and looked around cautiously. "There are also desert thieves lurking the sands.   Perhaps one of them is responsible for this. We should not remain here longer than necessary, my lord."

Amsi saw an amulet of wood laying against the exposed breasts of the woman.   Amsi looked closely at the amulet.   "It's the Buckle of Isis! This woman was under the protection of the Divine Mother."

Beside the woman laid a bag made of hide.   He cautiously reached for the bag and opened it to examine its contents. "This woman was robbed. Perhaps the thieves of the desert found her and killed her for her belongings."

Amsi looked at the gold jewelry decorating the woman's arms and fingers. "Why wouldn't they take her gold?" Amsi's nose wrinkled at the stench from the body.   "The Nobility of Heliopolis wear amulets of Rā and the Aten.   There are no Temples of Isis near our city."

"Qamra worships Isis, Amsi.   She gives offerings to her daily behind our home. Maybe she would know where a Temple of Isis is located."

"Why would they leave the woman's gold jewelry and steal her belongings? It makes no sense. The thieves could have taken her jewelry and her clothing.   I know her gold would have brought the thieves at least one hundred dînars, if not more."

Nakia shook his head as he looked around the area.   "We should leave, Master Amsi.   Should the murderers be nearby, I do not wish for you to be their next target."

Amsi removed the Buckle of Isis from the woman's neck.   He examined the wooden object closely and saw writing on the back of the amulet with some of the text corrupted by carvings.   "Do you think Azizi killed her because she is a Noble Woman?"

Nakia raised an eyebrow at Amsi's question. "That is a question your father would ask, Amsi.   Azizi may know something about this as he knows all the happenings in the world of thieves.   We need to find him."

Amsi mounted Naji and looked towards Azizi's oasis.   "I think we need to pay my friend a visit."

Nakia mounted Hamza and looked down at the dead woman laying in the sand.   "I hope she rests in Uala with her sisters."

Amsi closed his eyes and bowed his head at the corpse. "May you see the face of Rā."

Amsi and Nakia rode towards the Oasis.   They saw one more corpse in the sand, its body covered with red patches and sores.   Amsi covered his mouth as he passed, not wishing to approach the body closely. The stench carried through the air, making Nakia cough in his saddle.

When they arrived at Azizi's oasis, they stepped through the foliage. Grass brushed across their sandaled feet as they stepped onto the lush, fertile soil. Amsi smiled as a cool wind blew across his bald head, a welcome respite from the scorching heat of the desert.

Thick leaves brushed across them as they made their way towards the lake, Azizi's favored sanctuary. They emerged from the bushes and stood beside the lake. A circle of stones smoldered with a whisp of smoke.

Nakia kneeled beside the lake and sipped from the cool water. He licked his lips with a smile. "This water is like a divine elixir!" Amsi looked on the bank of the river and saw the toys he had given Azizi on the day of his mother's death. The little gesture of compassion had solidified their friendship. Azizi had never forgotten the sacrifice by his friend.

Amsi walked beside the ball and sat beside it. "I can't believe he still has this, Nakia."

Nakia looked at the ball that Amsi held in his hands. "It reminds him of you, Master Amsi. It was a kind gesture of you."

Amsi leaned back, his hand sinking slightly into a hole. He looked back and saw his hands buried in the soil. "What is this?" Amsi pulled his hand from the soil to find a handful of gold coins resting in his palm. "Nakia! Money! Look!"

Nakia looked at the gold dînars in Amsi's hand. "That must be where Azizi buries the gold he steals."

Amsi kneeled beside the hole and reached his hand into the soil. A rope was wrapped around his finger. He tugged on a rope and a small pouch rose from the dirt. Amsi opened the bag and his

eyes widened. "Nakia!" Nakia looked at the pouch of money and reached into the bag. Gold dînars, silver coins, and precious lapis lazuli sat upon his palm.

"I never knew Azizi had so much money!" Amsi exclaimed as he sifted through the pouch.

"Halt, thieves!" a voice growled angrily as a cloaked figure jumped from the brush.

Amsi dropped the pouch of money and swallowed nervously at the sword pointed towards him and Nakia. "We're not thieves!"

The cloaked figure advanced slowly towards Amsi and Nakia. The figure narrowed angry eyes at Amsi and his slave. Amsi felt the intruder's sword against his throat. Amsi quivered in fear as the figure glared at him with fury. A black cloth wrapped around his face revealed only his eyes.

"Do you expect me to believe your lies?"

Nakia raised his hands into the air. "Honestly, stranger! We were not going to steal anything! Please do not kill my lord and I!"

The figure looked at Amsi's golden jewelry. "What is a Noble Blood doing in the house of a Commoner?"

Amsi swallowed nervously. "Nobody lives here!"

"Where is Azizi Keket? I know you know him, Noble Blood! Speak!"

"I do not know where he is!" Amsi said defiantly. "I wouldn't tell you even if I did!"

"Then you forfeit your life, Noble Thief!" The figure raised his sword above his head.

Nakia watched with horror as Amsi closed his eyes, ready for the blow. The figure swung the sword toward Amsi's head and stopped inches from the Noble teen's flesh.

Amsi clenched his fists, his face covered in sweat. His chest rose and fell sharply. He cautiously opened his eyes and saw Azizi pulling back the cloth covering his face.

Azizi pierced the soil with the blade of his sword. He chuckled as he leaned against its hilt. "Noble Blood Amsi Al-Sakhir Ibn Kaemwaset, what brings you to my home and digging in the dirt for my hard-earned bounty?"

Amsi took a deep breath and ran his hand along his head. "I thought I was going to die, you horse's ass!"

Nakia stood on his feet. "You frightened us to death, Aziz!"

"Had I been a member of Pharaoh Runihura's forces, they would have killed you," Azizi said sternly. He approached Nakia. "You have a very strong master." Azizi looked down at his friend and put his open hand on Amsi's head. "One whom I am proud to call my friend and ally," Azizi added with a grin.

Amsi raised his head and stood on his feet. "It is good to see you again, my brother. Why do you insist on frightening me?"

Azizi chuckled as he pat his black horse's neck. "You passed your test." Azizi removed his black cloak, revealing his bare torso and his tattered white skirt to the slave and master.

"You almost cut my head off today!" Amsi protested.

"You know I would not have harmed you. The pharaoh, as you well know, would not stay his hand."

Amsi lowered his head and nodded silently. "I know. I'm glad to see you, Azizi."

Azizi and Amsi put their hands on each other's chests in greeting. Azizi's hands moved to Amsi's shoulders with a smile and a slight bow of his head. "Welcome to my home, Al-Sakhir." Azizi released Amsi's shoulders and kneeled beside his open money pouch. "Why were you looking through my possessions?"

"My hand sunk into the ground and I found a few coin."

Azizi replaced the coins into the pouch and tied the bag closed. "I should not have been so careless with my hard-earned money. I need to find a better place to hide it."

"I might have a small chest I can give to you. It would be more secure than hiding your money in a hole," Amsi said.

Azizi nodded and buried the small pouch, digging into the soil with his hands. "Thank you, my friend."

Nakia sat beside the lake and splashed cold water on his head. Azizi crawled to the edge of the lake and sipped with great thirst from the cool water. The teen splashed water on his head and his bare back. Azizi rolled onto his back and closed his eyes as he laid beside the lake.

"Azizi, I have a serious question for you."

Azizi brushed his forehead with his fingertips. The thief smiled as the water cooled him from the desert heat. "You have only to ask."

"Did you kill that woman in the desert?"

Azizi opened his eye and turned his head to his friend. "No. Why?"

"She was robbed and murdered. I found this in her neck," Amsi held the dart towards Azizi. "I believe it's a *Nuu* dart, but the thieves of the desert use them, as well. The *Nuu* do not murder innocent travelers in the desert. They are a hunting folk, not thieves."

"Careful, Azizi. The tip is poisoned," Nakia warned.

Azizi took the dart from his friend's hand. He held the dart to his eyes and rolled over on his side. He sniffed the dart and examined the wooden end closely.

"The woman still had her jewelry and this Buckle of Isis," Amsi said, holding the wooden object toward Azizi.

The teen sat and took the wooden amulet from Amsi's hand. He closely examined the markings upon the wood. "I cannot read the writing. It might be in Noble Tongue. You try to read it."

Amsi took the wooden item from Azizi and looked closely at the writing. He squinted his eyes to see the small hieroglyphics. "I can make out some of it. It looks like Noble Tongue, but it is somehow different."

Azizi jumped to his feet. "If you cannot read it, I know of one wise woman who may be able."

"Who?"

Azizi grinned. "It is time that you meet the Oracle of the Clan Osiris."

III

Language Of The Gods

Azizi lead Amsi through the streets of *Iunu*, his eyes keeping a constant vigil in the night. Azizi rode his black stallion with his black cloak concealing his body and face. Master and slave rode a safe distance from their companion as they made their way through alleys and abandoned streets.

Nakia saw a figure in the shadows watching him from an alley. He turned his head and the figure was gone, only to reappear in another alley. Nakia stopped his horse and looked at the figure, who returned the silent gaze. "Do I know you?" Nakia asked the dark figure.

Amsi stopped Naji and turned his head to see Nakia staring into an alley. "Nakia, come!"

Nakia's grip on Hamza's reigns weakened as he looked at the quiet figure in the night. "Nassar?"

"What do you see, Nakia?" Amsi asked, approaching Nakia.

The figure in the dark darted away as Nakia reached out to the alley. "Wait!"

Amsi watched the shadowed figure run away quickly. "Nakia, who was that?"

"I think it was my brother."

"The two of you better hurry or Kaphiri's gang will find us. You never know when they will strike," Azizi warned, gripping his dagger firmly. "Hairdar lurks these streets at night. Hurry!"

Amsi and Nakia continued along the streets. Azizi saw a woman down the road with a sheathed scimitar hanging on her belt. Amsi watched as Azizi revealed his right arm to the moonlight and pulled down a golden armband revealing the Mark of Osiris. The woman at the end of the streets bowed her head and pulled aside her black cloak to conceal her weapon.

"This is Halimah's district. She won't harm us," Azizi said.

Amsi watched as they approached Halimah. The young woman was leaning against a building, her breasts exposed to the moonlight as a thin, white veil covered her hips below her belly.

Azizi dismounted his black horse and stood beside Aneksi's hut. Amsi and Nakia dismounted their horses and looked around them uncomfortably. Nakia shifted close to Amsi, the hairs on his arm standing on end as they stood in the unfamiliar territory. Amsi watched as a drunken man stumbled by grumbling at the ground. In the distance, happy singing could be heard through the quarter as well as a baby crying. The scent of cooking meat hovered in the air.

Azizi knocked on the wooden door and pulled down his golden armband again. The door's tiny window opened and Azizi revealed his tattoo to piercing, dark eyes.

"Greetings, Darwishi," Azizi said with a grin.

The window on the door closed and Nakia turned to Azizi. "Do you always get such a warm reception?"

The door opened and Nakia's eyes widened at the tall, muscular man standing before him. He gasped and ran behind Amsi.

"Greetings to you, our king," Darwishi said, bowing before the teen thief. Darwishi looked at the teen decorated in gold jewelry and fine clothing. "You bring a Noble Blood into a den of thieves, my lord? Why do you bring Noble Vermin to our home?"

"Guard your tongue!" Amsi growled.

Azizi pointed his golden dagger at Darwishi's stomach. "He happens to be my friend and a valuable ally in our fight against the pharaoh! I do not appreciate my companion being treated in such a foul manner."

"He is not welcome here," Darwishi said adamantly.

Azizi sheathed his dagger and glared at Darwishi. "If my friend is not welcome, then I can see that I am not welcome as well. Goodbye. Let's go, Amsi."

"Wait, my king!" Darwishi exclaimed.

Azizi spat at Darwishi's feet. "You have disrespected me and my friend! Why should I wait a second longer?"

"Azizi Keket, why do you cause such raucous in the streets?" Aneksi asked as she stepped beside Darwishi.

"Darwishi disrespected my friend and I will not tolerate such behavior!"

Aneksi looked at Amsi in the moonlight.   The teen stood before her dressed in fine, white linen. Amsi avoided the woman's gaze.   Amsi's golden ankh and golden jewelry adorning his body left no doubt in her mind as to the boy's heritage. Amsi's white cape swayed gently in the night breeze.

"The Anointed Companion of Rā has arrived," Aneksi whispered with eyes wide and mouth agape.   "So the lore is true!"

Amsi looked around him.   "I beg your pardon, my lady?" the teen looked confusingly at Aneksi.

"Darwishi, allow them to pass," Aneksi said, running into the hut.

Azizi glared at Darwishi. "He has fed me and given me clothing. He has won my allegiance and my respect.   I expect you to show him the same if not more reverence to him than you show towards me."

Amsi and Nakia quickly passed the glaring thief and sat beside the fire. Azizi took a loaf of bread and tore a piece for Nakia and Amsi.

"Thank you," Amsi said, bowing his head in gratitude.

Aneksi watched Amsi from across the fire. "After fifteen years, my eyes finally gaze at the Anointed Companion of Rā! Praise be to Un-Nefer, the Lord of Eternity, Osiris!"

Amsi looked at Nakia and back towards Aneksi. "The pharaoh has called me Anointed Companion of Rā. How do you know about that?"

Aneksi closed her eyes and lowered her head with dismay. "The pharaoh knows of your identity as the Anointed Companion of Rā, Amsi Al-Sakhir. That is very dangerous."

Nakia put his bread on his lap. "How do you know my lord's name?"

Aneksi looked at the slave. "I have studied the Common Texts which told of the birth of two boys destined to fight the pharaoh. One boy was born of Noble Blood and ordained into the service of Rā, the Sun God. Those of Common Blood would be saved by a child bathed in blood and given the Mark of Osiris, Lord of the Dead. They battle the pharaoh together."

Amsi nodded. "The pharaoh has a mural of a battle between two people. Rā and Osiris hover above two men standing alone. I couldn't read the words of the mural because they have been chiseled away. I still see the mural when I visit the palace."

Azizi wrapped his black cloak around him and scooped a cup of water from a bucket. "The pharaoh is probably trying to prevent the prophecy from happening. If there were words of protection over the two people, he would have chiseled away the protective spells."

"What if there was a victor in the battle and Pharaoh Runihura didn't win? He would not want to face defeat," Nakia said. "By carving away the victor's names, maybe he hopes to prevent his loss from happening."

Aneksi looked at Nakia, passing him a bowl of water to drink. "Never ask a deranged mind to explain itself in a rational manner. Pharaoh Runihura's madness makes sense only to him and to those whom he has brainwashed into believing him. Fanaticism preys on weak minds."

"The Eye of Horus undoubtedly has made his brainwashing attempts much easier," Azizi said, licking his lips from the warm water.

Nakia sipped from the bowl and passed it to Amsi. "How can Master Amsi and Master Azizi fight the entire army of the pharaoh?"

Aneksi nodded. "The Anointed Companion of Rā will be inseparable from the Blessed Servant of Osiris." Aneksi grasped a handful of herbs and tossed them into the fire. She watched as the sparks rose into the air. "I see that you will be challenged. Your bond will be tested. I see blood. I feel pain. Fire races through my veins. I sense death! Oh, Blessed Osiris! The pain!"

Amsi and Azizi exchanged worried glances. Amsi swallowed nervously as Nakia took his hand. Azizi watched as Aneksi gripped her head and screamed into the air.

"One of you will die." Aneksi closed her eyes and raised her hands into the air. "To save his life, you must sacrifice your own!"

The thief turned to Aneksi as the woman's wail rose into the air.

"Aneksi!" Azizi exclaimed as he put his hands on her shoulders.

Aneksi's body jolted as she stopped screaming. She lowered her hands and her body quivered. Her eyes widened in fear as she turned her head towards Azizi. She gasped and reached for the teen thief's face. She cradled Azizi's face in her hands. "Azizi Keket, son of Ghazi!"

Azizi swallowed nervously as he saw the fear in Aneksi's eyes. "I'm here, Aneksi."

Aneksi took a deep breath and lowered her hands. "I fear for you both."

Amsi stood and scooped a cup of water for Aneksi. He kneeled beside the woman and handed her a drink. "Here, take this."

Aneksi bowed her head with gratitude and drank quickly from the cup. "Azizi has spoken of you fondly for a very long time, Amsi."

"We came to show you something important. Amsi, show her the Buckle."

Amsi removed the necklace from around his neck and offered it to Aneksi. "Nakia and I found a dead woman in the desert. This was around her neck."

Nakia swallowed a piece of his bread. "The lady's belongings were stolen, but the robbers never took her jewelry."

Azizi removed his dagger from its sheath and proceeded to clean under his fingernails. "That would mean that the murderers were not interested in her gold. The thieves had other plans for her."

Aneksi examined the piece closely as she sat beside the fire. "There are writings on this piece. Azizi, did you read this?"

Azizi chuckled and rolled his eyes sarcastically. "It's written in Noble Tongue. I can stare at the thing for the next thousand years and not comprehend it."

"I don't believe it is of Noble dialect. I can only read some of the words. We were hoping you would be able to read it."

Aneksi's slender fingers brushed across the wood. "The sacred protection spells to Isis have been defaced. It is writ in Holy Tongue, also known as Sacred Script, Amsi."

Amsi gasped as he stared wide-eyed at Aneksi. "Do you mean the language of the gods? Why can I read some of the words? I am not a priest nor have I learned sacred doctrine."

Aneksi looked at the Noble boy sitting beside the fire. "Pharaoh Runihura has modeled the language of the priests and priestesses using the language of Noble Tongue. Holy Tongue is spoken only by the higher echelons of priests, priestesses, and the pharaoh himself. That is why you can read some of the script, Amsi Al-Sakhir." Aneksi looked at Azizi. "Since Common Folk are not worthy of the favor of the gods, we are not meant to learn such a deified language. That prohibits us from entering paradise."

Amsi shook his head with dismay. Azizi crossed his arms defiantly. "The pharaoh is inventing a new language. This is bad." Amsi shot Azizi a quizzical look. The teen thief turned towards his friend. "You can read Noble Tongue. If the pharaoh wanted to prevent you from discovering his plans, he would need to devise a script that you cannot read. Using Holy Tongue, he can communicate to the Priest Sect, Scribes, and Nobility. This is unfortunate."

Amsi felt a chill run up his spine. "We won't be able to discover his next move unless I learn Sacred Script. I don't think Sawaret will teach me how to read the text, especially if the pharaoh does not want me to learn the new language."

"Why would someone defame a holy object?" Nakia asked.

"They did not want the victim to have the protection of the Divine Mother," Darwishi interjected. "Rā and the Aten have been worshiped in Heliopolis for millennia. However, Pharaoh Runihura has been seeing to the fragmentation of the temples dedicated to those gods. Pharaoh Runihura wants to see Sekhmet worship exclusively throughout the lands."

Amsi narrowed his eyes. "He will not succeed! Rā will smite him for such blasphemy! Rā is all powerful and will deliver his faithful children from these dark times. Rā will triumph once more with Horus at his right hand and-."

"Sekhmet at his left," Azizi added quickly, making Amsi stop suddenly. Azizi watched as Amsi fell silent. "Sekhmet will accompany Rā again to destroy humankind, Amsi. We cannot allow Sekhmet to succeed." Azizi paused to sip his cup of water. "So, the pharaoh wishes to start a holy war between the followers of Rā, Osiris, and Sekhmet. Un-Nefer, Beloved Osiris, Lord of the Dead, shall not submit." Azizi looked down at his clean fingernails and blew the dirt into the fire.

Amsi looked into the fire and closed his eyes. "My father will not turn from sun worship. I will not give up the faith I have in my god. Faith in the Sun God will see us through any time of darkness. Ascribe praise to Rā, the Lord of Heaven, the Prince, Life, Strength, Health, Creator of the gods! Adore ye him in his presence beautiful!"

Azizi folded his hands before him, closed his eyes, and bowed his head towards the fire. "Praise be to the Lord of the Dead, Osiris, Lord of everlasting, traversing millions of years in the duration of his life, Prince of gods and men."

"This woman who had worn this necklace, Amsi, was well-dressed?"

Amsi nodded. "She was dressed in gold and fine linens."

Aneksi looked at the two teen boys. "This woman was a priestess of Isis. Only those who worship the Divine Mother could have worn this amulet with the protective spells."

Azizi and Amsi exchanged quizzical glances. Darwishi sat beside the fire. "There are no temples of Isis around Heliopolis. One temple lies near Aswan while another lies far to the north in the land of the *Hnn-pht-k*. That is a far distance away for a solitary woman to travel."

"Why was she traveling to Heliopolis?" Azizi asked. "Why would she want to walk into the lion's den?"

Amsi's eyes widened as he snapped his fingers. "She came to the lion's den to see the lion-monarch himself. She was coming to see Pharaoh Runihura!"

"We do not know that for certain, Amsi," Aneksi said.

Darwishi laughed. "Boy, why would a priestess of Isis want to come to see the pharaoh? Do you think she was going to hand the pharaoh a sacred relic?"

"Why else would she travel so far from her temple?" Azizi grabbed the Buckle of Isis from Aneksi's hand. "Perhaps she came to give him this."

Amsi looked at Aneksi. "If she was traveling a long way, why was she alone?"

"Nefertum would not attack a solitary woman. However, he could have taken her belongings."

Amsi raised a curious eyebrow. "Who?"

Azizi poked the fire with a thin palm branch to keep the fire blazing. "Nefertum is the leader of the desert bandits. He might know something about the woman's death."

Nakia swallowed nervously. "Azizi, we can't just walk into a camp of desert thieves!"

"You are sitting within a den of thieves right now," Darwishi said with a grin. "What difference be there if it is in the desert or here?"

"My people will not harm you, Nakia," Azizi said. "They already know about you and Amsi. I have instructed them not to shed your blood."

"Well, that's comforting," Nakia said uneasily.

Azizi stood and looked at the Buckle of Isis in the fire's light. His black cape dragged the ground behind him as he walked slowly around the fire. "If the pharaoh is pursuing the relics of Isis, could this help him find them? What if he is once again on the move, my friend?" Azizi asked looking at Amsi.

The fifteen-year-old Noble stood beside his friend and looked at the Buckle of Isis. "We have to find them before he does."

Azizi gripped the Buckle of Isis tightly in his hands. "I need to speak with Nefertum. I need to hear what he knows."

"I will keep my ears open, Azizi," Amsi said. "I don't know why that woman was murdered. She may even had been traveling to Heliopolis for some unrelated reason."

Nakia stood beside Aneksi. "Then why would her prayers be defaced, Master Amsi? The pharaoh would want her to complete her journey."

"Someone wanted to prevent her journey. Amsi, keep your ears open for any movement of the pharaoh's army or any plans for special journeys through the desert. If you hear anything, send me word or to any member of my clan. Be certain not to give information to those tattooed with the Mark of Seth. They are Kaphiri's clan members." Azizi looked at Nakia. "Keep him safe."

Nakia bowed his head. "I will, my lord."

Aneksi read the rest of the prophecy.

The Scroll of Isis waits upon life's dying breath.

Bear you the Circlet of Isis

Possess the glory of the Divine Enchantress

Look to the Scorpion for healing wind

For plague and drought from Circlet rescind.

A Trial of Faith shall you pass with heart

For if you fail, shall ye be torn apart

Aneksi looked up with fear. "Who will face the Trial of Isis?"

Azizi and Amsi exchanged uneasy glances. "Pharaoh Runihura places no faith in the gods besides Sekhmet," Amsi said.

Aneksi dropped the scroll. "I was afraid of this.   Fate has told me of your deaths."

Azizi clenched his fists tightly. "I decide my own fate, Aneksi."

Aneksi looked at the two boys. "Have faith in each other or you will not survive."

"I trust Amsi with my life. There are few whom I trust. He has won my allegiance and loyalty."

Amsi nodded and looked at his friend. "Azizi means much to me. I will not abandon him. I should return home. My father has no doubt noticed my absence."

Azizi nodded with a yawn. "I shall find Nefertum and warn our people, Aneksi."

"You are both very brave boys," Aneksi said, smiling at the teens. "Both of you beware: Your friendship means your deaths should you be discovered."

Darwishi opened the door for the two boys. "Be careful in the night, Noble Blood. Should you not watch your back, an arrow may find its way into it."

Amsi narrowed his eyes at Darwishi. "I wish you no ill-will. I am fighting along side you as an ally."

"You have not earned my allegiance yet, Noble Blood."

"But he has won mine," Azizi interjected sternly. "I owe Amsi my life, Darwishi. If you do not trust him, trust my judgment."

Darwishi bowed his head. "I trust the King of Thieves absolutely."

Azizi mounted his horse. "Then trust my judgment."

Amsi mounted Naji while Nakia took his place on Hamza's back. They followed Azizi through the streets of *Iunu*. Ahead of them, a group of soldiers marched towards them. "Who goes there?" a soldier asked.

Azizi quickly lead Amsi and Nakia into an alley as a group of soldiers raced towards them. Azizi jumped off his steed and crouched low in the shadows. "They're coming, Amsi! Go! Leave!"

Amsi jumped off Naji and kneeled beside Azizi. "You can't fight them all." He could barely hear Azizi breathing as they hid in the shadows.

"What are you doing? Run!"

"I'm not leaving you to fight alone," Amsi said.

Azizi smiled in the darkness as he turned his head towards the entrance to the alley.

Naji whinnied loudly in alarm at the sound of the soldiers approaching.

"My lord, what shall I do?" Nakia asked anxiously.

"Sit on Naji! Calm him!" Azizi whispered sternly.

Amsi turned to Nakia. "Get your bow, Kelile!"

I don't know how he can live like this, hunted like an animal, Amsi thought as he listened to the advancing footsteps. Sweat formed on his forehead as he thought of the impending battle. If they were captured and brought before the pharaoh, they would be executed immediately.

His heart beat faster as the clanging of metal quickly approached. *This is it, Amsi. Your first real battle!*

Nakia jumped off Hamza's back and ran to mount Naji. "Quiet, boy! Nakia's here!" Amsi watched Nakia remove his bow and an arrow from his quiver. The slave was responsible for his master's welfare and he knew the penalty for failing in his duty. "Master, we should leave!"

"I'm not leaving Azizi to fight alone!" Amsi whispered stubbornly.

"They went that way!" Amsi heard raised voices approaching faster.

"Are you armed?" Azizi asked quickly looking at his companion.

Amsi shook his head. "No! Nakia and I were just going for a ride."

Azizi reached behind him and removed a silver dagger. He handed it to Amsi. "I hope Sawaret taught you how to fight."

Amsi swallowed nervously. "I just began my lessons!"

Azizi gripped the hilt of his golden dagger tightly. "Darwishi gave you the first lesson of being a master thief: Watch your back or something will find its way into it." Azizi narrowed his eyes and grinned, his body tensing as their prey approached. "Osiris, protect your humble servant and guide my blade in your holy name."

Amsi swallowed nervously. "Azizi, I don't think I can do this," Amsi's voice quivered as he gripped the hilt tightly.

"Thinking will get you killed, my friend."

"I've never killed anyone in my life!" Amsi's heart beat wildly as the footsteps sounded around the corner. *Rā, please help me!*

"There's a first time for everything," Azizi whispered as his body tensed, preparing for battle.

Four soldiers appeared in front of them, raising their swords. "It's Azizi Keket!"

Azizi felt a quick wind beside his ear and a soldier collapsed onto the ground as an arrow pierced his chest. Azizi jumped up and lunged at the next soldier. The soldier's sword and Azizi's dagger clashed.

Amsi saw another soldier ready to stab Azizi in the side. He lunged towards the soldier, tackling him onto the ground

"You are Al-Sakhir's son!" the soldier gasped in amazement.

Another soldier fell from Nakia's arrows, drawing attention towards him. The soldier watching the skirmish between Amsi and the soldier raced towards him. Nakia screamed in alarm as the soldier raised his sword. Naji reared loudly as the soldier approached. Nakia pulled on the reigns as the horse turned to run. "Naji, we can't leave Master Amsi!"

The soldier aimed for Nakia, but Naji turned suddenly, the sword impaling him in the right shoulder. The horse whinnied painfully and began to fall. Nakia was thrown onto the hard ground.

Hamza growled behind Nakia and dashed for the soldier. Amsi turned his head to see Nakia laying on the ground. Hamza reared and kicked the soldier with his front hoof. Nakia looked upward and saw the tall black stallion hovering above him. "Nakia!"

Nakia held his head as the horse's hooves slammed on the ground angrily around him. The slave lifted his head slowly when Hamza's hooves stopped landing harshly around him. The blood of the fallen Naji and the soldier pooled around him. He rolled over and grabbed the soldier's sword. Nakia rose to his feet and ran towards Amsi grappling with the soldier on the ground.

Nakia held the sword to the soldier's neck, panting and sweating. "Stop right there!"

The soldier narrowed his eyes. "You are Amsi Al-Sakhir!"

Nakia glared at the soldier prone on his back. "You will not harm my lord!"

Amsi turned his head to see the soldier kick Azizi in the ribs. "Nakia, stay here!"

Amsi saw the soldier bring his sword down quickly towards Azizi's head. Azizi fell to his knees from the force of the soldier's strike. Amsi raised his dagger and buried the blade into the back of the soldier. The soldier gave a gagging scream and fell to the side.

Azizi watched the soldier fall lifeless to the ground. He looked upward at Amsi, panting heavily. "Thank you, my brother."

Amsi took Azizi's hand and helped him to his feet. Amsi put his hand on Azizi's shoulder. "Are you alright?"

Azizi nodded, gripping his bloody dagger. "I will be fine."

Amsi removed his hand from Azizi and found his palm covered in his victim's blood. Amsi's eyes widened in alarm. *My father can't see me with blood on my hands!* Amsi reached down and dried his hands on the dead soldier's skirt. *Sweet Rā, I killed him!*

Nakia turned towards the fallen horse with tears coming down his eyes. "Naji wasn't so lucky."

Amsi turned towards the dead horse and ran towards it. He kneeled beside the bleeding horse and began to pet it solemnly. Amsi closed his eyes and leaned over the horse. "Naji has been my horse since I was a little boy. Why, Naji?" Amsi leaned over, sobbing over the dead horse.

Azizi staggered to the soldier laying on the ground. Azizi held his side as he reached for the hilt of Nakia's sword. "Give me the sword, Nakia."

Nakia handed Azizi the sword and ran towards Naji. Nakia kneeled in front of Naji, petting the horse's cheek. "He saved my life, Master Amsi. I'm going to miss you, Naji," Nakia sobbed, giving the horse one last kiss on the cheek. "You were a wonderful friend."

Hamza slowly walked towards Nakia and nudged him with his nose. Nakia heard a sad whimper come from the wild beast beside him.

Azizi glared angrily at the soldier and placed his foot on the soldier's chest, pressing down on the ribcage. "What do you know of the pharaoh's plans to obtain the ancient relics?"

"The pharaoh is searching for the relics of Isis!"

"Did you and your men kill that woman in the desert?" Azizi asked, pressing the tip of the blade against the soldier's throat.

"You'll have to kill me before I tell you anything, boy. The pharaoh will become invincible and you will crumble to your knees, begging for mercy!"

Azizi stabbed into the man's shoulder angrily, making the man cry out in pain. Azizi twisted the blade with a sudden motion. "I will never fall on my knees before that butcher!" Azizi twisted the blade again. "You are a fool if you believe that he is your savior!"

Amsi stepped beside Azizi and watched the loathing in his friend's eyes. The man's final breath left his lips as Azizi grinned with satisfaction. *I'm glad he doesn't look at me with that kind of disdain*, Amsi thought. He wiped his forehead covered in sweat. "We should leave before reinforcements come."

Azizi removed the sword harshly from the corpse. Amsi watched as the man's blood pooled beneath him.

"Azizi, did you have to kill him?"

"Would you rather him inform the pharaoh that you were in my company?" Azizi offered the sword to Amsi. "You should keep this. You earned it."

Amsi looked at his friend. "If I have a soldier's sword, my father will wonder where I found it. You keep it for now."

Azizi nodded. "If you need a sword, I will keep this for you. You will need it eventually."

Nakia lowered his head and cried over Naji. "I can't leave him, Master Azizi!"

"Then the soldiers will find you, return you to the palace where you will be interrogated, and killed by the pharaoh himself. It's your choice," Azizi said, searching for money pouches on the soldier's belts. With a satisfied grin, he held five small pouches of coins in his hands. "My work here is done," the thief said casually.

Amsi walked over to Nakia and put his arms around his slave comfortingly. "Let's go, Nakia. It will be alright."

Amsi and Nakia followed Azizi out of Heliopolis. Azizi stopped before the gate to the Al-Sakhir lands. He turned and stood before his friend.

"Thank you for saving my life, Amsi."

Amsi looked at his hands. "I never killed anyone before, Azizi."

Azizi looked into Amsi's eyes. "You are now a wanted man like myself. You have just committed a most heinous act of treason. You have just killed your own kind."

Amsi's eyes widened as the reality of his actions was realized. "You're right, Azizi! I just killed another Noble!"

"He could have killed you had you not struck him down. You did what you had to in order to survive, Amsi. That is the law of combat and living on the streets."

Amsi reached for Azizi's shoulders and gripped them tightly. "You are a strong person, Azizi."

Azizi looked at the Al-Sakhir mansion. "I have to be strong, Amsi. You are good in battle, but there will be more difficult battles ahead."

Amsi nodded. "I will be right by your side."

The thief pat Azizi's shoulder with a smile. "I would have none other."

"May Rā shield you with his light," Amsi said.

"May Osiris protect you," Azizi said reverently.

Azizi turned and mounted his black horse. "Keep your eyes and ears open, Nakia."

Nakia nodded. "I will."

Amsi and Nakia watched Azizi ride into the darkness of the desert.

"I'm going to miss Naji, Master Amsi. I don't know how I'm going to tell the others."

Amsi nodded as he looked towards the house. "I don't know how I'm going to tell my father."

Nakia walked solemnly beside Amsi, his eyes were cast to the ground. The slave watched as his feet lightly touched the dirt as he walked. *How am I going to tell the others about Naji? Naji was a good horse. He loved running free just as myself. Now he has the best pasture in which to run. Perhaps I should be grateful for that.*

Amsi saw Hamza nudge Nakia with his nose. "Hamza doesn't want you to be sad for Naji, Nakia."

Nakia rose his head to look at his master. "How am I to explain Naji's absence from the stable to Kaemwaset?"

"I will discuss this with my father. Put Hamza back in the stable and rest. It has been a very long day."

Nakia nodded slowly. "Yes, my Lord Amsi."

Amsi wrapped his arm around his slave. "Please don't be sad, Nakia."

"I will try," Nakia said quietly.

"Goodnight, Nakia."

The slave raised his head to see Amsi walking along the dirt path towards the Al-Sakhir family home. Hamza whinnied quietly and nuzzled Nakia. The slave pet the wild horse gently. "I know you'll miss him, Hamza. I'm lucky you are still here."

Nakia walked Hamza to the stable and brushed him. Nakia gave him fresh water and grain. Hadi's head leaned over the door of his stall and blinked his eyes at Nakia in a silent query. Nakia looked at Naji's empty stall and opened the door slowly.

The slave quietly walked into the empty stall and kneeled on the hay. His eyes filled with tears as his fingers brushed across the prickly hay. *My parents are gone. My brother is dead. Now Naji has been slain.* Nakia raised his head to the roof of the stable. His fists clenched tightly. Nakia's eyes saw a rope dangle from a metal circle. It dangled in front of his eyes slowly; Side-to-side it swayed in the gentle night breeze. Nakia lowered his head, burying his face in his hands. "What more will you take from me, Night Goddess?"

IV

Band of Thieves

Azizi opened his eyes as the sun's first rays crept across the sky, bathing the desert in red, blue, and purple hues. He laid upon the soft fertile grass of the oasis and rubbed his eyes free of sleep. The teen rolled onto his stomach and sipped from the small lake beside him.

His dark eyes peered through the palm trees of his home as the wind blew through his hair. The teen removed his skirt and sighed with fatigue. He jumped into the lake and began to swim, the cool water refreshing his hot skin. *Did the pharaoh order that woman's death? If the pharaoh wanted to see her, he would want her alive.* Azizi emerged from under the waterline and splashed his chest with the water. He rubbed the water around his dark skin to wash away the sweat, dirt, and sand.

Azizi plunged under the water once more. *Perhaps she had a secret. Maybe she had knowledge of a way to stop the pharaoh. Perhaps she came to find me.*

Azizi emerged from under the water and saw Qeb standing beside the lake. "Qeb! What are you doing here?"

Qeb bowed his head as he held his bow in his hand. "I offer my apologies, Lord Azizi, but I have some unfortunate news from our quarter."

The naked teen stepped out of the lake and wrapped his frayed linen cloth around his bony hips. "What has happened?"

"Your companion's horse has been found dead in one of our alleys. Kaphiri says that he has killed your friend." Qeb bowed on one knee before the teenager.

"Amsi is not dead," Azizi said calmly. "Amsi and I were attacked last night by the city guard."

"Giladi has followed the pharaoh to the Al-Sakhir family lands."

Azizi gasped as he glared at Qeb. "Giladi is only an eleven-year-old child and you sent him to follow that tyrant alone? Giladi will be killed!"

"Giladi returned to me safely in the quarter. Jamila found the beast and warned me that Kaphiri was gloating about Amsi's death."

"Amsi's death is exaggerated, but if the pharaoh is with him as well as his father, I fear for him."

"What shall we do?"

Azizi sheathed the golden dagger and fastened it to his belt. *Amsi doesn't stand a chance against his father and the pharaoh if he is alone with them.*

"Qeb, find Nefertum in the mountains. Tell him to be here at sunset. Be wary of the *Nuu*. I still do not know who killed that priestess of Isis and I want answers, Qeb!"

Qeb bowed his head to the ground before his leader. "I will find Nefertum for you, my king. I shall not disappoint you."

"I will not allow Kaphiri to rejoice in my friend's death." Azizi narrowed his eyes and growled at the prostrate Qeb. "I must rescue Amsi from his father and the pharaoh."

"Yes, my king," Qeb said, standing before Azizi.

Azizi reached under a bush and removed a small chest. "Be careful, Qeb." Azizi removed a dress and rolls of linen from the wooden chest decorated with an image of Hathor, goddess of beauty. Below the lid was inscribed 'Ife' as well as text writ in Noble Script which he couldn't read. A row of cosmetics and perfumes sat below the clothing contents. *I knew these would come in handy someday.*

*   *   **

Amsi's eyes snapped open as a piercing scream echoed through his ears.   His mother's frightened scream joined the chorus of angry voices filling the hallway. His heart leapt into his throat at the sound of his father's furious threats.

"Tell me what I want to know or I will beat you more!" Runihura's voice filled the hall.

"You know what we did to your twin brother! I think it's time you suffered the same penalty for your disrespect!" General Gahiji's voice resonated through the air.

"No! Please! I don't want to lose my tongue!" Nakia pleaded, his voice raised in panic.

Amsi quickly rolled out of bed as he heard Qamra and Imani's screams begging for mercy. Amsi ran down the hallway towards his father's office.   His mother and Qamra were standing outside the room as two soldiers held them back. Amsi pushed his way through the two guards and saw Nakia on his knees.   Kaemwaset, General Gahiji, and Pharaoh Runihura were hovering above their restrained prey.

Nakia turned his head in alarm as two soldiers held him by his arms. "Master Amsi!   Tell them what happened last night!"

Amsi clenched his fists tightly and walked to the soldiers angrily. "Let my slave go! He is innocent!"

Kaemwaset stepped beside Nakia and grabbed Amsi by his arm roughly. "Why was Naji found dead in *Iunu*, boy? Were you mingling with your little thief-friend? I told you never to speak to him! You deliberately disobeyed my orders, didn't you, Amsi?"

Pharaoh Runihura blinked, his golden eyes clinking as they glared at the frightened teen. "Do you know the punishment for what you have done? I would chance that you are conspiring against me, Amsi Al-Sakhir Ibn Kaemwaset."

Kaemwaset glared at his son. "You must be taught a lesson, my boy."

"Your Will is no match for a holy relic, Amsi! Horus shall teach you a lesson you will not soon forget," Pharaoh Runihura glared at Amsi and grabbed him by the throat. "Mighty Horus, give me power over my enemy that he may become my loyal servant!"

Amsi closed his eyes as a bright light filled the room. He felt his mind tearing itself apart. He gripped his head as a stinging pain flooded his senses. *The power of the Eye of Horus commands you to follow Pharaoh Runihura! You are powerless to resist!* Amsi grit his teeth against the discomfort. *I am not loyal to the pharaoh! I do not want to live the life my father wants for me!* Amsi saw the metal eyes blinking and clinking before him angrily. *Yet you continue to abide by the law of your father.*

The bright light diminished in the room as the pharaoh released his grip on Amsi's throat. Gahiji caught the Noble teen before he could fall on the ground. Amsi gripped his head in pain as he screamed.

"The boy is confused, Kaemwaset. He questions his loyalties, but he is not a lost cause. A piece of his mind remains loyal to us yet."

Amsi swallowed nervously as they heard loud banging on the front door. The pharaoh, Gahiji, and Kaemwaset raised their heads quickly. Amsi held his breath as he turned towards his mother.

"Has my little prey come to rescue you, Amsi?"

Gahiji threw Amsi to the floor. Nakia was released and brought Amsi into his arms. "I will dispose of your visitor and then your slave, Amsi."

Imani held up her hand. "I do not wish to be rude to a guest who calls, General Gahiji. I will not have you frighten away my visitors. It may be one of the field slaves in need of Nakia's help. I will see who it is."

Amsi looked at his mother pleadingly as Nakia clutched onto him desperately. *This is a bad time, Azizi. Run!*

Imani and Qamra walked down the hall slowly towards the front door. Qamra stepped beside her mistress. Qamra opened the door and she saw Ife standing before them. A long, white gown adorned her from head to toe. Her white veil covered the right side of her face. The figure bowed in front of the two women. "I came to visit Amsi, my lady. I wish to take him sailing on the Nile." Ife swallowed uncertainly.

Qamra leaned over and looked into the eyes of the teenager before her. "Azizi?"

Imani and Qamra watched the figure shift its eyes uncomfortably. Imani looked at the figure's slender hands. There was a gold ring on the person's hand, but the fingertips looked unkempt.

"Azizi Keket? What are you doing here?" Qamra gasped.

Azizi looked at Imani. "Is Amsi safe?"

"Who are you?" Imani asked.

"Azizi, you are not safe here!" Qamra said as she stepped towards him. "The pharaoh is here now."

"That's why I am here. I'm here to rescue Amsi."

Qamra giggled. "Dressed in women's clothing?"

Azizi brushed his sleeve free of sand with a mischievous grin. "I stole this from Ife when Amsi told me where she lived. I figured the gown would come in handy someday."

"Azizi, you are the boy for whom the pharaoh searches," Imani said, approaching the teen. The woman reached out her hand slowly and touched Azizi's cheek. "You are the boy whom I used to see beside the Nile with his mother. I hope she is well."

Azizi narrowed his eyes. "My mother is dead. The pharaoh beheaded her when I was a child."

"I'm sorry, Azizi. Your mother was a wonderful woman," Imani said.

The trio heard a scream come from Kaemwaset's office. Azizi swallowed nervously as his head turned towards the pharaoh's horses lined beside the home. "As far as you know, I am Ife," Azizi growled as he stepped between the two women and into the home.

Azizi looked around the corner and saw two soldiers standing guard by the door. Azizi turned the corner and walked towards the office slowly. "Ife, straighten your back, girl," Imani said. "Remember your posture, young lady."

Azizi straightened his back. *How does Amsi do this every day?* "My apologies, my lady," Azizi said, trying to mimic a female voice.

"Ife would never run," Qamra said as she watched Azizi begin to dart for the room.

Azizi stood in the doorway and saw Pharaoh Runihura slap Amsi across the face with his open hand. The teen fell to the ground holding his cheek. Amsi lifted his head to see blood dripping onto the carpet. Nakia kneeled beside his fallen master and draped his body over Amsi.

"Please, my lord, do not hurt Master Amsi!"

"Shall we punish you instead?" the pharaoh growled, pointing his sword at Nakia's shoulder.

Ife cleared her throat, attracting the attention of everyone in the room. "What are you doing to my future husband?" Ife asked, pushing between the two guards and running to Amsi's side.

Gahiji and Runihura glared at the newcomer. Kaemwaset clenched his fists angrily. "Ife, this is not a good time."

Ife kneeled beside Amsi and winked with a grin at Nakia. The slave's eyes widened as he pulled back from his master and stood beside him. "My beloved Amsi, are you hurt?" Ife cupped Amsi's face in his hands and gently caressed his bruised cheek. "My poor Amsi." Ife leaned forward and gave a light kiss to Amsi's cheek. "Play along," Azizi whispered into his ear.

Amsi opened his eyes and looked at Ife kneeling before him. "Ife?" Ife touched Amsi's chin where a drop of blood trickled slowly. Amsi looked into Ife's familiar dark eyes. The teen's eyes widened. *Azizi!*

"Who are you and what is the meaning of this intrusion?" Gahiji growled at the new arrival.

Ife stood up and glared at the pharaoh. "Why are you beating my future husband?"

"Your future husband has forgotten his place," Runihura said slowly. "He has been consorting with criminal scum, much like yourself, Azizi."

Ife gasped. "How dare you compare me to street filth! I am Ife Re-Nefer! I am a most beautiful woman!" The 'girl'ran her hands along her breasts and hips. Ife turned to Kaemwaset. "I should tell my father that you are allowing the pharaoh to beat my future husband, the father of my future children!"

Amsi swallowed nervously. *I think he's spent too much time in the desert sun.* Amsi struggled to his feet with Nakia's help. "Ife, what are you doing here?"

Ife turned to Amsi and took his hands. "Father said I could take you on the Nile."

The pharaoh grabbed Ife by the collar and brought 'her'close to him. Amsi looked at his father when Pharaoh Runihura grabbed Ife and turned her around violently.

"I know you are Azizi Keket!"

Ife gasped in fear. "I am not him! I am Ife Re-Nefer! Beautiful jewel of the Nile! Princess of Re!"

"My pharaoh, she is my son's betrothed!" Kaemwaset gasped. "Besides, my pharaoh, that garbage would not show his face around here!"

Amsi watched with fear as Runihura turned and slammed his friend against the desk, pinning him by the neck. Ife grabbed the pharaoh's wrist holding him down. Pharaoh Runihura pressed himself against his pinned victim.

"My pharaoh! Please, stop!" Amsi called out as Gahiji held the teen back.

Ife kicked her legs and screamed under the pharaoh's hand. The pinned victim looked into the eyes of his assailant. *"I'll be a good boy, my pharaoh,"* he heard his old words echo through his mind the last time the pharaoh was ready to kill him. Azizi felt his body tense as he felt the pharaoh's breath caress his face.

Pharaoh Runihura grabbed Ife's veil and ripped it away.   The pharaoh glared at the lack of scarring on his victim's right cheek.   "I know you are Azizi!"

Kaemwaset grabbed the pharaoh's wrist and tugged harshly. "If her father should find that she has been violated, my pharaoh, Mahoma will break off the wedding arrangements and I lose the dowry!"

Amsi narrowed his eyes at his father. *The pharaoh is pinning my friend to the desk and all he cares about is the dowry?* "My lord, don't harm her!"

Amsi watched as Pharaoh Runihura grabbed Ife's breast harshly, making Ife cry out in pain. "My pharaoh, you have gone too far!"

"My pharaoh, the girl is a virgin!" Imani cried out in alarm. "Do not spoil her purity!"

"I will not spoil her purity yet. I will indulge in that pleasure later." Runihura released his victim angrily, making Ife sit on the desk and cry into her hands. "She should feel honored to have my hands upon her body."

Amsi watched as a tear trickled from between Ife's fingers. *Azizi, is he really crying?Is this still part of his act?* Kaemwaset watched as the girl cried on the desk, her body shaking and trembling with fear.

Azizi shuddered as he sat on the desk. *I feel so...unclean. It wouldn't be the first time I felt this way.*

"I have never felt so mistreated!" Ife sobbed into her hands.

"Boy, you always tell me how much you dislike her!" Kaemwaset growled.

Amsi rushed to Ife's side and held her tightly. "I may dislike her, but she doesn't deserve such treatment!" He turned his head angrily towards the pharaoh. "How dare you put your hands on my future wife, my pharaoh!"

"I am the pharaoh, Amsi Al-Sakhir Ibn Kaemwaset! I can have anyone I wish! I can have anything that I desire! I can touch anyone that I wish! I need not explain myself to you, traitor!"

Amsi narrowed his eyes. "I am not a traitor!"

Runihura glared at the Noble teen. He approached Amsi and Ife slowly. "You became a traitor when you first decided to converse with street vermin, pests that should be exterminated and crushed beneath your feet." Pharaoh Runihura glared at Ife. "Such creatures are hardly human like you or I, Amsi. They are expendable, slovenly creatures best left dead to rot."

Ife cried harder. "I am not street vermin! My father shall hear of your cruel words, my pharaoh!" Ife's eyes rose to look at Kaemwaset. "How could you allow the pharaoh to put his hands on my body? I am not some brothel whore to use for your pleasure! My father will hear of this!"

Amsi held Ife close. "Ife needs some air, father," he said as he helped Ife off the desk. Nakia stood on Ife's opposite side and helped Amsi hold the shaking body stand. "Ife and I are going boating, father. My pharaoh, I will not have my guests treated poorly!"

Pharaoh Runihura glared at Amsi. "You do not command me, boy!" the pharaoh growled loudly.

"Nakia, I will take the price of that horse out of your hide!" Kaemwaset fumed.

Ife cried loudly. "I want to leave! I feel so violated!"

Amsi leaned into Ife. "Azizi, you're being overly dramatic," Amsi whispered.

Ife cried louder. "I have never been so poorly treated in my Noble life! My name has been soiled!"

Amsi and Nakia helped Ife out of the room and down the hallway. Nakia looked behind him to see the guards watching them intently. "Keep going. They're watching us," Nakia whispered.

"We're almost there," Amsi replied.

"I need a bath!" the Ife-imposter cried loudly.

The trio turned the corner and breathed a sigh of relief. Amsi and Nakia released Azizi from their grasp. Azizi turned his head to Amsi. "What did you think of my performance?" The King of Thieves asked with a grin.

Nakia looked around the corner and saw the guards marching towards them. "We're not safe yet, my lords."

Nakia and Amsi grabbed Azizi again. The slave and master helped Azizi out of the door of the Al-Sakhir home. The trio walked down the path towards the gate.

Khentimentiu watched as Amsi passed the garden. "Good day, Master Amsi!" the boy called to him.

Amsi waved to the little boy and continued to walk beside his friends. Nakia looked over his shoulder and saw the guards watching them from the front of the home.

"Keep going," Nakia said, facing front.

"Azizi, how did you know that the pharaoh was here?"

Azizi kept facing forward, wiping away the makeup hiding the scar on his right cheek. "Qeb found me in my oasis. He told me the pharaoh knew about Naji's death. One of the orphans followed him here."

The trio passed the gate and all of them sighed with relief. Azizi pulled the long gown over his head. Amsi saw a sash wrapped around Azizi's chest. The thief removed two rolled pieces of material from the sash.

"So that's how you deceived the pharaoh!" Amsi exclaimed.

Azizi chuckled as he threw the "breasts" into a bag on his horse. The thief placed the robe into the cowhide bag. "I am a master of disguise."

"Azizi, you could have been killed!" Amsi gasped.

"I wasn't joking about needing a bath," Azizi shivered in revulsion. Amsi watched Azizi's hand quiver as it gripped onto the bag tightly. "The pharaoh is the last person I want that close to me." *That man's hands and his breath smelled of wine in the bordello. I suddenly don't feel very well.*

"Aziz, are you alright?" Amsi asked, seeing his friend shudder with disgust.

Azizi's head sharply rose as if awakened from a dream. "You and Nakia are not safe here," Azizi said removing his black cape from the bag. Azizi tied the cape around his throat and mounted his horse. "Come with me."

Amsi and Nakia followed Azizi into the city. Amsi watched as Azizi wrapped his black cape around himself. The black hood covered his head as they made their way slowly through the streets. Amsi watched as a woman ran beside Azizi's horse.

The young girl looked at Amsi with her sparkling green eyes. She watched Amsi nervously as she took Azizi's hand.

"Fear him not, Kahla," Azizi said, leaning over.

"Aziz, Qasim came to Mbizi's. He's asking many questions of us. He claims he is looking for a priestess of Isis," Kahla whispered.

Azizi held Kahla's hand. "The priestess is dead. Amsi found her in the desert. Has he asked for your services, Kahla?"

Kahla shook her head. "No, but he has paid for Lakia's services. He beat her. She knew nothing of the priestess."

Azizi narrowed his eyes. "Qasim will answer for his actions, Kahla!"

"Kaphiri's clan is searching for the priestess. I have spoken with Jamila and she said that Kaphiri's clan has stolen from three of the shops in your territory."

"Take care of yourself, Kahla. Keep me updated on Kaphiri's movements."

Kahla's green eyes sparkled as she looked at Azizi. "Be careful, my king."

Amsi watched as Azizi leaned down and kissed Kahla on the lips tenderly. Azizi's brushed her cheek lightly with the back of his hand. He closed his eyes and placed his forehead against hers lightly. "I shall," he whispered. "Be careful of Qasim." Kahla's eyes shifted to the wealthy teen sitting beside Azizi. Kahla bowed her head and began walking with the crowd. Amsi watched as Azizi coaxed his horse forward.

"Who was she?"

"Kahla is my girlfriend," Azizi responded. "She works for Mbizi along with the other women of the night." Azizi lowered his head solemnly. "When my mother was upstairs, sometimes they would just hold me by the fireplace. I would look into the flames for hours waiting for my mother to return downstairs. Mbizi sometimes would-." Azizi fell quiet. *He smelled of wine...* Amsi watched his friend slouch slightly in his saddle. He watched his friend shudder. Azizi bit his lip and shook his head. "I do not wish to discuss this further."

Azizi turned his companions into an alley where four people were gathered. The youngest member of the group ran to Amsi and held out his hands.

"Master Amsi Al-Sakhir! Dînar for some food, sir?" the little boy asked with large eyes.

"I don't have any money on me," Amsi responded.

"But, I'm hungry!" the boy pleaded.

Azizi dismounted his steed and kneeled beside the boy. "Jamila will bring something for you later, Saqr."

The nine-year-old sighed and watched as Azizi approached the group.

"Kahla told me that Qasim has been at Mbizi's looking for the priestess of Isis," Azizi said as he stood before the group.

A little boy holding a rope nodded. "I overheard Marid talking to Qasim near the butcher. I took some of Marid's money from his pouch," the little boy giggled as he held out a handful of coins.

Azizi pointed to Saqr. "You should give a dinar to Saqr, Giladi. He is hungry."

"I'm hungry, too!" Giladi protested. "I stole this myself! Saqr can steal his own money!"

"We must help each other, Giladi. When your money is gone and Saqr has money, he would give you money if you were hungry." Azizi watched as Giladi clutched the money in his hand. "Do you remember Ferryn? If someone shared a dinar with him, his life could have been saved. He never would have been killed by Qasim while looking for food. We are all brothers, Giladi."

Giladi looked at the coins in his hand and into Saqr's eyes. The nine-year-old kneeled before Giladi pleadingly. "Please, Giladi?"

Giladi handed Saqr a coin slowly. Saqr took the coin and kissed it happily. He wrapped his arms around Giladi tightly. "Thank you! Thank you!"

Qeb stood before Azizi. Amsi watched with amazement at the respect with which the other street thieves treated their leader. "I found Nefertum in the desert, my king. He will be at your oasis when the sun has fallen." Qeb turned to Amsi. "I also bring news to you, sir," Qeb said, lowering his head.

"Please don't bow to me. I'm no king," Amsi said.

"You are of Noble Blood."

Azizi raised his head quickly as a woman's scream echoed through the quarter. "What was that?"

"Renet-Ka must have found her mother dead. She was sick with the 'Red Fever,'" Jamila said. "She has been coughing at night and she has been screaming in pain for the last two days."

Amsi looked down at Qeb. "What news have you for me?"

"Nefertum has said that a Bedouin caravan is traveling through the desert and will be here shortly. He has commanded me to give this to you," Qeb reached into his robes and offered him a small pouch. "Nefertum told me to give this to Amsi Al-Sakhir Ibn Kaemwaset of Heliopolis."

Amsi took the pouch into his hand slowly. He untied the string holding the pouch closed.

"I think it's from your girlfriend, Amsi," Azizi chuckled.

"She's not my girlfriend!"

Azizi chuckled. "Of course she's not! Just because you couldn't stop talking about her for months after the last time she left is a clear indication that you have no feelings for her whatsoever! Amsi, you cannot fool Azizi Keket Ibn Ghazi."

Amsi reached into the opening of the pouch and removed a gold bracelet decorated with a single pearl. Woven into the gold were tiny strings of silver. "Zahra," Amsi whispered with a smile. "She still remembers me."

"I'm always sending gifts to people for whom I have no feelings," Azizi snickered.

"She and I are friends, Azizi," Amsi said.

Nakia looked at the bracelet with wonder. "Amsi, that is beautiful! You should wear it!"

Amsi placed the bracelet around his wrist. "I can always say I bought it in the city. Father would never suspect."

"The pharaoh is after the next ancient relic. I have a dead priestess in my desert and I have no answer as to why. Kaphiri has been stealing from my territory. Qasim beat one of the women of the brothel and needs to be taught a lesson," Azizi said to Qeb. "Kaphiri also seems to delight in the falsehood that he killed my friend. Kaphiri must pay for his lying tongue!"

Qeb stood on his feet and put a hand on the fifteen-year-old's shoulder. "Let us deal with Kaphiri's trespass."

The group heard the sounds of chariots racing down the street. Jamila ran to the end of the alley and peeked around the corner. "The pharaoh is returning! Azizi, quick! Run!"

Amsi watched as Jamila returned to the group quickly. *There's nothing blocking the pharaoh's view!* Amsi grabbed Azizi's wrist and pulled him to his feet. "Come, let's see Nefertum!"

Azizi watched as Qeb, Giladi, and Saqr dashed down the alley's exit. "Follow them, Jamila. I will return shortly. Hopefully, I'll have answers. Keep your eyes open for Kaphiri's clan."

Azizi mounted his horse and looked down at his friend. "Follow me."

Nakia followed his master and his companion through the end of the alley and towards the entrance to the city. From down the road they could see the pharaoh's entourage racing through the entrance. When the chariots had passed, Azizi lead his companions through the gate.

V

<u>The First Casualty</u>

Pharaoh Runihura stepped from his chariot and saw Timin working with the lettuce. The child was pouring a small jar of water over the green leaves. The little boy kneeled on the ground, his thin legs almost sinking in the irrigated soil. The two-year-old's fingers dug into the soil as his father had taught him.

"Timin! Come here!" Runihura bellowed towards the child, making him startle. The boy stood up slowly,took a few cautious steps towards the pharaoh, and stopped.

"I didn't say stop there! I told you to come here, you deaf mule!"

"You will come to the pharaoh's side when you are called!" Gahiji growled, clenching his fists angrily. "Get over here before I drag you!"

The child walked on unsteady feet towards the pharaoh and his General. The naked boy looked down at the ground as he stood before the pharaoh. The child's hands went behind his back as he looked at the grass beneath his feet.

"Get on your knees, you disrespectful child!"

The boy put his finger in his mouth and continued to look at the ground. Runihura narrowed his eyes at the child and kneeled before the wavering boy. He put his hands on the child's shoulders and pushed down, forcing the child on his knees. "Stay there where you belong in my presence. Your father should be teaching you better respect for people who are better than you are and who are better than you will ever be."

"Hamadi will hear of this, my pharaoh," Gahiji said, bowing his head.

Pharaoh Runihura stood on his feet. "See that he does, Gahiji. I will also speak to him about training his little seed to be more respectful."

"My pharaoh! My pharaoh!" Kazemde ran down the path. Kazemde raised his wooden staff in alarm.

Pharaoh Runihura looked down at the boy. "Get back to work, little mule."

Kazemde arrived before the pharaoh and bowed before him. "My lord. Hakim has passed into Tuat!"

Pharaoh Runihura glared at the physician angrily. "You did not save him, Kazemde?"

"My lord! Your Grace! I have done everything within my power! I have recited every chant! I have given Hakim elixirs of healing, but the fever was too great."

"Has the priestess of Isis arrived?"

Kazemde shook his head. "She has not arrived, my lord. The *Nuu* should have arrived with her by sunrise."

Pharaoh Runihura growled low in his throat. "The fools had better return safe with her! Prepare Hakim's body, Kazemde."

"Yes, my pharaoh."

Runihura walked slowly towards the entrance to the palace. "The Al-Sakhir boy troubles me, Gahiji. There was something not quite right about his intended bride. All the women in Egypt would be honored for a chance to have my hands upon them."

"She is still a virgin, my king," Gahiji said.

"Even a woman untouched would not hesitate to have my hands upon her. No woman can resist me. I will be the most powerful being in the world when I acquire all of the ancient relics."

General Gahiji grinned. "Women will be willing to fight and die to provide you an heir to the throne, my pharaoh. It would be quite entertaining to watch them fight for a chance for you to take them to your bedchamber."

Runihura licked his lips slowly. "It would be entertaining, indeed."

"What do you propose we do about the Al-Sakhir boy?"

"I cannot kill him outright. The Nobility will boil in outrage that I slaughtered one of their own. Kaemwaset would certainly not approve. I will catch that boy in the act of deception one day, Gahiji. When that day comes, he and his friend Azizi Keket will die together. Their deaths will not come swiftly."

Runihura walked solemnly towards Hakim's room where priests were kneeling around the bed and chanting spells of protection and guidance. Runihura stood beside the bed and looked at the red patches of skin covering Hakim's corpse. Hakim's mouth was opened wide in an eternal, silent scream.

One priest said as he bowed his head, "His soul left him as he was screaming in agony, my king."

"The priestess of Isis has not arrived, my pharaoh. We had hoped that she would bring her Djet and heal the High Priest with her magicks."

Runihura looked down at Hakim. "I have plans for her upon her arrival. She will reveal to me the secret location of the Scroll of Isis and the Circlet of Isis."

"My pharaoh, you remember the strong ferocity with which the people of Edfû protected the Eye of Horus. The priestesses of Isis will not willingly offer their sacred relic without a fight."

Runihura chuckled. "I need not fight them. They will make perfect little house slaves when we take them prisoner. Besides, one of them is under my command. She has looked deeply into my eyes and now I control her mind," Pharaoh Runihura stepped towards Hakim's body and covered it with the thin white linen. "Give my regards to my mother, Hakim. You and I have made her proud in the afterlife." The pharaoh left the room and walked towards the throne room.

Pharaoh Runihura walked towards the altar and opened the Scroll of Thoth. His metal eyes blinked as he focused upon the hieroglyphics.

Bear you the Circlet of Isis

Possess the glory of the Divine Enchantress

Look to the Scorpion for healing wind

For plague and drought from Circlet rescind.

"With Hakim's death, Gahiji, we must find a way to protect ourselves from this ailment."

"Many people in *Iunu* are suffering from Hakim's burned skin. The gods must be angry."

Pharaoh Runihura narrowed his eyes. "Should I obtain the Circlet of Isis, I can become impervious to sickness. I can save my people from the afflictions which corrupts our people." The pharaoh grinned. "The gods are not angry. Can you not see, Gahiji? Sekhmet is helping me rid Heliopolis of the scourge of parasites that inflict our city. She has blessed me in my cause."

"Why did she strike Hakim? Why would she strike one of our own people?"

Runihura chuckled. "Hakim was an old man. He was frail in body."

"We must send for a new High Priest, my pharaoh."

The pharaoh nodded. "Yes. Hakim must be replaced as soon as possible."

Gahiji and Runihura turned to the entrance to the throne room. Heh bowed and calmly stepped into the throne room. Heh kneeled before him.

"My gracious pharaoh, I have located the priestess of Isis."

Runihura looked up and failed to see the woman behind the *Nuu*. "Well bring her in, Heh! Don't keep me waiting!"

Heh lowered his head solemnly. "She is dead, my king."

Pharaoh Runihura clenched his fists angrily as he stood before the kneeling man. "What? Who killed her?"

"I know not who killed her, my king. The thieves of the desert did not rob her of her gold, but her belongings were gone."

Runihura narrowed his eyes. "Did you find her Buckle?"

Heh shook his head. "The Buckle was not around her neck, my king."

"The thieves of the desert must have stolen it! I need that Buckle!" The golden eyes flickered in the light of the torches beside the throne. Runihura's fists clenched tighter as he scowled at the abyss before him. "Azizi! Azizi Keket is responsible! I will find him and humiliate him!"

"Wouldn't the boy-thief take the priestess'gold?" Gahiji asked, trying to diminish the fury of his sovereign.

Runihura turned angrily towards Gahiji. "He has spies throughout *Iunu*! He gets his news from those who lurk in shadow."

"The *Nuu* who had accompanied her said that the woman had questionable ties to her temple. She said that she was in fear for her life. Several priestesses of Isis followed them for miles through the sands, killing one of her guards. The priestess became separated from them."

Runihura stepped in front of the High Priest. "Execute them in my Temple of Sekhmet!" The pharaoh grinned. "Gahiji, you shall take a battalion and travel north to the Temple of Isis. These women must explain themselves. They must not know with whom they are meddling."

Gahiji bowed his head. "My men do not know the way to the Temple of Isis."

The pharaoh growled as he walked toward his altar to Sekhmet. "There must be a way to know the path to the temple! Find a way!"

Heh raised his head and grinned. "My men and I have found *Bedu* approaching Heliopolis. They are nomads who travel from lands far from here. They must know the way!"

Runihura chuckled as he turned towards the General. "Borrow one of them to accompany you on your journey. I doubt they will volunteer their services politely."

Gahiji nodded. "What shall I do with the women and their Temple?"

Runihura grinned. "Burn their Temple until not one rock remains standing. As for the women, bring them to me. I will need to add to my harem. Our 'borrowed' *Bedu* can be added to my list of servants. I care not if you grab male or female for my use. Their screams are equally melodious."
"Yes, my lord."

Runihura crossed his arms against his chest. "You will find the Circlet of Isis while you are in the temple, Gahiji. You will bring it back to me.

The Scroll of Thoth states that the Scroll of Isis lies in holy rest. The
Temple of Isis must have it! Find it and bring it back. The Circlet of
Isis will be mine!"

Gahiji bowed his head and walked quickly from the throne room.
Pharaoh Runihura looked at the thin hunter before him holding a spear.
"Have you seen the Al-Sakhir boy riding in the desert, Heh? He rides
with his body slave, the boy Nakia of the defeated Enzi tribe."

Heh bowed his head. "Many Nobles hunt in the wilderness of the
desert, my pharaoh."

"I want your men to keep a vigilant eye on the boy's moves within the
desert. I know he is conspiring with Azizi Keket. The Blessed
Servant of Osiris believes he can hide from my powerful hands. Find
him, Heh. You will find that boy and bring him to me!"

Heh kneeled before Runihura. "My men have dug up the sands in
search of him. He has eluded us. We have searched the many oases of
the desert. We have explored the burial chambers of your ancestors
and have found the boy has vandalized some of them."

"The desert bandits know of his whereabouts. You will find them and
offer one thousand dînars for the boy's capture. I want him alive.
Such a price can certainly not be refused."

"You are most generous, my king," Heh said reverently. "What if we
find the Al-Sakhir boy and your nemesis together?"

Runihura poured himself a golden chalice of beer. "Bring them to me alive for their deaths will be at my hand," he said with a smile.

* * *

Nakia remained behind at the Al-Sakhir family lands to help Baruti construct new tools for the upcoming planting season. Amsi held onto Azizi as the black horse charged through the desert. Azizi's black cape fluttered around him as the friends sped through the desert.

"I hope Nefertum has answers," Azizi said. "Who killed that woman and why? Did the pharaoh order her death? Why take her belongings and not her gold?"

"Maybe her belongings were better than the gold she wore!" Amsi exclaimed.

"What could be better than gold?" Azizi asked casually. "I found several good pieces of gold in the tombs of the pharaohs and sold them to willing buyers. If I was the murderer, I would have took her gold and left the belongings with her corpse."

"You would have taken her gold. Not 'took.'" Amsi narrowed his eyes. "Did you kill her?"

"I already told you no," Azizi responded adamantly. "Besides, I don't use darts as weapons. I prefer the satisfying slice of a blade."

Amsi groaned with frustration. "There must be some reason why that woman is dead!"

"Do you believe she died from the sickness which is sweeping through *Iunu*'s streets?"

"I don't remember seeing any marks on her."

Azizi gripped onto the reigns of his horse tightly as the oasis came into sight.   The horse trotted through the foliage of the oasis and arrived beside the lake.   Amsi saw a tall man holding a scimitar in his tight grip.   The man grinned as he watched Amsi dismount from the horse.

"You have brought one laden with gold, my king! Perfect. There will be no witnesses to his murder!"

Azizi dismounted his black horse and held up his hand. "No, this is Amsi Al-Sakhir. You will not harm him!"

"My blade thirsts for Noble Blood!"

Amsi gasped as the thief stepped toward him holding his weapon.

Azizi removed his dagger and pointed it in front of him. "Stand down, Nefertum! I have called you here to discuss a mysterious death in the desert."

Nefertum chuckled. "The desert claims many lives with the heat of Aten."

Azizi kneeled beside the lake and began to scoop water into his mouth. Amsi walked over to Azizi, who sat beside the lake. Amsi's eyes remained fixed on the desert thief.

The sitting teen looked up at Nefertum. "Did you kill the priestess of Isis in the desert?"

"I did not, my king."

"Did you see who did?" Amsi asked.

Nefertum lowered his head. "No, I did not see the death happen."

"Nakia and I saw a poisonous dart in her neck. Do you know who would be interested in her belongings and not her gold?"

"The woman was traveling with the approaching Bedouin tribe. She abandoned them and continued ahead. My men and I saw her break from the Bedouin formation in the middle of the night."

Amsi's eyes widened with surprise. "Is it Zahra's tribe?"

Nefertum nodded. "It was the same tribe which had given me that bracelet. Did you receive the gift from Zahra Kah'Li?

"I did receive it. Thank you."

"The Bedouin tribe may be able to tell you more."

Azizi laid on the grass beside the lake. "Do you believe the *Nuu* could have done it? They use darts for their weaponry."

"Why would the *Nuu* confiscate the woman's belongings and not her gold?"

"Her belongings could be used by the pharaoh," Azizi said.

Amsi looked down at Azizi. "The pharaoh would not turn down more gold, my friend."

"That is true. Do the Bedouin use darts as weapons? Perhaps she stole from the tribe and she was killed while trying to escape."

"Would Zahra's clan do that?"

Azizi yawned. "We need to know why she died. If the pharaoh is looking for the Circlet of Isis, I believe it is important to find out why a priestess of Isis lies dead in the middle of my desert with her gold still on her and her sycamore amulet defaced. Maybe she had clues as to the location of the Circlet."

"I will keep my eyes open, my king," Nefertum said, bowing his head reverently. Amsi watched as the bandit mounted his horse. "I will send Desta for answers."

Azizi nodded and waved Nefertum away casually. "You may go now, Nefertum. Thank you."

Amsi watched as the bandit rode away. "When Zahra's tribe arrives, I'll ask her what she knows. She would have information from lands far from Heliopolis. She may hold the key to the Circlet of Isis' location."

"Warn her of the pharaoh, Amsi. Should the pharaoh discover that her tribe knows something about the circlet's location, she will be a target for his wrath."

Amsi nodded. "I will do so. I must return home. I have no doubt that my father is anticipating my arrival."

"Be careful, Amsi. I must rest. I am tired."

"Thank you for helping me this morning, my friend."

Azizi nodded with a smile. "You need not offer me gratitude. You have helped me more than I can say."

"May Rā smile upon you, Azizi."

"Osiris keep you safe, Amsi, my friend."

The sun was setting low in the horizon, mixing reds and purples among the sky as he rode towards his family's lands. Amsi looked around him in the wilderness of the desert. The Al-Sakhir family lands slowly came into view from the distance. He shuddered with a sudden chill that made him stop and look back into the desert. His eyes looked towards Azizi's oasis. *Be safe, Azizi. I need to make it home before darkness falls. I looked down at the bracelet that Zahra gave me. I am glad she still thinks of me. I miss her. Perhaps she and I will*

dance again just as we did two years ago.   May Rā smile upon our
reunion.

VI

Noble Warrior Amsi Al-Sakhir

Shen pinned Amsi to the ground roughly.   Amsi struggled as his
wrists were pinned above his head.   Sawaret looked down at his pupil
calmly as sounds of struggle echoed through the arena.   Amsi inhaled
deeply, the foul smell of sweat permeating his senses. Shen chuckled as
his large hands pinned his prey into the sand and rocks below his
victim.   Amsi grunted as he tried to force the large man off him.

Sawaret leaned on his staff calmly watching the wrestling battle in front
of him.

Gahiji stood beside the Al-Sakhir tutor with his arms crossed,
chuckling at the success of his warrior overcoming his opponent.
"Where is Azizi Keket? Do you expect your friend to come help you?"
Gahiji laughed as he watched the futility of Amsi's struggle.

Amsi grit his teeth angrily as he tried to move his wrists.

"Overpower me," the large, muscular sweaty man said with a grin.
"You struggle like a female!"

Amsi glared at the man hovering above him.

"He has poor balance, Amsi," Sawaret said calmly. "Trap his ankle with your own and roll over."

Amsi moved his leg over with much difficulty. He trapped Shen's ankle against his own body and rolled, sending Shen onto his back. The soldier's eyes widened as he looked up at Amsi. Amsi punched Shen across the face and jumped to his feet. Sawaret tossed his staff at Amsi.

"Shen, stand up!" Gahiji growled.

"Yes, sir!" The large man grunted as he regained his footing. Gahiji tossed Shen a wooden staff.

Amsi's heart beat fiercely as he gripped Sawaret's staff in his hands. Shen smiled, revealing some missing teeth on his upper jaw. The large man's muscles twitched with anticipation of another battle ahead.

"You must defeat him," Sawaret said with a serious glance at Amsi.

Amsi looked at his tutor. "Yes, Teacher Sawaret!"

Shen slowly advanced towards Amsi. "I will teach you a lesson that you will never forget, boy!"

Amsi slowly backed away, his body tensing, readying himself for the large man's assault. Shen raised his staff quickly and struck viciously towards Amsi's head. Amsi raised his staff quickly to block Shen and kicked the man in the stomach.

The warrior laughed as he regained his footing. "Try again, boy!"

Amsi raised his staff to strike his opponent. When Shen raised his staff to block his strike, Amsi quickly jabbed the end of the staff into Shen's ribs. Shen grunted and leaned forward. Amsi raised his staff and swung towards Shen's head. The tall warrior blocked Amsi's strike and lunged at the teen.

Amsi fell to the ground from the muscular man's charge. Amsi rolled away as Shen's staff slammed into the ground beside him.

"You will never defend the honor of the Great Pharaoh Runihura while laying on your back, Amsi," Sawaret said calmly. "Kill or be killed."

Gahiji snickered. "This boy couldn't kill a dead mouse, scholar!"

Amsi narrowed his eyes at his opponent. Amsi jumped to his feet, clutching the staff in his hands tightly. His muscles tensed, waiting for his opponent to strike.

Shen curled his lip in disgust. "You are not worthy to protect Heliopolis against invading enemies, Amsi Al-Sakhir, son of Kaemwaset. An infant battles better than you can hold your weapon!"

Amsi raised his staff, ready to strike Shen's head. His opponent raised his staff to block when Amsi quickly turned the staff and slammed the end of the weapon into Shen's ribs. Shen grunted and leaned over. Amsi jumped to the side and slammed the staff across Shen's back.

The large man swept the staff towards Amsi's legs, tripping the teen. Amsi kicked Shen's knee, making the man topple over onto the sand. Amsi jumped to his feet and pressed his foot against Shen's staff. He pointed the blunt end of the staff against Shen's throat, panting heavily. "Surrender."

Shen glared at the teen and released his staff. "You won this time, Al-Sakhir."

Gahiji grinned. "Hamadi!"

Amsi watched as a thin soldier stepped into the arena. Hamadi held his spear as he approached his superior. Amsi didn't see the same lust for blood in this soldier. The soldier's sunken eyes and skeletal figure lusted more for food than warfare.

"Fight," Gahiji growled.

Hamadi readied his spear as he looked at Amsi. "Prepare to fight."

Amsi gripped the staff tightly. "I'm ready."

Hamadi pointed the blade of the spear at Amsi and lunged for the teen. Amsi dodged and swiftly struck towards Hamadi's back. Hamadi turned and blocked the strike, kicking Amsi. Amsi forced himself forward, toppling Hamadi onto his back. Hamadi's spear toppled from his hands. Amsi dashed for the fallen weapon when Hamadi grabbed his ankle. Amsi fell and Hamadi crawled on top of Amsi, struggling to reach for his weapon.

Amsi punched Hamadi in the face, stunning the soldier.

Shen and Gahiji laughed as they watched the brawl between the soldier and student. Sawaret yawned as he watched Amsi fight. "Amsi, you are showing your opponent mercy!"

Hamadi grabbed the spear and felt Amsi's hand wrap around his neck, pressing him into the arena sand. Hamadi released his grip on the staff as Hamadi's fist collided with Amsi's head.

Amsi screamed in pain as he held his head. Hamadi grabbed the spear and staggered to his feet. Amsi looked up at the soldier pointing the spearhead at his throat.

"Finish him!" Gahiji growled.

Sawaret uncrossed his arms. "My lord, that boy is the only child of Kaemwaset!"

"He should have learned to better protect himself. Teach him a lesson, Hamadi!"

Hamadi's hands quivered as he held onto the spear. "He deserves another chance!"

Shen clenched his fists angrily. "Soldiers don't show mercy towards their foe!"

Amsi swallowed nervously as he looked at the blade inches above his chest. Sweat dripped from his forehead as he held his breath.

"You are testing my patience, Hamadi!" Gahiji snarled.

Hamadi raised the spear slowly and stepped backward. "I can't kill you."

"Kill him!" Shen called as he stamped towards Hamadi.

Hamadi raised his head, watching the large man thunder towards him. Hamadi held the spear tightly in his hand. Shen grabbed Amsi's staff and raised the weapon angrily.

Amsi watched as Shen brought the staff down angrily towards Hamadi's head. Hamadi blocked Shen's strike and jumped backward to avoid a potential strike from his opponent.

Shen watched Hamadi waver on his feet. Shen stabbed the staff into Hamadi's rib as the soldier's weapon began to drop. Hamadi fell backward onto the ground. The spear fell from Hamadi's grip.

Amsi watched as Shen beat Hamadi with the staff. The soldier yelled in pain as the staff crashed against his head and back. "Stop! You'll kill him!"

"This will teach you to show mercy!" Shen screamed angrily, beating the soldier on the ground.

Amsi grabbed Hamadi's spear and blocked the assailant's strike. "There's no honor beating an unarmed opponent to death!"

Sawaret heard Gahiji snarl beside him. "The boy is right, General."

Hamadi rolled onto his stomach, his body trembling from the assault. His head rested on the sand as he heard his son calling his name from the entrance of the arena.

"Father? Father?"

"Don't come here, Timin!" Hamadi called as loudly as he could.

Shen laughed. "Come see your father beaten by his weakness, child!"

"Leave, Timin!"

Shen's foot slammed onto Hamadi's back. Timin watched his father on the ground and began to cry. Shen's foot rested on Hamadi's spine as Amsi grit his teeth angrily. Amsi kicked Shen, making the large soldier lose his balance. Shen fell on his back and felt the spear's blade press against his neck.

"Your cruelty just killed you," Amsi said angrily.

Shen narrowed his eyes again. "You don't have the stomach to slay me!"

Amsi grabbed the staff from the ground and lowered the spear. "Unlike yourself, I cannot kill in cold blood." Amsi ran to Hamadi and kneeled beside the fallen soldier.

Hamadi's eyes opened weakly and he looked at the teen hovering above him. "Thank you."

"How badly are you hurt?"

Hamadi clenched his fist and he winced in pain. "You saved me. Why?"

Amsi saw a shadow hovering above Hamadi. He looked over and saw a little boy standing over the fallen soldier.

"Father?"

Hamadi winced as he rolled onto his back.

Amsi helped the soldier sit on the sand. "I cannot kill a father in front of his son."

The soldier gathered the boy against him in a tight embrace. "Timin, I told you to leave."

Timin looked up at Amsi and began to suck his thumb.

"Amsi, it is time that we leave," Sawaret said. "I suggest that you keep perfecting your skills. You fight with honor, following the old ways."

Amsi stood on his feet and approached his tutor. "My opponent should be able to fight fairly."

"Amsi, fairness is admirable, but not always found on the battlefield. You must slay your opponent first before he has an opportunity to strike you."

Amsi looked back at Hamadi and the boy. Hamadi was watching Amsi carefully as he held the toddler in his arms. Hamadi struggled to his feet cradling the child against him. Hamadi staggered toward Amsi and bowed his head. "I owe you my life, my Noble Lord."

Amsi shook his head. "No. You do not."

Hamadi looked down at the boy in his arms. "I can be here for my son because of your kindness. I owe you a debt."

Amsi shook his head. "No, don't thank me."

Gahiji glared at Hamadi. "You disobeyed my direct order!"

Shen stood behind Hamadi and chuckled. "You know what that means." Hamadi held Timin tightly against him.

"The pharaoh will hear of your insubordination," Gahiji said angrily. "It is time for us to leave," Sawaret said. "Come, Amsi."

Amsi looked at the shaking soldier watching him with fear in his eyes. Amsi put a hand on Hamadi's shoulder. "I look forward to fighting with you again, Hamadi."

Hamadi nodded slowly. "May Rā grant us the opportunity."

Amsi reluctantly followed Sawaret out of the arena and down the garden path towards the chariot.

"You are improving, Amsi. Your father would be proud of your progress," Sawaret said.

"Teacher, shall we tell my father of Gahiji's demand that Hamadi kill me?"

Sawaret stepped onto the chariot. "Your father will be most displeased to hear of Gahiji's demand. I will speak to him about this privately upon our arrival."

Amsi stepped onto the chariot and Sawaret coaxed the horse into a light trot. The palace gates opened and the horses pulled the chariot along the road. Amsi watched as women bore laundry in baskets towards the entrance in the hopes of washing their linens in the swollen waters of the Nile. Amsi watched Saqr skip among the crowd with a smile. The little boy saw Amsi and discreetly waved to him.

The chariot stopped to allow a wagon to be loaded with another victim of the plague. Amsi watched with pity as an old woman mourned the death of her husband. "Sawaret, what do you believe is causing this illness?"

"I cannot say, Master Amsi. Someone has angered the gods. Perhaps a sacrifice would appease them."

Amsi heard Saqr scream from within the crowd. "Kaphiri! Haasib!" He watched as the child ran from the chariot in fear. Amsi looked to the right and saw another teen around his age. The teen glared at him with great loathing. The teen wore a black linen skirt, a long, red cape wrapped around his shoulders and draped over his head. The teen's arms crossed defiantly against his chest as the cold eyes pierced him with invisible blades. Around the teen's neck bore an amulet of Seth.

Amsi gripped the chariot tightly. "Sawaret, we must leave now."

"The wagon has not yet departed, child. The woman still weeps."

The glaring teen's lip curled into a menacing smile. His hand glided up his arm, moving the red cape around his shoulders. Amsi's eyes widened in surprise as a tattoo of Seth was marked on the teen's left arm. The teen closely resembled Azizi's description of Kaphiri Seti, Leader of the Seth Thief Clan.

"Sawaret! We must leave!" Amsi said earnestly.

"I will speak to the cart driver. Perhaps if he moves the cart, we will be able to move by him."

Amsi watched as Sawaret calmly walked off the chariot. "Wait! Don't leave me, Sawaret!"

"I will not be long, Master Amsi."

The red-cloaked teen uncrossed his arms and slowly approached the chariot. Amsi grabbed his staff tightly in his hands. Kaphiri chuckled as he approached the chariot.

"You must be Amsi Al-Sakhir, eldest son of Kaemwaset."

"You must be Kaphiri Seti."

Kaphiri chuckled low in his throat. "The Beloved of Seth will destroy the Clan of Osiris, Amsi Al-Sakhir. Don't look so surprised that I know your name. It is no secret among both thief clans that you are the Noble Blood who sympathizes with those who worship Osiris, God of the Dead. The Thief-Clan Osiris does not stand a chance against the mighty God of Night and Chaos."

Amsi glared at his friend's nemesis. "You keep to your territory, Kaphiri! Your clan is nothing but a clan of bullies who frighten small children for entertainment!"

"We seek nothing less than complete control of *Iunu* and *Khasekhemwy*." Kaphiri chuckled. "Should you decide to fight against us, you will perish with them."

"Azizi will be victorious, Kaphiri."

Kaphiri laughed. "Azizi's corpse will be dragged through the streets of Heliopolis as a testament to our superiority. You will tell me where he lives."

"I will not betray my friend to a pig such as you, Kaphiri."

"Then you will join that poor priestess in the desert!" Kaphiri growled, reaching for his twin swords.

Amsi swiftly struck Kaphiri in the head with his staff. Amsi grabbed the reigns and forced the horses into a quick gallop. "Sawaret! Come!" Amsi grabbed Sawaret and pulled him onto the chariot. Amsi looked behind him and saw Qasim and Marid in pursuit.

"Who are they, Master Amsi?"

Amsi swallowed nervously as the horses quickened their pace away from the two teens. "Street thieves!"

"Savages!" Sawaret exclaimed as the chariot crossed the boundary out of the city.

Amsi took a deep breath as the chariot entered the Al-Sakhir family lands. The slaves raised their heads to see Amsi coaxing the horses quickly. Khentimentiu raced for Amsi when the chariot came to a stop. The child hugged Amsi's leg tightly. "Welcome back, Master Amsi!" The smile faded from the boy. "You look ill."

"I'm fine, Khenti."

Khentimentiu gasped and jumped away from Amsi. "Did you see a crocodile by the Nile?"

"No."

"Did you see a spirit?"

"No."

The little boy gasped. "Did you see Seth?"

Amsi swallowed nervously. "I believe I did."

"Oh, that is terrible news! I'm glad you made it back here safe! I hope he did not follow you here. That would be bad."

Sawaret stepped off the chariot. "Return to feeding the lambs, child."

The child slave returned to the livestock enclosure where he continued to feed the goats and lambs. Khentimentiu pet the sheep as one ate from his hands.

Sawaret entered the home with a reverent bow. Amsi looked towards the entrance to the family lands. *Kaphiri knew about the dead priestess in the desert. Kaphiri's clan must have killed her! Kaphiri's clan would take her belongings, but why would they not take her gold? His clan could have used that gold to bribe soldiers or to buy food or shelter. It doesn't make any sense. Any thief would take gold from a victim. Why would Kaphiri choose to leave the most valuable objects on a victim untouched? I don't know if anyone in Kaphiri's clan uses a dart as a weapon. I don't know anything about his clan other than they worship Seth and are at war with the Osiris Clan.*

Amsi looked at the bracelet around his wrist. "Zahra's tribe will be here shortly. She won't know about Kaphiri's clan, but her people did have contact with the dead priestess. Azizi will want to talk to her, too. Perhaps we then we shall get some answers."

VII

A Happy Reunion

Amsi waited until the darkness covered the land before creeping cautiously from the family home. He stepped into the darkness and saw a glow from a distant fire rising above the walls around the family lands. A smile crossed Amsi's face at the anticipation of seeing the Bedouin tribe and Zahra.

Amsi ran through the arch and saw the tribe had not settled near the swelling banks of the Nile. Amsi walked into the desert where he saw a large group of people and carts gathering around a fire.

"Xeres, intruder!" Amsi heard someone call to the tribe. Loud, angry voices broke the silence of the desert night and he stopped suddenly.

Zahra appeared between the two watchmen, her gold glistening in the fire's light. "Amsi Al-Sakhir! Is that you?"

"Zahra!" Amsi exclaimed excitedly.

Zahra smiled as she ran towards him with open arms. "Amsi! How long has it been?"

Amsi caught her in his arms and hugged her tightly. The fire's light barely illuminated her mature features. Her eyes were lined with black ochre. Her lips were painted red. A gold amulet glistened delicately against her cleavage.   Amsi breathed in her flowery perfume.

Zahra looked at the bracelet around his wrist. She took his hand gently and smiled at the ornate gold. "You wear my gift.   Does it please you?"

"Thank you, Zahra.   I shall cherish it as I do our friendship."

Zahra giggled and blushed, rubbing the top of his hand. "I thought you would have forgotten me. I'm glad to see that it is not the case."

"I could never forget you, Zahra."

Zahra took Amsi's hand and slowly walked with him towards the camp. "We have traveled far, Amsi.   We have seen the Nile is beginning to flood its banks.   Our camp should be a safe distance from its swollen tides."

"The Nile waters will soon flood our fields. My father is hoping for a successful crop this year. Last year the crop was poor and my father was irate."

Zahra lowered her head. "Your father frightens me, Amsi."

The watchmen lowered their weapons when they saw Amsi and Zahra approach. "Your daughter approaches with a guest."

Xeres watched as Zahra and Amsi walked into the fire's light.   He was helping to erect the Tent of Elders that housed the tribal council. The leader of the tribe smiled when he saw his daughter approach with the Noble teen. He offered the Egyptian a respectful bow of his head.

"My Friend Al-Sakhir, the gods bless our reunion," the Bedouin man said, extending his hands towards Amsi.

The Egyptian teen bowed his head and clasped the man's arms in greeting. "The Land of Rā welcomes you."

Xeres looked into Amsi's dark brown eyes. "Word has spread that this is the Land of Sekhmet, the Realm of Typhon, and the Territory where the Evil Serpent Reigns Supreme."

Zahra stood beside her father. "Other tribes are wary of settling here. They say that a giant cobra has awakened in the land of Egypt which seeks to swallow the world."

"He won't succeed, Xeres. Egypt is not a land of war and bloodlust."

"Your pharaoh does not share your sentiment," the leader said raising an eyebrow. "He thirsts for blood of men and women and he eats the flesh of infants."

Amsi took a deep breath and sighed sadly. "I still believe that Egypt can reclaim the glory it once held in its hand. Rā's light will shine upon us once more."

"I am relieved to hear that the darkness which has shrouded this land has not blinded your heart to their corruption, Amsi Al-Sakhir. My people have traveled a long road and I must help to construct our tents."

Xeres bowed and returned to helping an old woman with her tent. Amsi saw Shera and Sumati cooking meat by the bonfire. "I'll tell Nakia that Shera is here. He will be excited to see her again."

Zahra chuckled. "Shera has been talking about Nakia since she learned that we were returning here. She is excited to see the Enzi who has stolen her heart."

Amsi smiled. *Wait until I tell Nakia that Shera has feelings for him! Whenever the tribe leaves, Nakia gets forlorn. I have found him sitting outside the family walls staring into the desert longingly. When I tell him of their arrival, his smile returns and he runs to greet them. When he wakes to help Qamra with the family's laundry, he'll see the settlement.*

"Nakia will be overjoyed to see her. He has been keeping an eye on the desert sands since your departure."

Zahra smiled. "Your friend's clansman found us during our journey. Qeb is well-mannered and gracious for a thief."

"Azizi's followers are just trying to survive. They are nice people."

Zahra nodded as she brought Amsi beside the fire. "He gave me his word that he would deliver the bracelet to you. I'm glad to see that he kept his promise."

Amsi sat beside the fire as Zahra offered him a handful of bread. He took the gift with a smile and began to nibble at the crust. Zahra sat beside him with a handful of grapes.

He watched her place a grape in her mouth as she watched the fire flicker in front of them. He broke off a piece of bread and chewed on it pensively.

"Zahra, Nefertum said that you encountered a priestess of Isis in the middle of the desert. Do you remember seeing her?"

Zahra nodded quietly. "She lost her way through the desert and we welcomed her to join our journey through the desert to Heliopolis. She had other traveling companions, but she said they had become separated from her during her journey."

Amsi looked at Zahra. "Did she say where she was traveling from?"

"She said that she traveled from the north. She said that she had come from the northern Temple of Isis."

Amsi nibbled at his bread. "Where is there a Temple of Isis located to the north?"

Zahra thought as she turned to Amsi. "There is one temple in Kadesh, but it is a journey of many moons."

Amsi sighed. "Azizi and I don't have many moons. We need answers as to why this woman was traveling alone. Did she mention the pharaoh during your journey?"

Zahra shivered beside the fire despite the warmth of the flames. "The priestess said she was determined to reach the pharaoh. She wanted an audience with him."

"Was she mad? Most people wish to get away from him."

"She said she had something very important to offer him."

Amsi gasped. "Perhaps she wanted to offer him a relic!"

"Then there would have been many people tracking her down," Zahra said. "It's not unknown that the pharaoh wields the power of Horus. They are afraid of him."

"With good reason," Amsi said, his head still aching from Runihura's strike. "Azizi and I are trying to stop him from acquiring the ancient relics."

Zahra popped another grape into her mouth. "We'll never know who killed her."

"I'll talk to Azizi tomorrow after my lessons."

Zahra smiled over at him. "What have you been learning?"

"I have been learning battle skills. It is required that all Noble males learn the art of fighting to protect the pharaoh at his command. It is a difficult art, but one that will be useful someday."

"I would think that the pharaoh would not need to train anyone if he has the power to control his enemies and make them obey his every whim. According to the rumor, that is the power that the Eye of Horus bestows upon its owner."

Amsi nodded. "It has also given him incredible strength. He can rip someone's head off if he wanted without effort." *Why did he leave me alive?*

Zahra stood beside the fire. "Wait here, Amsi." Zahra disappeared into the tent she shared with her father. Amsi watched as members of the tribe finished setting their tents and feeding the livestock. Zahra emerged with parchment in her hand. She sat beside Amsi and shifted close to him. The woman unrolled the parchment and pointed to the writing. Amsi examined the strange writing by the light of the fire. The writing composed of symbols was unlike anything he had seen.

"This is from our land many suns travel from here. It foretells of ancient objects which can possess a person's mind and transform him into something horrible, a being without mercy, bent on destruction and chaos."

Amsi looked closely at the images of a monster with clawed hands and dark eyes black as night. "Zahra, where did you get this?"

"It is a book of legend. Stories tell of the deceased who walk among the living. They long for death, but it will not come. They are immortal, yet their bodies never decay."

Amsi looked at Zahra. "When Azizi followed the pharaoh into the Cave of Horus, he said that he met a man who had been dead for centuries, yet appeared as mortal as you or I."

"Did you see him? His body did not decay?"

Amsi shook his head. "No. I was at my Coming-of-Age ceremony. Azizi went alone."

Zahra looked through the scroll, shaking her head. "Much of this knowledge has been lost throughout time."

Xeres approached the teens and handed Amsi a small ceramic cup. "Drink, Al-Sakhir."

Amsi smiled and took the cup with a bow of his head. "My gratitude, sir." The Egyptian sipped the beer from the cup and licked his lips. "This is well-brewed. Thank you."

Xeres sat beside the fire with his cup of clay. "You look troubled."

"Zahra told me about the priestess of Isis which traveled with your clan. My friend found her dead and we are wondering what business she had with the pharaoh."

Xeres sipped from his cup casually. "She was wandering in the desert and we gave her food and water. I warned her about Pharaoh Runihura and his watchdog, General Gahiji. She said the pharaoh would not harm her and she seemed confident in her belief."

"Did she tell you from which temple she had left?"

"She had come from the temple near the northern sea."

Amsi gulped from his cup and wiped his lips dry. "Where is this temple?"

Xeres took a wooden stick from a pile of wood and drew in the sand. Amsi stood and moved beside Xeres. Zahra held her scroll as she stood beside Amsi. The teens looked down as Xeres drew in the sand with the stick.

"You must travel north across the land bridge and follow the sea's coast. You must travel through the land of Canaan towards the city of Kadesh. There you will find the Temple of Isis from which the priestess departed."

Amsi whistled. "It must have been a very important audience with the pharaoh to make her travel so far a distance. I wonder what could have been so important."

"She would not say. She said that she feared her sisters of Isis following her. She told us that they had raised their staffs and chased her like a thief at market."

"Did she steal from them?"

Zahra shrugged. "She said she had something valuable that she had saved from the Temple."

Amsi's eyes widened with surprise. "What if she was transporting a relic of Isis to Runihura? What if she was giving him the Circlet of Isis? Perhaps that Buckle was a clue to the location of the relics of Isis."

"We saw no circlet upon her head."

Amsi's heart leapt into his chest. *If this priestess had the Circlet of Isis in her possession and she was traveling to Runihura, would she had given the relic to him? That would explain why her belongings were stolen, but not her gold! Whomever has her belongings, must have the Circlet of Isis!*

Xeres drank from his cup. "The Circlet of Isis?   What is that?"

"The Scroll of Thoth says that the Circlet of Isis gives the bearer 'healing wind'and the power to expel plague and drought."

Xeres'eyes widened. "Those are powerful abilities, too powerful to be in the hands of a madman."

"Xeres, there is a plague in *Iunu*. It is spreading throughout Heliopolis. Please be careful when you are bringing your possessions to sell at market."

"We will be careful."

Amsi looked up at the stars. "I should return to my family's lands." The teen looked at the girl standing beside him. "It is good to see you again, Zahra."

Zahra smiled and put her hand on his arm gently. "You honor us with your presence, Amsi."

"You know, that is a very long travel through the desert for my friend to go alone."

Zahra nodded. "The trip can be made by crossing the Great Green. If you sail, it will be shorter."

Amsi chuckled. "I don't know how good Azizi is at seafaring. My family does have a boat to travel down the Nile."

"Remember to pray to the Sea Goddess for a safe journey and she will grant you a pleasant sail."

Amsi turned to Zahra and took her hand. "I wish to remain here, but I yet I cannot let Azizi travel alone."

Zahra pressed a single finger gently to Amsi's lips. "Go with your friend. Keep him safe. I will still be here upon your return."

Amsi reached out slowly and hugged Zahra tightly. "I'm happy that you have returned," he whispered in her ear.

Zahra smiled as she rested her head against his shoulders. "You are a good friend. The gods smile upon our reunion."

Amsi reluctantly released her from his arms and began walking slowly towards his family home. *How am I going to convince my father to allow me to take the boat?*

VIII

<u>The Bride of Pharaoh Runihura</u>

Qeb, Khalil, Darwishi, and myself waited anxiously for the arrival of the enemy. Our eyes narrowed as we watched the road before us. The Eye of Rā was slowly rising and warming the cold streets of *Iunu*. They owe me an explanation for their arrogance! Kaphiri can attack me all he wishes. I will fight the ambassador of Seth until the end of my days. I will not tolerate his attack on my friends!

It is a rare occasion when our two clans collide without weaponry. When I see him in front of me, it takes me every ounce of control I have not to cut him. He steals from my territory, he steals from my clan, and now he has resorted to ridicule. Kaphiri had best watch his tongue or he shall lose it.

"Do you think they will come, my king?" Khalil asks.

"Kaphiri may be despicable, but when he says he will arrive, he will arrive."

Khalil shifted closer to Qeb, who was gripping his bow tightly. The clan archer lowered his hand and placed it on Khalil's shoulder. I could see the boy shivering as he held onto Qeb's skirt.

"Today is the feast of Hapi. Soon these streets will become impassable with revelers. Kaphiri had better be prompt."

I clenched my fists angrily. "He will come or I will drag him from his snake-hole personally."

Khalil looked up at Qeb. "The crowds will pack the streets of *Iunu*! Many pockets will be left unprotected! Qeb, will you come with me through the crowd?"

I lowered my head to look at the eager eleven-year-old. "With the streets so populated, escape will prove difficult. Be careful not to be caught."

Khalil nodded excitedly. "Qeb taught me well! Didn't you, Qeb?"

Qeb narrowed his eyes as his lip curled into a sneer. "The pigs have arrived."

From the end of the street, I saw the rival Seth Clan approach. Kaphiri's sandals tapped lightly on the ground as his red cape spread behind him. Around his neck, I could see the amulet of Seth and a gold necklace. That despicable creature dares to walk these streets bearing the Mark of Seth on his bare chest.

Behind my rival, Amari, Ini-Herit, Chakir, and Idogbe held their weapons, ready to strike. Darwishi and Qeb raised their weapons. From the corner of my right eye, I saw the blade of two swords and Qeb's arrow from the corner of my left.

Kaphiri appeared unalarmed by the threat posed by Darwishi and Qeb. "Greetings, Death-Worshippers."

"Your feet profane this sacred district which honors the God of the Dead, Kaphiri," Darwishi said with disgust.

Kaphiri chuckled. "It is you who desecrate these streets which rightfully belong to the God of Night and Chaos, the Beloved Seth!"

Chakir laughed. "Osiris was not fit to rule Egypt! The Great Seth will once again destroy those who oppose him such as you!"

"You dare mock the God of the Dead? I will send you to him!" Darwishi growled and raised his weapon.

"HALT!" I exclaimed, holding out my arm. "Stop this! I am here for answers."

"Then please, by all means, Azizi, let us get to business. I don't like the stench of vermin around here," Kaphiri said, looking at the child clinging to Qeb.

I lowered my arm and stepped towards Kaphiri. My eyes narrowed at my enemy. I do not fear him. He returns my same menacing glare.

"Why have you been stealing from my district? Your district is *Khasekhemwy*."

"Our district is *Iunu*! It has always been *Iunu*!" Kaphiri growled at me. "Seth bows to no one! We take what we want! We need not answer to you."

Qeb and Darwishi growled behind me as Kaphiri's clan laughed. Kaphiri dares to mock Blessed Osiris? He shall pay for his blasphemy when my dagger finds its way into his belly!

"*Iunu* is my territory, Kaphiri! The next time that I find one of your clan members in *Iunu* they will pay a hefty price!" I grabbed my golden dagger and held it towards Kaphiri's chest. "Do not cross me, Kaphiri Seti. Your clansman who finds his way into *Iunu* again shall have his entrails removed by my hand personally."

Kaphiri looked at my dagger and smiled. "You will also pay should I find another home in *Khasekhemwy* robbed by one of your men."

Darwishi spat on the ground at Ini-Herit's feet. "I would sever my feet from the ankle should I decide to step foot on your corrupted soil."

Ini-Herit clenched his fists and raised them towards Darwishi. "I dare you to dishonor me again!"

"My men do not violate our boundaries!" I said, stepping backwards near my men. Darwishi was ready to strike our foe before I could obtain the answers I want. You'll get your chance, Darwishi.

"There have been homes robbed in my quarter!" Kaphiri growled.
"Your men are responsible!"

"Where is proof?" Qeb asked calmly, holding Khalil against him
protectively.

"He ran away before we could catch him! His feet were swift."

I glared at Kaphiri. "Until you have proof that one of my clan has
robbed you, do not accuse me falsely. You must cease using your
forked tongue to spread vicious rumors.   Amsi was not killed by you
or your clan!"

Kaphiri chuckled. "Did I hit a sensitive nerve, Azizi?" The demon
crossed his arms.   "I don't see why you should care about the safety of
Amsi. He is simply one among many other Noble vultures." Kaphiri
stepped towards me. "He will be the death of you, Azizi Keket."

"You are a monster, Kaphiri! Amsi is my friend! Amsi has given me no
cause to doubt him!"

"Do you think he cares for you, Azizi? Do you think that should the
soldiers capture you and drag you to the pharaoh's palace that he would
risk his life to save you? For what reason would he come to your aid?"
Kaphiri grinned.   I tried to control my fury, my rage.   What Kaphiri
said couldn't be true! Amsi would help me should I find myself in the
pharaoh's dungeon!   I have saved Amsi from the anger of his father
and the pharaoh, knowing that I was flirting with death.   Amsi would
risk the same for me. Right?

"Amsi would lose nothing should you perish."

"Hold your tongue!" I growled, fighting back my urge to strike him.

Kaphiri smiled at me and grabbed my wrist. Kaphiri leaned into my ear and whispered. "I hope that you enjoy your friendship with him now, Azizi. Because when you die, only the rats will mourn you."

Stop it! A burst of rage sent my hands against Kaphiri as I shoved him onto the ground. My body trembled as I clenched my fists tightly. "Silence!"

Kaphiri rose to his feet. "You are so convinced of his loyalty.   He is of Noble Blood. Why would he care about a death-worshipper such as yourself? He worships the Sun God.   The rays of the Aten bless him each day.   The sun shines upon him, bathing him in radiance and purity." Kaphiri grabbed my tattered, white skirt. "Your clothing is covered in sand and mud and is torn. A simple rope holds your skirt around your starving body. What could you possibly have to offer him?"

Qeb stepped forward by my side. "How dare you mock the King of Thieves!"

"What did the belongings of the priestess in the desert have to offer you, Kaphiri?" I asked him.

Kaphiri grinned. "We have heard of soldiers speak of her death, but I don't recall what they said."

I reached into my money purse and dropped five dînars at his feet.

"My memory is very uncertain. There was something that the pharaoh's guards said about the priestess and why the pharaoh was anticipating her presence. If only I could remember!"

Another ten dînars landed at his feet and he smiled at me.

"I remember now," my enemy said, rubbing his chin. "The pharaoh is searching for a suitable mate."

Darwishi, Geb, and I exchanged glances. The pharaoh desires a male heir who would continue his father's legacy of domination.

"If the pharaoh becomes immortal, he will have no need of children," I said.

Qeb looked down at me and shook his head. "No, he will still need children. If he fathers enough children, the pharaoh's reach can extend throughout the world.   He will have agents in every city, every Nome who would be willing and able to do his bidding!"

"The pharaoh has no sister or mother with whom to mate and produce an heir for him," Darwishi said. "The pharaoh is seeking women from elsewhere."

"What are you talking about?" Khalil asked, too young to follow our discussion.

I turned to Kaphiri. "Why would he choose a priestess of Isis for his mate?   Wouldn't he prefer a priestess of Sekhmet?"

Kaphiri shrugged. "I do not dictate the pharaoh's lust.   He seems to have eyes for women of power and Nobility."

"The pharaoh would not want to mate with the harlots of your clan," Idogbe said.

"I'm not so certain of that, Idogbe," Kaphiri said. "The pharaoh's eyes may turn to Kahla and his hands may find their way into her house."

I raised my dagger and lunged for Kaphiri. "You do not dishonor my Kahla!"

Qeb quickly loaded his bow and fired an arrow at Idogbe, hitting him in the chest. Kaphiri grabbed one of his swords and raised it above his head. I kicked him in the chest, sending him to the ground. Jumping on top of him, my hands gripped his wrist and slammed his hands on the ground. "How dare you talk about Kahla in such a vile manner!"

I heard Chakir and Amari above me as well as the clash of swords. Darwishi was engaging them in a battle of steel.   Ini-Herit's fist struck against my head, knocking me off Kaphiri. I gripped my head in pain as Ini-Herit picked me off the ground. He held me in the air with one hand and felt his massive fist collide with my stomach. My assailant threw me to the ground. My hands went to my stomach, groaning as it burned.

Khalil's ball hit Ini-Herit and landed on my head. Kaphiri rose to his feet, lingering above me. He pointed his sword at my throat and smiled down at me. "I will be the one to collect the money on your corpse!"

My foot connected with his knee, sending him staggering backward and limping.

Qeb readied his bow again as Chakir and Amari grabbed their staggering leader and helped him limp away from our brawl.

"You will not get away with this, Death-Worshippers!" Kaphiri called as he raced away.

How dare Kaphiri even suggest that the pharaoh would have eyes for my Kahla! She belongs to me! She says that she has eyes for none other. I believe her. I hate you, Kaphiri! My Kahla would never invite the pharaoh, the Butcher of *Iunu*, into her bed!

Those sons of jackals raced down the street and disappeared into their quarter.

My body fell back on the ground as I held my stomach. It burned from Ini-Herit's assault. Those fists have won him many alley fights in *Khasekhemwy*. His fists can shatter wood and slice through mud-brick.

Darwishi and Qeb stood beside me as I rolled onto my side. Khalil kneeled beside me and touched my shoulder.

"Azizi, can you stand?"

"The streets will soon become alive with revelers to the God of the Nile."

Darwishi and Qeb grabbed my arms and pulled me to my feet. My hands wrapped around my waist as my stomach burned. "My King, we should take you to Aneksi."

"No, before I see Amsi, I must visit Kahla. If the pharaoh is looking for a mate, she could be in danger, especially if the pharaoh becomes desperate."

IX

Festival of Hapi, God Of The Nile

Amsi groaned as he felt Nakia's familiar hands rouse him from his sleep. "Master Amsi, it is time to wake! Your father requires that you bathe and dress quickly. Today is the Festival of Hapi, God of the Nile! Master Amsi, awake!"

Amsi groaned as he rolled over on his bed of feathers and expensive linen. His head peered out of the window at the dark night. "The sun has not yet risen, Nakia."

"Lord Kaemwaset says that you must prepare yourself for your prayers!"

Amsi yawned as he sat on the bed. The teen tiredly rubbed his eyes. "It's too early."

"Hurry, Master Amsi!"

"Where are we going?" Amsi asked, pushing the light blanket off him.

"Your father has commanded that we go to the Temple of Hapi!"

Amsi splashed some water on his face from a green glass bowl. Amsi took a small glass bottle of scented oil and rubbed his chest. "I must find Azizi and speak with him."

"I do not know how you will find him. The streets will be crowded today with revelers offering food and flowers to Hapi."

Amsi rubbed the oil into his legs and donned a clean linen skirt. Amsi fastened the golden ankh necklace around his neck. "Azizi and I must travel to a Temple of Isis across the wide waters. He must be somewhere in *Iunu*. You may return home, Nakia."

Nakia stepped towards Amsi. "Do not send me away, my lord. Let me accompany you to see your friend."

"You need to rest. My father has granted all servants a day of rest."

"Amsi," Kaemwaset said as he appeared at Amsi's door. "Prepare for our journey to the Temple of Hapi. The Nile has given you many blessings in this life, Amsi, and you must worship him."

I have to see Azizi! Perhaps I must stall my arrival. "Father, I have much studying for Sawaret to complete before I leave for the Temple."

Kaemwaset narrowed his eyes. "You are required to pay homage to the Nile God, Amsi Al-Sakhir. You cannot miss this glorious event or you shall incur your God-King's wrath as well as the wrath of Rā and Hapi."

"If I do not study my scriptures, I will fail to please you, father. I do not wish to be the subject of your disappointment." Amsi bowed before his father as Kaemwaset looked at him harshly. *I do need to study my scriptures. I was awake too late last night to commit the passages to heart. Sometimes I think that Azizi is lucky not to have to memorize my lessons.*

Kaemwaset slowly approached his son. "Without the bounty of the Nile, all things will perish. Your crops will wither from the rays of the Aten. Your livestock will perish from lack of water. You will suffer the pangs of hunger from lack of food and Rā will burn your back with fire should you not worship the Nile God."

Amsi bowed his head. "I shall arrive promptly for morning prayer to Hapi."

"Very well, Amsi. I will anticipate your arrival at the temple. I will not have you taint the name of Al-Sakhir with tardiness, Amsi."

Amsi bowed his head. "Yes, father! I will not fail you!"

"Bring Nakia with you to the temple." Kaemwaset tipped Amsi's chin up gently. "If I discover, my boy, that you and Nakia do not come straight to the Temple upon completion of your studies, you will have disappointed your father." The father's eyes glared down at his teenaged son. "Do you know what will happen should you disappoint me?"

Amsi swallowed nervously as his father's breath brushed across his face. "No, sir."

"Disappointing your father may cause him to do something very bad to himself or those around him. Do you understand, my boy?"

Amsi nodded quickly, his face beading with sweat and anxiety. "Yes, father!"

"Then do as I command," Kaemwaset whispered.

Nakia and Amsi swallowed nervously as the large man slowly turned and left the room. "Amsi, take his threat seriously! He is capable of anything!"

"Let's make haste, Nakia. We have to find Azizi before the crowds become too cumbersome."

*   *   *

Zahra smiled as she heard singing rising from the Al-Sakhir lands. A loud, booming voice shouted towards the sky, 'Praise Anubis, for we have a day of celebration and revelry! Long live Master Amsi!'

The girl holding the rope tapped Zahra on the shoulder. "Minoru needs this rope for the goat today, Zahra."

Zahra turned toward Chahna quickly. "I'm sorry."

"You are thinking of your boy, no?" the fourteen-year-old girl said with a happy giggle.

"I find him very handsome. It made me happy to see him again."

Chahna leaned towards Zahra and whispered, "Have you kissed him?"

"No," Zahra blushed, lowering her head with a smile. "We have not kissed."

"Do you harbor love for him? You should kiss him, Zahra! Then you will know if you love him!"

Zahra sighed, the smile melting away from her face. Zahra continued to braid the rope of thread and beads. *His father is evil-hearted. I asked Amsi who that girl had been at his Coming-of-Age celebration. The girl had said that she was not Amsi's wife yet. He insisted that he didn't love her. Her shrill, angry voice still echoes in my ears. She shoved me backwards and threatened to beat me. What if he marries her? Maybe Chahna is right.*

"I kissed Gyasi and told him that I love him. Our parents are discussing the dowry tonight."

Minoru called to the two girls. Zahra and Chahna looked at the thin fifteen-year-old waving his shepherd's staff from a distance. A goat and several sheep crowded around the teenager. "Zahra, do you have my rope yet? Kerem needs his lead!" Minoru looked towards his ankles as he felt the goat head butt his leg. "Ow! Kerem! Naughty goat!"

The girls giggled as they watched the goat bite onto Minoru's skirt. Zahra smiled and shook her head. She stood and walked into the desert towards the nearby shepherd who disconnected himself from the goat chewing on his skirt. "Here is your rope, Minoru."

The teen shepherd kneeled beside the goat and tied the beaded rope around the beast's neck. Kerem shook his head in protest. "It's not tight, Kerem. You will be fine."

Kerem looked towards the city as Minoru pet him on the head. "Thank you, Zahra."

Zahra smiled at the shepherd and turned her head, hearing the hooves of approaching horses. General Gahiji rode swiftly towards the Bedouin camp. "Gahiji! Minoru, the camp!" Zahra ran towards the camp, her dress flying behind her.

"Xeres! The pharaoh's General approaches!"

Xeres raised his head in alarm. Minoru grabbed his shepherd's staff and stood protectively in front of his flock. "Zahra, be careful!"

"Grab one of them!" General Gahiji screamed loudly.

Minoru watched in horror as the Egyptian army charged through the camp, slashing tents with their swords. Women ran screaming from the army's swords and arrows.

General Gahiji turned his head towards the lone shepherd standing before his flock. "You shall do nicely!" The General's horse charged towards the defending shepherd.

Minoru struck Gahiji's hand with his staff. "I will not let you harm my flock!"

The sheep and Kerem scattered from the battle, calling loudly in alarm.

"You're coming with me, boy!" Gahiji laughed, pointing his sword at the teenager. "Shen!"

Minoru turned his head and saw a soldier on a chestnut mare racing towards him. Minoru struck the hand of Shen when he felt Gahiji grab him by his cape. "Let go of me!" Shen moved his horse beside Gahiji, trapping the youth between the two horses.

Shen grabbed the teen's wrists as he struggled to break Gahiji's grip. "You belong to the Pharaoh from this moment, boy!"

"Help! Somebody help me!"

Shen quickly tied Minoru's wrist with rope and draped the captive in front of him. "We now have our volunteer, my General."

"Leave the encampment! We ride to the Temple of Isis!"

Xeres turned his head to see the teen shepherd draped over the horse of an Egyptian soldier. "They are taking Minoru!"

Gahiji's army swiftly withdrew their attack and rode into the desert. Zahra and Chahna saw the animals scattering and watched helplessly as the prisoner was carried into the desert by the Egyptian army.

*   *   *

Amsi and Nakia rode towards the city, hearing the sounds of revelry. Nakia's eyes scanned the multitude of people along the banks of the Nile to celebrate the Inundation.

"All praise to Hapi!   Hail to him, bringer of food!" a priest exclaimed, throwing a handful of flowers into the Nile waters.

"It's going to take a miracle to find Azizi in this crowd, Master Amsi!"

"Azizi is in the city. He's not near the banks."

Nakia looked at his master. "Why do you believe that?"

"There are not enough pockets for Azizi to pick.   He's in the city where people are drunk with beer and the crowds stand arm to arm." *Now I'm beginning to think like a thief!*

Amsi rode Hadi through the streets cautiously. Women and men danced with celebration, flowers encircling their heads.   Their voices rose into the air as statues of Hapi were carried through the streets.

Nakia pulled on Hamza's reigns as the horse stamped his feet impatiently as he tried to navigate the wave of celebrants. "Patience, Hamza. It's okay."

Azizi could be anywhere in this crowd. Amsi and Nakia's noses wrinkled as a foul odor surrounded them. Amsi turned his head to see a fresh corpse rotting in Azizi's alley.

"The Temple of Hapi is ahead, Lord Al-Sakhir," one of the soldiers said standing guard in front of Azizi's alley.

"Thank you," Amsi said. *I couldn't tell if the dead man was one of Azizi's men or Kaphiri's clan.*

It was difficult to see anyone in the ocean of humanity around them. People were throwing garlands of flowers onto a platform where the statue of Hapi was carried by priests. Some revelers placed apples and food on the statue to offer gratitude to the God of the Nile.

The palace enjoys our bounty which my father provides. My father considers it an honor to feed the god-king. Every year I travel to the temple and pray to Hapi to keep our crops healthy and plentiful.I worship the gods faithfully every holiday, every season. Amsi looked around the crowd to find Azizi.

Where is Azizi? I don't see him anywhere. I would think that with the amount of people in the road and the multitude of empty houses that he would have his clan scattered across Iunu. Azizi, where in the name of the Tuat are you?

Amsi and Nakia tied their horses to a post in front of the Temple of
Hapi. Amsi looked around at the dancing women and children before
the temple. The men were playing flutes and harps as women danced.

"You should get inside before your father drags you into the sanctuary
himself."

Amsi climbed the stone steps with Nakia following close behind.
Four tall stone columns decorated the front of the temple. Each
column was carved with a prayer to the Nile God for his continued
blessings upon Heliopolis. Nakia saw the slaves of the Nobility
standing outside the doorway.

One of the slaves opened the door for Amsi, who turned to Nakia. "I
will be quick."

Nakia nodded and sat on the stone steps. As a slave he was prohibited
from stepping through the temple door. The other slaves watched the
celebrations from a distance.

Amsi stepped through the door. An opening through the ceiling of the
temple allowed the rays of the sun to shine onto a garden pool on the
temple floor. Amsi's sandals tapped lightly on the polished floor.

The teen walked through the garden room, lined with statues of Hapi
and torches. Two large fountains flanked a door to the inner sanctum
where prayers to Hapi were heard.

He stepped through the archway and saw a large number of Nobility on their knees. They bent over, placing their foreheads on the ground in supplication to a statue of Hapi.

Sweet incense filled Amsi's senses as the dim room was lit by two torches on either side of the crowd. The smell of myrrh filled the room as the Priest of Hapi anointed the statue with oil.

"Homage to thee, O Hapi, thou appearest in this land, and thou comest in peace to make Egypt to live. Thou art the Hidden One and the guide of the darkness. Thou art the friend of bread and thou art the creator of barley. Thou art the bringer of food, thou art the mighty one of meat and drink, thou art the creator of all good things, the lord of divine meat," the Nobility prayed.

Amsi kneeled on the ground and touched his forehead to the polished floor in submission. "Thou fillest the storehouses, thou heapest high with corn the granaries, and thou takest heed to the affairs of the poor and needy. Thou makest thy strength to be a shield for man."

Amsi heard the door in the garden room open and close quickly. He closed his eyes and clenched his fists as he raised his body. The Nobility straightened their backs as they raised their hands in praise. Amsi raised his arms as his gold bracelets shimmered in the light of the nearby torch. "When the Inundation riseth, the waterfowl do not alight upon the fields that are sown with wheat. For millions of years, the repose of thy fingers hath been an abomination to thee."

Amsi heard a click against the ground and felt something touch his ankle. The Nobility raised their voices to sing a hymn to the Nile God. Amsi crossed his arms over his chest and joined the song only to feel something click against the ground again and knock into his ankle.

Amsi looked down and saw two small rocks sitting beside his leg. *Azizi!* Amsi turned his head and saw Azizi peek his hooded head around the corner. Amsi removed his sandals and rose to his feet. He crept quietly from the room of echoing voices.

He quickly turned the corner and saw Azizi hiding behind one of the pillars. "What are you doing? Only the Nobility is allowed in here!"

"That never stopped me before, Amsi. I go where I want."

"How did you get in here?"

"The door. How else?" Azizi asked with a grin.

Amsi sighed and shook his head. "I guess I walked into that one."

"According to Kaphiri, the pharaoh is looking for a mate. That is why the priestess was sent to Runihura."

Amsi wrinkled his nose and crossed his arms. "Why in the Tuat would she go there? Did she know what kind of tyrant he is?"

"The pharaoh was anticipating her arrival, but I'm certain the *Nuu* have already told him of her death. Kaphiri apparently didn't know why Runihura was seeking a priestess of Isis and not one of Sekhmet."

Azizi leaned against the pillar, holding his stomach. "We need answers and the only way we will get them is by traveling to the Temple of Isis."

"I spoke to Zahra about the priestess. She says there is one temple to the north beyond the wide waters. We must travel through the land of Caanan towards Kadesh. There we will find the temple. Zahra said the priestess was afraid of being followed by the other women of her Temple and she had something to offer the pharaoh."

Azizi wrapped his arms around himself and rose his face towards the ceiling decorated with murals of Hapi and his female counterpart, Isis. His eyes focused on Isis' picture hovering above him. She was offering jars of scented oils to the god drawn with blue waves representing the waves of the Nile. "Why is Isis painted in a Temple to Hapi?"

Amsi raised his head to look at the ceiling mural. "Isis gives the Breath of Life as Hapi offers the waters of life. Why would she not be included?"

"What else did Zahra tell you?"

"Zahra has a scroll which foretells of ancient relics which can possess a person's mind and transform him into a monster, a merciless being wreaking havoc on mankind."

Azizi felt a shiver of cold crawl up his spine. He shivered in the shadows as he thought of the pharaoh wielding such power. "Great Osiris, Amsi, what can we do?"

"It doesn't stop there. Zahra's people tell stories of the dead who walk among the living. They long for a death that will never come. They do not decay even after millions of years."

Azizi sighed. "We have to go to that temple beyond the Great Green."

Azizi and Amsi tensed as they heard the garden gate door open. Azizi turned his head as Amsi shifted close to him. Amsi clutched onto Azizi's shoulders as he looked around the corner.

Pharaoh Runihura stepped through the door, his golden eyes blinking and sparkling in the room's light. The king stopped, his metallic eyes surveying the room around him. Azizi and Amsi huddled together behind the pillar, holding their breath. Azizi's face dripped with sweat as the pharaoh's head slowly turned to the right.

'Don't let him approach...' Azizi prayed as his hand slowly reached for the pharaoh's golden dagger hanging on his hip.

Amsi held his breath as the pharaoh stood silently and motionless in the grand garden room. Amsi felt Azizi tensing as the thief readied himself for a battle. Azizi's right hand gripped onto Amsi's arm as they waited for the pharaoh to move.

"When thou shinest upon the earth, shouts of joy ascend," the prayer in the inner sanctum continued. "For all the people are joyful, and every mighty man receives food."

Pharaoh Runihura walked towards the edge of the garden and looked into the blue sky above him. The pharaoh's eyes shimmered as he turned towards the left row of pillars.

He stepped towards the pillar slowly.

Amsi licked his dry lips. He held onto Azizi tightly. The pharaoh's footfalls stopped.   Azizi's left hand gripped the handle of the golden dagger tightly. The two friends held onto each other, preparing for a hasty escape.

A single breath can alert the pharaoh that we are inches away from him. Amsi wiped sweat from his cheek and held his breath.

The pharaoh's steps turned as he entered into the inner sanctum. Azizi and Amsi peeked around the side of the pillar and sighed with relief.

"That was close," Amsi whispered.

"Too close," Azizi winced. Amsi looked down and saw a large bruise on his friend's stomach.

"Aziz, what happened to you?"

Azizi released his grip on Amsi's arm. "My gang and I met with Kaphiri and Ini-Herit punched me."

Amsi saw a fist dart from the right side of the pillar and pulled Azizi out of its path. The fist embeded itself in the stone. The friends watched with horror as Pharaoh Runihura stepped from beside the pillar and pulled his fist from the stone.

"I thought I smelled a rat!" the pharaoh growled as he glared at the teens. Runihura struck the pillar again, sending stone fragments flying towards the thief and Noble. A twisted smile curled on the pharaoh's lips.

Azizi covered his eyes as rock dust crept under his eyelids. Azizi lowered his head as he tried to rub the rock dust from his eyes. Amsi saw the pharaoh grin and race towards them. Runihura raised his fists and punched towards Azizi. Amsi grabbed his friend's cape and pulled him backwards. Runihura's fists slammed into the polished tile.

The Nobility ceased their prayers in the inner sanctum and began muttering among themselves.

Azizi raised his head as the pharaoh grabbed him and Amsi by their necks. Azizi's fearful gaze focused into the metal eyes blinking at him. Azizi gagged and choked as the pharaoh gripped tighter around his throat. Amsi gasped for air from the pharaoh's tight grip.

"You boys don't look so good. You may want to lie down."

Runihura tossed Azizi and Amsi across the floor of the temple. The teens slid across the polished floor, crashing against the pillar on the right side.

Amsi and Azizi laid on the tile breathing heavily. Amsi opened his eyes weakly to see Azizi slowly stirring and struggling to his feet.

Runihura laughed. "I must say, boys, I'm enjoying our little game of cat and mouse."

Azizi reached down to Amsi and helped his friend stand. Azizi held his ribs as he stood on his feet. The thief removed his golden dagger. "You won't kill me that easily."

"I accept your challenge, Azizi Keket."

Runihura lunged for Amsi as Azizi pulled his friend away from the path of the fist. Runihura buried his fist in the pillar, sending chunks of rock and dust flying through the air. Azizi and Amsi ran out of the temple door as fast as their injuries would allow.

Azizi held his right ribcage in pain as he caught his breath. "That could have gone better."

"My Master, are you finished praying already?"

"Let's go, Nakia! The pharaoh found-."

The pharaoh burst through the wooden door, splinters of wood flying into the air. "KILL THEM!"

Amsi and Azizi watched as the celebrants stopped their dancing. Their voices calmed and a heavy silence hovered around the temple.

Azizi and Amsi watched wide-eyed as the statues of Hapi were lowered. Musicians placed their instruments on the ground. Azizi grabbed Amsi's arm with his right hand. "Amsi Al-Sakhir?"

"Aziz?"

"We are in serious trouble."

Nakia clenched his fists. "I will protect you, Master Amsi."

"KILL THEM, MY SUBJECTS! PLEASE YOUR MASTER!"

Throngs of people ran up the steps towards the two boys and Nakia. Nakia charged towards the crowd, shrieking a familiar war cry that Amsi had heard as they rode through the desert. The people grabbed Nakia, punching him as he returned their punches.

Azizi saw a figure on a rooftop firing arrows into the crowd. *I wonder how Qeb knew I needed him. I owe him much when I see him next!*

"Quick, Amsi, we must get to our horses!" Azizi said, charging down the steps.

Amsi followed his friend, kicking two men down the steps who were grabbing onto Azizi's cloak. The two men knocked down more people racing towards them.

Azizi pulled back his arm and sliced his dagger in front of him, sending six of his assailants falling down the steps and spraying his chest and face with blood. Azizi chuckled at the temporary victory as he raced down the stairs.

Amsi saw Hamadi at the bottom of the steps. The guard handed Amsi his sword.

"Take this! Leave this place!"

Amsi looked at the guard and bowed his head. "Thank you."

"Go! Hurry!"

Amsi raced towards Hadi. A woman grabbed onto Amsi's arm and pulled on him. Amsi elbowed the woman in the face, sending her onto the ground. One man grabbed Amsi's cape and pulled him to the ground.

Amsi pierced the man's stomach quickly as the man raised a stone to crack his skull. The man fell dead beside him. Amsi rose to his feet and saw a woman pulling on Azizi's black hair. Two men had grabbed Azizi's arms.

Azizi's head flew back, breaking the woman's nose behind him. She released his grip on his hair and he struggled with the two men holding his arms.

Amsi rushed towards the men, slicing through one. Azizi's foot slammed against the other man's foot, making him cry out in pain.

With his left hand free, he punched the man holding his right. Another arrow flew towards them, killing two women behind them.

Azizi raised his head and saw a figure on the rooftop point towards the entrance. "Let's go, Amsi."

Nakia mounted Hamza, the large horse bucking his feet behind him to stop the crowd's approach. Azizi mounted his horse and looked towards the pharaoh with hatred. Amsi mounted Hadi as the two teens sliced through the crowd. People fled from the side of the Noble's horse. Azizi looked behind them as the crowd dispersed. Amsi watched Azizi lean forward on his horse and lower his head.

"Azizi, are you alright?"

"Yes," the teen whimpered in pain.

Nakia watched as he saw the figure down the road disappear around the corner.

Azizi watched the figure's disappearance. *That wasn't Qeb!*

The crowds away from the temple continued to celebrate freely, unaware of chaos in the square. They were continuing to chant prayers to Hapi.

"We should return to the Al-Sakhir family lands," Nakia said.

"We can hide better in the crowd," Azizi said, prodding his horse towards the mysterious ally who had disappeared behind the corner.

Azizi lead his friend and Nakia towards the alley where they saw a lone figure standing, a long black cloak covering his body and a black hood covering his head and face. Azizi looked at the figure. "You! I have seen you! You are the one who is stealing from Nen-Re's bakery!" The figure stood silently. "Why did you help us?" The figure stood motionlessly with his head lowered.

Azizi and Amsi jumped off their horses and looked at the silent figure. "Aren't you going to answer the King of Thieves?" Azizi asked.

"Azizi, we owe him our lives," Amsi said calmly.

"Who are you?" Azizi asked again, approaching the figure.

Nakia dismounted Hamza and stood beside Amsi to protect his master. "Azizi, calm down."

"Answer me!" Azizi growled, standing before the figure. Azizi grabbed the man's cloak and shoved him onto the ground. "Show me your face."

Nakia and Amsi watched as the figure pulled back the hood concealing his face. Nakia's eyes widened in shock. His hands went to his mouth to hide his scream of surprise.

"Ah-E-ah?" the man on the ground asked sadly.

Nakia staggered towards his brother sitting on the ground. "Nassar? Is that you?"

I thought you were dead, Nassar. Nakia extended a hand towards his twin. "Ulan?"

Nassar grabbed Nakia's hand and rose to his feet. Nassar looked into the eyes of his identical twin brother. Nakia's eyes filled with tears as he flew into Nassar's open arms.

"Where were you? Kaemwaset said that he killed you! He told me that you were dead! Why did you not come back to me? Why?" Nakia punched Nassar's arm and sobbed against his brother's chest. Nassar wrapped his arms around Nakia and held him tightly against his body. "I thought you were dead."

"Nassar, is that really you?" Amsi asked, standing beside Azizi.

"Yef, Ma-er Am-i. He-o."

Amsi smiled and hugged Nassar and Nakia. "My father said you were dead! I was very sad to hear of your death."

Nakia trembled in his brother's arms. "I've missed you so much! I love you!"

Azizi crossed his arms. "Were you stealing from Nen-Re, Nassar?"

Nassar nodded. "I hu-gee."

Amsi turned to Azizi. "How else was he supposed to eat?"

Azizi sighed. "Very well. Just leave me enough to take when you decide to raid his shop. He's leaving less on the shelves. Of course, if his bread weren't so delicious, he wouldn't be robbed as much."

Amsi released the twins and stepped beside Azizi. "We owe Nassar a debt of gratitude."

"Thank you for helping us, Nassar," Azizi said.

Nassar nodded. "I keep Ah-E-ah a-wife."

"Nassar, you can come back with me and we can be a family again!" Nakia said excitedly. Nassar shook his head. "Why not? Nassar, I have been waiting to see you for years! I thought you were dead! I want you to come back with us!" A tear crept down Nakia's cheek. "Please, Nassar! I need you!   We belong together! We're brothers! We are the last of our tribe!"

Nassar nodded. "We a-way be buffah, Ah-E-ah."

Nakia wrapped his arms around Nassar again. "I just got you back." Nakia's hands gripped Nassar's cloak.

"Nakia," Azizi said, approaching the embracing twins. "My Clan can take good care of Nassar for you.   He is welcome to join the Osiris Clan."

Nakia looked into Nassar's eyes. "The *Bedu* tribe has returned. Sumati will be happy to hear from you, brother!"

Nassar chuckled and nodded. "We go kee er-omie."

Nakia looked at Amsi and released Nassar. He approached Amsi and stood before his master. "Do you wish me to journey with you to the Temple of Isis?"

"Azizi and I can do this by ourselves. Our journey will be dangerous."

Azizi turned his head as the crowd continued to celebrate the festival. "I would suggest that you not catch up here."

"Azizi, did you see Gahiji at the temple?"

"I was more preoccupied with the pharaoh's fists slicing through solid rock to notice the pharaoh's lapdog."

Amsi looked at Azizi with alarm. "Perhaps the Gahiji has left for the Temple of Isis!"

"If the pharaoh knows that the priestess was killed, he would seek retaliation."

Azizi brought his hand to his mouth and coughed hard. Nakia and Nassar watched with concern.

"Aziz, are you alright?"

The thief nodded as he regained his balance. "Yes. Maybe I breathed in too much of that dust. We need to get to the Temple of Isis before Gahiji."

"Zahra says we have to cross the land bridge and-."

"It will take us too long by horseback. Besides, we must get to the Scroll of Isis first."

Amsi nodded. "Our family has a small boat. It's not as large as the pharaoh's ship, but it will do."

"How long will it take us to arrive?"

Amsi shrugged. "It took Men-Kheper-Re ten suns to march to Gaza. Gahiji's army will travel his route."

"We don't have much time, then." Azizi crossed his arms. "Gahiji will not stop to allow his army to rest.   He will drive them until they collapse in the desert from thirst and hunger. You go home and get ready. Pack what provisions you need. When the sun sets, we set sail."

Amsi nodded. "Be at my family's lands at dusk."

Azizi mounted his horse. "I must say goodbye to my favorite girl before I leave."

Amsi smiled as he looked at his bracelet. *So must I.*

X

<u>First Kiss</u>

I watched Azizi ride towards the crowd and disappear.   Rā, please keep him safe.   We barely escaped with our lives. My hands rubbed my back where Azizi and I collided with that pillar. For a moment, I was grateful that Sawaret is giving me my battle lessons. People swarmed us like flies. It was difficult to move and even more impossible for me to avoid taking more lives. I have little doubt that the pharaoh is informing my father of my transgression.

Let him be angry with me! I should be free to befriend whom I choose! My doubts lie whether my own father would pull me from the path of the pharaoh's angry fist. When the pharaoh slapped me in my father's office, it felt more painful than anything I have ever experienced. His fists felt like granite covered in warm flesh. My father raised not one fingernail in my defense.

I watched the twins' reunion, grateful that Nassar was alive. Azizi will take care of him. He will prove a valuable ally in the fight against Runihura. Qeb may want some archery competition within Azizi's gang. The Osiris Clan will adopt him into their family.

"Amsi, let's take Nassar to Sumati. She will be happy to see him and you can visit Zahra! Come!"

Nassar smiled at me and walked towards me. "I happy oo kee you, Ma-er Am-i."

I hugged my former slave, delighted to see him again. "You are always welcome at my home, Nassar. Never forget that."

Nakia mounted Hamza with Nassar behind his brother. I rode Hadi towards the entrance where more revelers celebrated the Festival of

Hapi by throwing bread into the Nile.   Azizi wouldn't appreciate that very much if he had seen that. He would have jumped in after the bread.   I'm certain if he could have one of his gang breathe underwater, he would have caught all the food which had drifted to the bottom of the Nile.

Zahra's camp came quickly into view.   I couldn't leave without saying goodbye to her. If her clan departed during my absence, I wouldn't get a chance to see her until her next arrival.

Our horses approached their camp and the same guards alerted the others that I was returning. From a distance, we saw the men scurrying about, calling into the desert with alarm. One woman kneeled in the desert sands some distance away clutching a shepherd's staff in her hands, crying towards the west.   Several tents had been demolished and food and items were thrown onto the ground.

"What has happened here?" I asked as the twins and I approached the encampment.

"General Gahiji kidnapped one of our young men and has traveled north towards the land of the Sea People."

Zahra stepped from her father's tent and ran towards me, tears streaming from her eyes. She threw herself at me, clutching onto me desperately. As I wrapped my arms around her I can feel her trembling like a reed in the wind. "Zahra, tell me where he went!"

"That beast took my son!" One man screamed angrily at Xeres, his body trembling with anger. "The pharaoh must pay! He captured my boy! He is only a shepherd!"

Xeres put his hands on the man's shoulders. "I will hold council with the pharaoh and demand an explanation for everything, Tamkinat."

The concerned father lowered his head and cried. "He's my only son, Xeres. Why did they take my boy?"

I hear a happy squeal of joy from Shera and Sumati when they see Nakia and Nassar dismount their horses. The twin girls threw themselves at my friends. Sumati cries as she kisses Nassar's lips. Her arms wrap around his shoulders tightly. Nakia and Shera watch the reunion.

"Nassar, I thought we were unable to save you!" Sumati exclaimed.

"You knew he was injured?" I asked.

Shera nodded as Nakia wrapped his arms around her waist. "He crawled near our camp on the banks. We called Onfalia to dress his wound. She wasn't certain if she could properly treat a cut throat. The wound was not deep nor was it wide. He disappeared one morning and we never seen him again."

"I faw Ah-E-ah kiwd by Kaemwa-et."

Sumati hugged and kissed Nassar again. Nakia and I watched Sumati take Nassar into a tent.

"General Gahiji has kidnapped Minoru and they escaped into the desert," Shera said sadly.

"What of the *Nuu*? Why are the *Nuu* not accompanying them?"

Zahra looked up at me as a lone tear trickled down her cheek. "The *Nuu* fired their arrows during the attack. Gahiji knows we *Bedu* wander the desert. He knows we can show him the way."

It appears that Azizi and I have another goal for our mission. We must save Zahra's clansman. "We will return him to you, Zahra."

"Amsi, what happened to you?" Zahra asked me as she looked at my disheveled appearance.

I relayed the story of the temple and the attack. She watched in amazement as I recounted the tale.

"Azizi and I will set sail tonight. I wanted to say goodbye if you leave while I am gone."

Zahra smiled as she looked at me. She took my hand and kissed it gently. "I will wait for you. Every day, every night, my thoughts will drift to you, my friend. Please return Minoru safe."

"Where do you and your friend travel?" Xeres asked as he stood beside us.

164

"Azizi and I travel to the Temple of Isis near Kadesh. We must find the scroll and the Circlet of Isis before General Gahiji arrives."

Xeres chuckled. "Your journey will be long indeed. If you need horses, I can offer you two of our finest stallions. Please return Minoru, Lord Al-Sakhir. If you bring back the boy safely, we will offer you much gold."

"Azizi and I are taking a boat onto the Great Sea. You do not need to pay us for returning him to you."

Tamkinat bowed before Amsi and folded his hands in prayer. "Please, Al-Sakhir! Please return my son to my wife and I. We will give you anything! I beg you to return our child to us."

Amsi nodded. "My friend and I will rescue him. You have my promise."

"Your journey will be perilous. Storms turn boats over and people drown. You can lose your way. Lack of Shu's blessing will keep your sails flat. You should pray to Isis for a safe journey."

Isis would surely bless our voyage. I shall pray that her gentle, life-giving wind will keep us moving toward our destination. We shall hear her moans on the Great Sea as we sail. Her fresh air from heaven will guide us as Rā's light warms our backs. The morning wind of Isis helps Nut give birth to the sun each day.

Zahra turned to her father. "Pae, Amsi ah a leoka."

Xeres bowed his head. "Amsi, I wish you luck in your journey and may the gods keep you safe. I must help my people replace their tents."

Xeres walked away from Zahra and me.   Zahra lead me into her father's tent.   Blankets were piled on the ground for their beds.   A small chest with strange markings resembling hieroglyphs sat in the corner, holding small vials, their contents making the air smell sweet. A mirror rested beside the chest along with a bowl of water.

Zahra sat on a blanket and motioned for me to sit in front of her. "Amsi, I worry for your safety."

"If Azizi and I can survive an attack by a mob under the control of a mad pharaoh, we can survive a journey over the waters of Hapi."

Zahra reached over and cupped my cheek in her hands. Her delicate hands caressed my cheek, sending pleasant shudders through my body. Ife never made me feel like this.

I reached towards her and placed my hands on her arms. "Amsi, I want you to take something with you."

I looked into her sparkling eyes. Her beautiful face seemed clouded with worry.   Zahra leaned towards me and placed her lips gently against mine. She closed her eyes as she shifted closer to me.   Her pleasant, sweet perfume filled my senses.

What do I do? I've never kissed a girl before. Zahra and I have kissed on the cheeks. I have kissed Azizi on the cheeks as a sign of friendship and brotherhood. What do I do?

My eyes closed as a feeling of calm surrounded me. The world outside the tent drifted away. We were the only two beings alive. The giggling and moaning in the other tent was just a fantasy. It seemed far in the distance as Zahra shifted closer to me.

I held her against me, focusing too much on her gentle lips.

My hands trembled from anticipation and anxiety. What do I do? Zahra deepens the kiss as I feel something I have never felt before when I saw Ife. My hands touched her back clumsily. Her hands rested on my shoulders and drifted down my chest.

Her skin is soft and her body smells of holy oil. The world is gone. Everyone leaves. I'm beginning to feel a tightness in my body that is strange.

What is this I am feeling? Is it love? My father has never discussed this with me. He has told me that I am in control. The pharaoh said that I must teach my wife her 'proper place.' I want to leave and I want to remain in her presence. Her arms decorated in gold bracelets and gold rings wrapped around me again. My trembling hands rested on her hips. Where do I touch her? Her breath drifts across my face; Her warmth surrounds me.

The sounds from the other tent slowly drifted into focus. Zahra hesitantly withdrew from our kiss. My eyes opened and I saw her smiling at me. My hand raised to caress Zahra's cheek tenderly.

"I wish that I could take an infinite supply of that on my journey," I said, my groin feeling uncomfortable.

Zahra blushed and kissed my forehead. "I shall eagerly await your return, my dear Al-Sakhir."

I looked into her glistening brown eyes. I leaned toward her again and kissed the side of her neck. She held onto me and tipped her head to the sky. I placed tiny kisses on her neck, a mysterious force keeping me near her.

Zahra sighed quietly as she held onto me, her body twitching under my hands. "Amsi," Zahra said sadly. "We must not continue."

I looked at her, my body tightening for some unknown reason. It was then that I noticed a tight sensation between my legs. What is happening? Why is this happening?

"Master Amsi!" I heard Nakia call from outside the tent. "Master Amsi!"

"What is it?"

Nakia stood outside Zahra's tent. "We must leave! You must prepare for your journey!"

Zahra stood up slowly and helped me to my feet. The tight sensation in my stomach didn't stop. Standing was extremely uncomfortable. For a moment, I wondered how I was going to ride Hadi back to the Al-Sakhir family lands.

"Nakia's right, Zahra. We must leave."

Zahra embraced me again and rested her head against my chest. "Please be careful and return home with Minoru alive."

I kissed her forehead again. "I will, Zahra."

Zahra and I left the tent and heard the giggling and moaning continue in the other tent. Nakia looked at me. "I think we're going to have to return home alone. It's not going to be easy to pull those two apart now."

"I'm inclined to agree."

"Goodbye, Nassar!" Nakia called to his twin.

"Bah, Ah-e-Ah!" Nassar's voice yelled loudly from inside the tent.

Nakia kissed Shera and mounted Hamza. He blew her a kiss and we returned to my family's lands, albeit uncomfortably.

Nakia saw me shifting on Hadi. "My lord, are you feeling okay?"

I swallowed nervously as I nodded. The sooner we get home the better. "When we get home, Nakia, check the boat and make sure that it is in good condition. Please prepare enough food for Azizi and I. Najam will ask questions. Tell her nothing of what we plan."

"Yes, Master Amsi."

When we arrived at the home, Nakia and I jumped off our horses. "One more thing, Nakia."

"Yes, Master Amsi?"

"Please pack my *Senet* board. Azizi and I will need some way to pass the time."

Nakia bowed and I watched him run towards the fields. He would need Baruti's help moving our boat.   During the Inundation of the Nile, it was easier to move and closer to our dock.   The craft was big enough for Azizi and me to move freely. My family used the craft to travel to Luxor during the annual Festival of Rā. People leave their work and celebrate the glory of the Sun God. They anoint the statue of the god and pay homage to the bounty he gives to us.   My father and I give praise to the sun, the Almighty Eye of Heaven! Life, Health, and Strength to Him! May he bless our journey and protect us with his Guiding Light.

I ran to my room and opened a small bag. Inside I placed three clean linen skirts and two white tunics, and a purple cloth interwoven with pure gold.   A small box would hold my gold bracelets and my small vials of scented oils.

"Where are you going in such a hurry, my son?"

I turned quickly to see my mother standing at my doorway with her hands folded in front of her. With my bag tied securely, I turned to her. She watched me closely as I approached her. My mother worried about me. Her eyes watched me intently as I stood before her.

"Amsi, where are you going?"

You will have disappointed your father. That may cause him to do something very bad to himself or those around him. My father will go to many lengths to command my obedience. Would my father hurt my mother? His rage would blind him so he wouldn't care who he whips or whom he strangles.

"Mother, you must not be here when my father returns. You must go, leave."

"Son? Where would I go? What has happened, my child?"

My bag fell to the ground as I grabbed onto her shoulders. How can I convince her? "Mother, there was some-unpleasantness at the Temple of Hapi. My father found me with Aziz! The pharaoh attacked us and we barely escaped intact."

My mother gasped and covered her mouth with her hand in alarm. "Amsi, are you alright?   Are you hurt?"

"Mother, please listen to me! You must leave! Have Nakia take you for a chariot ride through the desert! Have Baruti and Qamra take you for a ride on Munir! Do anything! Father said that he would do harm if he did not see me in the temple."

"Did you go to the temple?"

I nodded. "Yes, and Azizi was there. We were hiding and the pharaoh found us."

"Why is your traveling bag packed?"

I sighed, shaking my head. "Azizi and I are going to Kadesh to the Temple of Isis. The pharaoh is after the relics of Isis and he will stop at nothing to obtain all of the ancient relics of power."

My mother looked around and sniffed. "Do I smell sweet perfume? Were you with a girl, my son?"

Swallowing nervously, I shifted on my feet, becoming slowly less comfortable again. "Mother, I do not have time to explain. You must leave here!"

I heard the sound of horses neighing nearby. Could my father have arrived?

"Master Amsi!" I heard Nakia crying in alarm.

"Surrender, Traitor!" I heard the pharaoh's loud voice booming.

"He's come for me! Mother, run!"

My mother kissed me on my cheeks. "I always knew you were destined for greatness, my son. Please return safe, my precious Amsi. Go. Do not worry about me. Go with your friend."

I grabbed my bag and quickly ran to the window. My feet landed on the ground as I heard Nakia's scream echo through the air.

"Nakia!" I heard Baruti calling.

My legs carried me swiftly around the home. My mother was kneeling beside Nakia on the ground. Pharaoh Runihura hovered over my mother as she cradled Nakia against her body. Baruti was standing in front of my mother, shielding her from the pharaoh.

"Give your son to me, woman!"

"Kaemwaset will hear of your disrespect, my king! My son is not here!"

I watched in fear as the pharaoh's guards pushed past my mother and invaded the home.   My feet raced into the fields. The height of the crops forced me to bend low to make my escape.   May the Sun God protect my mother and keep her safe.

*   *   *

The crowds fill the streets like flies on rotten fruit.   They buzz all over, landing on you no matter how many times you swat them away.

With much effort, I arrived in front of Mbizi's Bordello. Lakia and Tabora stood outside, enticing drunken men to honor the Nile God by emptying their pockets inside.

Lakia smiled and embraced me when I jumped off my horse. "Well, if it isn't the King of Thieves! Are you here to celebrate with Kahla, Azizi?"

I chuckled. "I'm here for a different reason. Is Mbizi around?"

"He's with Maysun in her quarters."

"Carry on, my pretty ladies," I said, kissing them both on the cheek.

Inside Mbizi's a few candles burned, casting dancing shadows against the wooden walls. Thana fluffed a pillow by the couch and smiled at me. "Hello, sir! Do you want a drink?" The little girl ran for her pitcher of wine. "No, my girl. I'm here to see Kahla. Does she have a drunken rat with her right now?"

"No, she's upstairs in her room."

"Thank you, pretty girl," I said, climbing the stairs. The air became sweeter as I ascended to the second floor. No doubt Mbizi had incense burning as familiar moaning and banging of wood echoed through the upstairs. There's an image I didn't particularly need burned into my brain today.

So many people have walked through Mbizi's door. I have seen those who look akin to apes. Many beautiful women have serviced men in these rooms. Some of them were not so handsome, but who had nonetheless fallen into the depths of despair and poverty. My eyes rose when I saw Room 8. My hands slowly reached out and touched the wooden door. This was her door.

I remember hearing my mother moaning behind this door and believing that she had taken ill. Mbizi was furious that I had interrupted my mother while she was working and he took me into his room to punish me. Sometimes sitting on the couch downstairs, I would hear her crying in her room. My ears could hear her screaming.

How I hated to hear her screams! I covered my ears as I cried that night. Maysun held me to her breast to feed me, then she rocked me to sleep. Now that I'm older, I understand my mother's sacrifice. May Osiris keep her happy until I can see her again and tell her I'm sorry that I had caused her pain. I'm sorry that I caused her death.

I walked to Room 6 and knocked on the door. "One minute!" a voice called from inside.

"It's me, Kahla!"

Kahla giggled on the other side of the door. "Who is 'me?'"

"The most wanted thief in all of *Iunu*!"

The locks unfastened on the door. "Who would that be?"

"The man who will someday make you his wife!"

Kahla turned the doorknob and opened the door with a smile. She leaned against the door post. Her soft hands, smelling of sweet oil, slowly rose to caress my cheek. "Azizi Keket, my dear future thief-husband."

Without notice, I grabbed her and pulled her against my body. I looked into her sparkling green eyes and smiled. She landed on her feet and hugged me tightly, constricting my injuries from the pharaoh's assault made me whimper slightly.

"I'm sorry, Aziz!" Her eyes looked me up and down. Her smile faded as she noticed my stomach bruised and bleeding slightly from my encounter with Runihura. "You are hurt!"

I nodded and walked over to the bed where I laid down with a groan of pain. "The pharaoh attacked Amsi and I. Ini-Herit punched me in the gut."

Kahla stood over me and took a vial of oil. She carefully placed some on her finger and rubbed it onto my stomach. I gripped her bedsheets and growled. "When I next see Ini-Herit, he will pay for this!"

Kahla sat beside me and caressed my cheek. "What happened with the pharaoh?"

My eyes closed as I winced with pain. My body burned as if it were on fire. My back was screaming for rest. Rest will have to wait. There is a mission I must complete before I can truly relax.

"He could have broke Amsi and I in half if he desired," I turned to look her in the eye. "Kahla, his fists went through solid rock."

Kahla's eyes widened and she took my hand. "Azizi," she sighed, caressing my cheek.

I closed my eyes, inhaling her sweet fragrance. Her soft, gentle hands touched me, comforted me in my hour of need. Kahla's kindness relaxed me as my eyes struggled to remain open.

I'm so tired. My body wants rest. Amsi and I have a journey to begin, one which may destroy us both.

"Rest, Azizi. I will be here." My body barely noticed her standing. She released my hand and I felt her shift into the bed beside me. Kahla's head rested against my shoulder. "Rest, Aziz. No danger shall fall upon you while I keep watch."

Kahla, I want to look at you, but I'm so tired. My back can still feel the stone of the pillar as Amsi and I slammed into it hard. I will not rest this well until we return.

My head turned to face Kahla slowly. I wrapped my arm around her as she lightly caressed my chest. "Kiss me."

Kahla tipped my chin towards her lips and she kissed me lightly. Her hands gingerly touched my skin, strategically avoiding the injury on my belly. As we kissed, I reached over and caressed her cheek tenderly.

Kahla kissed my cheek and my shoulder. My fingers buried in her soft, black hair as she kissed my chest. I don't want to fall asleep on Kahla. I want to be awake for her, but somehow that seems doubtful.

I felt her kiss lower, giving my stomach injury a light touch of her honey-sweet lips. My aching back arched as I squirmed. Kahla's hands caressed my hips as her head kissed towards my shoulder once more.

Her sparkling green eyes pierced through my half-closed eyes. "Azizi, I love you."

My body was fighting my exhaustion as sleep threatened to arrive. "Amsi and I must travel to Kadesh. I don't know when or even if we will return."

Kahla watched me with worried eyes. Her thumb traced my jaw as tears pooled in her eyelid. "Why?"

"The pharaoh is after the Circlet of Isis. He needs to be stopped. You and I of all people know that is true."

Kahla lowered her head and slowly nodded. "Promise me one thing."

"You know I don't make promises that I can't keep."

Kahla's arm wrapped around me and touched my skin lightly. "Promise me that you will come back alive."

"I promise to return, my beautiful." I touched her shoulder and pulled her close to me. "I love you, Kahla," my hand caressed her cheek as I looked into her eyes.

Kahla kissed my lips again lightly with a smile. "Close your eyes and sleep, my king. A long journey awaits you."

My eyes closed, unable to fight the battle of consciousness anymore. Before I drifted into slumber, I heard Kahla whisper, 'I love you, Aziz. You will always be my king.'

XI

My Brother In Arms

Azizi awoke and found that Kahla had fallen asleep beside him. He leaned over and kissed her cheek. "Be safe from the pharaoh. May Osiris keep you safe." The thief stood up from the bed holding his sore back. "I'll be feeling that for a few days." Azizi fastened his dagger's sheath to his rope belt and watched Kahla turn over in her sleep. The moonlight illuminated her naked form to his eyes. Her chest barely rose and fell as she slept deeply. *I wish I could stay with you this night, but my duty lies elsewhere. I don't want to leave her. It pains me to leave your side, bnt fear not, Kahla, I shall return to you. Sleep sweetly, my dearest.*

Azizi slowly opened the door to Kahla's room and walked down the stairs. With caution, he slipped from the brothel and raced down the street toward the city entrance. An oil lamp burning on the bank was the only beacon for him to follow. Azizi ran towards the boat docked beside the Nile. It was a small raft with a single small shelter large enough to fit himself and Amsi inside. A single oil lamp dangling from a short mast provided the only light source. Two oars connected to the sides of the boat provided manual locomotion.

He stepped onto the ramp as Amsi pulled on a rope connected to a sail. "Welcome aboard the 'Rā-Rises-In-Glory', Aziz!" Amsi smiled, tugging hard on the rope.

The Noble teen struggled to unfurl the sails. Azizi watched Amsi grit his teeth and his muscles flex with his burden.

"How do you feel after narrowly escaping the pharaoh's clutches?"

The sail unfurled and Amsi wiped his sweaty brow. "Like a piece of pulverized meat." Amsi grabbed a harpoon and placed it beside his seat.

Azizi grinned. "Kahla and I enjoyed some quality time together. I truly hope that our departure is not extended."

Amsi nodded. "Me, too. I want to get back here to spend more time with Zahra before she leaves."

Azizi stepped to the bow of the small craft and looked into the dark void ahead of him. He wrapped his cloak around him to shield himself from the cold night air. "Amsi."

The Noble teen watched his friend stare into the night before him. The thief's cloak flowed behind him in the wind. His shoulder-length black hair blew in the breeze. "What is it?"

"Do you think we will return alive?"

Amsi dropped the rope and slowly approached his friend. Amsi stood beside Azizi and stared into the unknown. "I don't know. There is always a possibility that we will not."

Azizi turned toward Amsi and placed his hands on Amsi's shoulders. "I would have none other fight by my side."

Amsi smiled and nodded. He took Azizi's hand and placed it against his chest. "You are my brother. I won't let any harm come to you, my friend."

Azizi grinned and nodded in agreement. "Let's sail for Kadesh." The thief grabbed the plank to the shore and hauled it onto the deck. Amsi pulled the anchor from the water and grabbed the oar on the left side of the boat. Azizi sat on the right side and grabbed the oar.

Both of the teens rowed from the banks, looking into the darkness ahead of them. Amsi watched Azizi from the corner of his eye.

The thief rowed quietly, his face bearing a countenance of great concentration.

"How will we find our way to Kadesh?" Azizi asked. "Did Zahra give you a map?"

"I am using the map from my lessons.   We continue straight until we reach the Great Sea.   Next we must follow the coastline. We will pass Megiddo below the Empire of the 'Sea People.' We follow the land north to their boarder."

Azizi raised a curious eyebrow. "You brought your texts with you?"

"I have to keep up with my studies," Amsi said.   "Sawaret would expect nothing less."

Azizi breathed the night air deeply as the sound of the water rippled lightly against the boat and their oars.   Torch light from cities ahead danced in the gentle currents of the Nile.   Azizi chuckled as he shook his head.

"What's so funny?"

"Darwishi told me of a major provincial tomb ahead before the Great Sea. Perhaps I should show you how to properly rob a royal tomb."

Amsi continued to row. "We are racing towards our destination and you want to stop to rob a tomb?"

"It's never too early to learn the tricks of the thief trade, Amsi. You fought well today." Azizi grinned. "You would make a great partner in crime."

"I don't know how to steal, Azizi! I don't know how to break into a tomb."

Azizi continued to row. "Do you think I came from my mother's womb knowing how to break into a tomb and steal the many pretty things therein? No! I had to learn my trade through practice just like you practice your reading and writing and whatever else you learn."

"History, astronomy, mathematics, reading, writing, combat techniques, Sacred Scripture, and Law is what I study with Sawaret."

Azizi raised an eyebrow. "That is quite a list!"

"I try to study hard to please my father."

"What about yourself? Do you study to improve yourself or do you simply do so for your father's sake?"

Amsi stopped rowing and cast his eyes on the deck. "That is a difficult question to answer, Azizi."

"No, it's not, Al-Sakhir. If you struggle for your own sake, that is your choice. If you push yourself to the limits to please others, your actions are misguided. Work hard to please yourself. Why would you want to please your father who has the heart of a cobra?"

"He is still my father!"

Azizi gripped the oar tightly in his hand. "I did not see your beloved
father racing from the inner sanctum to help you in your hour of need,
Amsi."

Amsi sighed and nodded. "I know."

"Live your life for yourself, Amsi. Do not live in the shadow of a man
who has lived his own. See your father for who he is and not the god
you have made him in your mind."

Amsi raised his head sharply. "You're right, Azizi."

Azizi nodded as he faced forward. Amsi began to row with the thief.
"You learn much on the streets, my friend."

"You are wise beyond your years, Azizi."

Azizi sighed. "There is little choice in the matter when you live on the
streets. I have orphans who depend on me to feed them and teach them
the finer points of thievery.   My Clan depends on me to stay one step
ahead of Kaphiri's plans to dominate our territory." Azizi's eyes gazed
at the waning moon. "Osiris peers down at us, Amsi. Behold!"

Amsi looked up at the waning moon. Stars twinkled in the sky as the
moonlight reflected off the surface of the water.   The swirling of the
water was quiet as he and Azizi rowed through the darkness. Scattered
along the surface of the Nile were flowers thrown into the water by

Hapi worshippers. "If we weren't in such hurry and if our lives were not in danger, this trip would be rather enjoyable."

"Am I not good company?" Azizi asked.

"No! I'm not complaining. This is the longest we have spent together. It will be a pleasant journey."

Azizi's eyes looked near the edge of the boat, wary of the aquatic creatures which could capsize their boat. The sails above them ripped as the wind aided their trip up the Nile. "Have you kissed Zahra yet?" Azizi asked, turning his head towards his friend.

"What?!"

"Did you kiss her? It's not a difficult question to answer. Tell me."

Amsi swallowed nervously and gripped the oar tightly. "Yes. We kissed for the first time today."

"Does she kiss well? Did you enjoy it?"

Amsi chuckled uncomfortably and tugged on his white cape. "I think I hear the enemy near!"

"You do not! You are trying to avoid answering my question!" Azizi laughed. "Tell me, Al-Sakhir! Did you kiss your girl?"

"Yes! I did! Happy?"

"Extremely. Did you enjoy her kiss?"

How could I not? She smelled sweet like a field of flowers. Her eyes were like those of diamonds. Her skin was soft and warm. If Isis herself was before me, I would not have noticed her. Does this mean I love Zahra?

"Rich-Boy, did you enjoy the kiss?"

"Yes, I did. These sensations are so new it's hard to give them words."

Azizi nodded. "Kahla and I have kissed many times. I told her that someday I would take her as my wife."

"Ife does not own my heart. I do not like her."

"To steal from her chambers was simple. She barks like a dog at her slaves so I can always tell when she is coming near the room."

Amsi looked at Azizi. "Be careful you don't get caught."

"I'm not worried about being caught. It's become a game."

"Ife is needlessly cruel. She wrote me a letter proclaiming her love for me. Below the letter she had written: Establish fear of yourself that you may be feared for a real magistrate is one who is feared."

Azizi pulled his cloak around himself as the wind increased in intensity. "A man's lifetime is but an hour. When a man dies, his deeds are placed beside him in heaps. If he gets there without sin, he will live like a god and march with the Lords of Eternity." Azizi turned and smiled at his companion. "I know the Osirian maxims well."

Amsi smiled with a nod. "Yes, I remember that scripture."

Amsi and Azizi watched as they passed a temple along the banks of the Nile. The moonlight illuminated the roof as they slowly drifted by the structure.

"Amsi, do you know what we are going to find at the Temple of Isis?"

Amsi stood up carefully and handed Azizi the handle to his oar. Azizi watched as Amsi disappeared into the small structure behind them and rustle through a bag. The thief's eyes and ears kept attentive as he heard rippling in the water.

Amsi returned to his seat beside Azizi and rowed with one hand. He opened a scroll on his lap and read by the light of the oil lamp. "Before Issâm died, he told the pharaoh that from the myth comes the power of the scrolls. The Scroll of Thoth had read to find the Scroll of Horus, one had to seek out where 'life fails to flower.' You found the scroll hidden in a cave in the desert mountains. I'm certain you are aware of the tale of Isis and Osiris. Isis is a mother-goddess. She used great wings to breathe life into her dead husband."

Azizi continued to row, keeping his eyes focused on the calm waters. "She searched for the body parts of Osiris and the wind carried her moans of despair and pain of losing her husband to Seth. She gives food to the deceased and breathes life into the Blessed dead."

Amsi leaned forward to read the hieroglyphs. "She is identified with the goddess of justice, Ma'at."

Azizi looked at the scroll on Amsi's lap. The hieroglyphics were illegible to him. "That looks like the writing on the walls found in royal tombs."

"That's because it's writ in Noble Tongue."

"It doesn't even look like writing!"

Amsi shook his head. "No, it's hieroglyphs. You just can't read it because you don't know the language."

"Perfect. Then here is your opportunity to teach me some Noble Tongue. I can teach you Common Script just in case you ever need to read something from me."

"That sounds reasonable enough." Amsi read the scroll. "The scorpion was sacred to Isis."

Azizi swallowed nervously. "I hope we don't have to travel through confined spaces as in the Caves of Horus. I could barely move, the air was thin, and traps could send anyone plummeting to their death. Give me snakes. Give me swords. Do not give me an enclosed area."

Amsi shivered as the wind rippled the sails again. He pulled his white cloak tighter around his body. "You are a member of the Osiris Clan. Has Aneksi taught you the myth of Osiris and Isis?"

Azizi chuckled and bowed his head as if in prayer. "Isis was a most affectionate mother and wife. She searched for any possible means to bring her lover back to life after his murder by his brother, Seth. I am familiar with the story. She had foolishly released Seth when Horus captured him."

"Isis was a lady of forgiveness."

Azizi looked over at Amsi with a cold glare. "Her forgiveness rewarded her with decapitation."

"I'm sorry, Azizi," the Noble Teen said quietly. An uncomfortable silence surrounded the teens as they continued to float up the Nile towards the Great Sea. Amsi heard Azizi muttering under his breath as his eyes wandered towards the crescent moon hovering above in the partly cloudy sky.

The boat gently rocked in the calm waters as a small village drifted by them. Amsi rolled the scroll and replaced it in the shelter behind them. Amsi rubbed his eyes and yawned. *I can't be tired now! We have such a long journey ahead of us! I must stay awake no matter what!* Amsi unrolled a blanket and placed it on the floor of the small shelter. He heard Azizi cough from outside. The teen stopped suddenly as he remembered the plague festering through the streets of *Iunu*. "Azizi, are you alright?"

"I'm just thirsty. Why?"

Amsi stepped out of the shelter and saw Azizi turn to him. "Are you becoming sick?"

"Your concern for me is much appreciated, but I am certain I am fine." Azizi watched as a thin veil of cloud failed to obscure the moon from view. "O Osiris, thou goest round about heaven, thou seest Rā, thou seest the beings who have knowledge. He goeth round the horizon of heaven."

Amsi returned to his seat beside Azizi. "Do you think we will arrive at the Temple before Gahiji?"

"We have to if we have any hope of obtaining the relics of Isis."

The Noble teen continued to row beside his friend. "Preventing Gahiji from obtaining the Circlet and Scroll of Isis is not our only duty at the temple."

The King of Thieves peered at his friend. "Do you mean stopping at Esbet-Rushdi and engaging in a crash course of tomb-robbing?"

"No! I'm being serious!"

"So am I. Let's go, Amsi, it could be fun!"

Amsi shook his head. "We have to get to the Temple of Isis before General Gahiji! He attacked Zahra's camp and kidnapped one of the young men of her clan!"

Azizi gasped and gripped the oar tightly in his hands. "Was anyone killed?"

"It didn't appear so, but we have to save him before Gahiji kills him! Zahra said that Gahiji needed a guide to the temple."

The thief sighed. "General Gahiji will not kill someone that he needs. His life is safe at least until they get to the temple. We'll get him back." Azizi licked his lips. *Perhaps his life will be worth a few dînars as a reward!*

Amsi looked up at the twinkling stars. He took a deep breath of the salty air. "You know, Aziz, we should do this more often."

The night wind ruffled the hair of the thief as he looked into the dark sky of night. The twinkling lights peered down at them from above. "It is very peaceful out here."

Noble and Thief continued rowing quietly along the Nile, the only sound emanating from the water gently rocking the boat.

XII

The Price You Pay

Pharaoh Runihura crossed his legs, sitting on his golden throne. He swirled his golden goblet of imported wine from Amathus. Semerkhet inhaled the sweet incense he had burned around the pharaoh's throne room. The torches beside the altar to Sekhmet were blazing, sending dancing shadows on the wall. The sweet smell of fresh flowers perfumed the altar's statue to the lion-goddess of destruction, the Eye of Rā.

"Semerkhet, when I obtain the Circlet of Isis, I shall cure those I choose worthy of the gift of health. I shall be the salvation of the worthy."

Semerkhet bowed before his pharaoh. "What of those who stand in your way?"

"I will crush them under my fist," Runihura said, clenching his fist tightly. "I had them within in grasp, High Priest. I could have crushed Azizi's throat had the pillar not stayed my hand."

Semerkhet smiled. "I have no doubt that your Lordship would have succeeded in slaying the boy."

Runihura chuckled. "It's not enough that I slay the boy, High Priest. I want to make a toy of him. My eyes wish nothing more than to see him bleed and hear his screams echo into the ears of his beloved Osiris. Death is a gift, Semerkhet. It is a gift not to be given in haste, but to be bestowed with mercy." Runihura sipped from his wine and licked his lips with a predatory smile. "I will humiliate Azizi before I grant him sleep eternal. I will show him that I am superior to him. His body will be a canvas for my blade. Sekhmet will smile upon me, knowing that I have proven my dominion over him. It will be glorious."

Semerkhet raised his hands in prayer before the altar to Sekhmet. "Praise be to Sekhmet!"

"So it is true," Runihura heard a voice from the Throne Room Entrance echo through the room. "Egypt is the Land of Sekhmet, the Realm of Typhon, and the Territory where the Evil Serpent Reigns Supreme."

Runihura stood before his throne, clutching the goblet of wine in his hand. A teenaged boy bowed beside two men standing in the doorway.

"My lord, Xeres, the leader of the *Bedu* has requested an audience."

"Neka, send them away!"

One man walked into the room defiantly and approached the pharaoh's throne. "Your army has taken my son! I demand his safe return this instant!"

Xeres stood beside the angry father and folded his hands in front of him. Runihura's lip curled in disgust as he scowled at both men.

"Neka, show these filth out of this throne room this instant, boy!"

"We will not leave," Xeres said calmly.

Runihura turned his head to his slave. "Come here, Neka." The shaking teen bowed and rushed beside the pharaoh. Neka bowed before him, kneeling on the marble floor. Neka pressed his forehead against the floor, making Runihura grin with pride. Runihura turned towards the men. "Where are your manners? Bow before me!"

Tamkinat spit on the steps leading to the pharaoh's throne. "I do not bow before a snake such as yourself!"

Runihura chuckled and licked his lips. "So my General Gahiji has plucked a boy from your garden of weeds. Delightful!"

"Return my son, pharaoh! You have no right to take my son from his flock!"

"Well, would you rather my beloved General take your daughter, *Bedu* filth?" Runihura asked Xeres as he calmly walked down the stairs. Xeres glared in disgust at the pharaoh advancing towards him. "I am looking for a female to bear my heir. Perhaps your daughter will prove an obedient and fruitful child-bearer."

Xeres clutched his hands tightly in fury. "You are a beast! You will never get your hands on my daughter and fill her body with your demon-seed!"

"Never say never, my good sir," Runihura smiled. "I am the pharaoh, the Great Runihura. I take what I want and I have no need to ask permission to enter your daughter's house."

Xeres stepped back from the pharaoh, fighting his desire to tear the cocky king asunder.

"I demand that you return Minoru to me!" the angry father exclaimed.

Pharaoh Runihura turned calmly and walked toward the altar to Sekhmet. He stood beside Semerkhet. "Leave." Semerkhet bowed and fled from the room.

"We *Bedu* are a peaceful people, Pharaoh Runihura. In no manner did we engage in hostilities with you."

"I care not about engaging in hostilities with you, my good King Xeres. You have no hope to defeat my army. Your people are weak farmers, nomads with nothing more than fleas and sheep."

Tamkinat stepped closer to the pharaoh. "Why did you capture my son? He is worth nothing to you!"

Pharaoh Runihura turned his head to the altar and took two coins. With a calm toss, he tossed them at the father's feet. "That is all your son is worth to me. Take your money for his life and leave."

"You are paying me coin for my son? Keep your money! I want my son returned to me!"

Xeres narrowed his eyes at the pharaoh. "Return my brother's son, Pharaoh Runihura! He is a shepherd, not a fighter!"

"Even a simple child can learn to fight for the Great Egyptian army! Your son belongs to me, Bedouin filth! He is no longer your concern!"

Tamkinat raised his fists towards the pharaoh. "For Minoru!" Tamkinat lunged forward, punching Runihura in the stomach. The pharaoh cried out in pain and fell to his knees. Runihura leaned forward, grasping his stomach. The furious father hovered over the pharaoh.

Neka raised his head when he saw the pharaoh kneeling beside him. "Move away from him!" the boy cried out in horror. "Jump back! Watch his fists!"

Runihura raised his head with a grin and slammed his fist against Tamkinat's stomach. Neka and Xeres watched as Tamkinat flew into the air and slid across the marble floor.

Runihura chuckled as he rose to his feet, looming over the kneeling slave. Xeres ran to Tamkinat laying on the ground, panting heavily.

"Tamkinat! Speak to me!"

Tamkinat held his ribs as he panted heavily. Xeres kneeled before his fallen brother and placed his palm on the fallen man's forehead. "Tamkinat, let us return to the camp! Onfalia will help you."

Neka's footsteps echoed across the floor as he ran beside the fallen Bedouin. "Can he move?"

Pharaoh Runihura shoved Neka to the ground as he stood behind Xeres. "Does he still want his money?"

Xeres looked up at the pharaoh. "Keep your filthy money, Pharaoh
Runihura!"

"Xer-es," Tamkinat struggled to say through failing breath. Xeres
looked down at Tamkinat sadly. "Don't speak. Conserve your breath."

"Minoru, I failed you," the fallen man struggled to say as he gasped for
air.

Xeres stood and glared at the pharaoh. "You leave my clan in peace,
you monster!

Runihura leaned down, returning the menacing glare of the Bedouin
leader. "Beware the hand of Sekhmet.   Her fists are mighty."

"Tamkinat simply wanted his son returned to him," Xeres protested.

"To prove that I am not without mercy, I shall offer you and your friend
a ride to your settlement.   I shall call the guards and they shall escort
you home."

Runihura called loudly for the guards who rushed into the room armed
with their spears. "Please return our friends to their camp. Be careful of
the dying one."

The guards grabbed Xeres by the arms and pulled him away from
Tamkinat. "Leave him alone! You hurt him enough!"

Runihura kneeled beside the father and dropped two more coins onto
the man's chest. "This is for your pain." Runihura watched as the man

swallowed, his eyes opening wide in fear as he gagged for air. "Take him away."

The pharaoh watched the guards drag the two men away. Neka began to stir on the ground. The slave's eyes peered beside him and saw the pharaoh's feet. The teen swallowed nervously as his eyes rose to see the pharaoh hovering above him. Neka's face covered in sweat as he held his hand out protectively. "No, please, my pharaoh!"

"Hello, Neka," the pharaoh said pleasantly.

*   *   *

Azizi opened his eyes, the world around him slowly coming into view as he heard Amsi's voice speaking from the bow of their boat. He felt himself rocking on the deck as he laid quietly in the little shelter. The thief yawned as his fingers felt a material covering them. He looked down and noticed that Amsi had covered him with a blanket while he slept. He rubbed his eyes and noticed Amsi kneeling, raising his arms towards the rising sun.

"Pilot who knows the water, Helmsman of the weak, who gives bread to him who has none. I take not a noble as protector. I associate not with a man of wealth. I place not my share in another's care. Amun who knows compassion." Amsi leaned over, touching his forehead against the deck of the rocking boat. "Hail to you, Rā, perfect each day, who rises at dawn without failing, Khepri who wearies himself with toil! Praise giving to Amun, I make for adorations in his name! I give him praises to the height of heaven."

Azizi sat up and watched his friend raise a bowl to the sun. The fiery dawn above Amsi was speckled with reds and purples. The thief looked beside him and saw Amsi's unguent box. He lifted the lid slowly and found a collection of expensive oils and cosmetics. Black ochre reeds would apply the makeup around Amsi's eyes. Azizi uncorked a vial and sniffed it. *This oil fetches quite a hefty price in the market place.*

Another box in the corner was decorated with blue and green lotus flowers. Squares were painted on the lid in varying colors. Images of a man hunting ducks decorated the sides along with patterns of hieroglyphics in Noble Tongue. Azizi opened the lid and examined the contents inside. Two sticks and wooden cones were arranged neatly. *What is this?*

Azizi heard a loud cry accompanied by a splash into the water. Azizi turned his head quickly to see Amsi missing. "Amsi!" The thief jumped up and raced out of the shelter to find Amsi swimming in the open water.

"Azizi! You're awake!" Amsi called as he emerged from under the water. "Greetings to you! I apologize if I woke you."

"I thought you fell into the water!"

Amsi shook his head to free the water from his eyes. "No! I finished my daily prayers and decided to swim."

Azizi sighed with relief and stretched. Amsi's eyes rarely saw the thief's tattoo on his left arm, the Mark of Osiris. Azizi had removed his gold bands from his arms before he fell asleep. The thief stood on the deck of the rocking boat, his flat stomach beginning to protest for food. His friend's ribs were clearly visible as he resumed his seat beside his oar.

"How long have we been in the Great Water?"

"We left our homeland not long after you fell asleep. I trust you slept well?"

Azizi nodded. "Yes. I can row while you rest. You need your sleep."

Amsi relaxed as he floated along the surface of the water. His eyes watched the clouds hover above the craft. Birds flew overhead as he breathed deeply. "I wonder if my father is looking for me."

"No doubt he is searching for you. He discovered you were conspiring with me," Azizi said as he stood and disappeared into the shelter. He emerged a moment later with a piece of bread and a handful of raisins from Amsi's basket of food.

Amsi stopped floating and swam to the edge of the boat. He crossed his arms on the side of the boat and looked up at Azizi with worry. "What if he hurts my mother?"

Azizi took a bite of bread and sighed. "She can divorce him or leave him. I wouldn't worry about your mother. Your slaves will take care of her in your absence."

"My father will definitely take his anger out on the slaves."

Azizi held his hand towards Amsi and offered him raisins. "You knew what could happen if you chose to follow me, my friend. Allying yourself with me, coming with me," Azizi paused as Amsi took two raisins from his hand. "Being my friend necessitates that you take a risk." Azizi turned to Amsi. The thief leaned forward, looking Amsi directly in the eyes. "We could be killed for our friendship." Azizi lowered his head sadly. "I wish that you not suffer punishment on my account. I wish that you not be hunted. My eyes do not wish to see another person I-."

Amsi watched as the thief fell silent. His friend took a big piece of bread into his mouth and chewed pensively. Azizi swallowed and began to eat his breakfast in silence. "Azizi, what were you going to say?"

"Nothing."

Amsi shook his head. "No, no, you were going to say something. Tell me."

Azizi looked up at the sky. The sun had risen above the waterline. The colors in the sky had faded, leaving blue and a collection of hovering clouds.   He offered more raisins to Amsi, who grabbed Azizi's wrist. "What were you going to tell me, Azizi Keket?"

"Release my arm."

"No, tell me what you were going to say."

Azizi finished the bread and looked at his friend. Azizi's eyes met the Noble Teen's directly.   "My eyes do not wish to see another person I care about be slaughtered by the pharaoh."

Amsi's eyes widened. "Azizi, I have never heard such sentiment come from you before!"

"As the King of Thieves, you don't know who is ready to come behind you and stab you in the back. I have to be strong. Leaders must show no weakness."

Amsi nodded. "I can imagine it is difficult." The Noble Teen swam backward from the boat. "I bet you as the King of Thieves, nobody has done this to you yet." Amsi splashed Azizi with the water and laughed.

"What was that for?" Azizi asked, his black hair and naked torso dripping wet.

Amsi shrugged and laughed. "I felt like it." Amsi splashed the King of Thieves again and chuckled.

"You're not going to get away with that!" Azizi grinned.

The thief jumped into the water as the Noble teen began to swim around the boat. Amsi's laughter rose into the air as Azizi pursued him.

"The King of Thieves cannot get me for I am too swift!" Amsi called.

Azizi took a deep breath and swam under the boat. Amsi had stopped, keeping a diligent eye around the sides of the boat for Azizi's pursuit. The thief grinned under the water and pulled Amsi under the water by his ankles. The teens pushed against each other and emerged from under the water grappling with one another.

Azizi splashed Amsi and turned to flee, but the Noble grabbed his ankle. Azizi felt Amsi pulling his leg, preventing him from escaping.

The thief kicked his leg near Amsi's face, sending a geyser of water in towards Amsi. Amsi released his friend's leg and wiped the water out of his eyes.

Amsi opened his eyes to see his friend laughing at him and pointing. "You had me there for a minute, Aziz." Amsi lunged for Azizi, throwing himself on top of the skinny thief. Azizi pushed Amsi away from him as he struggled to reach the surface. Azizi shook his hair when he emerged from the water. Amsi chuckled as he swam to the surface and saw Azizi.

"You took me by surprise, Rich Boy," Azizi chuckled, shaking his head again free of water droplets.

"Me? I surprised the King of Thieves? You must be getting slow in your old age, my friend!"

Azizi splashed Amsi and swam towards the edge of the boat. He pulled himself into the craft and looked at his friend in the water. "Perhaps you would be willing to pull the boat along Gaza and Megiddo so these old bones can rest."

Amsi swam to the boat and climbed onto the deck. He grabbed Azizi's shoulders and sat him on his seat.   Amsi disappeared into the shelter and emerged with Azizi's cape and gold bands. "I don't wish you to get sick."

Azizi slipped the gold bands onto his arms and covered his Osiris tattoo.   He tied his cape around his neck and bowed his head to Amsi. "It's your turn to sleep. I will wake you when I spot land."

Amsi yawned and stretched as he pat his stomach. "I'll grab something to eat before I fall asleep. Call if you need me."

"Sleep well." Azizi grabbed the oars and continued rowing. *Amsi disappeared into the little shelter and sifted through our basket of food. He brought a good amount of dates, raisins, bread, and duck for our journey. He brought enough food for both of us. When he had eaten his small ration, I heard him settle on his blanket and begin to snore. My, how he snores! It's like thunder!*

I wonder how Kahla is dealing with our temporary separation. When I return, it's my intention to stay in her warm, windless room.   The warm, crackling fire and my Kahla in bed would be a welcoming sight! Her smile comes to mind, making me miss her all the more. Her smooth skin touching my own, her gentle hands massaging my aching shoulders, and most of all, the gentle kiss she places on my forehead fills my heart with longing for her.

Sacrifices must be made, unfortunately. The Circlet of Isis cannot fall into the hands of my enemy. We must find a way to set Zahra's tribesman free. The Temple of Isis would know the location of the Scroll and Circlet. Hurry, Shu, carry our boat forward quickly!

I turned my head and saw Amsi sleeping. His head rested upon the same pillow he had given me. With my seat abandoned, I crept into the shelter and covered him with the same blanket with which he covered me as I slept. I kneeled beside him and watched him sleep.

His eyelids fluttered as his fingers twitched with deep sleep. He looks peaceful. Sleep, the sister of death, had claimed him in her delicate embrace. As my eyes watched him, I couldn't help but worry about Aneksi's prophecy. 'Have faith in each other or you will not survive,'*she said. In the past, my heart questioned Amsi's intentions.* "Why am I worthy? You could befriend any of Heliopolis'Nobility. Lavish parties, tables full of meat, hunting expeditions, are at your fingertips. Why me, Amsi Al-Sakhir?" *He continued to sleep, unaware that I was watching him as a gazelle watches over her newborn fawn. With nothing on its mind, but protecting its young, likewise here I kneel*

*beside my friend wondering why he is willing to follow me into danger
from which we might not return.*

*Who am I, Amsi? Sometimes, I don't know who I am or understand why
destiny has chosen us to fight against this menace. Are we destined to
fail in our quest?* Azizi took Amsi's hand in his sleep. *I'm afraid, Amsi,
but I wish to worry you not with my troubles. I must remain strong.*

*Perhaps I am being foolish. You have eyes for Zahra. You have
dedicated your heart to her, Amsi. I will assure you that one day you
shall stand with her for eternity. I trust you, Amsi. My lips cannot
say to your face what I wish to say. My heart fears what you may say
in return. I want to tell you that I am afraid neither one of us may
return from our journey. I am afraid of General Gahiji capturing us
and dragging us before the pharaoh. Darwishi taught me that thieves
know no fear. Strong men fear not. Darwishi says that weakness can
get men killed. I cannot be weak, for many depend on me. That
dependence frightens me, but it is a burden which I bear willingly.*

*There are other things that I wish to say to you, but I know not how you
will respond. I am an orphaned boy who has learned not to trust his
heart to any soul. It is my fault that my mother was slaughtered. My
soul roams alone in this world of many. Your heart beats like mine.
Your lungs breathe like my own. And yet, we are removed from each
other. I may seem distant at times and for that, I apologize.*

"Zahra," Amsi moaned in his sleep as his hips shifted. The teen's free
hand drifted to the front of his white, linen skirt.

Azizi covered Amsi with the blanket and stood over his friend. *Be quiet, my heart. Be silent, my tongue. Return to the rowing. Light the oil lamp. When the sun falls, my prayers in worship of the Death God, Osiris may begin.*

XIII

The Darkness In The Heart of Kaemwaset

Pharaoh Runihura looked over the city as Janani stood beside him. The gentle wind blew his cape as he crossed his arms defiantly towards the Bedouin camp. Runihura's lip curled in disgust. "That man should have taken the money for his son. I wonder if his injuries have claimed his life."

Janani looked below in the garden where Timin was walking happily unaware of the predator hovering above him. A smile crossed her face as the little boy pulled a small toy on wheels. Neka followed the little boy with a bucket to water the garden. The house slave filled the bucket with water.

"Timin, help me scoop water onto the flowers like your father showed you," Neka told the boy.

"Father?" Timin looked around the garden. When he saw his father missing, the young boy looked up at Neka. "Father?"

Neka handed Timin his tiny cup. "Pour water over the celery, for they are thirsty."

Timin took the cup into his hands and sniffled. "Father? I want my father!"

Neka kneeled before the little boy who slowly began to cry. "Your father is away, Timin. Trust Neka. Your father will return." Neka hugged the child and caressed the child's hair. "I promised your father that I would take good care of you until his return. You must help me with the garden to make your father proud."

Janani sighed as she watched her son water the vegetables. Timin was too young to understand that his father had no choice but to leave with the army. *One of these days, Hamadi, Timin, and I will leave this horrible place. We will leave and never look back. While we might not have much, we will have each other.* Janani smiled. *Hamadi and I will settle beside the Nile and enjoy our lives with our children yet unborn. Hamadi, I await your safe return, my love.*

Janani heard the front gate to the palace screech as it opened to allow the Al-Sakhir chariot entry. The familiar slave sat behind the horses, shaking the reigns with haste. Runihura and Janani looked into the court and saw Kaemwaset step off his carriage.

"After all that I have done for that boy, this is how he repays me!" Kaemwaset bellowed as he stomped angrily past Neka and the child.

"I'm sure your son is around town somewhere, your Lordship!" Nakia exclaimed, running behind his furious master.

"By the hand of Rā, I will whip that boy and seal him in his room for eternity when I find him!"

Runihura scowled at the furious landowner. Runihura's finger tapped his chin as he thought. "Kaemwaset's heartache is exploitable."

Janani followed Runihura into the throne room. "Why does Lord Kaemwaset come here with such anger?"

Runihura grinned. "He knows his son has allied himself with the boy for whom I seek. We have known of Amsi's affection for the thief for many years. Despite my many threats, he insists on helping his friend foil my plans. His father finally sees the light, but it will be the darkness of disappointment in his heart which will cloud his mind. I shall see to it personally."

Janani watched as Kaemwaset burst into the throne room, pushing the large doors apart angrily. Nakia followed him closely as the man's sandals echoed through the Royal Hall.

"My Lord, my son is gone! I have not seen him since the brawl at the Temple of Hapi!"

Runihura watched the large man breathe heavily. Nakia dabbed his master's face with a white cloth to capture his sweat. "You do know that I had found your son conspiring against me in the Temple of Hapi?"

Kaemwaset bowed his head before the pharaoh. "I saw him on the ground after you tossed him and that worthless rat of a thief. I have forbidden that boy to speak to that little whelp, but it appears he has ignored my command."

Pharaoh Runihura glared at Nakia with his metal eyes. He stepped towards the slave, who quivered under the hypnotic eyes of the pharaoh. Nakia took a step backward for every step the pharaoh gained on him. The pharaoh's lip curled into a glare of disgust. "Where is your Master, you wretched dog?"

Nakia felt his knees quake as his chest began to tighten. His hand went to his chest as his legs grew weak. "Please, don't hurt me, my pharaoh," Nakia pleaded as he began to wheeze.

"Tell me where you have hid him or your entrails will not stay within your body for another night," Runihura glared, his golden eyes glowing red with fury.

Nakia fell to his knees before the pharaoh and fell forward, covering the back of his head with his hands. "Please, have mercy! I know not where he is at this moment!"

Kaemwaset stood beside the pharaoh. "Imani has stated that our son has left. Our family's boat is gone! Where has he gone, Nakia?"

"I don't know!" Nakia screamed in fear.

Runihura reached for Nakia's wrist and grabbed it harshly. He clutched tightly onto the wrist, making Nakia straighten his body. "Where is he?"

Nakia screamed as the pharaoh began to twist his arm. "Stop! Please!"

Janani ran beside Nakia. "My pharaoh, please don't hurt him! He doesn't know!"

"Leave here. Command Wosenret to come to me."

Nakia watched Janani leave, his heart beating wildly. "My Lords, I do not know where Master Amsi is now!"

Pharaoh Runihura threw Nakia to the ground and placed his foot on the slave's chest. Nakia grabbed Runihura's ankle, struggling to remove it from his body. Pharaoh Runihura was not a large man as Kaemwaset, yet the foot felt as a rock upon his breast.

"My Lord, I can't breathe," Nakia strained to say through his wheezing lungs.

"Then you had better tell me what I wish to know before my foot crushes you," Runihura growled.

Kaemwaset glared at the slave. "I know you are harboring his whereabouts! Where is he? He is not at the Bedouin settlement! He is not on our land! Where is he, Nakia, son of a defeated people?"

Runihura leaned over, placing more pressure on Nakia's chest cavity. "It would be a shame if your bones pierced your heart and you suffocated on your own blood. Where is he?"

"I have asked the other Nobles if they have seen him. Not one eye has seen him. Where did he go, Nakia?"

"I can't breathe," Nakia barely said as the pharaoh placed more of a weight on his chest.

Runihura chuckled. "His gagging is quite entertaining, is it not, Kaemwaset?"

Kaemwaset stood beside Nakia and pointed an accusatory finger at him. "You will tell us what we need to know or I rid myself of you permanently!"

"Boat," Nakia whimpered. "Temple."

Runihura removed his foot and watched as Nakia wrapped his arms around himself protectively. The slave wheezed, struggling to breathe through his compressed lungs.

"Where did they go?"

Tears fell from Nakia's eyes. "Amsi went with Azizi to the Temple of Isis near Kadesh."

Pharaoh Runihura glared at the slave struggling for air. "Are you certain?"

Nakia nodded silently, crying. "I'm sorry, Master Amsi."

Runihura looked down at Kaemwaset. "It appears that it is not enough that your son has chosen to openly defy your command. He now travels with the boy."

Kaemwaset glared down at Nakia. "How could you let him go, you little wretch?"

"Amsi wanted to go!"

Kaemwaset shook his head solemnly. "The boy for whom I have prayed to the gods is a traitor to his father! He has disobeyed my command! How could my own child do such a cruel thing as disrespect his father's wishes?"

Runihura grinned as he put a hand on Kaemwaset's shoulder. "Your son has been blinded to the truth. Your wife has poisoned his mind against you and your wishes." Runihura leaned into Kaemwaset's ear. "Your wife is to blame. She has softened his heart and has made him weak of mind, weak of character, weak of loyalty to his people."

Kaemwaset clenched his fists. "I knew she would corrupt him! My wife is to blame!"

Nakia struggled for breath as he looked at his master. "Mistress Imani…is…merciful. Hatred and anger have enveloped your heart in darkness where they fester like a disease!"

Kaemwaset leaned over to the wheezing slave. "I care not for your tongue, Nakia! I should have known that my son would do this to me! How could he turn his back on his people?"

Runihura grinned. *If Amsi is indeed the Anointed Companion of Rā, this is my chance to eliminate him.   Killing of another Noble would turn the Nobility against me. I cannot afford that. However, if there is a valid reason to slaughter him, nobody will question my real intentions.* Runihura put his arm around Kaemwaset and leaned into the large man's ear. "Your son is officially guilty of High Treason and Conspiracy, Kaemwaset."

Kaemwaset turned to Pharaoh Runihura and narrowed his eyes. "I have no son! My son is dead to me!"

Nakia's eyes widened as he watched he master.   His hand covered his chest as he gasped for air. "Master Kaemwaset...he is your son."

Wosenret stepped through the open doors and bowed before the pharaoh. "My lord, what do you wish of me?"

"Send a battalion into the desert to search the Red Land of Seth! I want you to look for Amsi Al-Sakhir and Azizi Keket! When you are finished with that task, prepare twenty of your men to scour *Iunu* and find the relics of Isis. We will search every temple in Heliopolis for our prize." Wosenret bowed and left the room. Runihura looked down at Nakia. "I trust not your words, heathen. They could have set free the boat in an attempt to deceive us."

Kaemwaset shook his head remorsefully. "I prayed for that boy. I prayed to Rā that He would bless me with a son. Amsi was to be the glory of my House! Amsi was to be my Legacy to Eternity! Instead, what I have is a son who would rather be a mule than a stallion! How could my son be so cruel towards his father?" A tear crawled down Kaemwaset's cheek. "My boy is a traitor to his people. How could this have happened?"

Runihura took Kaemwaset's arms and looked the wealthy landowner in the eyes. "Your son does not love you. Your wife hates you with every breath your lungs take. She and your son are your enemy. You are my ally, Kaemwaset."

Nakia shook his head as he watched the pharaoh look into the eyes of his owner. He struggled to his knees and winced in pain as his sides throbbed with pain.

Kaemwaset looked into the golden eyes of the pharaoh. The clinking of the blinking eyes echoed through the silence of the room.

"You know what I must do," Runihura said. "He must not be allowed to live."

Nakia looked up at the pharaoh. "No! You will not harm Master Amsi!"

Runihura calmly looked at Nakia. "How are you going to stop me? You are struggling for air. You are weak, Nakia. Try to stop me."

Nakia struggled to his feet and felt his ribs throbbing with every movement. He took one step and crumbled to his knees holding his sides. Nakia coughed as he leaned over. A whistling sound came from the slave's lungs as he tried to breathe. Runihura and Kaemwaset watched as the slave coughed blood onto the marble tile. Nakia fell onto his stomach, panting heavily. The slave moaned as his lungs wheezed. "Master…"

"Is there no other way to save my son besides his death, my Great Pharaoh?"

"He has already been corrupted beyond repair, my Lord Kaemwaset. Death is the only option for him. He is a traitor. His feet corrupt the land upon which he walks. Should you decide not to give him to me for his punishment, the palace will seek its produce from another Noble family. Your purse will ache for coin, Kaemwaset.   You do not wish for me to withdrawal my patronage of your lands, do you?"

"No, my pharaoh! You bless my lands with your financing! Your glorious feet bless my crops when they see you in your chariot."

Runihura sighed sadly. "I do enjoy your lettuce, Kaemwaset. It would be a pity if I must choose another family to grow my food. You would not be able to feed your wife. Your slaves will suffer and starve. Nobody will purchase food from a traitor's father. Heliopolis will call your lands and your crops cursed and inedible. You will lose your dwelling and live in the streets with the thieves you so abhor."

"I cannot allow that, Great One! How will I survive?" Kaemwaset
shook his head. "Perhaps I can rehabilitate him.   Perhaps he need not
die."

"Your son is a lost cause, Kaemwaset. He wants the throne of Egypt for
himself. This I cannot allow. Your son and his friend shall perish by
my hand."

"I can only hope that my son is not beyond repair. I can fix him, my
pharaoh. If I can't, I will do the deed myself."

Nakia's eyes widened in shock. *Master Amsi...no!*

Runihura grinned. "You would kill your son, the product of your *Ka*?"

"My son acts as one un-befitting of his station. He has turned his back
on his family and his people. He has thrown our traditions and our
family name into a pile of manure. Amsi has disgraced the name of the
Nobility. Better a dead son than one who will soil my name and
disgrace the name of 'Al-Sakhir.'Though his death shall leave Ife
Re-Nefer with no husband."

Runihura stepped from Kaemwaset. "If Amsi cannot appreciate a good
wife, then bring her to me.   She could bear my heir, the next king of
Egypt."

Kaemwaset bowed. "If my son does not fulfill his duty to my House,
then she will be brought to you, my pharaoh. I will give my son one

last chance to do as I command. If he fails to please me, I will eliminate him."

Runihura looked down at Nakia. "He has heard every word. What shall I do with him?"

Kaemwaset stepped to Nakia and glared angrily at the slave. "If I lose the sponsorship of the pharaoh, Nakia, my boy, you will be the first I will send to meet Anubis. If he reveals any of our words today, his fate will be in your hands, pharaoh."

"Delightful," Runihura said, chuckling low in his throat.

XIV

The Dawn Of A New Age

Ma-Amun raised his hands as the morning's first light filled the courtyard of the Temple of Rā.   The priest had woken early to anoint the statue of the sun god in expensive oils and wrap the statue in the finest linen available.   The priest bowed as he placed the best fruits and meats before the statue's sanctuary. "Glorious Rā, who blesses his people every morning with his beautiful light, who defeats the evil serpent Apep, shine your healing, heavenly light upon your faithful! Amun-Rā, may my prayers be heard by your divine ears."

Carim watched from the top of the temple wall, looking down at the bowing priest.   A gentle breeze brushed across his skin as he watched the priest worship his god's sanctuary.   The teenager heard thundering hooves race from the Temple of Hapi. A golden shimmer of the pharaoh's chariot made him crouch low on the wall to prevent being seen.

Twenty soldiers, including Wosenret, raced behind the pharaoh. *What brings the pharaoh and his entourage out in such big numbers?*

The pharaoh and his men stopped before the Temple of Rā. Carim grabbed his bow and saw the soldiers swarm towards the door. The pharaoh climbed the stairs and Carim jumped as the door to the courtyard was forced open by Runihura's fists.

Ma-Amun turned quickly as he saw the pharaoh calmly approach. "My Great Pharaoh!"

Carim glared as the priest bowed before Runihura. *This can't be good. The priest has nobody to protect him from that jackal.*

"Where are they, priest?" Runihura asked quietly.

Ma-Amun cautiously raised his head. "What are you looking for, Merciful One?"

Carim tightened his grip on his bow as he stared wide-eyed at the priest. *Run, you fool! Don't kneel before him!*

"I am searching for the Scroll and Circlet of Isis. Give them to me and I will spare your life."

"My pharaoh, I know naught of what you ask of me."

Runihura turned to Wosenret. "Tear it apart."

Carim watched as the soldiers spread themselves around the courtyard and into the temple. "What are they doing?" the priest asked nervously.

"Finding what we came for, priest," Runihura said, calmly walking toward the sanctuary of the sun god.

Carim heard smashing of glass and stone within the temple. Soldiers in the garden grabbed small statues of Rā and smashed them on the ground.

"Please stop!" Ma-Amun pleaded as he rose to his feet. "This is an abomination to the Sun God!"

"The time for talking is over, old man," Wosenret said as he stood beside the priest calmly. "We do not ask twice for what we desire."

Carim watched the soldiers swarm like bees, breaking wooden and clay offering bowls. *Run, you foolish man! The pharaoh will kill you even if he finds what he seeks! Run!*

Ma-Amun saw Runihura reach for the god's sanctuary. "My king, do not open the home of the god! You are defiling holy ground with your violent assault upon my temple!"

"Don't touch him!" Carim exclaimed in alarm as the priest grabbed Pharaoh Runihura. "Run, you fool!"

Wosenret and the soldiers raised their heads to see Carim standing on the wall. "Kill him!"

Carim ran across the wall as the soldiers fired their arrows. Carim saw a boomerang race towards his head. The teenager ducked as another volley of arrows raced towards him. Carim lost his balance and fell off the wall.

"Get him," Wosenret growled to two of his men.

Pharaoh Runihura glared at the priest with his shining eyes. "Who are you to tell me that I am defiling holy ground? I am your god on earth!"

"Why would objects of Isis be hidden within the Temple of Rā? Search the other temples!"

Runihura growled low in his throat as he opened the doors of the stone house of the god. "The sanctuary of the goddess is empty." Runihura reached into the sanctuary and grabbed the statue of Amun-Rā.

"My pharaoh, please replace the Great Sun God into his sanctuary."

Runihura turned to the priest and whipped the statue across the priest's head, causing some of the statue to break off. Wosenret watched calmly as the priest collapsed onto the ground motionless. "Well done, my lord."

"This temple belongs to Sekhmet now. Destroy all images of Amun-Rā and bring my artisans to create murals to the Great and Powerful Sekhmet."

Runihura threw the statue onto the priest, flattening the man's face from the impact. "Take this into the alley. The feral dogs will enjoy the meal."

Three soldiers returned to Wosenret. "The kid disappeared."

Runihura grinned. "Forget him.   If he manages to tell the other temples that I am searching for the relics of Isis, perhaps they will be more cooperative."

*   *   *

Amsi slowly stirred as he heard Azizi's voice speaking softly.   Azizi was kneeling on the deck of the boat, bowing to the stars. "Hail to you, Osiris, Lord of Eternity, king of gods, of holy forms. The imperishable stars are under his rule, the unwearying stars are his abode." Azizi turned towards the west and bowed his head. "His sister was his guard. Mighty Isis who protected her brother, who sought him without wearying, who roamed the land lamenting, not resting until she found him, who made a shade with her wings and created breath with her wings, guide our journey into the dangerous night."

Amsi rubbed his eyes and looked down at the blanket covering him. His eyes watched as Azizi sprinkled herbs into the water.   The sails flapped above Azizi as he prayed. Amsi emerged from the shelter and pulled on the rope for the sail.

Azizi watched the Noble teen tighten the rope and tie the rope to the mast. "Greetings."

Amsi looked into the darkness surrounding the boat. "Greetings. Do you think we'll hit land soon?"

Azizi nodded. "If Shu's wind continues, we will hit land sooner than we planned."

Amsi held his breath as the water gently splashed against the boat. Azizi stood, his eyes gazing into the night. The oil lamp flickered, sending a few feet of light ahead of them.

The creaking of the boat was all that was heard around the two boys as the wind became still.

"It's quiet," Amsi whispered as he stood beside his friend.

Azizi nodded silently as he stepped backward, bumping into Amsi. "Too quiet."

Amsi felt the wind brush against his cheek again. "I have something that can help pass the time." Azizi watched Amsi disappear into the shelter and emerge with the decorated box he had earlier examined. The teen sat on his seat and opened the box. He placed the several throwing sticks in front of the thief and pulled two cones of different color. "We'll play *Senet*."

Azizi raised a curious eyebrow. "I've never played this game."

Amsi placed a white cone and a black cone on the lid. "It's simple. You see before you a grid of three rows of ten squares. You must win the 31st square at the top beside me to win where you will stand in the Hall of Osiris. Do you want to be the white or black cone?"

"I'll take the black," Azizi said as his eyes widened. Some of the squares had been painted with heads of demons. One of the squares had been decorated with ripples representing water.

"Take the sticks and throw them on the deck. The carved lines will tell you how many squares you move."

Azizi took the throwing sticks and dropped them onto the deck. Three sticks displayed a total of three lines. "So I move ahead three spaces?"

Amsi nodded and watched Azizi move forward three spaces. Amsi leaned over and saw the markings on the space. "You have reached the First Arit in Amenta. Who is the watcher of the First Arit?"

"Meti-heh, the herald is Ha-kheru."

"You are safe, then. I'm surprised you know that, never having read the Book of the Dead."

Azizi continued to row as Amsi picked up his throwing sticks. "I worship the God of the Dead. I am the leader of the Osiris Thief Clan. I had better know the names of the gates, their watchers, and their heralds."

Amsi threw the sticks on the deck and rowed with his left hand. Amsi moved five spaces as indicated on his sticks. "'You will be blessed with a happy marriage.' That was a fortunate throw for me! Get a two, Azizi. You and-what's her name?"

"Kahla."

"You and Kahla will be blessed with a happy marriage, too!"

Azizi grabbed the sticks and dropped them on the ground. Azizi moved his cone ahead six spaces. Amsi picked up the black cone and read the script. "It says that you will obtain what your heart desires."

"What do I desire?" Azizi asked, looking at his friend.

Amsi shrugged. "What is it that you want?"

"I want to defeat the pharaoh and see the old code return. I want to take Kahla away from Mbizi. I want-." Azizi turned his head and looked at Amsi. The Noble teen continued to row, looking at him quizzically. "I want to-."

"What do you want, Aziz?"

Azizi shook his head, quickly silencing himself. "I want to get to the Temple of Isis before Gahiji."

Amsi nodded as he grabbed the sticks. Amsi threw the sticks on the deck and moved his piece ahead two spaces. "Oh No! Apep is after me! I must roll again! I need a six to outrun him!" Amsi quickly picked up the pieces and threw them onto the deck again. Amsi moved his cone ahead eleven spaces with haste. He looked at the space and sighed with relief. "I am in the Land of the Scepter! I'm safe!"

Azizi chuckled. "You are lucky, my friend." The thief grabbed the sticks and tossed them onto the deck. He moved his black cone eight spaces. "What does it say?"

Amsi picked up the cone and read the text on the square. Amsi's smile faded from his face. "The Eye of Horus is upon you."

Azizi and Amsi looked at the board with bewilderment. Azizi sighed deeply as the clouds parted from the moon, allowing the moon to shine upon them. "Even on the Great Green, the Eye of Horus remains fixed in our direction."

Amsi replaced the cone on the space. "Perhaps the board means the hawk-god, Horus, and not the pharaoh."

"The pharaoh is the Living Horus, Amsi. How am I to know if Horus, Avenger of his father Osiris, approves of my actions?"

Amsi looked into the eyes of his friend. "Rā has created this world and from his tears were born men and women. It is we, Azizi, who are trying to save his children. We are fighting for much more than our own lives. We are fighting to save the world from a man whose anger, hatred, burns in his heart. Rā smiles upon you as his son. His rays protect you. If you were trying to save my child, Azizi, I would love you because I love my child. There is no doubt in my mind that the gods love you because you are trying to save their children. Rā wishes none of his children die."

"Isis loved her husband and hid her son, Horus, from the prowling eyes of Seth. The bond between parent and child is strong. I hope that one day, Amsi, that should the gods bless me with a son, I will never treat him as your father has done to you."

Amsi took the sticks in his hand. "Azizi, do you love Kahla? Do you want to have children someday?"

Azizi rowed the boat as he looked forward into the night. "I want to make Kahla my wife. I hope someday to have children. She understands what I must do to ensure the safety of our child."

"I do not love Ife. Zahra is beautiful, her manner, jovial and kind. When I kissed her, I felt a strange sensation in my belly and I don't know what it was."

Azizi watched as Amsi tossed the sticks on the ground and move his piece ahead nine spaces.

Amsi looked at the square. "By Ammut! I landed in the House of Rebirth! I must return to the fifteenth square."

"What sensation did you feel?"

Amsi fell silent as he placed his cone on the fifteenth square. Azizi watched his friend blush and avert his eyes.

"Tell me! What did you feel?" Azizi asked, picking up the throwing sticks.

Amsi swallowed nervously. "My belly felt tight.   My body became stiff between my legs."

Azizi chuckled and smiled. "Are you talking about your manhood?"

"Shh! Don't say that!"

"Why not? Did your father never sit down with you and discuss intimacy with women and your growing body?" Azizi tossed the sticks and moved his cone ahead nine spaces

Amsi looked at the square. "You have seen Aaqet-qet in the Hall of Horus.   No, my father has never sat with me."

Azizi laughed, leaning forward on the handle of the oar. His face turned red from laughing hysterically. He wiped away tears raining down his cheeks.   "I cannot believe it!"

Amsi pushed Azizi's shoulders and grabbed the sticks. "How am I supposed to know what was never discussed with me?"

Azizi straightened his back and took a deep breath. "You excel in the knowledge of books and scriptures, but you are ignorant of the life around you. Raise your nose from your books, Amsi, and you will experience more of life."

Amsi threw his sticks and moved ahead three spaces. "I may not understand much, but I do know that I have been invited to eat bread and drink beer with Qeq-hauau-ent-pehui! You have passed my square, so you may not indulge in beer and bread!"

Azizi picked up the sticks. "I've had to learn all of this on my own. Aneksi discussed this with me only in passing. Kahla and I have kissed before. Sometimes, we lay beside the Nile, hidden in the reeds, and we kiss through the night. Her lips are like honey. When I think of her, my heart leaps with joy. She has touched me where a wife touches her husband." Azizi smiled peacefully. "Her lips have blessed my stomach with her kisses. She worships me with her lips. I have loved her as a man loves his wife."

"Have you felt the same tightening?"

Azizi nodded. "When you feel love, when your belly becomes aroused, your manhood will react and become stiff."

"Does that mean I love her?"

Azizi looked at Amsi in the eyes. "Would you die for her?" *As you would die for me?*

Amsi nodded. "Yes, I would die for her."

"Would you suffer the pains of millions of arrows just for a glimpse of her?"

"Yes. I love her, my friend.   My heart leaps for joy. Lovely is the look of her eyes. Sweet is the speech of her lips. Joy has he whom she embraces."

Azizi threw the sticks, moving his piece ahead to the 31st space. "I am in the presence of the Almighty Osiris. I have won."

Amsi gathered the sticks in his hand. "You played well for someone who has never played *Senet*."

"Have you told Zahra that you love her?"

"No, I am nervous."

Azizi put his hand on Amsi's shoulder. "Don't be afraid. What is the worst that could happen?"

"When she greets me, she smiles and throws herself at me with joy."

"She loves you!   I encourage you to reveal yourself to her. Kahla knows I love her. I have told her many times.   Someday, Amsi Al-Sakhir, she will be my wife. We will establish a home and a family.

Many children will be blessed to us by Osiris. With every *Akhet* season, a new babe will be born to us!" Azizi smiled and spread his arms wide. "I will be the leader of a new gang of thieves, all of whom will be happy to have been born of my body."

Amsi laughed. "Do you plan to repopulate *Iunu* single-handedly?"

Azizi grinned. "Well, I am the King of Thieves and the other women of Mbizi's would be more than happy to give me a hand with that plan."

"I know when I father a son, I will not burden him with my desires. I have told my father I cannot live the life that he wishes me to live. I want to live my own life."

The thief nodded and pat his friend's shoulder. "You have made me proud with that statement. You shall make a wonderful father and a desirable mate, Amsi."

Amsi smiled at his friend. "You believe so?"

Azizi bowed his head. "I know that to be true. When we defeat the pharaoh, our children will behave as their forefathers. Beggars and Nobles will sit at the Table of Plenty and share beer and lamb. Our sons and daughters, Amsi, will begin the dawn of a new age. Our sons need not war as we must."

Amsi smiled and covered Azizi's hand on his shoulder. "I look forward to that day, Azizi Keket." Amsi held Azizi's hand as the waves gently rocked the boat. "We will sit beside each other as brothers with our wives and children beside us."

Azizi nodded. "May the gods bless that day."

XV

Thoth's Legacy

My son is a traitor. He has betrayed his lineage, his family, and most importantly, my memory. How could my son, my flesh and blood, my legacy betray me? When he was fashioned in his mother's womb, he was perfect. Amsi was my child who would set offerings at my tomb and continue the Al-Sakhir name.

Now the Al-Sakhir name is tarnished! My heart! My son! How could you turn your back on your father? You betrayed your own father who placed you into his mother's womb! Your name tastes of fetid meat! The name of Amsi Al-Sakhir once smelled of fine perfume, but no longer.

Nakia stopped the carriage. He's nervous. He knows I will hand him to the Great Pharaoh should he decide to speak of our plans for my child. Baruti stands in front of the slave home, waiting for the prodigal slave to return. Baruti glares at me sternly. The only reason I keep him around is his strong back. Otherwise, he knows I would rid myself of him. Qamra stepped beside him, no doubt waiting to welcome home the lonely twin.

I would rather slay my servants than release them from my charge. The fine would be minimal. They belong to me. If I lose the patronage of the pharaoh, she will be the first slave to go. Though her body be entertaining, she would not like to see the slaughter of the children. I will spare her the pain of seeing me kill them.

I passed the pasture as I walked toward my home. My home was built to reflect my greatness. It is truly fit to be the home of the Nobility! When I stepped into my home, I saw the murals of Rā on my walls. My ancestors painted on the wall will forever pass the challenges of Osiris.

Who is in my garden? The digging of a trowel sounds nearby. When I approached the archway, I saw Khentimentiu kneeling among the cucumbers. The eight-year-old boy hacked at the soil with the small shovel. No doubt his father and mother were awaiting him outside. The child was humming softly to himself.

"What are you doing in the garden this late at night?" I asked, looking down at the child.

Khentimentiu dropped the shovel and looked up at me with fear. He jumped to his feet. "Najam asked me to finish harvesting the cucumbers for your breakfast, sir."

"Khentimentiu!" Baruti called for his son. "Come here, my son!"

I walked towards the boy and hovered over him. The child took a hesitant step backward. "I'm helping Najam! I promise!"

"Do not let me catch you stealing from my private garden or I will tie you to the post for seven suns!"

Khenti shivered as I looked down at him. "Yes, sir, I'm sorry!"

"Get out of here before I beat you!"

The little boy ran through the gate. I walked behind him as he raced away.   Through the iron bars of the gate, I watched the little boy run into the waiting arms of his father.

Baruti put his arms around his son and glared at me through the bars. I watched him kiss his child on the head.   I heard the child cough as he disappeared into the house with his family.

"Where have you been?" I heard my wife's voice behind me.

I turned to her and crossed my arms sternly. "I went to the pharaoh. Imani, tell me where our son has gone."

Imani folded her hands in front of her. "My husband, our son is in danger."

"He is in danger from that thief-rat he calls his friend!"

Imani stepped towards me. In the moonlight, she remains as beautiful as when I first brought her into my home. "My good lord, the pharaoh is evil, can't you see? His intentions are cruel. His hand is wicked. Why can you not see he means harm to our son?"

"Our son is dead to us, my wife!"

Imani looked up at me as I saw a tear creep down her face. "Do the Sacred Scriptures not say 'If you are a man of worth and produce a son by the grace of god, do for him all that is good for he is your son, your *Ka* begot him. Do not withdraw your heart from him?'"

"The Sacred Scriptures also say if he strays, neglects your counsel, punish him for all his talk! His guilt was fated in the womb!"

Imani took my hand and pressed it to her breast lightly. "My dear Kaemwaset, he is our son. I suffered through the pains of labor to birth him. My heart weeps at his disappearance. You would choose your sovereign over the flesh of your soul?"

It is not easy for me to condemn my son to the pharaoh's list of victims. However, our good name would be synonymous with treachery and betrayal. I would be ruined. "Think, my wife, of all that the Nobility will say of our name! Our lands and vegetables are corrupted! The pharaoh will no longer purchase food from us! We will not afford our taxes and become beggars in the streets!"

"Certainly you cannot choose your Noble status over your son, Kaemwaset Al-Sakhir!"

"It is a decision not easily made, my wife.   Perhaps the gods will bless our family again with a new son."

Imani stepped back from me. "I refused to share a bed with you fourteen years ago and I still refuse to allow you into my house.   I shall never share a bed with you again, Kaemwaset. My body belongs to you in name only, not in my heart."

"Then I shall command Qamra to my bed again!"

Imani looked at me angrily. "Maybe I should take Baruti to my bed! He loves his children and protects them! His seed is strong and would easily give me a son! Perhaps he would make me feel pleasure unlike you who are selfish and uninteresting in the bedchamber!"

My eyes glared at her. "You would be guilty of infidelity and thrown to the crocodiles!"

"You have already committed that crime!   Should I hear from Qamra or Baruti that you have taken her by force, we will no longer share more than a bed.   I will take Qamra, Baruti, Khentimentiu, Meskhenet, and Laila with me."

"Najam, Nakia, and Akilah cannot work the fields, dress me, and cook my dinner alone!"

"I will be taking Nakia with me. You have beaten that boy enough."

"A boy's ears are on his back. He hears when he is beaten! Besides, Pharaoh Atenhotep has given Nakia to me! He belongs to me! You cannot take him."

"Then the local vizier will hear us and decide who shall take him. I will not leave that boy here with you alone."

Najam stepped through the archway to the kitchen. "My Lord and Lady, do you need me?"

"No, Najam. We are sorry for interrupting your sleep," Imani told her.

Najam bowed as I heard another cough come from the slave quarters. I bet you that Nakia brought that plague from Iunu here with him! Nakia coughed as he left the barn. His lungs almost made a screeching sound as he coughed.

Imani turned towards me angrily. "Ipa-witu will decide who will get the slaves! Qamra is my body slave and I can choose to take her with me."

"Baruti belongs to me and since his children come from his loins, they belong to me, too!"

"You are a selfish man choosing between your son and your wealth! Never would I have believed that my husband would treat his son so poorly!"

I crossed my arms defiantly. My wife will not win this argument! "If you take Baruti to your bedchamber, you may find yourself a new home and I promise to hang Baruti from the same balcony as Jinan!"

"Goodnight, my husband," Imani said, turning and walking away calmly.

I turned towards the slave home, my lip curling in disdain. I will not allow Imani to intimidate me.

My slaves belong to me.   If I can't possess them, nobody will!

*   *   *

Amsi watched his friend examine the scroll carefully.   Azizi glared at the text on the papyrus, trying to pronounce the words.   The thief had learned ten hieroglyphics and three words.   The Noble teen grimaced when he heard his friend slowly say the word.

"How can you read these eight hours every day?" Azizi asked with frustration.

Amsi shrugged. "It is expected that I learn how to count, read, write, pray, record, and do calculations of bushels and livestock.   I must learn this to oversee my father's lands."

"Do you know how to pick a pocket?" Azizi asked, his teeth showing in a menacing smile.

"No."

The thief laughed. "Now we're even."

Amsi rowed with his left hand as he pointed to the scroll on Azizi's thighs. "The territory of the '*Hksw hsswt*,' the Hyksos, lies to the north of Kadesh. Is there a Common word for them?"

"*Hnn-pht-k*, the Children of Strength."

Amsi raised a curious eyebrow. "That's an interesting term."

"I have heard Aneksi speak of rulers past and I have seen carvings in tombs. There are carvings near a Noble's tomb in Nekheb which depict the struggles between Neb-Pehty-Re and the Hyksos invaders. There are murals in the Noble's tomb which depict the siege at Sharuhen. They were strong adversaries."

Amsi narrowed his eyes at Azizi. "You broke into the tomb of a Noble?"

"I was bored."

"Why don't you do something constructive rather than break into the tomb of one who has served his country well?"

Azizi shrugged. "Do you have any suggestions?"

"Read?"

"I can't read."

Amsi asked, "Learn a skill?"

"I already know how to pick locks and pick pockets. What else would I need to know to survive?"

"What about learn a trade?"

"That's boring."

Amsi sighed with resignation. "You really are the most frustrating student I have ever had the misfortune to teach."

"I'm here trying to learn your language, aren't I? I can't be a total loss," Azizi said casually. "One of these days, I'll take you with me. We'll go together and you'll see the thrill of adventure."

Amsi stopped rowing. "Do you realize what will happen to you if you were captured? Gahiji will take your hands and the pharaoh will cut your throat! He'll drink your blood and offer your corpse to Sekhmet! His dogs will chew your bones!"

Azizi nodded. "I know what will happen if he catches me. Nobody patrols the Valley of the Dead. You will come with me one day. You honestly do not lust for adventure, Amsi? I know you want more out of life than establishing a family, being the Lord of your lands, and reading this book-ish nonsense all day."

Amsi continued to row. "Yes, but-. Azizi, I would be dishonoring my family if I engaged in such activity!"

"Don't be afraid of dishonoring your family. Your family will never know. You will come with me on one of my expeditions and you will have more fun than all the banquets and *Wag*-feasts combined!"

Amsi watched as the oil lamp's flame flickered in the darkness. *Perhaps Aziz's right. Watching the women dance and listening to the music is enjoyable, but shouldn't there be more excitement to life? When Azizi and I were fighting the pharaoh in Hapi's temple, it was exhilarating. The battle with the soldiers in Iunu tested my skills. I have never taken a man's life before that night, but my heart beat wildly. My lessons with Sawaret never entailed so much danger. That night in the alley, I could have been killed. Azizi could have been butchered at my side.*

As partners, we fought well as a team. At the Temple of Hapi, Azizi and I barely escaped with our heads intact. I still do not know how we escaped. Nakia's help was valuable. Nakia...Nassar. I wonder how they are doing. My hope is that Nakia has not succumbed to my father's wrath. No doubt he has noticed my disappearance.

"Amsi, do you trust me?" Azizi asked as he looked into his friend's eyes.

Amsi swallowed nervously as he looked at his friend. "What?"

Azizi reached out and put his hand on Amsi's shoulder. "Do you trust me?"

Amsi nodded. "I do."

The thief smiled. "Then trust me to keep you safe."

"I trust you, my friend.   I question not your intentions. I do question whether you intend to rob from my tomb after my death."

Azizi chuckled. "If you are buried with only your school books, I would not rob from your tomb."

"That's a relief."

"Because if all that I had to steal from your sarcophagus was your school texts, I would die of boredom."

Amsi sighed as he heard Azizi chuckling beside him.   "Very funny."

"I would join you in death because I would open your coffin and say, 'Behold! My only booty will be instructional texts! My mind has seized with tedium from such academia! I die on you, Amsi!' I would then proceed to collapse on top of your corpse and breathe my last breath."

"What if I had gold and coins? Would you take them first and then die?"

Azizi continued to row and removed his hand from Amsi's shoulder. "I would pocket the coins and then die on you not from boredom, but from incredible sadness and despair. I would have stolen from you, but your coin would go nowhere."

"Don't rob my tomb when I am dead," Amsi said sadly.

"You need have no fear of me robbing your tomb, my brother."

"Why is that?"

Azizi slowly rowed the boat forward. "Should the pharaoh capture us together, we die together."

Amsi nodded. "Can you read the second word, Azizi?"

Azizi looked down at the scroll again. "*Sdmyw?*"

Amsi smiled and nodded. "That is the Noble word for 'Judges.' The term means 'the listeners.'"

"In Common Tongue, the word for 'Judges' is '*khefta.*' It means 'enemies.'"

Amsi repeated the word. "What will you do should I perish first, Azizi? Would you really die of sadness and despair?"

I would lose my brother, my best friend. Even should I not pocket your gold and die on you, I would wish for a venomous snake to bite me and spread fire through my veins. I would use my dagger and plunge its blade into my heart. The pain in my chest would be nothing compared to the pain in my heart that I would feel from your absence. I will lament as a mother mourns for her dead child or a husband for his wife. My body will ache. My heart will leave me. How could I bear your absence?

"Honestly?"

Amsi nodded. "You look in pain. Do you need to lie down?"

"No, Amsi. Should you die, I would lament deeply. My grief for your death would be none less than a man who has lost his wife. Osiris himself would hear my cries. Like Isis, my wailing would carry on the wind. My cries would not cease until my lips are forever silenced, my brother. I couldn't bear this life without my best friend." Amsi's eyes widened as he looked at the pain on Azizi's face. The thief wrapped his cloak tightly around him. His bottom lip trembled and his body shivered. Amsi saw the stoic, strong thief display a moment of vulnerability. "It is not easy for me to speak of such emotion and loss," Azizi said. "I hate myself for admitting it."

"Don't hate yourself, Azizi. I would make certain you were anointed with the best oils. The rays of the Aten forever would be darkened. The world would be as barren as the desert because I would not have my friend by my side. My life would no longer know joy, only pain without your presence."

Azizi smiled from his seat. "My parents are awaiting my return in the Hall of Osiris."

"Issâm will greet me from beside the seat of Thoth."

"Return to the shelter and grab your flute. This is our third day on the open water. The night sky protects us under her veil of shadow. Play so that our hearts will be merry."

Amsi stood and returned to the shelter. He emerged with his flute and sat before Azizi on the deck of the boat. The thief grabbed Amsi's oar and resumed rowing while Amsi commenced playing his instrument.

*   *   *

Nakia coughed as he entered the slave home.   Khentimentiu was sitting on his mother's lap, coughing and leaning against her.   The children were taking bread from their father's offering hand as they looked up at him.

Nakia took a piece of bread and sat beside the fire quietly.   His eyes stared into the fire, thinking of Nassar in *Iunu*. *I can't believe he's still alive!   I wish he were here with me now.   Master Kaemwaset wants to see his son dead. Surely, he can't wish that!   What father would wish to see their son die? Kaemwaset was so happy when he heard that his child was a boy. How he could wish his child dead is a mystery.*

Baruti sat beside Khentimentiu and brought his son into his lap. "You do not feel well, my son?"

"Najam wanted me to help her in the garden. Perhaps I should have told her that I could not because I'm tired."

Nakia's eyes raised as he watched the father cuddle his son against him. Baruti kissed his son's forehead and rocked him gently.   *I can never see Baruti treating his children with such malice. He loves his children. He and Qamra are waiting to see once more if the barley sprouts again.*

"Nakia, are you feeling alright?" Qamra asked. "You have been very silent as of late."

"You've hardly eaten," Akilah said as she sat beside the fire.

Nakia heaved a heavy sigh. "I found Nassar."

Qamra and Baruti's eyes widened in shock. "You found your twin? Where is he?"

"Why didn't you tell us this earlier?" Qamra asked. "Why did you not bring him home with us?"

Nakia lowered his head. "Because he is better where he is."

"Where is he?" Meskhenet asked.

"He has become one of the thieves of *Iunu*. Azizi's clan found him."

"Why did he not return here with you?"

Nakia looked up at the fellow slave. "Father Baruti, Nassar is better where he is. The Osiris Clan can take care of him. He can help Azizi. Why would I want him to return here where-." Nakia fell silent quickly, cutting off his own sentence abruptly.

"Where what?" Qamra asked.

Nakia shook his head. "Why would I want him to return here? At least on the streets he can steal food. He's been surviving that way for two years. It's better than what we have here, isn't it?"

"But he has you here, Kelile," Baruti said.

"No, my brother is safer away from Kaemwaset's lands." Nakia bit into his bread. *If you only knew the fate from which I am saving him.*

Qamra watched Nakia eat. "Did he appear healthy?"

Nakia nodded. "Azizi welcomed Nassar into his clan and told him to see the woman, Aneksi."

Meskhenet turned to her father. "Where is Master Amsi? I haven't seen him in the fields."

Qamra looked into the fire with concern. "Mistress Imani told me that the Little Master is on a long, dangerous journey to the Temple of Isis in Kadesh."

"Why in the Tuat is he going there?"

"He's trying to stop the pharaoh from achieving the godhood he so desires. I pray to Isis that he returns safe."

Nakia slammed his fist against the floor. "I should have gone with him! My place is at my master's side!"

Qamra looked over at Khentimentiu, hearing the boy wheeze and cough in his sleep. "I hope that they are not too late to stop him." The mother reached over and caressed the boy's cheek in his sleep. "Khenti feels hot, Baruti. Perhaps he spent too long working today."

Nakia's eyes widened. "Khenti has the illness sweeping *Iunu!*"

"What illness?" Baruti asked.

Nakia watched the sleeping boy with worry. "People are sick in the city. They are coughing and dying with rashes on them! I have seen them in the city! Khentimentiu is going to die!"

"Nakia, don't say such things!" Qamra scolded. "He just needs to sleep. He worked hard today."

"I hope Master Amsi can find what he needs."

"Khentimentiu needs his rest. I can make him medicine in the morning. Get some sleep, Kelile."

Nakia coughed into his hand as he watched Baruti lay the child on the ground. The father draped his arm over the sleeping boy and closed his eyes. *Master Amsi, you cannot fail.*

XVI

The Landing

Azizi rushed into the shelter to rouse Amsi from his sleep. The thief shook Amsi's shoulder with excitement. "Open your eyes, my friend! There is land nearby!"

Amsi groaned as he opened his eyes slowly. "Why did you wake me? I was sleeping well."

"There is land nearby! A small city sits on the bank where we can refresh our supplies! Wake yourself, Al-Sakhir!" The thief ran out of the shelter and grabbed both oars.

Amsi slowly raised himself to his feet and yawned. "You are like a child who has received a present!"

"Our food is running low and we have been on the water for four days! My legs ache for land."

Amsi stepped into the light and stood behind the teen thief. He squinted to see the shoreline slowly coming into focus. Several small vessels lined the shore. Sailors were carrying jugs of wine and crates of clucking chickens. Their vessel was shrouded in darkness as a large fishing boat crossed their path.

Azizi felt the boat rock as the tall fishing boat passed them. "Be careful with your oars!"

"Our apologies! We could not see your minnow of a boat!" one fisherman called. "Perhaps we should see if your tiny boat can fit in our nets!"

Azizi growled as he glared at the laughing men on the boat. "Perhaps you would like to come here and tell that to my face! This way, I can see the fear in your eyes as I offer your soul to Osiris!"

Amsi put his hand on Azizi's shoulder. "Do not repeat calumny, Azizi, nor should you listen to it. Your silence is better than chatter. Leave him be."

"I will not allow him to speak with such a vile tongue!" Azizi exclaimed, shaking his fist angrily and stepping forward. Amsi wavered as the boat rocked from Azizi's sudden movement. "You will rue the day that you decided to pass so close to my boat!"

"Azizi Keket!" Amsi yelled as he nearly lost his footing.

"May Osiris feed you to Ammut!"

The men laughed and raised their oars. Amsi's eyes widened as the seven oars splashed into the water at once, sending Amsi's boat rocking wildly. Azizi grabbed onto the violently rocking boat and heard a splash behind him. The thief turned his head and saw Amsi missing from the deck. "Amsi?"

Amsi surfaced from under the water line, coughing and sputtering. The men on the large fishing boat laughed as they continued to make their way towards shore. Azizi looked over the edge of the boat.

"Are you alright?"

"I was better in the boat," Amsi said.

Azizi reached into the water and helped Amsi onto the deck. "I apologize."

"You don't need to apologize," Amsi coughed. "They started the fight."

Azizi glared at the large fishing boat docking by the shoreline. "They won't get away with this!"

"Azizi, we can't have the Syrian soldiers chase after us. We can't obtain the Circlet of Isis or her scroll if we are rotting in a dungeon."

Azizi and Amsi rowed to the shoreline. Amsi gathered his bow, quiver, and sword. He placed his ointment box in his bag. Azizi placed the food in the bag and disembarked when the fisherman who had accosted them earlier approached Azizi.

"I believe you wanted me to mock you to your face, stranger?" the man asked.

"Azizi?"

Amsi watched as the fisherman's crew surrounded them. "Azizi, this is exactly what we didn't want."

"Your little friend is correct," the fisherman chuckled. "What should I mock on you first? That tattered rag you call clothing?" the man laughed as he pointed at Azizi's torn and frayed linen skirt. "Shall I mock your body? What are you? A skeleton granted mobility by the Death God himself? You could punch a fly and the fly would hurt your hand!"

Azizi narrowed his eyes and pulled his cape over his shoulder, revealing his bare shoulders and his golden armbands. Amsi could hear the vicious growl bubbling in Azizi's throat. He saw Azizi's body tensing. *Azizi, don't attract attention to us!*

"Have you nothing to say to me, Walking Bones?" the fisherman laughed with his companions. He leaned over and looked Azizi in the eyes. The man shoved Azizi angrily. "What if I beat you? Would you sail home to your mother and cry to her?"

Azizi's fist connected with the fisherman's nose, sending the man to the ground. Amsi winced with the crunch of bone as his friend's fist connected with the man's skull. Three of the man's companions lunged towards them. Azizi grabbed his dagger and raked the blade across one man's stomach, sending him collapsing to the ground.

Amsi punched the face of a man who grabbed his white cloak. Amsi brought his knee into the man's face as he leaned over.   Amsi felt an arm wrap around his throat and a blade touching his back. Amsi felt the man hold him close to his body.

"Stop struggling or I will run you through," the man snarled in his ear.

Amsi watched as Azizi threw a man to the ground and slice through the man's throat with his golden dagger. Azizi smiled with satisfaction at the dying man, his chest rising and falling rapidly. "Azizi!"

Azizi stopped as he saw his friend held hostage by the fisherman. The foe laughed as he held the dagger to Amsi's back. Amsi gagged as the man's arm constricted against his throat.

"Stop right there or I slay him!"

"Release him!"

The man smiled as he pressed the blade against Amsi's skin, making the teen scream through his squeezed throat. "I will kill him!"

Azizi heard the approaching sounds of metal armor. He turned and saw soldiers advancing towards them. "There go our plans for a quiet entry."

Amsi grit his teeth and threw his head back quickly. The back of his head collided with the face of his captor. The man dropped his dagger as he screamed in pain. Amsi grabbed the man's shirt, threw him over his shoulder onto the ground. Amsi grabbed the man's dagger and pierced the man's chest.

"I suggest we make our escape," Azizi said calmly.

Amsi and Azizi ran from the shoreline as people scurried out of their way. Amsi turned his head to see the soldiers gaining ground on them.

"We'll need horses!"

Amsi grabbed his arrows and his bow. He turned quickly and fired his arrow towards the soldiers pursuing him and his friend. The soldiers ran behind large clay pots to avoid the arrows. Azizi cut the ropes of two horses in front of a shop.

Azizi mounted the black horse and turned to Amsi. "Care to join me, my brother?"

Amsi quickly handed Azizi the bow and arrow as he mounted the white horse. Azizi fired the arrow, but it fell to the ground. The Noble teen grabbed his bow and arrow from his friend.

"Remind me to teach you archery, too!" Amsi said as he coaxed his horse forward.

A mischievous smile crossed Azizi's face as he looked behind him. "I hope they learned their lesson well."

"I should say they didn't have too long a time to learn their lesson, my friend. They're all dead." Amsi looked behind them as they left the city. 'Sidon'was written on a sign outside the city limits. "We rise northeast toward Kadesh!"

Azizi raised his bloody dagger into the air with a howl of victory. "To the Temple of Isis, Al-Sakhir, and the Scroll of Isis! Raise your weapon with me!"

Amsi looked at the blade dripping with his captor's blood. "Amun-Rā has guided my blade! I hope our boat is there when we are finished our work at the temple. If I return without my family's boat, my father will be irate."

Azizi shrugged. "If we lost your boat, we have the boat of our rivals. I'm sure they will not need the boat where they are going." The thief added a final chuckle as the couple raced into the desert.

*   *   *

Nassar held onto Sumati's hand as they walked through the streets of *Iunu*. Sumati kept her body close to him as she saw people sitting on the sides of the road asking for money or food.   Nassar watched as one woman collapsed onto the ground. The woman's body gave a final shudder and she died. Her skin was covered with red patches that appeared as burns.

"What is this?" Sumati asked. "I heard people cheering the other day. They were celebrating the Festival of Hapi, correct?"

Nassar said quietly. "Cough kiw peepiw."

"Nassar, why did you bring me here?"

Nassar turned to her. "You ko away. I cwy becaw I mi-you."

Sumati smiled and caressed Nassar's cheek tenderly. "You are sweet, Nassar. I miss you, too, when we are apart."

The former slave wrapped his arms around Sumati in a tight hug. "I wuv you, U-Ma-i."

His left arm stung as the new tattoo on his upper left arm burned. The new mark would officially bind him to the Osiris Thief Clan. Nassar released Sumati and kissed her cheek.

"Let go of me, you pig!" Nassar heard a woman protest from the alley.

Sumati and Nassar looked into the nearby alley where he saw Kaphiri pressing a woman against a wall. Nassar saw the young woman who had kissed Azizi in the streets.

"With the King of Thieves gone, you have nobody to protect you. Shame," Kaphiri grinned.

"Let go of me, you pig-faced demon!" Kahla protested as Kaphiri held her wrists against the wall.

Kaphiri grinned. "I can finally have you all to myself. Azizi is such a selfish bastard, keeping you all to himself."

"The only bastard is you, Kaphiri! You will not have my body!"

Kaphiri looked down at Kahla and smiled. "I can be a better lover to you than Azizi. Let me show you how good of a lover I can be," Kaphiri grinned, pulling Kahla into a fiery, hungry kiss.

Kahla punched Kaphiri and pushed against him. Nassar and Sumati stepped into the alley as Kahla tried to fight back against her aggressor.

"You leave her alone!" Sumati exclaimed.

Kaphiri turned his head and saw the couple standing in the alley. "Leave us!"

"Kah-a, rum," Nassar said, grabbing his bow and arrow.

Kahla pushed against Kaphiri and ran behind Nassar.

Kaphiri narrowed his eyes at the Nubian archer. "You have no call interfering, stranger! Kahla, get back here now, you whore!"

"No!"

"You are a rude little rat! You don't speak to a lady with such vile words!"

"Kahla is no lady! She is a whore! She pleases a man for coin! There is a big difference. Kahla is no lady and she will never be one!"

Nassar fired an arrow towards Kaphiri. The Seth Clan leader raced away from them.

Sumati put her arms around Kahla. "Don't cry."

Kahla looked at Nassar, wiping away a tear. "Thank you, stranger."

"His name is Nassar," Sumati said.

"Thank you, Nassar," Kahla said with a small smile.

Kahla and Nassar turned abruptly when they heard the marching of soldiers. Nassar pulled Sumati into the alley to hide. Kahla watched as the soldiers rode through the street, looking at her suspiciously. After the soldiers passed, Nassar and Sumati stood beside her.

Kahla turned to Nassar and Sumati "Thank you for helping me."

"Who was he?"

"That was Kaphiri. He is the leader of the Seth Thief Clan. With Azizi gone, he is trying to acquire *Iunu* as part of his territory. He has sent Qasim to the bordello with the intent to threaten Mbizi.

Ini-Herit comes with him and grabs Tabora every night. Tabora cannot be treated so roughly."

Sumati pointed to Nassar's arm. "He just received the mark of the Osiris Clan."

Kahla looked at the bandage on Nassar's arm. She offered the Nubian a smile. "Well, it is nice to see a fellow clansman. I hope Azizi makes a hasty return." Kahla's smile faded. "I miss him," Kahla sniffled sadly. "I ache for him."

"I not wet Kaphiri wu *Iunu*," Nassar said.

Kahla nodded. "Thank you again for your aid. I should return to Mbizi."

Nassar and Sumati watched Kahla return to the brothel as a cry from down the road echoed through the streets. Sumati turned her head to see a well-decorated carriage pulled by two horses trot down the street.

Nassar jumped into the alley, quickly recognizing the carriage. Sumati watched as a father and his daughter sat comfortably in the back of the carriage.

When the carriage passed by, Nassar cautiously emerged from the alley. "I mow her. Mafer Am-i wiw mawwy her!"

"Who was that?"

Nassar narrowed his eyes. "Ife wif Mahoma Re-Efer."

"Ife-Re-Efer? Who will she marry?"

"My Mafer Am-i."

Sumati watched as the golden chariot turned the corner down the road. *Zahra has told me that she has committed her heart to Amsi Al-Sakhir. Has Amsi been lying to her? Does she know that Amsi is meant to marry that girl?*

*　　　　*　　　　*

Runihura sat in the garden with Nusair purring around his ankles. With a contemplative mind, he reached down and pet the cat's belly. *General Gahiji better not fail me in his mission. If all goes according to plan, Kaemwaset will murder his own son and my hands will be clean. I can murder the Anointed Companion of Rā without placing one finger on him. Murder is such a messy business.* Runihura reached beside his chair and plucked a lotus blossom from its stem. He held the flower to his nose and breathed the sweet aroma.

Semerkhet briskly walked down the garden path towards the pharaoh. When he arrived beside the pharaoh, he kneeled on the grass. "Your Greatness, I bring word from-."

"Don't ruin the peaceful mood that I am in, Semerkhet. Choose your words wisely," Runihura said, tapping the blossom against his bare chest.

"Historical texts have noted Isis has been worshipped in Heliopolis for many years."

"Then why are there no temples of Isis within our boarders, Semerkhet?"

Semerkhet bowed his head. "There was a revolution and all of her temples were converted. Her priesthood was scattered throughout our lands."

Runihura chuckled. "So will all temples in Heliopolis worship Sekhmet when I disperse their priesthoods."

"My king, perhaps the Circlet of Isis remains in our boarder! The relics of the gods lie where their worshippers would offer their tributes!"

Ten priests stepped into the garden and kneeled on the grass before Runihura. "Great and Powerful pharaoh, we are humble before you. You have summoned us into your Great Presence for what purpose?"

"The Circlet of Isis is no good without the scroll. I want all of you to return to your temples and search your texts for whereabouts of the Circlet of Isis. Isis has been worshipped in Heliopolis since the dawn of time. Her relic must be here in Heliopolis! Find them!"

The priests bowed their heads reverently and scurried out of the garden. Runihura saw a golden carriage enter the grounds. A servant girl stepped from the carriage and opened the side door. Mahoma Re-Nefer stepped from the carriage with his staff. Ife stepped from the carriage, intentionally moving her sandaled foot to step onto the bare foot of her servant girl, making her wince quietly.

"That will teach you to keep your feet out of my sight," Ife laughed.

Mahoma lead Ife towards the pharaoh and bowed his head reverently. "My pharaoh, this is my daughter, Ife."

Ife bowed her head. "It is an honor, my pharaoh."

Runihura stood and handed Ife the lotus blossom. "Your daughter is quite beautiful."

Ife took the lotus blossom in her hand and smiled. "Yes, Re Himself has blessed me with beauty unequalled. As you can see, the dwarf-god Bes has blessed my servant with his ugliness and foul appearance." Ife turned and pushed her servant onto the ground, laughing.

Runihura grinned. "Ife, this is the start of a most harmonious relationship."

XVII

The Temple of Isis

Amsi and Azizi watched as a large temple enclosed by large walls loomed before them.   The primary temple was large with numerous pillars around the perimeter.   The roof was flat and shimmered as gold in the morning sun. Several smaller structures rose above the walls of mud-brick.

As they approached the surrounding walls, their eyes gazed at the painted columns and the figure of Winged Isis painted on the face of the temple. People were walking through the iron gate and bowing before the temple.

"This is holy ground, Amsi," Azizi said. "The followers of Isis have come for her healing wind and her blessing."

Amsi dismounted his horse and stepped through the gate with Azizi. A blacksmith was banging metal with his hammer.   Near the blacksmith's hut stood a home with a sign displaying the symbol for 'healer.'

Some women were sitting at their looms weaving material near the entrance to the temple.

Azizi tensed as he saw a group of soldiers marching through the streets. Amsi put his hand on Azizi's arm.

"Don't startle. They may think you have done some crime."

"It's a habit," Azizi said covering his head with the hood of his cloak. The black cloak acted as a shroud to protect him from view of the soldiers. Amsi lead Azizi towards the fountain near the temple stairs. Azizi watched with curiosity as Amsi quickly bathed himself and rubbed his skin with perfumed oil. A fresh coat of black eye paint lined his eyes. He changed into a clean, white tunic and washed his mouth.

"Why are you doing that?"

"I have to purify myself before going into a holy temple. It's Holy Law."

Azizi raised a curious eyebrow. "Why?"

"If I enter the Temple of Isis unclean, it's blasphemy. You should clean yourself, too. You are a mess."

"I'll be fine," Azizi said casually as he wiped sand off his leg. "Let's get the answers we came for."

Azizi and Amsi tied their horses to a plank of wood. The friends walked up the steps towards the wooden doorway chiseled with protective prayers of Isis.

Azizi removed his hood as he looked behind him. He sighed with relief as the soldiers ignored his passing. Amsi opened the door to the temple and stepped inside with the thief.

The walls were high. Pillars lined the walls inside the temple where murals depicting several scenes from Isis' myths were meticulously painted. One mural depicted Osiris facing towards them, holding the staff and flail. Lotus flowers were encircling him. Torches stood upon stone pedestals placed strategically around the room. Azizi looked down at the polished stone floors.

"Good morning, travelers," a female voice echoed from the other side of the large room. Amsi and Azizi were approached by a young woman dressed in a long tunic of white, fine linen. A golden belt surrounded her thin form. Her black-haired wig fell around her shoulders. Around her head she bore a golden circlet adorned with blue, green, and red stones. Amsi saw the same eye-paint around her eyes that he wore daily.

"How do you know we are travelers?" Amsi asked.

"Because your faces tell a tale of a journey of a great distance. Welcome to the Temple of Isis, for she will cast your troubles into the wind. Welcome, my Noble Sir and to your slave, as well."

Azizi narrowed his eyes angrily. "I am not his slave, woman! We need to speak to the High Priestess."

The young woman bowed her head. "My Lady is occupied, sir."

"It was not a request," Azizi said, crossing his arms defiantly.

Amsi stepped in front of Azizi quickly. "What my companion means, my lady, is that we have traveled very far and we would like to request an audience with her as soon as she is available."

"Why do you request a hasty audience with her?"

Azizi reached into his bag and removed the Buckle of Isis. "We've come for answers."

The young woman jumped backwards and covered her mouth as if in fear. "Where-Where did you get that?"

"Your friend had it around her neck when she traveled to Egypt."

The young woman's eyes widened in terror and her body began to shake. "Why did you bring that cursed artifact back here?"

Amsi stepped towards the terrified woman. "What is cursed about it? Why do you fear it?"

The woman turned and ran away quickly. Azizi and Amsi looked at the defaced Buckle in the thief's hand. Amsi took the necklace into his hand. "I do not see anything evil about it."

Azizi stepped close to his friend. "My intentions were not to frighten her away." The thief scrutinized his surroundings cautiously. His body tensed as he waited for the arrival of soldiers or another angry mob. "Somehow I get the feeling we will not be welcomed by the High Priestess."

Amsi walked toward the mural on the wall. "Aziz! Come here!" The mural before him depicted two figures fighting a large gold scorpion. Azizi walked slowly towards his friend and gasped.

A great wall of fire blazed behind the combatants and the scorpion. A winged Isis was painted above the two fighting figures. Amsi stepped close to the mural and examined the hieroglyphics carved into the rock.

"It's written in Noble Script. It says: 'The emissary of –shall prove victorious.'"

Azizi raised a curious eyebrow. "The emissary of who?"

"I cannot read it. The rock has been defaced."

Azizi looked at the Buckle of Isis in Amsi's hand and at the rock. "Look! The scratches are the same! Whomever has defaced the Buckle also defaced the mural." Azizi reached towards the mural and touched it, gliding his fingertips over the rock. "Who would deface a carving in so sacred a place? Who would defile holy ground?"

Amsi held the Buckle of Isis tightly against his chest. "It is sacrilege of the highest order."

"Does that mean the woman's killer resides here?" Azizi asked.

Amsi shrugged. "Perhaps the priestess herself caused these scratches before she left. But why would she defile her own sacred item? We must keep our guard up, my friend."

"Why have you come here? You are not welcome," a female voice growled from behind them.

Azizi and Amsi turned to see the High Priestess of Isis standing before the archway leading into the inner sanctum. The two teens stood before the woman clad in a single belt of solid gold with a thin veil that failed to conceal her naked body from view.

"We came to ask you questions about this amulet worn by a priestess who had supposedly come from this temple."

The priestess'eyes narrowed at Azizi. "Remove yourself from this place, you pestilence-ridden son of Seth."

Azizi growled and clenched his fists. "I am no worshipper of Seth!"

"Sir, control your slave," the priestess said.

Azizi clenched his fists. "I am nobody's slave!"

"Azizi, speech is more effective than fighting," Amsi said calmly.

The High Priestess grabbed Azizi's cape and shook him violently. "You defile this hollowed ground with your vile feet, traveler!"

The golden bands on Azizi's upper arms fell onto the floor. The surrounding priestesses gasped and chattered in their language which Amsi could barely comprehend.

"Look, Priestess!"

The High Priestess of Isis saw the Djet, the backbone of Osiris tattooed onto the thief's left arm. "By the gods! He bears the Mark!"

Amsi watched as the woman dropped Azizi on the floor. Azizi grabbed his golden armband and slipped it onto his right arm.

"Where are your manners, woman?" Azizi asked heatedly.

Amsi helped his friend to his feet and watched as the woman slowly backed away from Azizi.

"What is my name?" the priestess asked as she looked at Azizi.

"High Priestess of Low Manners, I should say!" Azizi exclaimed angrily. The priestesses surrounding the standing woman fell on their knees before Azizi. "Your friends have better respect than you, do!"

The High Priestess continued to look at Azizi. "What is my name?"

"How should I know? You never told me your name and we just met! You were too busy throwing me on the floor and accusing me of being a worshipper of the Pig-God, Seth! I would never worship that-."

Amsi stepped forward and held his hand up, causing Azizi to abruptly fall silent. "I am Khepera in the morning, Rā at the time of his culmination, and Temu in the evening."

Azizi raised a curious eyebrow as Amsi responded in Noble Tongue. The High Priestess smiled and bowed her head. "How is it she is not picking you into the air and throwing you on the ground?"

"So, the follower of Rā has come as was foretold." The woman turned her head to Azizi. "You have arrived with the worshipper of our brother, Osiris, the Great Lord of Eternity."

Amsi turned to Azizi. "The Instruction to Merikare teaches us speaking is stronger than all fighting."

"Tell that to her! She's the one who threw me on the ground before I had an opportunity to explain why we are here!"

"Why have you come with that cursed relic in your hand?" the High Priestess inquired.

The women bowed before Azizi. "Praise be to the follower of our brother, Osiris. Life, Strength, Health to him!"

Amsi held the Buckle in his hand as he bowed before the priestess. "My Lady, I was in the desert when I happened upon the body of a priestess in the desert. I was told that she had come from a Temple of Isis to the north. This remained around her neck, a Buckle of Isis with the sacred prayers defaced."

269

The High Priestess held out her hand to examine the wood. Her fingers glided across the carved wood. "So it would seem. Our sister did travel from this temple."

Azizi stood beside his friend. "Why did she travel to Egypt? It would appear she was traveling to Heliopolis to see Pharaoh Runihura."

The priestesses kneeling on the ground raised their heads in alarm and rose to their feet. "Why would she go see Him?" Azizi asked.

"The pharaoh of Egypt is a dangerous person, my Lady. Why would a Priestess of Isis wish to travel into the Lion's Den to see him?"

The High Priestess lowered her head and folded her hands in front of her. "It is a sad tale. She had made her decision, much to my disappointment."

"Her decision led her to her death," Azizi said, glaring at the priestesses. The women in the room exchanged worried glances and backed away slowly from their leader.

Amsi looked at the High Priestess. "We wish to know why she was traveling to see the pharaoh and why would someone deface holy prayers."

"Who killed our sister?"

Azizi shook his head. "She was poisoned by a poisoned dart, we believe.   There was no other damage to her body."

The woman looked down sadly at the floor. "Our sister had been plagued by nightmares. She had claimed Isis was telling her to reveal the location of the Circlet of Isis to Sekhmet's favored crusader."

Azizi crossed his arms. "Do you realize she could have endangered people's lives with her actions?"

"She wanted the nightmares to stop. Certainly, you can relate to that, Follower of Osiris."

Azizi lowered his head solemnly. "I know how it feels to be plagued by nightmares, by thoughts which will not cease."

Amsi watched Azizi step away from him and lean against a nearby pillar with his arms crossed against his chest. Amsi looked at the High Priestess. "Can you tell me where the relics of Isis lay? We are on a quest to stop the pharaoh from obtaining them. The pharaoh's army will be arriving to procure them for their lord."

"You have both traveled from far away Egypt. You must need rest."

"We came for the relics. Please tell us where they are," Azizi stated.

The High Priestess'nose wrinkled. "Your friend needs to bathe."

"He may have an aversion to cleanliness, but time is of the essence. Please tell us where the Scroll of Isis and the Circlet of Isis are located."

"I must insist that you rest. There is a library here where you may examine the ancient texts. You appear to be a literate and well-spoken man. One can see that you are not of Common Blood."

Amsi bowed his head politely to the woman. "My name is Amsi Al-Sakhir, Son of Kaemwaset, Worshipper of the Sun God Rā, Creator of All, and the Aten, Eternal Lord. You are indeed correct. I am of Noble Blood, well-versed in the art of Speech and Writing. However, time is of the essence, my lady."

The High Priestess turned her head towards Azizi. "You who linger near the shadows, what be your name?"

Azizi kept his head lowered, but raised his eyes to glare at her. "I am Azizi Keket, Son of Ghazi, Worshipper of Osiris, the Lord of the Dead, King of Gods, Eldest of Geb, who set Ma'at throughout the Two Shores."

The High Priestess slowly walked towards Azizi. "Mighty Isis was her brother's guard. She sought him without wearying, breathed life into him through her wings." The woman reached towards his cheek and caressed it tenderly. She smiled at him pleasantly. "She raised him, received his seed and bore him an heir, the Mighty Horus, Avenger of his father, Osiris."

Azizi looked into her eyes and felt his body relax. His tense muscles weakened. His breath stalled as he felt a wave of dizziness overcome

him. Her thumb traced his jawbone with affection. *What is she doing?
What is happening to me?*

"Amsi..." Azizi felt the room spinning around him as he opened his
mouth.

The woman pressed a light finger to his lips. "Shh, my boy.   Quiet."

Azizi's eyes rolled back into his head as his body fell onto the floor.
Amsi ran to his friend and hovered above him.

"Aziz! Wake up!" Amsi kneeled beside his friend and touched the
thief's cheek lightly.

The High Priestess stood slowly and backed away from the
unconscious thief.

"Azizi, speak to me! What did you do to him?" Amsi asked, turning to
the woman in anger.

"Your friend is tired from your long journey. He needs to sleep.   We
have a room where you both can rest. While you fill yourself with lamb
and beer, he can sleep."

Amsi looked down at his friend with worry. *I've never seen Azizi take
ill so suddenly.   Our journey has been long. Perhaps I should let him
rest.* Amsi carefully brought Azizi into his arms. The thief slept quietly
with his head against Amsi's chest. *He weighs hardly more than a
feather!*

"Follow me," the High Priestess said.

Amsi followed the woman through the archway and into the inner sanctum. She lead him through a side door of sycamore wood. A large antechamber was decorated with couches covered in soft red material. Jugs of wine stood in the corner beside a table with goblets of silver and gold. Paintings along the walls depicted Isis and her place beside her brother-husband, Osiris.

Another archway lead into a hallway lined with doors. The High Priestess stopped beside the first door and lead Amsi into a room with two beds. Mattresses of cloth and feathers cushioned the wooden frames. Beside the wall, a small table was adorned with a single white candle.

Amsi carefully placed Azizi on one of the beds. The teen untied the cape around Azizi's neck. He placed his hand on Azizi's chest. "I will return with food for you." Amsi turned to the priestess. "What did you do to my friend?"

"I have told you that your friend is weary from your travels. Being well-versed in Scripture, you know of the works of Isis. You know she is the Mistress of Magic."

Amsi nodded. "I know many things. I know she has the gift of Charm."

"I saw that your friend needed sleep, so I gave that to him."

Amsi's eyes widened. "Are you saying you cast a spell on him?"

"If that is what you would believe, who am I to stop you? The Magic of Isis can do many things."

Amsi swallowed nervously as he stood in front of Azizi. The unconscious thief gasped in panic in his sleep. "What is your name?"

"My namesake is Meraset, Noble Amsi Al-Sakhir."

"I will wait for my friend to wake before I partake in a meal."

Meraset smiled as she took his hand. "The duck is warm and the lamb is tender."

"Meraset, if General Gahiji arrives with his troops, he will not stop his slaughter until he has the Circlet and Scroll of Isis.   He will kill anyone who stands in his way.   Your lives are in danger!"

"Lady Isis will protect us."

Amsi shook his head as he grabbed her arms. "Lady Isis will not appear from the sky and help you! He will kill everyone, please! My friend and I will protect you, but we cannot do anything without the Scroll and Circlet."

"How can you protect us? You claim to have knowledge of Scripture, yet you are clearly violating the lessons taught to you by your teacher."

Amsi released the woman. "What do you mean?" he asked defensively.

"'Keep away from a hostile man. Do not let him be your comrade.
Befriend one who is straight and true.' Your friend, I can sense much
from his mind. His behavior is nothing less than a wild stallion,
untamed and untrained. You should return to your station and forget
him.'"

Amsi took a deep breath. "'Do not set your heart on wealth. There is no
ignoring Fate and Destiny.'Azizi and I must stop the pharaoh at any
cost. He may be wild and his temper may flare, but we cannot ignore
that we must fight this battle together. Now, we need your help. Azizi
and I must stop Pharaoh Runihura, Son of Sekhmet, from obtaining the
ancient relics."

Meraset straightened her back and looked at the sleeping teen in the
bed. "You may use our library. The Scroll of Isis'location may be
hidden in the texts. It may offer some clues as to the Circlet of Isis'
whereabouts. The Library is the last door to the right."

Amsi sighed with resignation. "Very well, Meraset. Thank you."

Amsi watched as Meraset stepped out of the room. The Noble teen sat
on the empty bed and looked at the mattress. The bed was a welcome
sight after sleeping on a ship's hard deck for four nights and the lack of
sleep in the desert.   He watched Azizi sleep in the bed. The thief's
fingers twitched in his sleep as he lay on his back.

*Did Meraset truly cast a sleeping spell on Azizi or did he simply
succumb to his exhaustion?   Only the gods wield true magic.   If only*

*the gods can wield true magic, what about the Eye of Horus? Runihura
made the army of Edfu slay themselves. How can we defend against
her magic if the need arises?*

If Meraset did cast a spell, that would mean she has a relic of a god.
Amsi's eyes widened. *Could she be knowingly concealing the location
of the circlet? What would her motive be for hiding it from us? If
she did cast a spell on Aziz and she does not have an ancient relic, from
where did she get her power? If she can cast magical spells at will and
create Charms imbued with Isis' power, the pharaoh would not hesitate
to exploit her powers. Her power could be an invaluable asset.*

"Amsi," Azizi whimpered in his sleep as his left arm flailed.

"I'm here, my brother," Amsi said, sitting beside Azizi and taking his
hand. The thief shifted on his side and clutched tightly onto Amsi's
clean skirt with his free hand. "Why did you leave?"

Amsi reached to Azizi's back and touched it lightly. The thief's grip on
his skirt slowly released as Azizi fell into a peaceful slumber. "I'm
right here."

Amsi looked out of the window of the temple to see the stars peeking
from a partly cloudy sky. Azizi continued to sleep quietly beside him.
What did Meraset do to him? The only sound coming from the
slumbering thief was his breath. "Aziz, wake up." Amsi heard the
thief stir then resume his deep sleep.

The door opened to the bedchamber slowly as a woman carrying a tray of meat and fruit entered the room. "Lady Meraset commanded that I bring you food since you and your companion did not appear at dinner."

Amsi bowed his head. "Thank you. He's still asleep."

The woman placed the tray on the table between the two beds. "Have you enjoyed your stay at our home?"

"Why is my friend still sleeping?"

The middle-aged woman smiled at him. "He is tired from your long journey."

"I've never seen him this tired. I'm worried about him."

The woman shook her head. "He will wake when he is ready."

Amsi stood and took a piece of lamb. He placed it under Azizi's nose in an effort to stir the thief to eat. With no reaction from the thief, Amsi ate the piece of meat. "A starving man does not reject food when it is offered to him."

Amsi turned to the priestess and grabbed her arms. "What did Meraset do to him? I demand to know what has happened to him! You will tell me or I will lose my temper!" the Noble teen's eyes narrowed as he felt himself tense.

The priestess'eyes widened in fear. "He is tired!"

"Unacceptable! You will tell me why my friend is still unconscious and why was that girl afraid of the Buckle of Isis?" Amsi shook the girl angrily. As he looked at the fear in the woman's eyes, he was reminded of how his servants were shaken by Kaemwaset. He had seen that fear in Nakia and Nassar's eyes. Now the woman stared at him, frozen stiff from his fury. The woman gasped for air and tensed as his fingernails dug into her skin. He pinned her against the table with the tray of food and growled at her. "Tell me right now or you will regret it!" Amsi raised his right fist in anger.

"Please, don't hurt me! I'll tell you everything!"

Amsi's eyes widened and quickly released her. He stepped back and looked down at his hands. His fingers were curled with anger. His tight grip had turned her arms red from his assault. *I'm becoming like my father. How can I become what I hate? How could I become like that beast?* Amsi looked at the terrified woman too afraid to move. *She can't defend herself just as the twins could not defend themselves against my father's wrath. He beat them. His fist deafened Nassar permanently in his left ear. How could I behave so cruelly to this woman? How can I become infected with the disease of cruelty that plagues my father's mind?* Amsi sat on the empty bed and buried his face in his hands. "I'm sorry. I'm so sorry. Please, forgive me."

The woman swallowed nervously, her chest rising and falling with fear. She looked down at the sleeping thief. "You care about him, don't you?"

Amsi nodded. "I do."

The woman kneeled beside Amsi. "You and your friend are in danger here," the woman said. "My name is Gysa and I want to warn you that the High Priestess means to turn you over to General Gahiji upon his arrival. You both must leave."

Amsi removed his face from his hands and looked at the woman. "Aziz and I can't leave. We have an important purpose here. Gahiji will come and slaughter all of you, do you not understand? He is under the charge of a maniacal madman unfit for his throne!"

The woman took Amsi's hand and looked back at the sleeping thief. "We cannot speak here while your friend sleeps. We will wake him."

"I've been trying to wake him, but nothing is succeeding!"

Gysa stood and brought Amsi to his feet. "Come with me. I will show you to the library. Your friend needs his rest. He is tired." Gysa saw hesitation in Amsi's eyes. "We are Priestesses of the Divine Mother. He is a worshiper of her brother, Osiris, and no harm shall come to him."

Amsi looked down at Aziz and sighed. I need to examine the ancient texts. Perhaps he will be fine. "I will be back shortly, brother." Amsi left the room with the woman and walked through the hallway.

"You care much for your friend," Gysa said.

Amsi stopped. "Why is that so shocking to you?"

"He is not of Noble Blood. You wear fine linen and are filled with the Speech of Thoth. He is not like you."

"I see beyond what others see. Rā keeps my eyes open to the Light of this world whereas Sekhmet seeks to blind it, Gysa. That is why we must stop the pharaoh. I must stop this ever-increasing darkness growing in the hearts of men. Do you support such darkness and hate, Gysa?"

Gysa stood silently and looked at the floor. "The darkness has covered our temple and our High Priestess' heart. Beware of her, Amsi. She wants to see you dead."

Amsi narrowed his eyes. "I won't let her succeed in killing Azizi or me. I will defend Azizi until my final breath."

Gysa lead Amsi into the library where shelves of scrolls lined the walls. Parchment books bound with leather and hide were stacked on tables. A number of candles provided light in the dark room. A blazing fireplace provided warmth and light which allowed shadows to dance upon the top of a nearby desk. A woven rug beneath the desk was the only covering on the wooden floor. A small kitten was sleeping peacefully on one golden seat.

Amsi slowly entered the small room and examined the scrolls piled on the shelves. "Are these writ in Holy Tongue or Noble Tongue?"

"Our scribes have not yet translated all of these into Holy Tongue. Some remain written in Noble Tongue."

Amsi removed one of the scrolls and sat at the desk. He unrolled it slowly as Gysa lit the seven candles on the desk. Their light illuminated the script on the papyrus parchment. A burst of wind entered the room through an open window. Amsi read the words of the parchment. "This is a medicinal scroll. It contains prayers to remove the venom from a scorpion sting."

"Those who defile the name of Isis will suffer the pain of the scorpion, Amsi," Gysa said. "It is good that you please her with your words and actions."

Amsi nodded. "I wish not to defile the name of any god or goddess. Though Sekhmet be evil, she is also a goddess who offers healing to those who ask for it." Amsi looked up at Gysa. "Could Isis cure a plague?"

Gysa raised her hands in supplication. "Mother Isis can do all for she sees all."

"*Iunu* is suffering through a terrible illness. People are dying and their bodies are piling in the streets. Red patches form on their skin and they cough. Their lungs struggle for air. Can we stop the plague with the Circlet of Isis?"

Gysa folded her hands in front of her and lowered her head. "The Ancient Relics, Amsi, are legend. They hold no real power."

"Pharaoh Runihura has the Eye of Horus. With it, he has commanded an army to kill themselves. The Ancient Relics are very much real and very much to be feared. The Circlet of Isis can remove plague according to the Scroll of Thoth. I need to find the Circlet and the Scroll which gives it power."

"We do not have either."

Amsi sighed heavily. "Pharaoh Runihura seems to think so because there is an army of soldiers and a captive who will be arriving to take them. They have to be here!"

Gysa turned her back to Amsi and stoked the fire. "Why are you trying to prevent Gahiji's arrival? Doesn't the Code say that a Nobleman cannot slaughter another of his own kind?"

"The pharaoh and his General have no mind for the Code of Honor."

"You will help him in his fight?"

Amsi narrowed his eyes at Gysa. "I would rather kill myself than be a puppet to the pharaoh! I will not help the pharaoh get the Circlet of Isis! I must concentrate. Please leave."

Gysa bowed her head and left the room. Amsi looked down at the scroll in front of him, rubbing his forehead. *What do I have to do or say to convince the women that they are in grave danger? Do they believe that Isis will protect them?* Amsi relaxed in the chair. *Why wouldn't they believe it? I believe that Rā protects me. Aziz's faith in Osiris is one of complete dedication.* The Noble teen's eyes widened as he continued to read the text. When he rolled the scroll further, an image of a town filled with corpses had been drawn. The corpses were painted in white with red patches on their skin. Blood flowed in rivers around the dead. His hands began to tremble as he watched the frozen faces scream at him from the papyrus. "Blessed Rā, it's Heliopolis," he whispered, not wanting to alarm any priestesses walking by the room. Amsi read the text under the image.

Sekhmet's pleasure is fulfilled when friend and foe alike are killed.

Tame the lion-goddess and worship her with might, only then can you break the circle and illness fight.

"Never!" Amsi exclaimed, slamming his fists on the table. "I will never bow to Sekhmet! I will never bow to the pharaoh! That is madness! I can't bow to him." Amsi read the final line of text. "'Break the circle?'Wouldn't it make more sense to be 'to break the cycle?'" He read the text again and shook his head. "No. Azizi and I have to break the circle. Do we have to destroy the Circlet of Isis? It would prevent the pharaoh from benefitting from the relic's power."

Amsi continued to read the text. "'Isis weeps for her fallen children, kneeling before her brother, Osiris. Descending into the Underworld, fraught with danger, she laments. She weeps as a mother for her dead child. She weeps as one in love who has lost her beloved. Isis breathes the Breath of Heaven into the lungs of her husband and she no longer weeps for he is born again.'"

Amsi continued to read the text until he could read no more. "This is Sacred Script." Amsi stood and returned to the shelf of scrolls. From the chair, the kitten yawned and opened its eyes. The tiny white kitten meowed at Amsi, grabbing the Noble's attention. "Hello, emissary of Bastet."

Amsi grabbed a scroll and opened it. The text was writ in Sacred Script. He carried the scroll to the table and laid the papyrus beside the other scroll. Amsi compared the writing in Noble Tongue and Sacred Script, searching for common strokes of the reed.

XVIII

Beggar Child

Azizi opened his eyes slowly to the room around him. He gripped onto the sheets as the room twirled and tilted around him. The thief coughed as his arm fell weakly onto the bed. A quiet groan accompanied the thief rubbing his forehead.

"So you are awake," a woman's voice said with pleasure.

Azizi groaned as his eyes scanned the spinning room. "Amsi. Where's Amsi? Where am I?" the thief asked tiredly.

"You are resting," the voice responded. "You are in the Temple of Isis."

Azizi saw a woman step into his line of sight. "Amsi?"

"No, my child. I am not him. I am Meraset, High Priestess of Isis."

Azizi winced as his head began to throb. "What happened?"

"I put you to sleep, my boy." Azizi tried to sit up, but Meraset pushed him onto his back and held him down by his chest. "You're not going anywhere, Azizi Keket Ibn Ghazi. I know the pharaoh searches for you."

Azizi looked up at her. "How do you know the pharaoh pursues me?"

"Isis herself has told me. She has told me of a beggar child who would walk into our midst with a follower of the Sun God.   You are in danger, Azizi."

Azizi rubbed his forehead. "When am I not in danger, miss?"

"You must stay here and not return to Heliopolis."

"I can't stay here, Meraset. I am responsible for my Clan in *Iunu* and I have Kahla waiting for my arrival."

Meraset smiled. "She will be protected, my boy. You love her, do you not?"

Azizi looked up at the ceiling. He smiled. "How could I not? My sister is better than all prescriptions. She does more for me than all medicines. Her coming to me is my amulet. My heart smiles when she is near me and I know true peace and happiness."

Meraset smiled and caressed Azizi's cheek. "You long for her body?"

"I long for her soul. I long to hold her in my arms." *I still remember her gazing down on me. Her smile illuminated by the candles on the table beside the bed. My arms wrapped around her, holding her close to me. My lips tenderly kissed her breast as she whispered words of love into my ear. Throughout the night, our souls and bodies were as one. Under the eyes of Osiris did I hold her and caress her. With reluctance and great sorrow did I part from her.* Azizi rolled over and sat on the edge of the bed. "I must complete my mission here before I return to her, Meraset. Tell me where the Scroll and Circlet of Isis rest. They cannot be allowed to fall into the pharaoh's hands."

Meraset folded her hands upon her lap. "The Scroll of Isis is protected by the Companion of Isis and cannot be defeated."

"Are you speaking of the large scorpion drawn onto the wall?"

Meraset nodded. "Selket is the great protector of Isis'relic. Isis was joined by seven scorpions on her journey through Egypt. They will not allow Isis'name to be defamed."

"I seek not to defame or speak sacrilege against Mother Isis. My brother and I want to prevent the pharaoh from acquiring the relics."

Meraset smiled. "Your brother is your better."

Azizi narrowed his eyes and stood. "Amsi and I are equal. Because I cannot read or have pockets lined with gold is no reason to treat me like a cur begging for scraps at your table!"

Meraset stood. "I apologize for my quick tongue. To find two men so dissimilar traveling together is rare. When one finds you traveling together, one automatically assumes that he is your master."

"Amsi is not my master. He has earned my trust and is one of few whom I consider 'friend.'"

"Your heart is divided, I see. Your beloved is in *Iunu* yet you call your companion your brother." Meraset paused.

Azizi narrowed his eyes. "You must leave now."

"You are confused. You know not who you are."

Azizi grit his teeth. "Get out of my room."

Meraset stood calmly before the seething thief. "You are looking for love, for acceptance, and to satisfy your own thirst for vengeance."

Azizi growled loudly. "I will make the pharaoh pay dearly for his transgressions! Now get out of my room!"

"You are hiding, Azizi Keket. You are young and on a journey of self-discovery. You are trying to find yourself."

Azizi glared at the priestess. "The pharaoh has been searching for me since he killed my mother. Many nights I laid starving in the alley, too hungry to move. By day, I saw other children with their parents." Azizi lowered his head to hide the tears forming in his eyes. "I watched as the mothers hugged and kissed their children. I wanted to go to sleep and wake up to find her beside me. I wanted to feel her arms around me and tell me that everything would be back to how it was. My parents were not around to protect me, to braid my side-lock of youth." Azizi's head snapped up. "I would have gladly died to give them life again!" Azizi nodded. "You're right, Meraset. I'm looking for acceptance and I may not know who I am. But one thing is for certain: If Amsi and I fail in our quest to obtain the Ancient Relics, everyone will die. Everyone will have no choice but to bend to the will of Pharaoh Runihura Atenhotep, Beloved of Sekhmet."

Meraset bowed her head. "I have heard of his cruelty."

"His General is on his way to obtain the Scroll and Circlet of Isis." Azizi grabbed Meraset's arms. "Tell me where the relics of Isis rest. Amsi and I can fight him when he arrives, but we must assure that the relics stay out of his-." Azizi felt his chest tighten as he began to cough. The thief lowered his head as his body tensed, coughing blood onto his arm.

I'm sick with the Red Fever! Azizi raised his head slowly. His eyes widened in alarm. "I have the deadly illness!"

Meraset smiled at Azizi and caressed his cheek again. "Soon you will see your beloved god, Osiris, Azizi Keket Ibn Ghazi."

"There must be a way to stop that plague, Meraset!"

"I shall request that the cook boil medicine for you. If you become hungry, the cook will feed you and your companion."

Azizi released Meraset's arms and sat on the bed. *I can't die! My quest isn't complete! I must stop Runihura.* Meraset disappeared from view and left the room. Azizi buried his face in his hands. "I have to get home to Kahla. I can't die in a foreign land."

"Aziz?"

Azizi lifted his head and saw Amsi standing in the doorway with two scrolls under his arm. "Where have you been, my friend?"

Amsi placed the scrolls on his bed and sat across from Azizi. "I was worried for you. Are you alright?"

Azizi nodded. "Where were you?"

"I was studying in the library. You should see how many scrolls are in there! Some texts are hundreds of years old!" Amsi said excitedly.

"I wouldn't be able to read any of it anyway," Azizi said sadly lowering his head.

Amsi put his hand on Azizi's leg. "Nonsense, my friend! You have learned how to read some glyphs on our journey across the sea. You are eager to learn. Be cheerful."

"Meraset was here," Azizi said as he stared at Amsi's well-pedicured feet.

Amsi's smile faded as he leaned forward and tilted Azizi's face upwards to look into his eyes. "What did she say to you, Aziz? You are upset. Talk to me."

"She said that you were my better."

"I don't believe that for one second. Azizi, something has been bothering you and I want you to know that you can talk to me."

Azizi nodded. "Thank you. Have you found anything in the library that could help us?"

Amsi reached to the scroll beside his leg. He showed Azizi the image of the town littered with corpses. Amsi pointed to one corpse covered in red patches. "This scroll speaks of the plague in *Iunu*. The text beneath it says to tame the lion-goddess and worship her. Only then can we break the circle and destroy the illness."

Azizi raised a curious eyebrow. "We have to break the circle? Is it speaking of the Circlet of Isis? Do we have to destroy her relic?"

"If we destroy it, the pharaoh cannot use it, correct?"

"How can we destroy a relic of a god? Is it even possible?"

Amsi shrugged. "Perhaps melting the relic may work. One of the priestesses didn't believe in the power of the relics. She said they were legendary."

Azizi rolled his eyes. "I should take her to Edfû and show her the mass grave dug for those soldiers slain by the Eye of Horus. That will convince her of the reality she faces."

Amsi rolled the scroll to a new section of text. "Aziz, do you believe that a loyal follower of a god should have doubts as to the power of their patron deity?"

Azizi rubbed his forehead with a groan. "Repeat, but use smaller words."

"Should a follower of Isis have doubt that Isis' relic is real or even that it exists? Shouldn't a follower of a god have faith?"

"Perhaps she only believes what she sees with her own eyes. If you had asked me ten years ago if I believed that a golden eyeball could cause hundreds of men to kill themselves, I would have laughed at you."

Amsi sighed. "It is true. I never would have believed that was real unless I saw it with my own eyes."

"You do believe me, right?"

"Friends believe each other, Azizi. I know you do not lie about what you have seen."

Amsi took the scroll and sat beside Azizi on his bed. "This text reads that Isis weeps for her fallen children kneeling before her brother, Osiris. It also mentions her breathing life into her husband. This could be related to the plague."

"Does it say how to cure the illness?"

"As stated before, it commands that we tame Sekhmet and worship her. Then we have to break a circle. Sekhmet may be cruel and lust for human blood, but she is also a goddess of healing. Perhaps we have to worship her as a deity of healing."

Azizi shook his head. "Isis also bestows healing powers onto her faithful. A few smart purchases at the amulet shop wouldn't be a bad idea." Azizi coughed into his hand.

Amsi's eyes widened as he put a hand on his friend's back. "Azizi, are you alright?"

"Yes, perhaps my throat is dry," Azizi said, sipping from a cup of water beside the bed.

Amsi put the scroll beside him. "Azizi, tell me you do not have the Red Fever."

"I will be fine, Amsi. We have to find the Scroll of Isis and find a cure for this sickness or the image on that scroll will become a reality. The Scroll of Isis is here and we have to find it. Meraset said that a companion of Isis guards the scroll."

Amsi grabbed the other scroll from the bed and showed the Sacred Text to Azizi. The thief scratched his head as he looked at the strange hieroglyphs. "I compared the text in the other scroll to this one. I do not completely understand all of the symbols, but I can get a basic understanding of some of the words. This letter is addressed to the priestess who died in the desert. The Buckle of Isis is a key to help open the path to the Scroll of Isis. The lines scratching out the sacred prayers marked a pattern to open a special door to the catacombs below."

"'The Scroll of Isis in holy rest.'It must be here! No wonder the pharaoh was so eager to get the Buckle!"

"The letter also spoke of a marriage proposal. He threatened the woman to arrive at the palace with the Buckle or he would destroy the temple and all the women within."

Azizi rolled his eyes. "The pharaoh will destroy the temple either way as soon as he achieves his goal, the Scroll and Circlet of Isis."

"It gets better, my friend. He says that there is one here who is under his control."

"Well, that is just perfect. I'm going to assume there are no names mentioned."

Amsi shook his head. "The perpetrator held the scroll up to a candle and burned away the name of the traitor."

Azizi chuckled. "I didn't see that coming," Azizi sighed with sarcasm. "Did any of the scrolls reveal the resting place of the Circlet of Isis?"

"No, but the Scroll of Horus pointed you towards Edfû, did it not?" Amsi rolled the scrolls. "How are we to find the entrance to the catacombs?"

Azizi yawned and held his stomach. "We can begin our search in the morning. Right now I'm hungry."

Meraset walked into the room with a cup of hot soup. "This will help your cough."

Amsi and Azizi looked into the bowl of red liquid. Amsi sniffed the liquid and wrinkled his nose in disgust. "That takes like fetid meat!"

"No matter how hard our cook tries, it is difficult to properly boil sheep brains and make it smell enticing."

Meraset placed the cup on the table between the two tables and bowed her head. "Goodnight, my lords."

Amsi watched as the lady left the room. Azizi looked into the bowl. With a slow, curious scoop of the provided spoon, he stirred the liquid.

"You're not honestly going to eat that, are you?"

Azizi shrugged. "I'm hungry. When you're hungry enough, you'll eat anything."

"Even boiled sheep brains?"

The thief sniffed the brew. "They added some mint leaves to make it more palatable."

Amsi watched with a groan as Azizi sipped the red liquid. "I don't know how you could eat that." Azizi sipped from the cup and turned his head to cough into his shoulder. "If it helps you fight that deadly illness, I guess it's worth it, isn't it?"

Azizi held the cup between his legs and looked pensively into the liquid. His fingertips tapped lightly on the clay cup. Amsi watched the thief stare into the cup, his eyes transfixed on the object of his scrutiny. "Amsi, you did a good job tonight," the thief said suddenly.

"Thank you, Aziz. I wish I could have found more, but I learned a little of that Sacred Script."

Azizi nodded slowly and raised his eyes to look at Amsi. "We must search for the entrance to the catacombs, but we cannot appear suspicious. If there is a sympathizer of Pharaoh Runihura Atenhotep nearby, we cannot let her obtain the Scroll of Isis."

Amsi yawned and laid on his bed. He turned to Azizi and rested his head against the soft pillow. "Do you want me to stay awake so you can rest?"

"I believe I have rested sufficiently. I still do not know what happened to me. Hopefully I can find some answers. You need your sleep and have earned your rest, my friend."

Azizi kept watch as Amsi slipped into slumber. The thief raised his head and peered out of the window. Thin veils of clouds spread across the night sky, partially obscuring the moon from his view. *Osiris, keep my companion and I safe from harm. For I fear we are two lost lambs caught in a den of wolves.*

XIX

<u>Holy Ground</u>

Azizi slowly opened his eyes as a ray of sunlight pierced through the window. He rubbed his eye with a groan. *The best part of darkness is that it never blinds you in the morning.* The thief turned his head and saw Amsi fastening his golden ankh around his neck and slipping his bony hands through the bracelets.

"Good morning, Aziz. I hope I didn't wake you getting ready for my morning prayers. Meraset invited us to the morning worship of Isis and the morning sun."

Azizi felt the open scrolls roll off his legs and onto the floor. The thief yawned and scratched his back. "I should use this opportunity to sneak around and do what a thief does best."

Amsi crossed his arms like a parent ready to scold their child for some naughty deed. The Noble teen shot his friend a stern glare. "Azizi Keket, this is a temple. This is Holy Ground. Theft is strictly forbidden."

"Did I say I was going to steal anything?" Azizi rose to his feet and tied his black cloak around his shoulders. "I said I was going to use this opportunity to sneak around. Until you wear priestly vestments, don't preach to me about Holy Ground."

Amsi narrowed his eyes at Azizi. "Don't you take that tone of voice with me!"

"What are you going to do about it, Al-Sakhir?" Azizi growled, pushing Amsi backwards onto the bed.

Amsi stood on his feet and glared angrily at his friend. "Push me once more and I break the hand that touches me!"

Azizi grinned wickedly. "Very well, Kaemwaset Al-Sakhir."

A flash of red sparked before Amsi's eyes. His vision darkened as he glared down at his friend. *I am nothing like my father! I'm not cruel! I'm not like him!* Amsi's body trembled with uncontrollable rage. *I will never be the beast that my father is! I don't want to be like him!*

I'm not like him! "Take that back, Azi!" The Noble teen's vision went black.

Amsi looked down and saw himself pinning Azizi on the ground by his wrists with one hand. Blood trickled from the corner of Azizi's mouth. The thief's cheek was red and beginning to swell. One of his hands was grasping Azizi's throat and strangling him.

Amsi released Azizi's wrist and throat quickly. "Azizi! What have I done?" Amsi stood up quickly and looked down at the thief, struggling to sit under his own power. "Azizi, are you alright?"

Azizi wiped his mouth with his arm. "This isn't the first time I have been punched in the face."

The Noble teen reached down a hand and helped Azizi onto his bed. "Azizi, I'm sorry."

Azizi winced with pain. "What I said was out-of-line. I was asking for it."

Amsi sat beside Azizi on the bed. He put a gentle hand on Azizi's leg. "I'm so sorry, Azizi. I don't know what came over me." The teen looked down sadly. *The power of the Eye of Horus commands you to follow Pharaoh Runihura! You are powerless to resist!* Amsi raised his head. "The pharaoh used the Eye of Horus on me."

"What!" Azizi gasped. "When?"

"Before you came to my home. The pharaoh was trying to turn me into one of his followers. He tried using the Eye of Horus on me, but it was unsuccessful."

Azizi looked at his friend with concern. "How did it not turn you into one of the pharaoh's loyal followers?"

"I am not loyal to the pharaoh."

"Neither were the thousands of his sympathizers before he turned his eyes onto them. Why were you immune?"

"I don't know. Maybe the pharaoh sent some of his rage into me." The Noble teen looked into the eyes of his friend. "You have my undying loyalty, my brother. But-." Amsi looked down sadly and folded his hands in front of him. "Maybe you're right, Azizi. Maybe I'm just like my father." *Perhaps I am just a cruel tyrant like my father. I have become everything that I hated, loathed, and despised. Maybe I will hinder Azizi's search for the Items of Legend.*

"Did you enjoy it?" Azizi asked, placing his right hand on Amsi's shoulder.

"Enjoy what?"

"Punching me in the face five times and trying to strangle me?"

Amsi shook his head sadly. "No."

Azizi covered Amsi's hand with his own. "Then you are not like your father. You are forgiven. Your father would never have offered me food, clothing, or coin. Your father tried to kill me with his chariot, remember? You should be getting to your morning prayers. I apologize again for what I had said. It was wrong of me. Can you forgive me?"

Amsi looked at Azizi. *I don't want to be like my father. My father is cruel. He shows no compassion towards the slaves or my mother. He torments them for his own pleasure and it is wrong. I try so hard not to be like him. Sometimes I must consciously lock that part of my mind in its cage. My eyes have seen enough suffering at my father's hands and at the hands of the pharaoh.*

If Azizi has become ill with the Red Fever, it could be affecting his mind. Perhaps that was the illness speaking to me. "How could I stay angry at you, Azizi? I know you are not feeling well. You should rest while I attend my morning prayers. I will be back as soon as possible."

Azizi nodded. "Be safe, my brother."

Azizi stood up and washed his face in the bowl of water sitting upon the table. *I don't know what came over me. Never would I say that Amsi was like his father. As my hands grasp the table, I can feel the urge to return to bed. There is no rest for those who have no time. Amsi and I must find the entrance to the catacombs and find the Scroll of Isis.*

Every day Gahiji's troops march ever closer to Kadesh. Gahiji will allow no soul to survive here. Their survival depends on our success.

With my dagger fastened to my rope, I cautiously leave the room. The chant of the women mingled with few men filled the hallway. They were chanting hymns to Isis. My feet crept silently along the hallway, not wishing to alarm any priestess not in Morning Prayer. The murals along the hallway depicted mythological scenes involving Isis, Osiris, and Horus. Mother Isis suckling the child Horus displayed on the wall in meticulous detail. The next mural depicted Isis liberating the murderer of her husband, Seth.

I came to the first doorway and opened the door. Inside the room were beds and tables much like the bedroom occupied by Amsi and myself. The next room to the right was the kitchen. A large archway lead to the outside of the temple where the cooks were preparing the next meal. One table lined with many chairs indicated a dining area.

The next room to the left was designed as a small chapel. An altar to Isis stood against the wall and was decorated with fine linens. The tiny stone sanctuary of the goddess stood in the middle of the altar. Many candles of white and green flickered with tiny flames. A pillow set before the altar helped the penitent be comfortable as prayers were offered to the Divine Mother. I lifted the pillow and the carpet underneath.

The entrance to the catacombs is not going to be easily accessible.   No shining light will appear pointing to the entrance.   If I have to turn this place upside down to find what I want, so be it.

While kneeling on the ground, my hands drift over the stone.   My fingertips trace the cracks looking for a switch or anything suspicious.   My fingers just traced the dirt between the rocks.   There's nothing here.

Cautiously I left the tiny sanctuary.   Across the hallway a closed door prevented me from peeking inside the room.   Chanting continued from the temple's main hall.   I could hear Amsi's voice clearly among the voices of the women.   If Sawaret taught him vocal lessons, Amsi has learned well.   If Amsi had to sing for his supper, he'd earn a banquet every night.

I slowly opened the door across the hall and what I had found was incredible! The walls were lined with scrolls.   Two tables stood against the walls with a large cauldron in the front of the room.   Stone tools laid on one table covered in Lapis Lazuli, gold jewelry, and silver.   A gem cutter must have abandoned her tools for her prayers. The other table was covered in papyrus, reeds, and inkwells with different colors.   I picked up one of the scrolls and was able to read the script.

Divine Mother protect me from the sting of my enemies

That their venom may not harm my bones of gold.

Another prayer implored Isis to protect an infant from sickness and death. A tall basket glimmered with finished amulets, gold bracelets, and rings. This is a magical enchantment manufacturing shop! Prayers, amulets of holy protection, and jewelry blessed by Isis herself were being fashioned for those willing to pay the price of the temple. Their customers spoke Common Tongue. Few of these are in a script I cannot read, though one amulet in Noble Tongue seems to want to protect the family's cat from cheese. I'm probably reading that wrong.

I hear clicking noises behind me as I turn around sharply. There's nothing behind me. I reach into the basket of amulets and remove a green emerald set against a silver sun. A smile crossed my lips as I thought of Kahla. I want to give her a present when we find a home together. This will do nicely. Sifting through the basket, I found another necklace with a green stone and placed it where my necklace had rested. Several of the amulets contained scorpions encased

in resin. Around their preserved bodies, protective spells against scorpion venom were chiseled into the gold or silver.

I know I told Amsi I wouldn't steal, but surely they will offer us a reward when we save their lives from General Gahiji's army. I'll take my payment now. Why wait for it? The green amulet fit well into my money purse tied behind my back.

The clicking behind me grabbed my attention again and I turned. A glass container of live scorpions clicked on one of the shelves holding the scrolls of protective spells. Slowly I approached the container, my

*eyes transfixed with the amount of clicking scorpions crawling over
each other. If Runihura should obtain these protective spells and
amulets, he could become even more powerful.*

*I left the room and crept towards the door at the end of the hallway.
Here is the library where Amsi studied. Perhaps there is a scroll
written in Common Tongue. I grabbed a scroll from the shelf and
brought it beside the window. A tall archway appeared with scorpion
claws reaching toward the heavens. My eyes focused on the Noble
Script written above.* Door…Osiris…Burn. *Worship beloved Osiris
where burn? Amsi will have to look at this. I examined the walls and
found nothing. My eyes sifted through the scrolls, searching for
evidence of the Circlet of Isis or the Scroll.*

*I don't know how long I was there before I heard a familiar voice speak
to me at the doorway.* "Weren't you supposed to be resting?"

"Amsi, come here. Take a look at this." Azizi rolled the scroll he had
examined on the table. Amsi stood beside Azizi and looked down at
the text. "I could read the words: door, Osiris, and burn. I think this
word is 'worship.'"

Amsi traced the script with his finger. 'Ausar Nes Tuat…Osiris flame
of the Underworld. It says, 'Worship my brother, Osiris, where the fire
burns. Descend as I into the dark Underworld to see my lover.
Follow my steps to that which protects my sister's power.'"

"We must find Osiris to gain entry into the catacombs? There is a mural in the main hall with Osiris! Perhaps that is the way!"

Amsi shrugged. "What do we have to lose?"

"Agreed. It's a good place to start."

"Did you see anything while you were prowling around like a thief at market in this holiest of sacred ground?"

Azizi shook his head as they walked down the hall. "No, but I saw an entire room filled with protective spells and amulets. My hands examined every crevice of the small sanctuary to Isis and found nothing."

Both teens stepped into the main hall of the chapel. A visibly shaken young man was surrounded by priestesses. "Please, you have to listen to me! The Great Army is upon us! We must leave Karnak!"

Amsi and Azizi exchanged worried glances. Amsi ran quickly to the crowd of women trying with futility to calm the messenger. The young man's eyes widened when he saw Amsi standing before him. "Where is the army now?"

"Our outposts report they have crossed the southern border near Tyre." The young man fell to his knees before the Noble teen and bent low to kiss Amsi's feet. "Please, my lord! Save us!"

Azizi casually approached the crowd and watched as the frightened man kissed his friend's feet. "Where is the army? How far away are they?"

"It is time for the Anointed Companion of Rā to prove his strength," Meraset said.

Amsi's eyes widened in alarm. "I'm supposed to prove my worth by fighting an entire battalion of the pharaoh's army? How am I going to beat hundreds of men?"

"You will command our swords and our archers to victory."

"Azizi?"

Azizi shrugged. "I hope you were paying attention during your lessons, my friend. In this test, there is no room for failure."

Amsi's sparkling brown eyes looked down at the worshiping man.   He looked around at the priestesses watching him intently.   *I have to rescue Zahra's clansman.   If I fail to return that poor shepherd alive, she will never forgive me.*   Amsi took a nervous breath and put his hand gently upon the back of the man's head.   "I will do everything possible to keep the Temple of Isis from falling into the hands of Gahiji's army. There is no need to kiss my feet and beg for my aid."

The man raised his head. "Please save our families!"

Azizi stepped away from Amsi and headed towards the door.

"Azizi! Where are you going?"

"I'm going for a little ride in the desert."

Amsi stepped around the man kneeling on the ground. He grabbed Azizi's shoulders. "You can't be serious! Gahiji is out there!"

"He's been pushing his army to the edge of exhaustion. Their exhaustion will play into our favor.   They will still be a challenge. Get the women and children to a safe place. Arm the men and priestesses."

Amsi shook his head. "We can't expect these women to help us, Azizi! They are of Holy training, not battle-mistresses!"

"We need every hand that can hold a sword," Azizi said, turning to face Amsi.   "I won't allow a child to watch his mother fight and die in battle. These priestesses can fight or they can protect the mothers and children in their safe place. The walls of Karnak will be our saving grace."

Amsi kissed each of Azizi's cheeks. "Please hurry back, my friend."

Azizi returned the friendly gesture and pat Amsi's arm reassuringly. "I will return shortly. I have faith in yourself and your capabilities." Azizi walked hastily out of the doors and ran down the steps. "We have an errand to run, boy!" Azizi's horse turned its head.

He removed the rope keeping the creature tied to the post. He brought the horse to the fountain where Amsi had bathed the day before and allowed his horse to drink. Azizi submerged his head into the water and removed it, shaking the water free from his shoulder-length wavy, black hair. Azizi mounted the large, black horse and coaxed it into a gallop through the gate.

XX

My Beloved Child

Qamra helped Imani into the bath filled with warm water scented with sweet citrus oil. Imani settled into the water with a smile and a sigh, the pleasant vapors filling the air around her. Qamra grabbed a cloth and proceeded to rub Imani's shoulders.

Imani rested her head against the headrest and closed her eyes as she thought of her missing son. "How much longer do you believe our Amsi will be gone?"

Qamra's cloth gently rubbed Imani's back slowly. The woman silently washed her mistress without responding.

"Qamra? Did you not hear me, my dear?" Imani opened her eyes and turned her head to see tears falling down Qamra's cheeks. "Qamra, what is the matter?"

Qamra wiped her eyes and sniffled again. Her cloth gently glided over Imani's buttocks as she shook her head despondently. "I do not know when Master Amsi will return, my lady. I hope he returns soon."

Imani turned and put a light hand on Qamra's shoulder. The Noble woman gently lifted Qamra's chin upward to look her in the eye. "My precious Qamra, why do you cry? Did you lose your baby?"

Qamra dropped the cloth into the warm water and cried into her hands. Imani looked with pity on the woman and slowly wrapped her arms around her, pulling Qamra close to her wet body. Qamra opened her eyes and slowly reached for Imani with trembling hands. Qamra rested her hands on Imani's shoulders and sobbed. Imani's gentle hands caressed Qamra's hair tenderly.

"My dear, tell me what has happened. It is not like you to be so upset. Has my husband improperly touched you again?"

"No, my mistress," Qamra said sadly. "The wheat has grown behind our little home."

Imani smiled. "A girl will bless your home, Qamra! That is wonderful news! The gods have blessed you and Baruti for a fourth time!"

Qamra wrapped her arms around Imani and held her mistress close to her. "I am very happy not to lose the baby, Mistress Imani," Qamra cried. "But Anubis may take one of them away."

Imani hugged Qamra. "Who is ill?"

Qamra began to tremble again in fear for her child's life.

"Khentimentiu, my first son, has fallen ill with the Red Fever. I have given him every medicine I can concoct. I have spoken all the prayers I know. Every amulet I can make by hand have I placed around him to protect him from evil spirits. Isis has told me she wants to welcome him into her arms, but how can I let him go, Mistress Imani?" Qamra slowly pulled back from Imani. "How can I allow the goddess to take him? I don't want my son to die."

"You have tried everything?"

"Yes, my lady, except-." Qamra paused. She looked at the fallen cloth and picked it up. "I have yet to take him to the *Bedu*. They may have a cure."

Imani's eyes widened with shock. "Qamra, those people are dangerous! You don't want to take your son to them. They have strange spells that can turn humans into snakes and can make a man's intestines emerge from his skin! Refrain from seeking their aid."

"What other choice do we have, my lady? Master Amsi has spoken to the *Bedu* and has befriended one of their own."

Imani sighed with resignation as she lowered her head. "That boy would walk towards a starving jackal growling at him and extend his hand in friendship."

"Your son has a loving heart, my lady." Qamra washed Imani's chest and her stomach. "Khentimentiu has a loving heart like his father. If

Baruti and I lose him, Baruti will mourn deeply. Baruti was devastated when I lost the last baby."

Imani released Qamra and settled into the water. "Kaemwaset was questioning Khentimentiu's absence in the garden. I told him that Khenti had to clean the slave quarters."

Qamra wiped her eyes solemnly. "I apologize for my tears, my mistress. I should not allow them to interfere with my duty."

Imani sighed and turned her head to Qamra. "Go home," Imani said softly.

Qamra raised her head sharply. "Mistress Imani?"
"Go home and be with your son."

"Are you certain?" Qamra asked, standing before the bathing tub.

Imani bowed her head. "I will be there shortly to see the boy."

The door to the bedroom flew open and Nakia ran inside. His eyes widened as he saw Imani in the bathtub and Qamra standing before her. Nakia gasped and fell on his knees before Qamra. He bent forward, touching his head to the marble floor. He folded his hands in supplication. "A thousand apologies for interrupting your bath, my Lady! Qamra, you need to return to the home right away! Baruti needs your assistance!"

Qamra bowed before Imani. "Thank you, my Lady! Let's go, Nakia!"

Nakia jumped to his feet and bowed again before the naked Imani. "Apologies again, my mistress!"

Nakia and Qamra ran out of the home swiftly. "Baruti needs more medicine for him!"

"Which potion?"

"He needs to open his lungs again," Nakia wheezed as he ran.

Qamra saw Laila standing outside the slave home, motioning for her mother to hurry. "Laila, boil a pot of water!" Qamra exclaimed loudly.

Laila, Qamra, and Nakia ran inside to find Baruti rocking Khentimentiu in his arms. Laila poked the fire in the middle of the home and poured water into a pot from a nearby bucket. She placed a pot of water over the fire and looked down sadly at her half-brother. Qamra kneeled before Baruti and lightly caressed the sick boy's forehead. "Khenti, my beloved, look at your mother."

The weak boy's eyelids slowly fluttered as he lay in his father's arms. Khentimentiu's face glittered in the fire's light with a thick veil of sweat covering his body. "Mother."

Qamra's bottom lip trembled as she watched the boy slowly open his eyes. She smiled uneasily and caressed her son's hot cheek. "Your mother is here, my child. Where is your pain?"

Khentimentiu coughed and breathed through wheezing lungs. With a sharp gasp, the boy tried to force air into his body. Khentimentiu's head fell back as he struggled to breathe. Qamra shook her head as the child laid limp in his father's arms. Red scabs now covered his body. "Laila, is that water ready yet?"

Laila looked into the water and nodded. "It is almost ready."

"Hold on, boy," Baruti whispered. "Anubis, don't take him. Please do not take him this night. Issâm, I pray to your *Ka*, keep death from our doorstep."

"Baruti, I don't know what else to do for him," Qamra whimpered. "I have heard people speaking beside the Nile. Anyone who has this disease is doomed to death."

Meskhenet and Akilah gasped as they looked at the sick boy. "Will Khenti truly die, mother?"

"I pray that it is not so, Meskhenet."

Baruti shook his head despondently. "I do not like to see him in pain."

"What shall we do, my love?" Qamra whispered. "Khentimentiu is suffering. We cannot take away his pain. There is no cure."

Baruti raised his eyes to look into the teary eyes of his wife. The field slave swallowed nervously, tears falling down his face. "I don't want our son to die, Qamra. There must be something we can do."

"Do you think I want to see our son die? Do you think that I am ready to bury another child?"

"Mother," Khentimentiu moaned through a congested airway.

Qamra looked at her son sorrowfully. "What is it, baby?"

Khentimentiu touched his mother's hand lightly. "Help me."

Qamra nodded slowly. "I'm trying, my son. Baruti, I don't know what else to do for him. There is nothing I can do to make this illness leave his body."

Laila stood beside Baruti. "Father Baruti, the water is ready for him."

Qamra placed the small pot of boiling water on the floor.   "Hover his head above the water." Baruti helped his son to kneel on the floor.

The child looked into the pot of boiling water and felt a cloth drape over his head.   He breathed the steam into his lungs as his parents held him steady.

"How much longer can he suffer, Baruti? He can't eat. He can't breathe. Those sores on his body trickle with white fluid and form once more."

Baruti felt the boy trembling in his arms. "There must be some cure."

"My love, there is none," Qamra rubbed Khentimentiu's back and felt his lungs become temporarily relaxed. "Good boy, Khenti." Qamra looked at her husband. "I only want what is best for our son. I know you hate to see him struggle like this."

Baruti nodded and wiped tears away that crawled down his cheeks. "I love our son so much, Qamra. I can't bear the thought of losing him."

Meskhenet and Akilah raised their heads to see Imani step into the slave home. Both of the little girls kneeled before the Noble woman. Nakia raised his head to see his mistress and kneeled before her.

"Hello, there is no need to bow." Laila, Qamra, and Baruti raised their heads to see Imani stand beside Qamra.

"I think the boy has had enough hot steam for now," Baruti said.

Qamra removed the cloth covering Khentimentiu's head as Baruti cradled the child against him once more. Qamra watched as Imani kneeled beside Baruti.

The field slave and the Noble woman locked silent gazes. Baruti held his son protectively against his body as Imani looked down. The father watched as his son shivered in his arms.

Imani placed a soft hand on the child's forehead. Baruti looked at the woman's finely manicured nails. Her fingernails were painted red which matched the red stones in her bracelet. The woman's hands were clean and smelled of sweet perfume. The woman's thumb delicately caressed the boy's hot flesh. As her thumb glided over a red blister, the child whimpered, his eyes-half opened.

"Khentimentiu, can you see me?" Imani asked.

The child's eyes wandered to Imani. "Mother?"

Imani smiled. "No, my child. You have a wonderful mother who loves you and a devoted father to whom you have been blessed."

"Mistress Imani, why have you come to see me?" Khentimentiu asked.

"Because I wanted to be assured that you were alright. When Nakia was sick as a boy, I would come visit him. I visit whenever any of our little helpers have taken ill," the Noble woman said with a tender voice.

Nakia folded his hands in front of him as he watched Imani compassionately caress the boy's cheek.

The sick boy smiled and let his eyes close slowly. Imani watched as the eight-year-old fell asleep in his father's muscular arms. Baruti shook his head sadly as he kissed the boy's forehead.

"I am sorry, Baruti," Imani said, placing her hand on his arm.

"Nakia, you said that the Bedouin have returned nearby?"

Nakia nodded. "Yes, Father Baruti. They are nearby in the desert because of the Nile has swollen beyond her banks."

"They may be Khentimentiu's only chance of survival," Baruti said, standing with his son cradled against him. "If they cannot help him, then-." Baruti stopped. "Then I will begin to dig his grave tonight."

Meskhenet began to cry and ran into her mother's arms, clinging to her tightly. "My brother can't die, mother! Please, make one of your potions and make him recover!"

Qamra held her daughter tightly against her. "My precious daughter, there are no other potions. I have sung every chant and have spoken every prayer. I have made every medicine which has been handed from mother to daughter."

Imani blocked Baruti's exit from the home. "Baruti, those people are dangerous! I tried to stop Amsi from approaching them, but he refused to listen to me."

"The *Bedu* are not dangerous," Nakia said quickly. "Zahra and her clan are our friends.   They are peace-loving and are skilled in the ways of medicine not known in our area.   They have spoken of tall mountains extending their reach for great distances.   They have spoken of protective dragons and a culture which seeks spiritual enlightenment. The *Bedu* write in a strange script that appear as hieroglyphs. Mistress Imani, because they are different does not mean they are to be feared. Did you not teach Nassar and I the same lesson when we were brought here as young children in chains?"

Imani sighed and stepped out of Baruti's path. "That girl who appeared at Amsi's Coming of Age Ceremony did not appear hostile."

"I must do this for my son, Mistress Imani. My son could die without their help," Baruti carried Khentimentiu through the arch.

Nakia walked beside Baruti to guide him to the Bedouin settlement. Baruti whispered prayers to Anubis as he solemnly walked. "Nakia, I pray the god of death does not take him."

"Zahra's people are wise. They know much from their travels across distant lands."

Baruti and Nakia saw two guards cry out in alarm when they stepped into view. Nakia held up his hands and the guards lowered their spears.

"We need to see Xeres," Nakia said quickly.

Shera heard Nakia's voice and ran to him happily. When she saw Baruti holding a limp child in his arms, her frown faded. "What is wrong with him?"

"My son is ill and requires your aid. Please help him."

Xeres stepped beside Shera and smiled at Nakia's arrival. "Nakia Enzi! What joy it is to see you!"

"Lord Xeres, my friend Baruti needs your help. His son is very sick. Baruti, this is Xeres, the leader of the *Bedu*."

Xeres watched as Baruti fell to his knees before him.

"Merciful Lord, please help my son. He has fallen gravely ill from the Red Fever sweeping across *Iunu*. My wife knows no more potions, no more spells, and no more prayers that can cure him."

Xeres approached the child and leaned over to inspect the sores and rashes. Xeres touched one sore and watched white fluid ooze from the raised skin.

Zahra gasped and covered her mouth. "Poor boy!"

"Onfalia!" Xeres exclaimed loudly. "We need your knowledge!"

Baruti watched as the Bedouin medicine woman ran to Xeres. The woman's eyes widened in horror at the sight of the dying boy.

"What manner of corruption is this? Zahra and Shera, prepare an ointment to dry the sores of their fluid," Onfalia said.

Onfalia looked at Baruti. "What is this ailment?"

Baruti held Khentimentiu close against his body. "He can't eat or breathe. These sores burst with white fluid and harden. He shakes like the corn in rough wind."

"Where is Sumati? She needs to help me make medicine to stop the child's inflammation."

Shera looked around for her twin. "She must be in *Iunu* visiting Nassar."

"Give the boy to me," Onfalia said.

Baruti looked down at his sleeping son and felt a tear creep down his cheek. "Please do not hurt him."

"We will not," Xeres said as Onfalia opened her arms.

Baruti hesitantly stood and placed the boy in Xeres' arms. "Can you help him?"

"We will do everything we can, Baruti," Xeres said.

"Chahna, find Shera's twin and return her here."

Nakia stepped forward. "Thank you, Xeres, but I will find my brother and Sumati," Nakia said. "I'll bring Baruti back here tomorrow night to check on the boy."

Baruti turned to Nakia and grabbed the Ethiopian's shoulders. "Please find them quickly, Kelile!"

Nakia nodded. "I will not disappoint you, Father Baruti." Nakia ran from Baruti's side.

"What is the child's name?" Onfalia asked.

"Khentimentiu Mer-User-Anpu Ibn Baruti."

Xeres bowed his head. "Thank you, Baruti. May your Anubis not arrive to guide him to the home of his forefathers."

Baruti watched helplessly as Onfalia laid Khentimentiu beside the fire. Members of the clan circled around the child. Baruti watched them as they looked at the child curiously. *My son's life is in their hands.*

*   *

*

I have done everything I can to prepare for the arrival of General Gahiji and his army.   Perhaps Azizi is right in that the troops will be weak from their long trek across the sands.   Few of the priestesses have told me they refuse to fight the pharaoh's army.   'We are holy women and refuse to take lives,'they told me.

They will be protecting the mothers and their children in the unlikely event Gahiji and his men will find them.   Men from Karnak have offered me their arms in battle.   My eyes gaze upon the tall colossi of Isis standing in the main hall. Its piercing eyes fixed on me.

Lady Isis, please tell me that there is nothing more to be done in preparation for our battle.   My hands lay my bow and arrow before me as I kneeled in supplication. I bowed before the large statue and was burning sweet incense upon the altar. What more can I do?   *Please guide the weapons of my men.   Grant unto us victory in our dark hour. Guide me, Beautiful Lady of the Heavens! Protect your children as we fight to protect that which you hold sacred within your catacombs.* A gentle wind blew against my left ear. How could a wind blow in a room with no open spaces?

"How do you know the catacombs hold something sacred?" a voice asks as Gysa stepped beside me.

My hands grabbed my bow and arrow. I stood beside Gysa. "Because I have read it in one of your texts. The Scroll of Isis is here."

"You are on a fool's errand, Anointed Companion of Rā. The Scroll cannot be here."

"And why not?" I asked with frustration. "I have found textual evidence to support my claim. After Azizi and I fight Gahiji's army, we are going to find the entrance and claim what we have came here for!"

I walked to the altar and grabbed a scroll and my flute. When I turned, Gysa was standing before me, trapping me against the altar.

Gysa looked at my scroll and my flute. "You are a scholar, not a fighter."

"I have brought my scholarly texts to study. I may have servants to answer my every desire and I may have wealth, but I will defend to the death something precious."

Gysa smiled at me. Why is she smiling like that? "And what is so precious to you that you would defend to the death?"

"I will not allow the relics of Isis to fall into the hands of Sekhmet. I will not allow innocent women and children to be slaughtered. Gahiji will mercilessly slaughter every man, woman, and child within Karnak for a chance to obtain Isis' relics. Once he discovers that Azizi and I are here, he will add us to his list of dead or he will drag us alive across the desert only to perish by the pharaoh's hands. I refuse to see Azizi hang."

I began walking towards the door.

"Would you sacrifice your life for his?" Gysa asked me.

I stopped, remembering Aneksi's prophecy. *To save his life, you must sacrifice your own.* According to Aneksi, one of us will die. I turned my head to Gysa and offered her a quizzical look.

"What did you ask of me?"

"Would you give your life for your friend?"

My head lowered. "I would give my life for him without hesitation."

"Would he do the same for you?" she asked as she stood in front of me. "How can you be so certain that he would die for you?"

"If Azizi wanted me dead, he would have been able to kill me years ago. Why would he deceive me?"

Gysa smiled at me and touched my arm lightly. "Why would he not want to deceive you? You have money. He has little that he can call his own." Gysa paused, waiting for my reaction. I can't deny that statement. "Azizi has been caught wandering the halls looking for little trinkets to claim as his own."

"Azizi has given me his word that he has not taken anything in my absence. I believe him."

I stepped around Gysa and walked out of the temple. Can I believe that Azizi is telling me the truth? He is a thief and survives through deception. Something is telling me to return to the room and search his belongings. What about trust? Can I trust that my companion has not stolen anything?

Azizi was honest about stealing from the tombs of the Nobles. As egregious as that sin may be, he plainly told me about his exploits. Azizi even invited me to rob a tomb with him. If that is not honesty and trust, why would I have a reason to disbelieve him?

I climbed the ladder to the top of Karnak's wall. Sitting on the heavy rock, I placed my scroll and flute beside me. My eyes stared into the looming darkness. From my quiver, I took an arrow and placed it into my bow, ready to fire at an unseen enemy.

Azizi, where are you? Did Gahiji find you?

Below my perch, men were discussing the imminent invasion. Men-Kheper-Re had invaded Karnak almost two hundred years ago. Today I had taken some time to read the inscriptions on the great black granite Victory stele which recounted the attack by the pharaoh's army. Men-Kheper-Re boasted how the king smote all before him. I copied some of the text and committed some of the text to memory. He boasted of his victory at Megiddo and Kadesh. Men below me speak of fearing the pharaoh's wrath. They have every right to be afraid.

The pharaoh's campaign lasted five moons as he conquered lands for Egypt's glory. Gahiji and his men will not stop their journey. He will allow men dying of thirst to lay in the sands.

What's that? I saw something move in the dark! I quickly knocked the arrow and aimed at the moving object in the night. What are you? Oh, it is a leaping gazelle. With a heavy sigh, I relaxed.

Perhaps Azizi is praying to Osiris in the desert. He is not accustomed to having a roof over his head. He lives in the open desert and alleys of the city. To him, it is freedom. To me, I would be uneasy. Jackals could attack or snakes can bite. Scorpions can sting and the sun would scorch my skin. I could be killed and robbed in my sleep. Never have I slept in the open night.

In the distance, a baby began to cry, perhaps already uneasy from the strife of tomorrow.

My head turned to see the men sharpening their spears. Archers were fixing their bows and preparing their arrows for battle. My bow, arrow, and my sword are ready for combat. My heart, though, is far from eager about taking lives. However, if they are going to kill me, I must kill them before they can kill me. *May Rā and the Aten protect us.*

What's this? Something approaches! I hear the whinnying of a horse. My eyes narrowed as I armed myself with my bow and arrow again.

Glaring into the desert, I was ready to protect Karnak from an early invasion. The sound of the horse raced ever closer…and closer. My nerves grew more unsettled. The night failed to reveal the traveler. Perhaps Azizi has arrived. It is difficult to see him as he blends into the veil of black surrounding Karnak.

"Halt!" I growled, pulling back my arrow.

"Put down your weapon, Rich-Boy!" Azizi called to me.

Azizi has finally returned! I watched as he rode through the gate towards me. He smiled up at me. "I have good news and bad news, my friend."

"What's the good news?"

"They still have your girlfriend's clansman."

"Azizi Keket, she is not my girlfriend!" I exclaimed. Why doesn't he believe me?

Azizi laughed at me. "Are you going to go into your tomb believing that lie?"

"What's the bad news?"

"They will be here by dawn."

XXI

The Battle For Karnak

Amsi kneeled before the figure of Rā and raised his hands in worship. "My lord is my protector, I know his might, to wit: A helper strong of arm, None but he is strong. Amun who knows compassion, who hearkens to him who calls to him. Amun-Re, the King of Gods, the Bull great of strength, who loves strength."

Azizi watched as Amsi bowed before the figure of his god. Amsi kissed the feet of the statue and bowed once more. His head turned toward the mural of Osiris. "All extol the goodness of Osiris! How pleasant is his love for us! His kindness overwhelms the hearts. Love of him is great in all. Great Father, protect us and shield us with your mighty hand," Azizi kneeled before the mural of Osiris and bowed to place his forehead on the ground.

Much to his amazement, a light breeze brushed across his hair. Azizi lifted his head and looked around. "Amsi, did you feel that wind?"

"All hail glorious Rā in his-No, Azizi, I did not.-All hail glorious Rā in his rising!"

Azizi raised a curious eyebrow and leaned over, touching his forehead against the marble floor once more. A light wind quickly flicked a few strands of hair. "Something is here, Amsi. The entrance to the catacombs is here! The scroll was right!"

Azizi rose to his feet as Amsi turned his head. Azizi kneeled against the wall as Amsi walked toward him. The thief brushed his hand at the base of the wall. "Feel that! Wind!"

A pair of dark eyes watched the thief and Noble from afar. The painted lips twisted into a predatory grin. *Thank you for leading me to the Scroll. General Gahiji will be pleased.*

Amsi kneeled beside the wall and placed his hand on the marble. A subtle wind brushed across his hand. "We found it, Aziz! We found it!"

Azizi nodded. "Now we need to know how to open it."

"We can't go into the catacombs now. Gahiji's men will be here soon and we have to prepare the men for battle."

The thief looked at the mural with awe. "We need to protect this mural, Amsi. If Gahiji discovers how to open the doorway, he will acquire the Scroll of Isis."

"What do you propose we do?"

"You will be leading the archers. I will be on the ground with the foot soldiers. Your job is to keep them from breaking through the gate. Should they break through, my troops will protect the wall."

Amsi heaved a heavy sigh. "I will be here, too, to help you. We cannot let Gahiji succeed."

Azizi nodded. "We should go out there, my friend."

Amsi watched Azizi walk towards the door slowly. The thief's black cape swayed gently behind him. *One of you will die.* "Azizi?"

Azizi stopped and turned his head. "Al-Sakhir?"

Amsi approached Azizi and stood in front of him. "Do you believe Aneksi's prophecy to be true?"

Azizi avoided Amsi's eyes and looked at Amsi's feet.   The thief swallowed nervously. "I don't quite know. Our fate is in the hands of the gods. Ever since I have heard Aneksi speak, it has troubled me. I pray that-." Amsi watched with pity as the normally stone-faced thief revealed a crack of fear.   "I'm afraid, Amsi." Amsi watched as the thief crossed his arms against his chest and lower his head.   Azizi's black hair fell in front of his face, hiding the faltering mask of fearlessness. "Terror. Doubt. I try so hard to hide them.   Nobody wants to see a leader unsure of himself."

"It's okay, Aziz. I'm afraid, too." Amsi grabbed Azizi's shoulders and pulled him into a tight embrace. "Should anything happen to you, I will avenge you."

Azizi swallowed nervously and cautiously pat Amsi's back. "Woe to the man who should slay you, Amsi, for their death will not come swiftly." Azizi offered his friend a small smile. "Let us win the day, my brother."

Amsi and Azizi stepped into the early light of dawn.   Archers were perched on the castle walls and rooftops of their homes.   Foot soldiers were poised before the large gates of Karnak.

Meraset approached the two teens and bowed her head. "Today you shall both prove your worth."

Both teens swallowed nervously as they saw hundreds of men look at them.

"Why are we relying on children to lead us?" one man asked. "They look hardly old enough to stop feeding from their mother's breast!"

Azizi narrowed his eyes and stepped forward. "You either follow my orders or you won't have a chance at defeating the pharaoh's army! Don't be a fool!"

The man glared at Azizi. "General Gahiji has years of battle experience, child. What accolades have you achieved?"

Amsi instantly drew his sword and pointed the blade at the man's chest. "Disrespect my friend once more and you will have no chance to prove your worth in battle!" The man and Azizi drew their weapons aggressively.

"Stay your hand, Corelis!" Meraset exclaimed. "We fight the enemy!"

Amsi slowly lowered his weapon and glared at the man angrily. "Do not test me, *peasant*!"

Azizi winced from the venom in the Noble teen's voice. The sound of disgust and revulsion resonated through the insult. *I wonder if he*

listens to himself sometimes. *It was as if Kaemwaset was standing*
beside me.

Amsi sheathed his sword and ran towards the ladder leading to the wall
where wooden barricades were constructed to protect the archers. The
Noble teen kneeled beside the archers.

"Sir, do we have a chance against their numbers?"

Amsi heard Azizi race up the ladder and stand beside him. The Noble
teen drew an arrow from his quiver as he held his bow tightly.

"May Isis help us protect her sanctum," Amsi said. "We have a
chance, comrade. Have faith that the gods shall favor us."

Azizi's ears perked as he heard the sound of numerous footfalls. The
clanging of hundreds of armor echoed through the barren wasteland
ahead of them. Azizi put his hand on Amsi's shoulders as he saw
hundreds of spears point toward the sky. A battalion of mounted
soldiers rode behind none other than General Gahiji.

"There are hundreds of men!" the archers gasped with fear. "We must
surrender, Lord Al-Sakhir!"

"No!" Amsi exclaimed. "Hold your position! We are the first line of
defense! The army cannot approach if our arrows rain upon them.
Think of your families!"

Azizi swallowed nervously. "I will fortify the gate, Amsi. Osiris bless you, my friend."

"Azizi, I trust you."

Azizi nodded and raced down the ladder.   He ran towards the gate and checked the blacksmith's chains binding the iron doors closed.   Azizi heard the thunder of the approaching troops.   Gahiji's army would have to encounter Amsi and his archers before they could approach the gate.   Azizi watched his friend from below as he looked at the frightened soldiers.

Azizi mounted his steed and peered at the sea of faces watching him. "Gahiji's army will stop at nothing to gain entry.   Protect the temple with your lives!   Your ancestors have defended this temple before! Make your forefathers proud to call you 'Warriors of Isis!'" Azizi grabbed the pharaoh's golden dagger and held it into the air.   "Protect your family from Sekhmet's fury!"

Amsi smiled as he heard Azizi encouraging his troops.   *Now I understand how Azizi felt two years ago when he saved his friend Sekani from the gallows.   My body is so tense! I can feel my heart racing. Staring at the throngs of soldiers, I almost feel as if this is a fruitless battle.   How can we win?*

How can we not? Think of the alternative, Amsi.   Zahra's clansman will perish. Azizi and I will either be executed on sight or dragged before the pharaoh where we face the death sentence.   My mother and

my father will mourn my demise as their only son. I stand to lose
everything if our small army loses today. Rā, Glorious Father, please
hear my prayer and guide my arrows in your beautiful name.

The large army stopped movement before the walls of Karnak. Gahiji
looked up at the soldiers peeking from behind their sanctuaries.

"Citizens of Karnak, open your gates and surrender to the great
Pharaoh Runihura Atenhotep! Your lives shall be spared!"

Amsi stood among the archers and gripped his bow and arrow tightly.
"General Gahiji, I will not allow Karnak nor the Scroll of Isis to fall
into your hands! I demand that you release Minoru!"

Gahiji chuckled as the unconscious shepherd remained draped over
Gahiji's horse. "Well, if it isn't little Master Amsi Al-Sakhir Ibn
Kaemwaset! Your dear father misses you terribly!"

Amsi growled. "Release Minoru and turn back to Egypt!"

"I will return your body home to your parents and the Scroll of Isis to
the great pharaoh, my boy! Slay every man and child, but keep the
women alive for the pharaoh!"

Amsi watched as the sea of humanity threatened to crash into the
temple. Amsi saw the Egyptian archers fire their arrows towards him.
The Noble teen ducked and nodded to his archers.

Azizi watched as Amsi and the others fired their arrows towards the invading army. Amsi repeatedly fired his bow and hid behind the wooden shields to protect him as he reloaded his weapon. With a silent nod to Azizi, the thief knew the battle of Karnak had begun.

"Gahiji's men are invading! Ground archers at the ready!" Azizi called as a line of men kneeled in front of him, ready to fire at the army who would rush the gates.

Amsi fired his arrow toward Gahiji, who held up his wooden shield to protect him. Other than appearing dirty, Minoru seemed unharmed much to his relief. *I'm going to return you to your clan, Minoru. Hold on.*

Amsi's archers fired another volley of arrows towards the invading Egyptian army. Egyptian archers returned the assault, firing their weapons into the air. Amsi saw a great number of arrows fire into the sky. The Noble teen raised his head and saw the rain of arrows descend upon him and the other archers.

"Look out!" Amsi exclaimed as he placed his quiver over his head and back to shield himself.

Archers screaming in pain toppled from the wall onto the desert sand below. Amsi trembled, struggling to bring himself to open his eyes and see the effects of the Egyptian rain of deadly ammunition. Twenty men landed in a silent, bloody heap below, bringing tears to Amsi's eyes. *What a senseless waste of life.*

The Noble teen loaded his quiver again and cleared his eyes of tears. "Protect the temple, Amsi! This is no time to mourn the dead."

Azizi heard the archers scream above and found many men falling onto the sand below. The thief looked up and saw a rain of arrows striking towards the archers and the soldiers on the ground. "Arrows! Guard up!"

The men raised their shields as the arrows pierced the wood. Azizi saw Gahiji among the soldiers struggling to burst through the gate. "Ground archers! Release!"

Archers on the ground released their volley into the attacking Egyptian army. Gahiji laughed loudly as he saw the teen in tattered clothing. "Azizi Keket and Amsi Al-Sakhir in the same location! Pharaoh Runihura will be pleased to see both of you."

"You shall disappoint him, Gahiji! We will not become your prisoners today!"

Egyptian archers fired through the gates toward the foot soldiers and the temple archers. Azizi watched the line of archers fall to the arrows. An Egyptian soldier's axe slammed through the chain.

"Will that chain hold?" Azizi asked the blacksmith standing beside him.

"I fired it twice last night. Horus himself would not be able to-."

The axe sliced through the chain. Azizi's eyes widened as the horse reared in alarm. "I thought you fired it twice!"

"That's impossible!" the blacksmith exclaimed. "Someone must have weakened it!"

The Egyptian army flooded into the temple grounds, their weapons held high. Azizi's dagger clashed with one of the soldiers. Azizi kicked the man in the face with his foot and slammed the dagger into the top of the man's skull. With a vicious tug, the blade removed itself from bone.

The temple soldiers ran toward the Egyptians, their battle cries echoing into the air. Azizi saw Gahiji's horse racing towards the temple. Azizi's heels dug into the horse's sides. The thief raced beside Gahiji and pounced on him, knocking horse, captive, and rider onto the ground.

"You little street-rat!" Amsi heard Gahiji call behind him. He turned and saw Azizi sitting on top of Gahiji, punching the General in the face angrily.

"You killed my mother!" Azizi growled, punching Gahiji with such force, the man's large form trembled. Azizi raised the pharaoh's golden dagger above his head.

A soldier raced behind Azizi and wrapped his arm around Azizi's throat, pulling the thief off the fallen General. Amsi's eyes widened when he recognized Azizi's assailant.

"Shen!" Amsi cried in alarm.

Amsi watched as Shen raised his fist and slammed it into Azizi's face. Shen stepped back and Azizi fell back onto the ground unconscious. The Noble teen raced down the ladder and withdrew his sword. "Azizi!"

Shen turned and saw Amsi racing towards him with his sword drawn. Shen and Amsi's swords clashed as the battle raged around them. Amsi kicked Shen backward as the muscular warrior lunged towards him.

"This time, Al-Sakhir, nobody will save you from my blade. Your concern for your friend will get you killed."

Amsi saw a trickle of blood creep down Azizi's nose as the thief laid motionless on the ground. "Azizi…"

Shen lunged for Amsi, swinging his sword and removing a second from its sheath. Amsi held tightly onto his own as Shen raced for him, slicing the air with the blade. Amsi turned and ran. *I need another sword and a plan! Quick!*

Amsi felt Shen's thick hands grab his cape and pull him back. Amsi fell onto his back and looked at the strong man smiling down at him.

"Goodbye, Al-Sakhir."

Amsi glared at Shen and thrust his sword into Shen's stomach. Amsi closed his eyes as blood trickled from Shen's stomach onto his face. Two swords dropped by Amsi's head. Amsi rolled away as Shen's body toppled forward, the sword skewering through the dead man's stomach.

Amsi panted heavily as a pool of blood spread beneath the body. "I want my sword back, Shen." Amsi turned the corpse onto its back and pulled the sword from the disemboweled man.

"Help! Help!" Amsi heard.

Gahiji was carrying Gysa over his shoulders and dragging Azizi by the wrist up the temple steps.

"Azizi! Gysa!" Amsi raced towards the pharaoh's General as five soldiers blocked his path. *I have to get to Azizi! Perhaps even more importantly, I have to protect the entrance to the catacombs! If Gahiji acquires the Scroll of Isis, he will know of the Circlet's location!* "Move aside!"

The soldiers chuckled as they grinned. "You don't stand a chance, Al-Sakhir!"

Amsi's sword clashed with two of his opponents. A third soldier lunged at Amsi, making the Noble jump back to avoid the blow. Amsi grabbed his own sword quickly and sliced through one of his opponents. The other soldier jumped backwards to avoid Amsi's strike.

Amsi locked threatening glares with the four remaining enemies. Amsi tensed as one soldier raced towards him. The Noble quickly ducked and tossed the soldier over his head. Amsi turned his body, keeping his eyes on the remaining soldiers. Amsi sword pierced the fallen soldier's chest.

Amsi grinned, his heart beating wildly, his blood pumping through his veins like a quick burst of wind. A chuckle emanated from the throat of the battling teen. Amsi's grip tightened on the hilt of his two swords bathed in crimson. "Who would like to feel my blade next?"

"Perish, Al-Sakhir!" one soldier exclaimed, charging for the enraged teen.

Amsi crossed his swords to block the soldier's strike. With a quick step, he kicked the knee of the soldier in front of him. Two remaining soldiers watched as their comrade fell to his knee. Amsi trapped the man's throat between his swords. With a quick slice, Amsi beheaded the soldier, who fell at his feet.

Maybe the pharaoh was right...

Amsi's body trembled as he raised his bloody swords with a grin. Sweat dripped from the Noble teen's tanned skin. His white skirt of fine linen was now dotted with crimson. Amsi felt himself laugh as he held his two swords towards his opponents. The silver blades trickled with the blood of Amsi's victims.

I determine their fate with my swords...Kill or be killed.

The battle raged around him. Men's screams of pain and the whimpers of the dying filled his senses. Light from the morning sun reflected from Amsi's gold as he glared at his opponents.

I cannot let Azizi fall to Gahiji! Amsi lunged forward quickly slicing through the two remaining soldiers. The Noble teen raced up the steps. *Hold on, Azizi!*

Amsi burst through the door and found Azizi laying on the altar to Isis. The thief's left arm dangled from the altar. Gahiji stood before the altar holding a dagger to Gysa's throat.

"One more step, Al-Sakhir, and I kill this girl," Gahiji smiled, holding the priestess in front of him. His arm wrapped around her throat as Gysa cried.

"She is a priestess of Isis, Gahiji! Do you want to incur the wrath of Isis?"

Gahiji grinned. "Retribution by the Mother Goddess does not concern me. Only the Scroll of Isis for the Great Pharaoh Runihura is my concern. Tell me, woman, where is the scroll?"

"I don't know!"

"Where is the Scroll of Isis, Al-Sakhir?"

Amsi narrowed his eyes as he saw Azizi's fingers twitch on the altar. "I don't know, Gahiji! Let her go!"

Gahiji chuckled. "Very well." Gahiji threw Gysa towards Amsi.

Amsi caught the priestess in his arms. Gysa looked up at him with sparkling eyes. "Are you alright, Gysa?" Amsi felt a piercing pain in his shoulder as he released Gysa. Amsi fell to his knees before the priestess. His left arm trembled as it raised slowly, trying to grab the dagger embedded in his back.

"Yes," Gysa smiled. "But you don't look so good, Anointed Companion of Rā. Perhaps you should lay down!" Gysa kicked Amsi in the face, sending the Noble teen onto the floor.

Gahiji and Gysa laughed as they watched Amsi grit his teeth with pain. "Now we have the Blessed Servant of Osiris and the Anointed Companion of Rā. Pharaoh Runihura will be pleased to see you boys."

Amsi watched as Gahiji's dagger hovered over Azizi's stomach. Runihura's General chuckled as he looked at his unconscious victim. "The pharaoh has been waiting for this moment for fifteen years."

Amsi watched as the unconscious thief slowly made a fist. Azizi groaned with pain on the altar. *Azizi! I need to get Gahiji away from him!* "The pharaoh is a butcher! He has sent his army to slaughter innocent men! You obey his every command like a common dog! But I know why you follow his every order, Gahiji. You are afraid of him." Amsi narrowed his eyes angrily. "You are a despicable coward, General!"

Gahiji's lip curled in disgust. "You should hold your tongue or I will remove it like your father removed the tongue of your body slave!"

Amsi smiled with a challenging glare. "You know the pharaoh wants Azizi and I alive. If we are returned dead, he will be quite disappointed."

Gysa slammed her foot on Amsi's stomach, making the teen shout with pain. "Prisoners do not speak!" Amsi held his stomach in pain as Gysa kicked his injured shoulder.

Amsi grunted as he weakly reached for the dagger embedded in his shoulder. Amsi opened his eyes to see Gahiji hovering above him.

The General grabbed Amsi's cape angrily. "The pharaoh wants you both dead." Gahiji smiled. "Your father offered me much coin to put you to your death."

Amsi's eyes widened as a tear fell from his eye. *What? My father wants me dead? Why would he want his only son dead? I thought…I thought my father loved me. This has to be a trick!* "You lie! My father would never want me dead!"

Gahiji laughed. "I heard the words from your father's own lips. You are a disgrace to the Al-Sakhir name. You have betrayed your family and the Nobility. Your father has signed your death warrant." Gahiji threw Amsi's body on the ground, making the injured teen scream in pain.

My own father wants me dead? I'm his only son! How could a father condemn their child to death? My mother would never approve of this! Does this mean that my mother is dead? My father has threatened her life before. I fear that my father is capable of anything, especially under the influence of beer and wine of which he is fond. Why would my father do this to me? I thought he loved me.

Azizi slowly opened his left eye to see Amsi on the ground, reaching weakly to remove a dagger embedded in his shoulder. Tears were falling down his friend's cheeks in rivers. *Amsi...I heard everything. Kaemwaset Al-Sakhir will regret this, I promise.*

"It can't be true," Amsi sobbed. "I'm his only son!"

Azizi groaned on the altar again and closed his eye. Gysa turned her head to see Azizi turning his head to the side.

"I think our little death-worshipper is not faring so well," she said, approaching Azizi slowly. She looked at the thin specter laying on the altar. With a careful hand, the priestess caressed the cheek of the thief.

"He is a handsome one," Gysa said tenderly. "It is unfortunate the pharaoh wants him dead. He would make a very handsome slave."

"You leave him alone, you traitor! It was you who defaced the murals!"

Gysa laughed as her hand seductively rubbed Azizi's chest. "Our sister had no chance against the collective might of our temple! She thought she could leave and take the key with her." Gysa smiled down at Azizi. Amsi watched as Gysa leaned down to Azizi's face. "Get away from him!"

"Silence!" Gahiji growled, kicking Amsi's injured shoulder again.

Amsi watched through glassy eyes as Gysa turned Azizi's head and kissed him romantically on the lips. Amsi narrowed his eyes at the amorous priestess.

Without warning, Azizi grabbed the priestess'head with both hands and broke her neck.

Gahiji turned on his feet to see Azizi sitting up on the altar and Gysa laying on the floor with her lifeless eyes staring into the abyss before her. "Common rat!"

Amsi brought back his leg and harshly kicked Gahiji in the back of his leg to distract him. Gahiji lost his balance and fell on top of Amsi. The Noble screamed with pain as the dagger was embedded further into his shoulder.

Azizi jumped off the altar and wavered unsteadily on his feet, his eyes full of tears from his broken nose. Pain radiated through his head as he staggered forward. The thief reached for the swords laying on the ground. His surroundings spun around him as he struggled to see through a fog ahead of him. Blood pulsed through his head, igniting fire through his senses. "How fitting that the same sword you used to behead my mother is the same sword that will now take your life, General Gahiji."

Hovering above him, he saw Azizi holding a sword in his hand. The thief pointed the blade bathed in crimson at Gahiji's chest. "Killing me will not bring your mother back from her grave," the General smiled wickedly. "You have nothing to gain by my death."

Azizi raised the blade of the sword toward Gahiji's throat. "You killed my mother, Gahiji. Now do I send you to Osiris, where Ammut shall devour your soul."

Gahiji smiled. "Send me to the God of the Dead, boy. The Great Pharaoh Runihura will achieve victory and will take great pleasure in killing you slowly."

Azizi pierced Gahiji's throat with the sword. The thief grabbed his golden dagger and stabbed Gahiji in the chest savagely. Amsi watched Azizi stab Gahiji's body repeatedly.

Amsi watched as Azizi glared at the corpse with disdain and disgust. Azizi's body trembled with fury and sadness as his mind relived that day. It was finally over. He had his revenge.

"Azizi? Help," Amsi whimpered as he tried to shift from under the corpse.

Azizi grabbed the dead man's legs with a struggle and helped Amsi from under the man. Azizi kneeled beside Amsi and helped his friend sit. The Noble teen saw tears falling from Azizi's eyes and concern in the thief's face.

"Hold still, my friend."

Amsi wrapped his arm around Azizi as the thief removed the dagger from his shoulder. Azizi saw Amsi's white cape stained with blood.

Azizi looked down at Amsi and saw a renegade tear falling from the Noble's eye. *Amsi has finally seen the disease that plagues his father's heart. His father has just condemned his son to death. He has struggled to please his father. I can only imagine what my friend is feeling in his heart.*

Had I heard that my parents wanted me dead, I would be devastated. How could a father maliciously order the death of his child? I cannot see how any father could be so cruel. Amsi is a kind person. His heart walks the path of Light, illuminated by the Sun God, Rā. My brother weeps. I can feel his pain. Amsi has just lost his father today. My heart aches for him.

With a gentle motion, Azizi brushed a tear from Amsi's cheek. Amsi looked up at Azizi, still holding onto the thief. Azizi slowly brought Amsi into a hug. "I'm sorry, Amsi."

Why would my own father do this to me? Why? I could never wish my son dead!

My hands tightly grasp onto Azizi. Pain in my shoulder spreads through my arm, but now that seems secondary. Azizi is like a brother to me. He is akin to family.

"You are welcome to join my family, Amsi," Azizi whispered. "I do not wish you dead." Amsi looked into Azizi's eyes and down at Gahiji. "He's no better than my father."

Azizi released Amsi and looked down at him as angry screams raged outside the temple doors. "We must join the battle. Are you up for it?"

Amsi stood as he grabbed his bow and arrow. "What of your injury?"

Azizi felt the room spin around him. His head ached from his injury. Blood trickled down Azizi's chin from his crooked nose. "We must ensure the retreat of the Egyptian army."

Amsi put his hand on Azizi's shoulder. "I will cover you, my friend."

Azizi took his golden dagger and opened the door. Amsi stood at the top of the temple steps and fired at the soldiers who lunged towards Azizi.

XXII

Longing

Amsi winced with pain as Loida stitched closed the wound in his shoulder. Amsi watched as Meraset supervised priestesses attending to Azizi's injury. Azizi laid unconscious on the bed as the doctor cleaned blood from his face. The doctor placed the small rolls into Azizi's nose. The thief had collapsed after the Egyptian army had left.

"Will Azizi be alright, Meraset?"

The doctor nodded as Meraset handed two small rolls of linen saturated with grease to the doctor. "He is one having a break of the column of his nose, an ailment which I will treat."

"You are very lucky, Anointed Companion of Rā. Our battle was fierce, but you have proved yourself worthy of your title."

Amsi lowered his head. "I couldn't get to Azizi before Shen broke his nose. I wouldn't consider that a victory."

"Your friend will need time to rest until the swelling reduces. He will need his wound treated with grease and honey until he recovers."

Meraset walked around Amsi's bed to examine his injury. The High Priestess placed a piece of meat on Amsi's wound. Loida wrapped the injury, placing an amulet of Isis into the wrapping.

Amsi looked down sadly. *Azizi and I won't be able to find the Scroll tonight. He needs his rest.*

"Why are you sad? You should be praising the gods that you have survived," Loida said, patting Amsi's left shoulder. "Many have not been so lucky."

"General Gahiji told me some very upsetting news before he died."

Meraset stood before Amsi. "What news has bothered you so?"

"My father wants me dead."

"That is absurd! What father would wish for his son's death?"

Apparently, my father is one who has commanded that it be so. Amsi sighed. "I just want to be left alone. Please." The women left the room with the doctor. *I don't want them to see me upset.*

Azizi, where are we going to go? What are we going to do? He has told me that should I die that he would seek me out in my tomb and perish with me.

The only son of a Noble Family abandons his wealth to join a commune of thieves. How can I truly abandon my family and my birthright? How can I abandon my mother to my father's cruel nature? I cannot leave her alone. What will mother say?

Azizi, we must find the Scroll of Isis. We must complete our mission and hurry home. I'm relieved that your injuries are not serious. Never have I seen Azizi collapse before. He continued to fight, even as I saw him in pain. My wounded arm struggled to slay his assailants with my arrows.

I laid on my bed, struggling to keep my eyes open. My shoulder burned, but the real heartache flared in my heart. My father has condemned me to death. Why is it that a thief from Iunu, *a homeless orphan, is more family to me than the man who placed me in my mother's womb?*

My eyes feel as if they are attached to large stones. Against my will, they're beginning to close. Azizi, I'm right here. Can't keep my eyes open anymore. I'm so tired. Sleep has come. Goodnight, my brother.

XXIII

The Breath of Heaven

Amsi groaned in his sleep as he felt a warm cloth touch his forehead and lightly press against his cheeks. A warm hand grasped his own as he whimpered in his sleep.

"You have sacrificed so much to rescue me from that horrid beast. I have caused so much suffering," the voice said to his right.

"May his soul be devoured by Ammut, Minoru," the angry voice growled at his left. "Our final duty is to obtain the Scroll and Circlet of Isis." A light hand caressed Amsi's palm. "I must return to my clan."

The cloth left Amsi's face and the Noble struggled to open his eyes.

"I cannot believe that we have slept for four days."

"The doctors came in to rub honey and grease on your injuries. You needed your rest after the battle."

Amsi slowly opened his eyes to see the Bedouin shepherd smiling down at him. "He opens his eyes! Lord Amsi! Praise the gods, you are awake!"

Azizi placed his hand on Amsi's stomach with a grin. "Hello, my brother. Look who I have found."

Amsi looked at Minoru, rubbing his eyes with his right hand. The Noble teen winced as the meat laid against his shoulder, touching his wound. "How are you, Minoru?"

"You have both earned a reward far greater than my family could pay. You have both saved me from the pharaoh's tyrant-beast! He kept me bound on his horse for days. He refused me water and food. Both you and Lord Azizi are my saviors."

Amsi sighed. "I'm no savior. I just did what was right."

Azizi chuckled. "A little hero worship never hurt anyone, Amsi."

"I don't want to be worshipped like a god," Amsi said as he tried to sit. Azizi stood and wrapped his arm around Amsi's back, helping his friend to sit comfortably.

"Aziz, have we truly slept for four suns?"

Azizi nodded. "The doctor woke me up the first day to ensure that I would waken from my sleep. That battle was terrible."

"How fared the women and children?"

"You did a wonderful job keeping their hiding places concealed. The women are back to making their bread and being mothers for their children."

Minoru nodded. "Karnak and my tribe owe you both a great debt."

Azizi looked up at Minoru. "Please get some food for him. He needs his strength for our next challenge."

Minoru bowed and stepped out of the room. Amsi looked up at Azizi and reached towards Azizi's shoulder. "I am relieved you have recovered."

"Well, a few more days and the discoloration will disappear. I cannot allow this to interfere with the real reason for our arrival. Do you feel strong enough to enter the catacombs with me?"

Amsi sighed. "I can't let you do this alone. Can it wait until nightfall?"

"Yes," Azizi said. "Tonight we shall enter the catacombs and obtain the Scroll. I wish to return to Heliopolis as soon as possible."

"Pharaoh Runihura will be furious when he discovers that his General has been slain."

Azizi nodded. "Precisely. I do not want him to ride through *Iunu* and repeat his massacre from fifteen years ago in retaliation. Kaphiri's clan would join in slaughtering everyone in my quarter."

"That's terrible! We have to hurry home!" Amsi tried to jump out of bed, but groaned with pain.

Azizi shook his head. The thief began to unwrap the bandages from Amsi's wound. "You need to stay in bed today. Minoru will bring you food."

Amsi relaxed in bed. "You need your rest as well. What are you doing?"

"Your wound needs to be treated with grease and honey. Inflammation from the stitching has reduced nicely."

Amsi winced as Azizi removed the meat covering his injury. "Where is the doctor?"

Azizi took a bottle of honey and lightly patted the sweet substance over the stitches. "He is very busy tending to others. Aneksi has taught me how to apply unguents and fix some injuries."

"Thank you, my friend."

Azizi nodded as he applied grease to Amsi's skin. "You are welcome."

Amsi raised his head as Minoru returned with a bowl of broth and bread slices. "Thank you, Minoru." Amsi took a bite of the bread and chewed slowly as Azizi applied new linen bandages to Amsi's shoulder. "Minoru, did Zahra speak of me during your travels through the desert?"

Azizi chuckled as he looked at the Bedouin teen. "Amsi insists she isn't his girlfriend, yet he speaks endlessly of her during her absence."

"Aziz! Ow!"

"Stop your whining, Rich-Boy."

Minoru folded his hands in front of him. "Yes, she does speak about you fondly while we are traveling the Long Road."

A smile crossed Amsi's lips. "What does she say of me?"

Azizi finished wrapping Amsi's shoulder and laid on his bed. He turned his head to watch the shepherd.

"Zahra thinks you handsome and very generous. She says you are a wonderful friend."

Amsi smiled as he laid his head against the pillow. "She likes me!"

"Xeres will surely reward both of you for saving my life."

"You have just given me my reward," Amsi said with a satisfied grin.

Azizi yawned and closed his eyes. *My reward would be to see the look on the pharaoh's face when he discovers that General Gahiji has been escorted into the Land of the Dead.*

That night, Azizi and Amsi stood before the mural of Osiris. Fire from two torches flickered beside the mural. Azizi reverently approached the image with his head bowed. Amsi watched as the thief kneeled before the mural. Amsi approached the mural and cautiously moved his hand over the image. Minoru watched from a distance, standing behind the altar to Isis.

"'Worship my brother, Osiris, where the fire burns,'" Amsi said, holding the scroll in his other hand.

Azizi bowed before Osiris and felt gentle wind move his hair. "Osiris, Un-Nefer, show me the way into the lair of your sister." Azizi's fingers traced the bottom of the wall where he found a crevice. He slipped his finger under the wall. "This wall is not sunk into the marble.   This wall must open somehow. Where is the trigger?"

Amsi's finger explored cracks on the plaster, hoping to find a switch. "Worshipping Osiris cannot make the door open on its own. There must be something around here to make it open."

Azizi brushed dirt from the crevice and felt something tug at his finger. "I think it's a spring. Stand back."

Amsi stepped back as Azizi grunted. The thief wiggled his finger against a thin rope.   "It's hard to reach," Azizi groaned as he pressed his finger against the string.

Azizi's finger hooked the string and tugged it.   Amsi jumped back as the wall began to shake and slowly open towards Azizi. The thief rolled backward, watching the wall open.

"Are you alright?"

Azizi rose to his feet and took one of the torches. "There are some benefits to thin fingers, I guess."

Both teens stared into the darkness ahead of them. Amsi felt the warm gentle breeze from the catacombs brush across his skin.

"How can breeze occur underground?" Amsi asked.

The thief turned his head and looked at the statue of Isis. "Isis breathes life into the dead. This breeze is not made by mortals. May the Mistress of the Divine help us."

Amsi opened the scroll and read the words. "'Descend as I into the dark Underworld to see my lover. Follow my steps to that which protects my power.'"

"Please be careful, Master Amsi and Master Azizi!" Minoru called.

"Stay close to me," Azizi said, holding the torch in front of him.

Amsi followed Azizi cautiously into the darkness. Azizi looked down at the floor and saw a spiraling stone staircase. The thief stepped down two steps and shivered. Azizi's nose wrinkled from a whiff of mold. The warmth of the breeze was replaced by a chill. "Do you feel that?" Azizi asked.

"Feel what? It's warm up here."

Azizi turned and saw Amsi standing at the top of the steps. "Step down here."

The Noble teen stepped onto the staircase and gasped. "What happened to the warm wind?"

"Isis descended into Tuat to see her husband," Azizi whispered. The thief looked into the void below. "We are going underground into the Land of the Dead."

Amsi wrapped his white cape around himself and shivered. "We cannot walk into Tuat. We're still alive."

Azizi swallowed as he cautiously lead Amsi down the stairs. "That can change very quickly, Amsi. Be careful. Stay alert. Don't look down."

Amsi looked below and felt his heart racing. Should the ground beneath their feet collapse, there would be nothing to save them from falling into oblivion. He felt his legs begin to quake with every step.

"I think this is a bad idea."

"I told you not to look down," Azizi said.

Amsi gripped the scroll in his hands nervously as the staircase twisted against the wall. Against his bald head, he felt a drop of water fall. "Azizi, I just felt water."

The thief raised his head, feeling a drop fall onto his nose. He saw the first spiral of stairs above him. Water droplets were beginning to fall into the abyss below. "Isis cries for her fallen lover. We must hurry."

Amsi followed Azizi into the next level of the spiral staircase when the water began to fall faster.

"Hurry, Amsi!" Azizi called. "Isis weeps at the loss of her husband!"

Amsi raised his head as a heavy cascade of water plunged against the stairs above them. Azizi huddled against the wall, raising the torch to conceal it under the stairs above them. Azizi raised his head to ensure the torch was sufficiently concealed so as not to be extinguished. Amsi pressed himself against the rock as two stairs across the wall were broken by the deluge of water. Heavy wind blew through the stairwell, spraying the water onto the two teens.

"Hurry! We must continue or the flame will go out!" Azizi lead Amsi down the stairs amid the flood of water around them.

Amsi followed Azizi down the stairs, pressing himself against the wall. Stone fell from above due to the force of the water. *I am the maker of the Waters. I am the Being whose name the gods know not. I am the creator of the fire of life. Glorious Rā, please placate the Great Mother!* Amsi jumped as a chunk of stone fell, smashing the stair beside him.

"The next step is missing!" Azizi cried out, barely able to distinguish the next ledge.

Amsi stepped forward to find it missing. Amsi dropped the papyrus and screamed as he began to plummet. Azizi grabbed Amsi's arm as the Noble dangled from his grip. "Azizi!"

Amsi grabbed onto the stair and pulled himself onto the staircase. "I dropped the scroll!"

"Don't worry about the scroll!" Azizi watched as another stair collapsed behind them. "Hurry!" Azizi watched as the torch's flame began to quickly diminish from the wind and water.

At the bottom of the stairs, they raced into an alcove. Water fell into a hole in the ground and disappeared. Azizi wiped water from his eyes as he panted. The wind had ceased its strength. Piles of broken stone lay on the ground around them.

Amsi breathed in a sweet perfume from the end of the tunnel. "I smell flowers. They're fresh." A smile crossed Amsi's lips. "It smells as sweet as Zahra's perfume."

Azizi watched as Amsi walked down the hallway. The thief breathed in deeply. "I smell something familiar. It smells like-." Both teens stepped into an open field of flowers, fresh grass, and radiant sunlight. "What sorcery is this?"

Amsi's eyes widened as he looked at the open field where wooden pillars stood reaching towards a blue sky. "Azizi, what magic is this? Where are we?"

Azizi turned and stepped through the threshold into the dark tunnel. "Come here. Read this for me."

Amsi stepped towards Azizi and looked where the thief was rubbing the wall with his hands. Amsi traced the hieroglyphics with his fingertips. "This writing is centuries old. 'Behold the glory of Tuat! Seek ye Melcarthus'desire.'"

Azizi stepped cautiously into the room where a gentle, fragrant breeze filled his senses. Amsi stood beside his friend and peered into the sky where the light glimmered overhead. "How can the sun shine? We are underground, are we not?"

Azizi reached down and let his fingertips brush through the grass. "This is an elaborate illusion. Unless…"

"Unless we really stand in the Elysian Fields."

Azizi stepped towards one pillar and touched it. "According to legend, Melcarthus made a pillar out of the tree which grew around Osiris'coffin. We have to find which pillar holds Osiris."

Amsi examined the pillar. His fingers brushed across hieroglyphics carved into the wood. "'Children Isis all praise devoted to mother to be her.'What is that supposed to mean?"

Clouds began to obscure the sun from view. Amsi and Azizi held their ears as a loud lamentation carried through the air. The sorrowful shriek pierced through their hands and throbbed in their ears.

Amsi's eyes widened as his heart raced with fear. *That voice is so full of sorrow and pain!* Tears came to Amsi's eyes. *I can feel the sorrow of the Great Mistress. I lost him. He was the one I loved. Seth stole my husband from my arms.*

Azizi turned to Amsi and gripped his left shoulder. "We have to cut open the pillars!"

"I lost my husband!" Amsi wailed with heartbreak.

Azizi winced, unable to hear Amsi's lament. The King of Thieves reached for Amsi's sword, his head throbbed from the piercing cry of pain. Azizi struggled to lift the sword over his shoulder. With quick strikes, he chopped through the pillar to find it empty.

"Amsi! Help me!"

Amsi rose to his feet, his legs shaking, and his cheeks flooding with tears. Amsi grasped his other sword and struck another pillar finding it empty. *My ears ring with the force of the cry. It's becoming louder with every failure to find the right one!* Amsi looked over to see Azizi struggling to stay on his feet. With two failed attempts to find the right pillar, the pitch of the cry became sharper.

The Noble teen staggered to Azizi and grabbed the thief's wrist. "Are you alright?"

Azizi shook his head pointing to his ear. He motioned Azizi to step aside. With a strong kick, Amsi kicked through the pillar. Volume increased on the cry.

Azizi felt himself stagger. Speaking to Amsi would be impossible. Azizi's hands shook as he held onto the sword. *We have too many pillars to keep attacking.*

Azizi stepped away to attack the next one. Amsi ran for his friend and gripped his wrist. *A different sequence of hieroglyphics adorned every pillar. This pillar says 'Isis be praise mother all children her to devoted to.' That doesn't make any sense. I grabbed Azizi and pulled him towards the pillar he last chopped. This says, 'Devoted children all praise to Isis to be her mother.' These are the same words on the last pillar, but in a different order. Perhaps the correct pillar has the same words in the correct pattern!* Amsi stood Azizi against a pillar and motioned for him to remain still. *The real pillar has to be around here somewhere! 'Children Mother all her praise be Isis to to devoted.' That sentence is a scribe's worst nightmare. If I wrote that sentence, Sawaret would have me beaten with my own ostraca. These other pillars don't make sense. Wait! I think I found it!* "Praise be to Isis, Devoted mother to all her children." Amsi raised his sword among the howling cry and struck the pillar.

Cries carried upon the wind had ceased. Gusts of wind and the clouds hiding the sun drifted away, revealing warmth and light. Azizi winced as his head rang from the pitch of the wail. Amsi held his head with a groan as he opened one eye to Azizi. "Are you alright?"

Azizi shook his head. "Never better," the thief said, returning Amsi's sword to him.

The Noble teen walked beside Azizi through the field as a gray door opened in front of them. Gold lettering sparkling like glitter appeared on the door. Amsi stepped toward the shining glyphs and shook his head. "I can't read this. It's nonsense."

"What does it read?"

"T'at'at sennu qeres kerh mitu neter. 'Dead god divine cakes night sarcophagus.'"

A corner of Azizi's mouth curled into a smile. "Very poetic. Are you sure that is what it says?"

"I have studied reading and writing for ten years. I know how to read. You try to read it."

Azizi stepped towards the door and focused on the shimmering letters. "Mrt htm neter iyt. 'Offer the gods your appropriate sacrifice.'"

Amsi's eyes widened as he looked closely at the glyphs. "It's writ in Common Tongue. Why would it be written in the vernacular?"

"Because every soul should be able to proceed to the Great Hall where Osiris, Isis, and Nephthys awaits." Azizi reached towards the metal ring and pulled to open the door.

A dense fog hovered in the air before the two teens. High in the distance, a beacon of light pierced through the darkness. Amsi shuddered as a cold burst of air pushed against them. Azizi took a deep breath and stepped through the doorway. He looked down as sand touched the sides of his feet. Amsi walked beside Azizi and looked at the large rocks arranged on a sandy beach.

Gentle rippling of water was heard as they followed the path to the shoreline. Water from the ocean crept onto their feet and receded. The fog covered the surface of the water.

Azizi narrowed his eyes as an object slowly crept from the cold mist. Amsi saw the object rocking on the gentle water.

"What is this we see, Azizi?" Amsi asked, watching his companion remain steadfast. *I have never seen anything like this! There's someone in the boat. I see a staff and a torch. His face and body is shielded by a hood and cloak much like Azizi's. The cold air stings when you breathe. Mist upon the water obscures any view of its surface. Azizi is standing his ground. What is he thinking?*

The boat crept towards the shore. Azizi watched as the figure stepped from the boat. A man removed the hood from his head, revealing a pale face and black eye paint surrounding his icy-blue eyes. Silver necklaces and a silver signet ring adorned his body. Fire from the torch flickered, casting dancing shadows upon the shore. Azizi saw the figure missing his toes.

The man's eyes shifted to Amsi, whose gold glittered in the fire's light. Azizi watched the man's lip curl into a snarl. Azizi's hand reached for the hilt of his dagger.

The stranger turned toward Azizi and held out an open hand. "What will you give me for ferrying you across to the Island-in-the Mist?"

Amsi reached into his money purse and placed two copper dinars in the man's hand. The figure narrowed his eyes at Amsi. *Where have I heard that before? It sounds familiar*, Amsi thought.

"Offering."

"I just gave you payment."

"Offering."

Azizi shrugged his shoulders. "Maybe he is not interested in money. What do you want?"

"Offering."

"We just gave you an offering," Azizi protested. "What do you want to ferry us across?"

The man stood silent with his hand extended to Azizi. Amsi swallowed nervously at the chilling gaze of the ferryman. Amsi placed two gold pieces in the man's hand.

The man raised his trembling hand slowly towards Amsi. His lip curled in fury.

"You offer me gold!" the man asked in rage.

Azizi gripped the hilt of his dagger as the man threw the money in Amsi's face. Amsi watched with horror as the man's eyes sunk into his sockets and a dark aura surround him.

"Gold is an abomination to Nemty!" the man growled.

Azizi gasped as a large jeweled scepter appeared in the hands of the ferryman. Amsi drew his swords as the man's empty eye sockets glowed with fire. "Gold was obviously not the offering, Aziz!"

Nemty slammed the scepter against the ground with both hands, making the earth shake below their feet.

Azizi sank to one knee as Amsi fell onto his back.

"I shall take my scepter of 4,500 pounds and kill one of you each day!" Nemty bellowed, raising his scepter.

Azizi lunged for Nemty as he quickly unsheathed the pharaoh's dagger. Nemty turned his head as Azizi stabbed him in the rib. "You offer me gold?"

Amsi watched as Nemty swung the Scepter towards Azizi. The thief expelled a puff of air as Nemty's arm knocked into him. Azizi fell onto the ground as Nemty approached him.

Amsi jumped to his feet as Nemty crashed the scepter into the sand with both hands. Azizi rolled out of the path of the scepter. Amsi sliced off Nemty's arm with a quick strike of his weapon.

Both teens saw Nemty waver unsteadily on his toe-less feet. Azizi rose to his feet and saw Nemty unable to raise the scepter. "It's too heavy for him to raise! Amsi, offer him silver!"

"Why?"

Azizi held his dagger in front of himself. "Look at him! He's covered in silver-not gold!"

Amsi quickly grabbed his money purse and held five silver dinars toward Nemty.

The fire extinguished from the man's eyes and his body relaxed. Azizi watched as his icy-blue eyes returned to their sockets.

"Please board my ferry."

Amsi shivered as Nemty returned to the boat. "Can we trust him?"

"Hide your gold and we should be alright."

Amsi wrapped his white cloak around him and boarded the craft with Azizi. Throughout the journey, Amsi kept a vigilant eye on Nemty. His body tensed as the ferryman rowed them across the gentle waves. *Nemty ferried Isis in disguise across the river. I should have remembered that myth. 'Offer the gods your appropriate sacrifice.' Gold is the color of the godly skin and represents eternity. I thought that would make an appropriate sacrifice. Isis offered Nemty a gold signet ring to ferry her across the waters.* Amsi turned his head to see

Azizi sitting beside him. The thief coughed into his hand and wrapped his cloak around him. Azizi was glaring at Nemty from behind. His menacing eyes fixated on the ferryman. *Without a doubt, Azizi is keeping himself ready should Nemty attack us again.* The torch fixed to the bow of the craft flickered, casting a light surrounding Nemty. *I can feel Azizi shivering as he sits next to me.*

As they approached the shore, the beacon in the sky dimmed. A large fortress surrounded by the veiling mist came into view. It was unlike any palace or temple either of them had seen before. Amsi's eyes widened in wonder as three tall spires rose into the sky. Azizi's eyes watched the gray stone come into view slowly. Black iron blades pointed towards the starry sky above.

Lights flickered in the windows of the spires. Stone sphinxes stood upon the walls of the fortress. Both teens felt the boat suddenly stop as it rested upon the shore.

"Disappear."

Azizi and Amsi stepped off the ferry and rose their heads to view the tall fortress. Amsi held his breath as he saw iron demons glaring at them from above.

Azizi slowly approached the walls of stone and touched the rock lightly. "This is strange."

"Did you find something?"

"No. I have never seen a temple or building in *Iunu* such as this."

"I know," Amsi said, slowly stepping towards the door. "Where are we?"

Azizi said quietly as he looked around suspiciously. "I wish I knew."

Amsi examined the entrance. "Do you see a plaque or any writing to give us instructions?"

Azizi looked closely at the door and shrugged. "I see nothing." Azizi reached for the door and opened it slightly. A great burst of wind threw open the door and knocked Azizi and Amsi onto their backs.

Azizi struggled to his feet and held his arm in front of his face to block the violent wind pushing him back. He grabbed Amsi's hand and helped him to his feet. Amsi stood beside him as the wind whipped in front of them and beside them.

"This is getting unbearable!" Amsi screamed.

"Don't give up! We can make it!" Azizi cried out, staggering forward on his trembling legs.

Amsi watched the wind push Azizi backwards even as he stepped against the current. Amsi gripped his friend's arm as Azizi's sandals scraped across the ground. Azizi raised his leg to take another step as a strong gust shoved him back again.

"Hold onto me!" Amsi called to Azizi.

Azizi and Amsi grabbed each other's wrist. Amsi grit his teeth as he pulled Azizi towards the door. The Noble teen struggled towards the doorway. A bright light emanated from the ceiling. A thin bridge lead to a doorway which appeared at the opposite side of the room. A powerful gust of wind shoved both teens against the side of the doorway.

Amsi lowered his head against the wind and saw two pits on either side of the bridge. "Azizi? Are you afraid of snakes?" Amsi's eyes widened in horror as hundreds of squirming, hissing snakes lined the pit.

"No, why?" Azizi grunted as he stepped beside his friend and looked into the room. The King of Thieves knocked into Amsi from the force of the whipping wind. Ahead of them the bridge was too narrow for both of them to cross walking beside each other. If one of them lost his balance, the slithery pit would become his tomb.

Amsi looked at the door looming before them on the other side of the bridge. The powerful wind shifted and suddenly blew into his face. "How are we going to cross this bridge without falling?"

Azizi clutched onto Amsi tightly. "We can do this! Don't stand straight while we cross! Keep your legs spread wide enough to keep your balance when that wind comes from the side."

Amsi stepped forward as he tried to ignore the hissing surrounding them. The wind pushed Amsi forward as he began to stumble. Looking down, Amsi's eyes widened in horror again as he saw the slithering pit shift and stare at him with hundreds of hypnotic eyes. "Azizi! Go back!"

"We can't go back!"

Amsi turned to Azizi quickly and grabbed his shoulders. "If we fall-."

"If you fall you won't have a chance to regret it. Keep moving!" Azizi narrowed his eyes at Amsi angrily. The thief grabbed Amsi's arms and stared into his eyes with determination and resolve. "I won't let you fall!"

The Noble looked into his friend's eyes as the wind whipped towards Azizi's face. "Promise?"

"Promise. Don't look down. Keep moving."

Amsi turned as the wind shifted and blew towards the teens from both sides. The Noble fell to his knee to prevent falling into the snake-filled chasm below. A powerful gale blew Azizi from his deep stance. Azizi fell to the ground and held onto the concrete.

Amsi crawled towards the door, followed by Azizi. Sounds of hissing and striking snakes below sent Amsi's heart beating and his hands damp.

Whipping winds stung their faces as they slowly made their way across the bridge. When they crossed the bridge, they looked back.

"Good job. We made it."

"That's all you can say? 'We made it?'"

Azizi nodded. "I knew you could do it."

Amsi leaned against the wall as he watched Azizi walk to the other side of the room and examine the walls. *I wish I had his strength. I guess living on the streets, you learn to control your fear. He's had to be self-reliant. My focus has been my studies, literature, and combat. Books and scrolls do not teach what I have seen in these catacombs.*

My heart is racing just as during my combat lessons. As unsettling and challenging as this experience has been, this has been exciting. Perhaps I should accept Azizi's offer and go with him on one of his exploits. Why should I continue to play the dutiful son when my father has betrayed me?

Azizi's hands glided over the rock as dirt crumbled at his feet. He raised his head to look at the rockface above them. "It appears to be a dead end."

"There has to be a way out of here," Amsi said, joining his friend and examining the jagged walls. Amsi swallowed nervously as he heard the wind stop its howling from the other room. He held his breath at the ominous silence around them. "Azizi," Amsi whispered. "The wind stopped."

Azizi stopped his examination of the walls. The thief and Noble turned their heads to see a young woman standing behind them with her hands folded against her chest. A golden circlet adorned her bowed head.

Fine, white linens wrapped loosely about her body covered one breast and her hips. A golden scorpion amulet rested against her small breasts.

Azizi grabbed his dagger and held it in front of him. "What do you want?"

Amsi held out his hand quickly. "Stop, Azizi! She bears an amulet of Isis!"

The woman raised her head with a smile. "My heroes have finally come after so many years of waiting."

Amsi saw Azizi tensing from the corner of his eye. "Who are you?"

"A priestess of the Divine Mother, sworn to follow her in life."

Azizi gripped the hilt of his dagger as his knuckles turned white. "Have you also chosen to follow her in death?"

The priestess smiled and bowed her head reverently. "Yes."

Amsi's eyes widened in surprise. "You are dead?"

"I had taken my own life to serve the Divine and Devoted Mother."

Amsi swallowed nervously. "How can you be dead? You are speaking to us."

"Yes, Anointed Companion of Rā, Amsi Al-Sakhir Ibn Kaemwaset, I am speaking to you."

A chuckle escaped from the thief beside him. "I told you the dead walk among us, Al-Sakhir. I had met a man in the Caves of Horus much like this woman here."

"By the hand of Rā," Amsi whispered as he approached the woman.

Azizi tensed as his friend approached the priestess. *What is he doing?*

Amsi slowly approached the woman and breathed in her sweet fragrance. She smiled up at him and reached slowly towards his face. Amsi felt her warm, gentle hand caress his cheek. "You're so beautiful."

"Isis is a beautiful lady and she has witnessed your deeds in protecting her Temple. Your trials, however, are not finished."

Azizi stepped forward. "We need to find the Scroll and Circlet of Isis."

"The Circlet lies in holy rest in her city."

"The Circlet lies in a temple?" Amsi asked.

Azizi scratched his head. "Which city was home to Isis'cult?"

Amsi opened his eyes wide. "Heliopolis."

"Are you telling me we came this way just for the scroll?"

"The Scroll was moved, remember? It seems the Circlet was never moved from its resting place."

The priestess smiled. "You have proven that you are both very brave. Now you must prove something beyond determination and bravery."

"What would that be?"

Amsi and Azizi heard rumbling behind them. A gray stone door emerged from the rock.

"Beyond this door lies the Scroll of the Divine Mother. Use your Buckle to unlock the door to the Scroll, but beware," the smile of the priestess faded. "Isis' protects her relics from those unworthy of her gift."

The teens watched the stone door open. Azizi and Amsi stood beside each other in front of the door. Amsi took a nervous breath and looked over at Azizi.

"Do you remember Aneksi's prophecy?" Amsi asked.

Azizi nodded slowly. "Have faith in each other or you will not survive."

"I have faith in you, my friend," Amsi said as he slowly walked through the threshold.

Azizi took a deep breath. "So do I, Al-Sakhir."

Both teens entered a large room with tall pillars arranged in a circle. A pit of flames illuminated the room and made them sweat from the heat. Smaller torches were mounted on the pillars, offering no haven for shadows. Two tall, naked statues of Isis towered beside a large, golden doorway with eyes.

Both teens looked around cautiously as they approached the golden door. Azizi coughed as the heated air entered his lungs. Amsi saw the thief wince in pain as he breathed.

Amsi put his hand on Azizi's back as the thief leaned over. Azizi grabbed Amsi's arm as he coughed. The Noble teen's eyes saw a red patch on Azizi's arm.

"You do have the plague," Amsi whispered.

The thief lowered his head and nodded slowly. "We have a job to do, Amsi."

"But-."

"Stop!" Azizi growled. "We're here to get the Scroll of Isis. This is no time to worry about me."

Amsi swallowed nervously and looked at the golden door. *The sooner I get the Circlet of Isis, we can save Iunu and I can save Azizi.*

Amsi and Azizi approached the door and saw an opening for the Buckle. Amsi removed the Buckle from his bag and examined the object. He looked at Azizi, gripping the golden dagger in his hand. With a nod of approval, Amsi placed the Buckle of Isis into the opening on the door. The object sunk into the door as a low growl emanated from the door. A series of clicks echoed in the room with a vicious snarl.

Amsi and Azizi backed away from the door. Amsi drew his swords as his body tensed. Azizi watched as seven scorpions scurried from the opening door. Each of the scorpions was large enough to stare the teens in the eyes.

Two scorpions rushed to Amsi who blocked both of the scorpion's claws with his sword. He raised his sword to block their tails from stinging him. Amsi dodged the claws of the other scorpion after he blocked the tail strike from the other. Sweat coursed down Amsi's chest as a third scorpion rushed to his side. *How are we going to defeat all of them? It's seven against two!* The scorpion to his left raised its stinger and stabbed where Amsi's right foot had been. It raised its tail again as Amsi jumped back. One of the scorpions dashed towards him from the front. The scorpion with the raised tail stung its counterpart as it suddenly moved in front of it. The stung scorpion released a squeal of pain and fell onto the ground twitching as it died.

Amsi sliced the sword in front of him, blocking the scorpion's claw. With a quick slash, he severed the scorpion's claw from its body. The creature squealed in pain, striking downward with its tail. The teen jumped to the left as the scorpion's tail struck the ground. Beside him, the scorpion raced for him, knocking him onto the ground. The creature squealed in pain above him as it was stung. Amsi grabbed his sword and stabbed the scorpion beside him.

Amsi felt his body tremble as it was pinned under the dead scorpion above him. The heat of the air and the weight of the insect above him made his head spin.

"Amsi! Where are you?" Azizi called loudly.

"Under the dead scorpion!"

Amsi winced as the heavy insect above him weighted him down. With great struggle, he pushed against the creature to make it move off him. Amsi breathed heavily as he saw Azizi fighting one of the scorpions. He sheathed his swords and grabbed his bow. With a quick shot, he fired an arrow into the body of the scorpion. Azizi stabbed the scorpion's head as it was distracted.

Two dead scorpions laid at Azizi's feet. Two clicking scorpions rushed to Azizi. Amsi fired an arrow and blinded one of the scorpions. The thief watched as the blind scorpion was stung by a swift stab of the other scorpion's tail.

The sole survivor raced towards Amsi. The teen fired an arrow at the snarling insect. Azizi darted for the scorpion and grabbed the insect's tail, stabbing it in the thorax. The creature collapsed to the ground with a squeal of pain.

Both teens breathed heavily in the searing heat of the room. Azizi nodded quietly as he leaned on the nearby pillar.

"Good...job," he panted as his skin dripped with sweat.

A long, low growl rumbled from the golden door. Amsi's heart raced as it seemed to jump into his throat. His hands began to tremble in fear of what would come from the large door. Azizi's eyes focused on the golden door as he held his breath. The ground began to quake under their feet.

Amsi shifted close to Azizi as he held onto his friend. "The scroll in the library said 'Follow my steps to that which protects my power.'"

Azizi's eyes gazed at the seven dead scorpions scattered on the ground. "Blessed Osiris!"

Both teens watched with stunted breath as they saw a large golden scorpion emerge from the doorway. Its tail grazed the rocky ceiling. With ease it stepped over the fiery pit bellowing intense heat. Its gargantuan claws snapped menacingly.

Amsi's eyes widened in terror as the scorpion glared down at both of them. "Great merciful Rā!"

The scorpion squealed with fury as it darted for both teens. Amsi and Azizi quickly raced away from the pillar. The creature threw itself into the stone pillar and roared in pain. Rock from the ceiling fell onto the creature, but it continued to roar and raise its snapping claws. Its eyes burned fiery red as it glared at the teens.

Running into stone didn't even stun it! Azizi tensed as he watched it turn towards him. *If it knocks every pillar down, the roof will collapse.* Azizi ducked as the claws snapped at his head and feet.

Amsi fired towards its body, but the arrow bounced off its exoskeleton. "That's impossible!"

Azizi jumped backward as the large tail crashed to the ground in front of him. Amsi watched in horror as Azizi fell to the ground. Amsi grabbed his sword and raced for the creature's legs. His sword severed one of the creature's legs. The creature slowly turned towards Amsi and growled.

Amsi jumped to the side as the tail crashed into the ground, sending rock and dust flying into the air. Amsi's sword blocked a striking claw as the other claw reached for him. The claw grabbed his cloak and held him in the air. Amsi watched the scorpion raise its tail to strike him. Amsi screamed as a rock bounced off its body.

The creature winced in pain and dropped Amsi on the ground. Amsi rubbed his arm as he saw Azizi throwing rocks at the furious creature. Amsi watched the creature turn towards Azizi.

Azizi ducked behind a pillar as the claws snapped towards him. Shrapnel of stone spread around him as the scorpion's claw cut through the pillar. Rock from the ceiling plummeted towards him as the pillar fell toward Amsi. Azizi raced from behind the pillar as rocks fell from above. Azizi panted heavily as he ran towards Amsi.

The yellow scorpion turned toward them on slightly staggering legs. Its claws snapped towards them as the tail rained down on them again.

The creature whipped its tail, sending Amsi flying backward towards the pit of flames.

Amsi groaned as his arm stung from the impact on the ground. He breathed heavily as his body felt exhausted. The pit's heat began to make his skin burn and blister. Steel from Azizi's dagger clashed with the hard claws of the scorpion. Amsi opened his eyes to see the creature's tail stab the ground beside Azizi. Azizi stabbed the creature's tail as it crashed beside him. The creature shrieked in pain as Amsi struggled to his feet. It snapped its claws at Azizi again.

Amsi watched in horror as the creature's stinger pierced Azizi's chest. The thief's eyes went wide as he shrieked in pain. Azizi's weapon fell from his hand as he sunk to his knees.

"Azizi!" Amsi bellowed as the thief's body tumbled onto the ground.

The creature turned towards Amsi with a victorious shriek. Amsi watched his friend trembling on the ground. *Sweet, Mother Isis...Azizi!*

The scorpion roared furiously as it rushed towards him. Amsi narrowed his eyes at the scorpion and charged towards it. Amsi's sword bounced off its claws when they collided. His sword bounced off its body when he stabbed it. Amsi watched as his blade broke in half. *There must be some vulnerable part on its body.* A painful groan echoed through the room. *I have to get to Azizi. When I blinded the smaller scorpion, it stung its companion. If I blind this one, he won't be able to see me.*

Amsi sheathed his sword and grabbed his bow. He jumped back and fired an arrow into the scorpion's glowing eyes. With his arrow embedded in the eye of the scorpion, it roared angrily, knocking its claws against the pillar beside it. Rocks from the ceiling fell upon it as its tail slammed into the rock above it. Amsi saw the creature's claws try to knock the arrow from its eye. Amsi narrowed his eyes and fired another arrow into the scorpion's other eye. The arrow pierced the creature's other eye, eliciting a painful shriek from the insect.

Azizi struggled to open his eyes as he laid on the ground. His chest burned with the sting and venom. His fingers twitched as he felt his heart struggle to beat. The thief struggled for air as he laid on the hot stone floor, his body dripping with perspiration. Azizi watched through cloudy vision as his friend raced toward the monstrous insect. Amsi sliced through the creature's legs. Azizi felt the ground shake under him as the beast crashed onto the ground. Falling rocks slammed on the ground beside him. Amsi's furious scream echoed through the room as he stabbed his sword between the eyes of the scorpion. Its claws and tail crashed onto the ground and its vicious growl now silent.

"Azizi!" Amsi called in terror as he saw his friend laying on the ground. "I'll help you!"

Amsi sat beside Azizi and gathered his friend's upper body into his arms. "Azizi, speak to me." Amsi's fingers caressed Azizi's cheek.

Azizi opened his mouth and drew a strangled, hot breath of air. "Is it dead?"

Azizi's chest was bleeding from the site of the sting. Amsi felt his friend trembling in his arms. Tears fell from Amsi's eyes as he watched his friend struggle for air and quiver. The hands of the Noble teen quivered as he tried to think of ways to help his dying friend. *I can't do anything for him. What am I going to do? What can I do for him?*

"Amsi," Azizi gasped. "Don't shed tears for me."

"Why shouldn't I?" Amsi asked, wiping away a tear from his cheek.

Azizi breathed sharply. "Because you are mourning a Common Thief."

Amsi held Azizi against his chest. Azizi closed his eyes as he felt his body burn with the venom. A hand buried itself in Azizi's hair and caressed the onyx strands lightly.

"No, I'm mourning my best friend," Amsi said sadly. A smile crossed the thief's lips out of the Noble's sight. Amsi rested his cheek against Azizi's black hair and felt Azizi gasp for breath. The thief closed his eyes. Amsi felt tears trickle down his cheek as he heard Azizi's breathing diminish into light gasps.

A shadow cast upon the floor before them. Amsi looked up as the priestess stood before him. "Please help my friend! He's been stung by the scorpion!"

The young woman smiled at him. "You can help ease his pain."

"I'll do anything to save him!" Amsi exclaimed. "Tell me what I must do."

The woman held her closed fist towards Amsi. When she opened her hand, Amsi tensed. A clicking scorpion stood in her hand. "To save his life, you must sacrifice your own."

Amsi swallowed nervously. "What must I do?"

"To save your friend's life, you must bite into the tail of the scorpion and place the venom on his wound."

Azizi raised a trembling hand toward Amsi's arm. Amsi felt the thief's cold hand on his skin. "Don't do it, Amsi," the thief pleaded through failing breath. "You'll die." Azizi whimpered as a tear crept down his face. "My mother died for me. I don't want you to die for me, too."

Amsi looked into his friend's eyes. "If I don't do it, you'll die."

"Let me go, Amsi," Azizi winced with pain. "I don't want you to suffer for my sake. Beat the pharaoh, Amsi." The two teens locked eyes. "I will always love you as my friend, my brother," Azizi whispered as a tear crept down his cheek. "Goodbye, my-."

Amsi watched as Azizi's head slowly drifted backward. Amsi held Azizi against his chest and sobbed. "No, Aziz..."

Amsi looked at the scorpion sitting still in the woman's hand. *If I don't bite its tail, Azizi will die. If I do bite into its tail, I'll die. Azizi can barely breathe. He will die if I do nothing.*

Amsi slowly reached toward the scorpion as Azizi's eyes closed. The thief relaxed in Amsi's arms. The Noble watched as Azizi exhaled a weak breath. "Azizi? No, you can't die!"

Amsi swallowed nervously as he looked at the venomous stinger.

"Your friend is succumbing to his injuries," the woman said calmly.

Amsi took a deep breath and brought the scorpion to his mouth. *For Azizi*...Amsi suddenly bit into the insect's tail.   His tongue and mouth burned with poison.   His body trembled as he grasped the thrashing insect and poured the venom onto Azizi's chest. The bitten insect shattered into pieces in Amsi's hand.

The Noble watched as the dying thief opened his eyes quickly and gasp for air. Azizi's head rested on his chest as the thief drew a desperate breath.   Azizi felt tears falling onto him as Amsi held him in his arms.

"Azizi, please don't die," the Noble teen sobbed.

Azizi slowly raised his hand and touched the bald teen's head. "Thank you."

Amsi raised his head and saw his friend smiling at him through half-closed eyes. "Azizi, you're alright! You're alive! Praise the God of Life! Praise be to Rā, King of the Gods!"

"You could have died. Why did you choose to save me?"

Amsi sniffled and hugged Azizi tightly. "Because I couldn't bear to lose you. Azizi, you're really alive!"

Azizi stiffened as he felt himself be crushed by the constricting embrace of his friend. "Thank you…Amsi. Can I breathe now?"

Amsi quickly stopped his tight embrace. Azizi sighed with exhaustion and licked his parched lips. "Water."

The woman kneeled in front of the teens and offered Azizi a cup of water. "I shall look after your friend while you obtain the Scroll of Isis therein."

Azizi looked up at Amsi. "Get the scroll."

Amsi reluctantly sat Azizi against the pillar. He watched as the woman helped Azizi drink from her cup. The thief looked weak as he leaned against the stone. *I have to get him into bed. Hopefully the doctor can attend to his wound.*

Amsi grabbed one of the torches and cautiously stepped towards the stone door. He held the torch inside the dark room where an altar of red jasper stood against the further wall. A golden box shimmered in the torch light as he entered the room. He cautiously opened the box as a bright light filled the room.

"Praise be to the Devoted Mother," Amsi prayed as he removed the Scroll of Isis from its resting place.

"Al-Sakhir! Look out!"

Amsi turned and saw the door begin to close. The Noble slid out of the room before the doors could close. Rocks from the ceiling began to fall around them. Amsi ran for Azizi and helped his friend to his feet.

The ground rocked violently under their feet as geysers of fire erupted from the stone floor. Azizi groaned in pain as he climbed over the pile of rocks before the door. Amsi pulled Azizi through the empty room where fire continued to burst from the ground randomly.

Azizi breathed heavily as they crossed the bridge and the open fields. Through the tunnel and up the circular staircase, both teens struggled to climb. The oven-heat of the fire room was replaced by the chill of the staircase. Azizi tried to ignore the pain as he jumped across gaps in the stairs left behind by the cascading waterfalls. He grit his teeth as his legs burned with fire.

Amsi wrapped Azizi's arm around his shoulder to support his staggering friend through the open door in the mural. Minoru and Meraset stood before the door amazed to see the two teens barely standing on their feet.

"You have obtained the Scroll of Isis?" Meraset asked calmly.

Minoru rushed to Azizi's side as the thief went limp on Amsi's side. "What's wrong with him?"

Amsi saw another red patch had formed on Azizi's shoulder. "He has the plague of Heliopolis," Amsi said with a quivering whisper.

"I shall find the doctor," Meraset said, walking swiftly from the temple door.

"Minoru, help me get him into bed."

XXIV

Sekhmet's Victory

Pharaoh Runihura emerged from the surface of his wading pool. Ife leaned against its edge with a pleasant smile. Janani stood beside the pool with a jug of wine and golden goblets. Timin ran towards her with a big smile.

"Hello, my beautiful son," Janani said, kissing her child and hugging him tightly.

Ife's nose wrinkled. "That boy stinks like ox manure. He needs to bathe."

Janani held Timin close as she narrowed her eyes at Ife angrily. "He's just a child."

"Yes, and a filthy little vermin at that," Ife replied.

Runihura waded towards Ife and smiled pleasantly at her. "Our son will be bathed in the best oils and he will be one born into glory."

Ife smiled as she touched the pharaoh's chest. "I am intended for Amsi Al-Sakhir, Great One. Should Amsi fail to prove himself worthy for my hand or fail in his duty to his family, my body and my soul shall belong to you."

Runihura reached for Ife's face and pulled her into a hungry, passionate kiss. Janani's nose wrinkled in disgust as the teenaged girl moaned into the kiss.

"Great Pharaoh's army returns!"

Timin's head quickly raised as he saw the multitude of soldiers march through the gate. A smile crossed his face as he saw one particular soldier return. "Da Da!" Janani put Timin on the ground and watched him walk towards his father. He held his open arms in front of him as he saw Hamadi break from the ranks to greet him.

Hamadi brought his son into his arms and kissed his cheek. "My beloved son."

Janani stepped toward Hamadi, but Runihura's growl stopped her from advancing. Runihura broke the kiss with Ife and stepped from the wading pool. He wrapped his linen around his groin and narrowed his eyes at the battalion. "Where is General Gahiji?"

The men shifted uneasy glances towards each other.

"Answer me, you pathetic wretches! Where is Gahiji?"

One of the soldiers stepped forward with quivering legs. "General Gahiji has not returned with us."

Runihura's lip curled in fury as his fists clenched with rage. "What?"

"He dragged the corpse of Azizi Keket up the steps at the Temple of Isis and he never re-emerged."

Pharaoh Runihura stepped toward the soldier and stared at him with golden eyes. "What did you just say?"

The nervous man's lip quivered. "General Gahiji dragged the corpse of Azizi Keket up the steps and he never returned."

A gratified smile played about the pharaoh's lips. "Azizi Keket is dead? Are you certain of this?"

"When I saw him last, blood was pouring from his head and his face smashed. I watched him collapse onto the sand from his wounds."

A low chuckle bubbled in Pharaoh Runihura's throat. He raised his hands to the sky. "Azizi Keket is finally dead! May Sekhmet relish the sweet taste his blood!"

Ife stepped from the pool and walked towards the army. "Was Amsi with him? Did you see him?"

The soldier nodded his head. "He had been injured in battle. He collapsed on the field of battle covered in blood."

"Give me the Scroll of Isis," Runihura demanded with an open hand.

"We-We never obtained the Scroll of Isis, my Lord! We were forced to flee."

Runihura's smile faded and was replaced by a bitter scowl. "You never found the Scroll of Isis?"

The man's eyes were wide with fear and his breathing was shallow. "No, sire!"

Runihura grabbed the man's throat and grabbed the sword of the soldier beside him. "You forfeit your life as payment!"

Hamadi and Timin watched in fear as Runihura pierced the man's stomach with the sword.   Timin screamed and clutched onto his father.

Ife smiled as the soldier collapsed motionlessly on the ground. "Wonderful punishment, my king."

Pharaoh Runihura smiled as he turned his head to Ife. "You enjoyed that, my little princess?"

Ife stood in front of Runihura and licked her lips suggestively. "I find it very stimulating. Allow me to punish one more in your glorious name."

Runihura smiled graciously and handed her the blood-stained sword. "If it please my princess to do so."

The men stood before the pharaoh watching Ife with fear and uncertainty. She smiled at the soldiers as she passed them. With a gentle hand, she caressed some of their faces as she walked past them one by one.

Hamadi held onto Timin as she approached him. Hamadi closed his eyes tightly as he held his child against him. Hamadi kissed Timin's forehead as his body quaked. The grass before him was stepped upon and a shadow cast over him.

"Please don't slay me," Hamadi pleaded as he hugged his son tightly.

"Not this one," the shadow said. "His blood belongs to Sekhmet."

Hamadi opened his eyes and saw Runihura standing over him. He tensed as Runihura's hand touched the top of his head lightly. Hamadi tensed as he heard the soldier beside him gag and collapse on the ground gasping for breath.

"Beautiful work, my dear," Runihura said tenderly.

"Da Da!" Timin cried.

"Your father's here, Timin," Hamadi whispered to the child.

"Take one of those filth and put it on my balcony. We may not have Azizi's body, but nobody will see him from the ground. Janani, bring

Wosenret to my throne room. All of you will spread the word that a royal proclamation will be made before sunset." Runihura grinned, licking his lips with predatory satisfaction. "Azizi Keket has fallen victim to Sekhmet's arrow."

*   *   *

The doctor and the priestesses filled the bedroom while they attended to Azizi's wound.   I watched as they placed amulets on his chest and raised their hands to the sky.   "Flow on, poison, and come forth from Azizi Keket; Let the Eye of Horus shine forth from the god and shine outside his mouth!" I couldn't see Azizi with the crowd of worshippers around him.   "I make the poison to fall on the ground, for the venom hath been mastered!"

Women were crying as they stood around my friend and asking Isis to deliver Azizi from his injury.

Minoru put his hand on my shoulder to comfort me. I felt my heart skip a beat as Azizi's arm fell from the side of the bed. His fingers didn't move and his skin appeared pale. Please don't die.   I need your help. If Azizi were conscious, he would probably tell everyone to leave and stop crying over him.   I know Azizi would not want to see anyone crying because he was injured. Sorrowful cries of the women continued as I clutched the Scroll of Isis in his hand.   This is the key to curing Azizi and Heliopolis.

I walked away from the wailing crowd towards the library. I can't allow anyone to see me worried about my friend. Light footsteps behind me informed that I'm not alone in my quest for solitude. In the library, I stoked the fire in the fireplace and sat at the desk to read the scroll.

"Do you think he will die?" Minoru asked me.

I'm afraid that Azizi will perish. He would not want me to mourn him, but I would. "I honestly don't know. My prayers to Rā can only help so much." I lowered my head. "'I am the maker of the heavens and the earth. I have made the Bull of his Mother. I have made the joys of-." I stopped and ran my hands over the papyrus. "'I have made the joys of love to exist. I am the creator of the fire of life.'May Rā protect him."

I unrolled the papyrus and leaned my head on my hand to read the text. Minoru slowly approached the desk and looked over my shoulder. "How can you read that?"

"I learned how to read."

"That is impressive, Master Amsi!" Minoru gasped.

Master Amsi? I never thought I would miss my slaves so much. I miss Qamra and Baruti. I miss Khentimentiu and Meskhenet. Akilah has not been with our family for too long, but I even miss her. How can I forget the twins? I hope the Osiris Thief Clan is keeping Nassar out of trouble. Nakia wanted to follow me so badly on this adventure. Perhaps I should have brought him along. However, if my father did not have Nakia around, he would have suspected that Nakia ran away and the other slaves would pay for his disappearance.

"Did I say something wrong?" Minoru asked.

"No, you didn't, Minoru," I said as my eyes perused the scroll. My eyes widened when I saw the circle hieroglyph. "Heliopolis! The Circlet was under our nose the entire time!" Why didn't the priestess simply take the Scroll of Isis with her? Did she not know the location of the entrance to the catacombs? She knew the Buckle of Isis was a key.   If the scroll is needed to give the items their power, why would she not bring the scroll herself?   There's another mystery that will need some solving.

Divine Mother Isis, who gives the gift of Breath

Shall save her children from Osiris'Grip of Death

The Circlet of Isis resides in city divine

City of the Sun, Temple of Water, Cut in twine

Break the Circle and Illness fight

Beware the sting of Sekhmet's bite.

A smile crossed my face as I read the incantation.   "This is it! This is what we need! We must hurry back to Heliopolis!"

"Your friend is in no condition to travel, Master Amsi.   His body is weak."

"Azizi would want to die among his friends. He wouldn't want to die surrounded by priestesses screaming chants around him. Get food and some medicine for Azizi. We'll be returning home without my father's boat." I still don't know how I'm going to explain to him how we lost the family boat.

"Yes, sir!" Minoru said with a quick bow forward.

I heaved a sigh and looked out the window. People were rebuilding their homes from the army's siege. Children were playing with their toys away from the chaos of the builders. When I return home, what am I going to say to my father? How can I even look him in the eye after what he has done? What of my mother? Is she safe? Has Baruti protected her from his wrath? A part of me is afraid to see the aftermath of my return. A groan of pain from down the hall sent shivers up my spine. That is an unhappy, but fortunate sign.

How am I to break the news to Kahla if Azizi dies? If what he told me about them is true, she will be heartbroken. What if I have to tell Darwishi that his King of Thieves has expired? I need not worry about confronting my father then because I know that Darwishi would kill me.

"Azizi, please fight it. I know you are strong. Please don't die," I covered my eyes to hide my tears that threatened to burst forth like the Nile.

"Your friend is resting," a voice said behind me.

"Will he live?" I turned to face Meraset.

Meraset bowed her head. "His fate rests in the hand of the Divine Mother."

"Meraset, answer me a question. Did your sister who was traveling to Heliopolis know of the catacombs which concealed the Scroll of Isis?"

The priestess shrugged. "I cannot say what she knew for certain. Knowledge of the below is forbidden to the laity.   Only select few of the priestesses knew what lurked below.   When she left, I woke to find the scorpion mural defaced and she had gone."

I narrowed my eyes at Meraset angrily.   Before I was aware of my action, I clenched my fists and dashed towards her. I grabbed her arms angrily and growled at her. "Are you saying you knew what Azizi and I would encounter down there and you never warned us about it?"

"The scorpion mural stated everything that needed to be said. I need not have warned you."

My knuckles turned white from the tight grip on the woman's arms. "If Azizi dies, I will blame you!"

"Isis will decide whether to tighten his throat."

I released Meraset angrily.

"If the priestess knew there was a scorpion, she wouldn't want to confront it herself.   She wouldn't have stood a chance.   Perhaps she was hoping Runihura would come here himself to retrieve the Scroll and the Circlet." My head began to ache. The journey through the catacombs and the battle had taken their toll on my mind.

Meraset stood before the teen. "You are tired, Master Al-Sakhir. You must return to your bedroom and rest."

I rubbed my temples lightly. "Tell me one thing before I lay down. If Isis is a central goddess of Heliopolis, why is the Scroll here in Karnak and not laying in a temple in *Iunu*, *Khasekhemwy*, or *Mer-Yet-Re*?"

"Men-Kheper-Re arrived here two hundred years ago and fought a great battle here at Karnak. His scribe, Thanuny, chronicled his exploits and his worship of Amun. Ten suns after his departure from your land did he arrive in Gaza to battle the rebellious prince of Kadesh. For five moons did he conquer Cilicia and so did he bring the Scroll of Isis to Karnak for protection."

"Why protection?"

"Maatkare, Great King's Wife of Akheperenre, claimed that she was conceived by Amun himself. She tried to remove all mention of the other gods of Heliopolis besides Amun-Re. The priesthood, in conjuncture with the young prince, decided to move the Scroll of Isis here should the queen decide to destroy it since it was not made by the hand of Rā."

I grabbed onto the chair beside me as the room began to spin. The Scroll of Isis slipped from my hands.

Meraset grabbed the scroll and held my arm. "You must be exhausted after your trial. Let me help you back to bed."

I could barely keep my eyes open as she lead me down the hallway. "You rest. I will wake you for the evening meal."

I laid on the bed and felt my body relax against the soft bed of feathers and linen. I wanted to roll onto my back, but felt too tired to perform that simple movement. My eyes opened and closed tiredly as I watched Azizi in the bed.

The thief's chest rose and fell quickly and sharply. Azizi's thin arm dangled from the bed almost reaching towards me. The sunlight peaking through the room made the sweat on Azizi's skin sparkle like diamonds. His black, wavy hair was wet as if he had stuck his head into the fountain at the bottom of the temple steps.

"Azizi? Are you awake?"

I watched as the fingers twitched. "I'm right here. I haven't left." His hand was cold and wet as I took Azizi's hand in mine. I wondered why I had never seen the signs of the fever. Then I figured it out. His rashes were hidden by his cape. Azizi never complained about being ill. Did he not wish to worry me? A blister on his arm looks like it's going to burst. Its white bubble raised above the skin while the blister beside it appeared covered in a sickly crust.

"Fight, Azizi. I will be right beside you." I watched as Azizi's breathing slightly calmed itself. "Always."

XXV

Gahiji's Sacrifice

Runihura poured the red liquid into his golden chalice resting upon the altar of Sekhmet. Semerkhet had consecrated the libation given him by the soldier who had failed to obtain the Scroll of Isis. Runihura sipped the bitter fluid and licked his lips. "May Sekhmet enjoy the taste of Azizi's blood."

"The dead has been adorned with a black wig sewn to his skin. He has also been dressed in appropriate attire to be shown to the crowd, my lord."

"I will be hailed as a hero by the Nobility for ridding the streets of a major threat. Petty thieves will be unorganized without their leader. Heliopolis is now safe for the rich to walk her streets."

Semerkhet took the half-empty cup of blood from Runihura and placed it before the statue of Sekhmet. "Gahiji has done a great service to his people by offering his life to eliminate Azizi Keket."

"Gahiji failed me, High Priest! He was an incompetent baboon! He couldn't kill a simple child the first time and he failed to return the Scroll of Isis to me. I hardly call that a great service," Runihura said, sitting on his golden throne. "His only accomplishment was killing the boy Azizi Keket."

Semerkhet smiled. "At least the boy is dead, sire."

"Now I have to contend with Amsi Al-Sakhir.   Nobody seems to know what has become of him."

"Perhaps he will perish in the desert. The jackals will make a feast of his corpse."

Semerkhet watched as the dead soldier's body was dragged into the room by Wosenret.   With a thud, Wosenret casually dropped the body on the floor.   Runihura pleasantly smiled as he approached the corpse. He kneeled down and examined the corpse's severed wrists. "Tell the Royal butcher that he did a thorough job and he will find additional coin in his purse for pleasing me."

"Are you certain this will work?" Ife asked as she stepped into the throne room with her slave.

Wosenret flipped the corpse onto its back.   Wide-eyes were frozen in time as they looked at the ceiling lifelessly.   "A black wig and some torn clothing will fool the masses.   Our soldiers have seen the capes worn by the thief clan."

Ife crossed her arms. "What of my future husband, Amsi Al-Sakhir?"

"Our soldiers have not seen the renegade Al-Sakhir.   The desert must have taken his breath," Runihura said casually.   "It matters not. What does matter is peace can now be restored to Heliopolis. Without the King of Thieves to coordinate their efforts, the criminal world of *Iunu* shall fall into disarray.   Children of the streets will have no one to turn to teach them lechery."

"Are you certain of this, my lord?" Ife asked. "What if the poor use this as a reason to revolt against your greatness?"

Runihura chuckled. "Fifteen years ago, the citizens of *Iunu* did not stand a chance against my mighty army. They are merchants and menial workers. They do not know the ways of war and combat. They will easily fall beneath my mighty fist." Runihura kneeled beside the corpse and caressed the cold cheek tenderly. "I shall make the streets of Heliopolis safe once more and eliminate all who stand in my way."

*　　*　　*

A flock of street children ran through the crowded streets of *Iunu* towards Central Square.

Saqr accidentally knocked into a man carrying a basket of smoked meat. "Sorry!" the nine-year-old boy called behind him.

"Watch where you're going, you little runt!"

Giladi giggled as he passed Khalil in their race. "Goodbye, Khalil!"

Jamila rushed from an alley ahead of Khalil. "I'll make it to the square first, Khalil!"

Khalil grit his teeth as he caught up to the thirteen-year-old girl. When the square was in sight, Khalil jumped forward and somersaulted on the ground. The boy laughed as he rose to his feet. "Khalil wins!"

Saqr and Giladi arrived at the square panting heavily. "We'll get you next time," Saqr said.

Jamila looked towards the rooftops for the Osirian archers.   Qeb, Nassar, and Carim were perched above the seamstress shop.   The young men sat with their bows leaning against their chests.   "Over there," Jamila said, taking Saqr's hand. She lead the group of orphans towards the gathering of the Osiris Clan.   Aneksi stood in front of the seamstress shop beside Darwishi and Halimah.

Sekani happily welcomed his little brothers Saqr and Khalil when they arrived. Khalil excitedly jumped up and down telling the tale of his racing victory over Giladi, Jamila, and Saqr.

Darwishi's eyes narrowed as he saw the Seth Thief Clan walk into Central Square as a group.   Kaphiri lead the pack with his father, Amari.   Gold jewelry and black leather cuffs adorned his arms. Their red capes flowed behind them. "The filthy swine have arrived," Darwishi growled with disdain. Saqr shifted close to his brother and clutched onto his leg.

Marid and Chakir looked in their direction and made an insulting gesture with their hands.   Qasim and Hairdar laughed at the insult.

"They are trying to incite us into combat," Aneksi said, taking hold of Darwishi's cape. "Do not retaliate."

"I should remove their hands for their insult!"

Sekani shook his head. "Darwishi, no! This place is crawling with soldiers and starting a battle here is foolish."

"It's never too young for these children to learn how to fight their enemy!"

Saqr shook his head vehemently. "I don't want to fight!"

"Darwishi, don't do this," Khalil pleaded.

Ini-Herit and Hairdar calmly walked towards the Osiris Clan. Nassar and Qeb loaded their bows, ready to strike. Ini-Herit stopped Hairdar from advancing. "Ho, Death-Worshippers! Where is your king?"

"You go away!" Saqr yelled at the muscular enemy.

Hairdar laughed as he tapped his club against his hand. "Do you want to come here and say that, whelp?"

Ini-Herit slammed his open fist into his other hand with a grin. "Hey, little boy, do you want to play a game with Hairdar and I?"

Saqr gasped and clutched tighter onto his big brother's leg. "No?"

"Get away from here!" Sekani growled. "You're only proving how much of a coward you are by tormenting a nine-year-old boy!"

Ini-Herit growled angrily. "Nobody calls Ini-Herit Seti a coward! You will pay for that remark, vile worm!"

"Ini-Herit, are you causing trouble?" Kaphiri asked as he calmly joined his clan members. "We shouldn't cause them grief today, for there will much grieving to be done by them today."

Giladi stepped in front of Sekani. "What are you talking about?"

Kaphiri chuckled. "A little piggy has told me a little secret in the streets of *Khasekhemwy*. You will find out in time. As for us, we have a celebration planned tonight on this glorious night of Seth's victory over his brother, Osiris."

"Leave now or you shall find yourself floating in pieces down the Nile," Darwishi growled.

The Seth Leader chuckled. "Just you wait, Darwishi. Tonight, Seth will celebrate his victory and rise to eliminate the competition in *Iunu*."

Kaphiri lead his clan members towards the Inn where they sat waiting for the announcement to begin. Nassar and Qeb relaxed, unloading their bows.

Mbizi lead the women into Central Square. Kahla stepped away from the group of women and made her way through the crowd to the Osiris Clan. Nassar saw Kaemwaset and Imani arrive in their gold chariot. His identical twin walked beside Imani. *I want to call out to Mistress Imani, but if I do so, Kaemwaset will see me. It's best for him to believe that I am dead.*

Kahla stood before Aneksi and Darwishi. "Does anyone know why we were summoned here?"

Aneksi lowered her head mournfully. A tear fell down her cheek. "What I feared has come to pass."

Kahla looked at Aneksi. "What did you fear, my lady?"

Halimah lowered her head solemnly. Aneksi shook her head. Kahla watched as the face of the clan leaders grow grim.

Kahla swallowed nervously. "What has happened?"

"I have prayed to Osiris that he would not grant Azizi entrance into the Land of the Dead. How I wish I was not cursed with this affliction!"

What has happened to Azizi? Has he returned? I pray every night that he returns to us safe. It is unusual for Aneksi to be so distraught. Kahla stepped towards Aneksi. "What has happened to our Lord?"

"Loyal subjects!" Pharaoh Runihura stepped onto his balcony, eliciting a combination of angry shouts and ecstatic cheers from the crowd. Wosenret and High Priest Semerkhet stood beside the pharaoh. "I have come before you this day with glorious news! Wosenret has been appointed Royal General of the Guard. General Gahiji has sacrificed his life in a great deed that shall be recorded in history's texts! Gahiji has given his life for the protection of the people of Heliopolis!"

Giladi crossed his arms defiantly. "He was nothing but a big bully."

"I've watched him through the gates of the arena and he wasn't very nice," Saqr added.

"Gahiji's statues shall record his sacrifice for future generations! Ten days shall Heliopolis mourn for her deep loss."

Qeb rolled his eyes. "I doubt his feelings of remorse, Nassar."

Nassar nodded. "I agee. He if a big wiar."

"What has Gahiji done to protect the citizens of Heliopolis? What indeed has this selfless man done to eliminate a threat to your safety and security?"

Khalil looked at the pharaoh and swallowed nervously. "Big brother, what is he talking about?"

Sekani put his hands on Khalil and Saqr's shoulders. "Stay with me, boys."

Kahla watched his horror as Wosenret held a caped figure into the air by its hair. Black hair dangled from the corpse's head. The black cape was torn from the figure and tossed below into the crowd.

"Citizens of Heliopolis! Azizi Keket, the King of Thieves, has been slain by General Gahiji!"

Many of the citizenry cheered with victory, hugging each other and raising their fists in the air. Other citizens threw dirt over their heads in mourning. Nassar watched as Kaemwaset clapped his hands in the air. The former slave's lip curled with fury.

Kahla gasped with horror and covered her mouth. Tears rained from her eyes as she began to tremble. *Azizi, my love! No. He can't be dead. Azizi...*

Saqr and Khalil began to cry against their brother. Sekani lowered his head and kneeled on the ground. He brought his little brothers into his arms as he tried to remain strong for them. Saqr sobbed into his brother's shoulder.

"Seth is victorious!" Kaphiri screamed into the air, holding his fists in the air. "Long live the God of Chaos and Disorder!"

Pharaoh Runihura grabbed his golden dagger and stabbed the corpse repeatedly. Giladi cried as he watched the desecration of the corpse. Halimah brought the crying boy against her and embraced him.

Aneksi wailed loudly into the air as she saw the crowd tearing apart the fallen black cape. "Their bond could not keep them together. The Anointed Companion of Rā has made his decision to follow the darkness in his father's heart. All is lost for the people of *Iunu*."

"May celebrations spread across Heliopolis! May the beer flow in rivers tonight!" Runihura exclaimed merrily. "Beautiful women, remove your linens and dance! Make merry in the streets for a great service has been done!"

Kaemwaset heard mournful wailing come from the seamstress shop and he turned his head. Above the shop sat a familiar face with a tattoo on his left chest. Kaemwaset narrowed his eyes, trying to focus on the figure. He broke from Imani's side.

Nakia turned his head to see his master leave his side. *What is he doing?* Nakia saw his twin perched above the seamstress shop with Qeb. *He's going to recognize Nassar!*

"Master Kaemwaset! Wait!" Nakia called after his owner.

Kaemwaset watched the figure on the roof closely as he pushed his way through the mourning and cheering crowd. *Nassar?*

Nakia reached Kaemwaset and stood in front of him. *I have to distract him from Nassar!* "Sir, you shouldn't leave your wife with all these thieves around!"

Nassar put his arm around Qeb to comfort the quiet archer. "Bon't cry, Qeb."

"His brave soul rests with Osiris," Qeb said sadly.

That is Nassar! I thought I killed him! I cut him like a sacrificial offering myself! How did he live? Kaemwaset narrowed his eyes and grabbed Nakia by the throat. "Nakia, did you know of his survival and you never told me?"

Nakia grabbed Kaemwaset's wrist and gasped for breath. "Yes."

The Noble pulled Nakia close to him. "That was a big mistake." Kaemwaset pulled Nakia towards the carriage.

Imani folded her hands before her anxiously. *What of my son? Where is Amsi? I know the boys sailed together. If he escaped General Gahiji, where is he? Could he be in the desert? Perhaps the Great Sea has swallowed him. Where is my beloved Amsi?* Imani saw Kaemwaset pulling Nakia towards the chariot angrily. "Release him at once!"

"Get in the chariot! We are leaving!"

"What about my son?   Perhaps the pharaoh will say something about our son."

Kaemwaset threw Nakia into the carriage and turned his head to Imani.

Imani gasped as tears pooled in her eyes. "What of our son, Kaemwaset?"

"Our son is dead! Get in the carriage!"

"Why did you not tell me before? What fate has befallen him?"

Kaemwaset and Imani locked eyes as Nakia panted heavily draped over his seat. Kaemwaset approached his wife. He brought her into his arms and hugged her tightly. "Amsi had escaped and became lost in the desert."

Imani sniffled. "But he had our boat. He wasn't traveling through the desert." Kaemwaset watched as Imani stepped backward from him. "You knew that, did you not? Why would he travel through the desert if he had our boat?" Imani watched as Kaemwaset lowered his head solemnly. "What have you done to your only son, Kaemwaset Al-Sakhir?"

"I didn't do anything, Imani! Why are you blaming me for his death?"

Imani walked past Kaemwaset and helped Nakia into his seat. "Nakia, we're going home." Kaemwaset walked to the carriage, but Imani held her hand out in warning. "You shall walk home!"

Nakia swallowed nervously as he saw his master's face turn red. *This won't end well.*

"I bought that carriage with my money! You can't leave without me!" Kaemwaset bellowed.

Nassar turned his head at his former owner's furious voice. Nakia clutched his chest in the front seat.

"I am calling a doctor for Khentimentiu, too, Kaemwaset!" Imani growled.

"You shall not waste my money on hopeless cause!"

Imani laughed. "And I am going to give the slaves threefold their dues in food today!"

"You're going to ruin me, woman!" Kaemwaset growled as he punched the carriage.

"Nakia, let's leave," Imani said, closing the door of her carriage.

Kaemwaset raised his fists in the air. "Nakia, I swear on Rā's name, that if you drive this carriage away without me, you will be chained to the post for a moon's cycle!"

Nakia pulled back on the horses'reigns. "Munir and Hamza, go!"

Nassar laughed as Kaemwaset's carriage rode away without him. *I hope he enjoys the walk home. He could use the exercise.*

Kaemwaset fumed with anger as he turned around to watch Nassar laughing on the rooftop. *You will not be free for long, my little prodigal slave.*

XXVI

Return To Your Family

A shrill scream made him open his eyes in alarm. Amsi saw priestesses and the doctors surrounding Azizi's bed. The thief was invisible behind the wall of priestesses. He rolled out of bed quickly and raced beside the doctor.

The doctor was applying paste to the resisting patient's injury which had swollen, puffed, and now bubbled. Priestesses pinned Azizi's wrists and legs to the bed as the patient struggled and thrashed in place trying to free himself.

"What are you doing to him?" Amsi asked the doctor angrily.

"I'm applying powdered snake skin onto his injury."

"Is it necessary to restrain him?"

Azizi's violent thrashing slowly stopped as he rested on the bed. Amsi watched as the sweating, heavily-panting figure closed his eyes with exhaustion. A bead of sweat trickled down Azizi's neck.

Amsi kneeled beside Azizi's head and watched the thief gasp for air. "Release him."

Priestesses surrounding the convalescent teen released his limbs and backed away. Azizi turned his head toward Amsi. "Morning."

"The doctor only wants to help you. He knows what is best."

"Your friend punched me in the face," the doctor said.

Azizi licked his parched lips as he gasped for breath. "He wouldn't go away."

"Don't you want the pain to leave you?"

Azizi gave his friend a small smile. "Never been to doctor."

The doctor stepped backward and recited a final prayer to Isis to remove the poison from Azizi's injury. When he finished, the priestesses followed him out of the room. Amsi took a cup of water and slowly brought it to his friend's lips. He supported Azizi's head to prevent the thief from choking on the water. Amsi watched as Azizi sipped the cold liquid quickly and acknowledged a small smile of gratitude from the other teen.

Azizi exhaled a puff of breath and closed his eyes. Amsi could see pain clearly on the thief's face. Amsi sat beside Azizi and took his friend's hand. "We're going home today. Minoru is gathering supplies for our journey."

Azizi sighed. "I want to see Kahla. Can you take me to Kahla?"

"Mbizi will turn you into the pharaoh. Why do you want to see her?"

Azizi looked into Amsi's eyes. "Because I love her."

Amsi sighed as he looked down at Azizi's hand. The teen caressed Azizi's hand with his thumb, taking care to avoid developing sores. "Azizi, I would be handing you into the hands of the pharaoh."

Azizi brought Amsi's hand to his chest. "As my best friend, my partner, my brother, please let me see her."

Amsi felt Azizi's cold, clammy chest. He could feel Azizi's heart racing wildly under his palm. "I can't deny your wishes. I will let you see Kahla. I promise that I will find a way to cure this disease. I won't let you die."

The thief closed his eyes and relaxed in bed. "Let's hope we're not too late."

"You rest. When Minoru and I have gathered our supplies and procured our boat, we leave." Amsi left the room and sighed. *Rā's blessings are great.* He walked down the hall towards the main chamber. As he walked toward the door, he stopped.

Amsi turned slowly towards the large stone statue of Isis. Her left arm was cross over her chest as her eyes stared ahead of her at some invisible object. Flowers lined the base of the statue as well as incense, coins, and other offerings of Karnak's citizens. *When Rā was stung by her sacred serpent, Isis 'words of magic and from her mouth came the breath of life. When that scorpion stung Azizi, I thought it was over for him. When I bit into the tail of the scorpion, I thought I wouldn't survive either. It is my hope that her words can heal the sick of* Iunu *and cure the disease which has claimed the lives of so many.*

Amsi ran out of the temple, finding Minoru haggling with the breadmaker. Minoru procured bread as Amsi stood beside him. "Master Amsi, I have bread and the priestesses have obtained necessary medical provisions for your friend during our journey."

"Have you found a boat for us?"

"I do not have money for that."

Amsi nodded as he looked around for the Boatwright. "I will find us a boat. We leave at high sun."

* * *

Sekani held his brother's hands as they walked beside Nassar. Khalil gripped his ball in his free hand, his eyes watching the ground where his bare feet touched. Saqr quickly stepped closer to his brother's side to avoid being stepped upon by passers-by. Three figures in the distance followed them silently.

"I can't believe he's gone," Sekani said in disbelief.

"I hope Maffer Am-i comes back," Nassar added.

Khalil looked up at Nassar. "Do you think he's alive?"

Nassar sighed with a silent shrug. Sekani stopped before the alley he and his brothers had called home for nine years.

"Nassar, could you please watch my brothers while I find some dinner for them? The shops are empty now and nobody will see me. I'll give you my ration if you would help."

Nassar saw the two little children look up at him with pleading eyes. Kaphiri's Clan would not give up the chance at eliminating their competition for food and money pouches. Nassar nodded as he saw Khalil enter the alley and sit on the ground, clutching his ball to his chest. Saqr ran to his brother and squatted in front of him. The younger boy put his hand on Khalil's shoulder, trying to cheer him up.

Sekani walked over to Khalil and caressed the boy's side-lock. "I will be back soon."

Khalil wrapped his arms tightly around Sekani's leg. "Don't go!"

"If I don't go now, you and Saqr might not eat tonight. Nassar will keep a good eye on you."

Khalil looked warily at Nassar and released his brother. "Alright."

"Saqr, stay here this time. No running off."

"Yes, big brother!"

Sekani pat Nassar on the back. "Thank you, my friend. Keep an eye on the little one. He's known to just vanish. He'll stay with you if you play with him."

Saqr crossed his arms. "A good thief needs to vanish at any time!"

"Not when the Seth Clan is out and about," Sekani said sternly before looking around the streets for Kaphiri's clan or soldiers. When he saw none nearby, Sekani ran down the road to the merchant bazaar.

Qasim peeked around the corner and watched Sekani run down the road. With a chuckle, Qasim stepped from the alley. "Sekani always disappears and reappears."

"That fool knows we are around! Why would he leave those infants alone?"

Falcon-eyes chuckled. "Because he thinks my slave can protect them."

Qasim drew his scimitar, its blade decorated with prayers to Seth. "How wrong he is!"

"Kaphiri will reward us greatly if we can eliminate two Osiris Clan members."

Kaemwaset stepped beside Qasim. "You will only get paid when I get Nassar back to my family lands."

"You better not cheat us out of money, old man, or you will need to be taught a lesson," Ini-Herit growled.

"Idogbe shall be avenged with the shedding of innocent blood," Qasim growled.

Ini-Herit and Qasim approached the alley cautiously.   Ini-Herit and Qasim approached the opposite end of the alley to prevent escape. Fifteen-year-old Qasim popped a date into his mouth and spit the seed onto the ground.   Ini-Herit cracked his knuckles with pleasure.

Kaemwaset slowly peeked an eye into the alley.   The little child crept toward Nassar, giggling impishly.   The boy reached for his wooden figure as Nassar tried to grab him.   Saqr jumped backward, giggling and bouncing on his feet excitedly.

Khalil sat against the wall of the alley hugging his ball tightly against his chest. His thin fingers caressed the hide of the toy. His eyes looked to the toy horse beside him. Khalil grabbed the rope and pulled the small object, watching the horse bounce up and down.

The youngest member of the Osiris Thief Clan watched as Nassar pretended to fall asleep. Kaemwaset watched the little boy tip-toe to the figure and place his hand on it. With a slow, cautious motion, he slid the toy from under Nassar's hand.

Nassar opened his eyes and grabbed the boy. "I gah you!" Nassar laughed as he hugged Saqr tightly. "Khalil! Help me!"

Khalil pulled the horse and watched it move, uninterested in his brother's game.

Saqr kicked his legs and squirmed in Nassar's arms. He slipped from the Nubian and stood beside him, grinning ear-to-ear. "I'm getting good at getting away, aren't I?"

"Yef, you are! You be a q-ick fief umday."

Saqr chuckled. "I'll be quick like the west wind!

"You'll need to be faster than that to escape from us," Qasim chuckled as he stepped into the alley beside Ini-Herit.

Khalil's head snapped up from his toy and he jumped to his feet. Saqr ran to Khalil when he saw Ini-Herit cracking his massive fists. "Sekani!" Khalil wrapped his arms around his little brother.

"He's long gone, boy," Kaemwaset said, blocking the only other route of escape.

Nassar gasped when he saw his former master approaching him. "Maffer Kaemwa-et!"

"So, you didn't die by my hand, Nassar. You escape the chains of slavery to babysit some feral children?"

"You ah mot my fami-y! You ah effiw!"

Saqr and Khalil whimpered as Ini-Herit and Qasim approached them from the end of the alley. "Sekani?" Saqr's voice quivered.

Qasim pointed his scimitar at the two young boys. "This is great! First the King of Thieves has been eliminated and now we have two little dead children from the Osiris Clan."

Saqr trembled as he cried. He looked up at the hovering enemy smiling down at him.

Ini-Herit restrained Nassar's arms and chuckled. "Kaphiri will be proud of us when he sees we have money and have eliminated two of our enemies."

"Weave fem awone!" Nassar exclaimed, stepping on his captor's foot.

Ini-Herit threw Nassar against the wall of the alley. Qasim chuckled as he glared at the two children.

Ini-Herit turned Nassar around and backhanded the slave, who fell to the ground unconscious. He turned around and looked at the two trembling children. "Kill them."

Khalil threw his ball in Qasim's face. He grabbed Saqr's hand and ran past Kaemwaset.

Qasim pushed Kaemwaset to the ground as he pursued the children.

The Noble grumbled as returned to his feet. "It's time to return to your family, boy."

XXVII

Solemn Promise

Amsi rowed with the Scroll of Isis unfurled on his lap. The stars above them were barely visible through gathering clouds. A gentle wind helped propel the craft along the shoreline. Amsi felt himself shiver in the night as a gust of cold wind brushed against his body. Gentle waves rippled against the boat's hull.

Amsi could tell Azizi was desperately trying to muffle his groans of pain. When asked about his discomfort, the thief would grit his teeth and say not to worry. Amsi could hear the thief struggling to breathe from the single shelter on the boat.

Minoru returned to Amsi's side and took his oar. "He's finally asleep."

"How is he?"

Minoru shook his head. "Pray for him. That is all that can be done."

Amsi gripped onto his oar tightly. "We must hurry. We have to find that relic."

"Do you know where it lies?"

Amsi looked down at the scroll. "It is in Heliopolis in the Temple of Hapi. Men-Kheper-Re separated the Scroll of Isis from Isis'relic to protect it from Maatkare. The priesthood and the young prince moved the scroll to Karnak, fearing the Great King's Wife would destroy it."

"Why would the Isis relic rest in a temple to a water god?" Minoru asked.

Amsi rowed faster. "The Temple had long been used as a temple to the Sun god and later to Thoth. However, the priesthood disbanded and the temple fell into disrepair. Over time, the Temple was rebuilt. Twenty years ago, the temple was consecrated to Hapi. Soon Pharaoh Runihura will disseminate that temple since it does not worship Sekhmet."

Minoru looked into the night. "Can a piece of metal cure the sickness in Heliopolis?"

"I have my doubts.   However, I had my doubts that Azizi would survive his injury.   If the Circlet of Isis does not save the people, I must find another way."

"What Zahra says of you is very accurate," Minoru said with a smile.

Amsi slowed his rowing and looked at the Bedouin teen. "What does she say of me?"

"She admires you for being brave and standing against the Demon in the royal palace."

Amsi chuckled nervously. "I'll have to thank her for her high opinion of me, but I'm just an ordinary person."

"Ordinary persons are capable of extraordinary feats and selfless acts. You risked your life to bring your friend out of the caverns below. You could have left him to die. Both you and him could have perished."

Amsi lowered his head. He gripped the oar so tight that his knuckles turned white.   "I know."   Amsi grabbed the scroll and stood. "I'm going to check on him."

Minoru grabbed Amsi's oar and proceeded to row.   Amsi entered the shelter and saw Azizi sleeping under several blankets.   Shadows hid Azizi's face from view as the thief slept.   Amsi reached toward Azizi's cheek and felt it damp with sweat.   Amsi gently dried Azizi's face with a cloth. A gasping breath from the thief informed him the other teen was still alive. *Divine Mother Isis, who gives the gift of breath shall save her children from Osiris'grip of death. Minoru says that I am brave. Azizi, you are braver than I. I can tell you are in more pain than you would want to admit to me. The only thing I can do for you is to break that Circlet. I will ensure that Pharaoh Runihura does not obtain the Circlet of Isis.* Amsi placed his hand on Azizi's chest. He could feel the thief panting heavily even during his sleep. A slow song from Minoru emanated from the bow of the boat. *You are brave. I know you can beat this, Azizi.* "I won't let you die," Amsi whispered. "I promised that I would not leave your side. I will fulfill that promise to the end." Amsi lowered his head. "I'm not going to let you perish without a fight. Common Thief or not, you are still my friend, my brother."

Amsi placed his hand lightly on Azizi's feverish forehead. "May Osiris bless you and Rā's healing fill your heart."

The Noble teen applied another unguent of crushed willow leaves, dung, and ibex grease to Azizi's chest. Amsi sighed and made certain the thief was tucked under the blankets. The Noble teen returned to the bow and washed his hands in the ocean.

"That unguent smells, but if it helps heal the diseased wound, it will be worth it," Amsi said.

Minoru continued to row. "I am amazed that you were willing to bite into the tail of a scorpion to save his life. Not many people would do such a dangerous feat. Weren't you afraid?"

Amsi splashed water on his face. "Is it not the highest honor of friendship to give one's life for a friend?"

Minoru nodded. "My father says to give one's life in service to another gives you an honored seat beside the gods."

Amsi sighed as he took his seat beside Minoru. "I wonder what my father is doing now."

"Your father has a temper. Xeres is convinced that he has demons inside of him."

Amsi nodded. "I have tried so hard to be a dutiful son, Minoru. I cannot please my father no matter how hard I try. I fear for my friends'safety in the slave home. When I arrive home, I do not know if my father will deny signing my death warrant or hand me to Pharaoh Runihura." Amsi turned to Minoru as he continued rowing. "If Pharaoh Runihura captures me, please tell Zahra that I shall think of her always."

"Do you believe the pharaoh will take you to his dungeon?"

"I don't know what will happen when we return home. All I do know is that I must find the Circlet of Isis within the Temple of Hapi." Amsi took a deep breath. "I hope Azizi can recover before then."

Minoru looked up at the stars. "If he has not perished before we reach Heliopolis, his chances of survival are greater. These first few suns are crucial to his recovery."

*   *   *

Khentimentiu held the cup in his hands as his father caressed his side-lock of youth. Qamra smiled as the little boy fed himself for the first time in days. Baruti wrapped his son in a blanket after Khenti handed his cup to his mother. "More, please!"

"That is your third cup of soup, my child," Qamra laughed. "You should get some sleep."

Baruti laid his son on his reed mat and kissed his cheek. "Sleep well, my boy."

Qamra kissed her son's cheek and placed his cup beside him. "What did the *Bedu* do for him?"

"They had given him a bitter tea and applied some liquids to his wounds. The *Bedu* said they encountered people becoming sick when exposed to livestock."

"Did they eliminate their livestock?"

Baruti shook his head. "They applied an ointment to their livestock to keep vermin from them. After they did so, their sick recovered. I have some that I'll place on our sheep and goats in the morning."

"Be careful," Qamra said, scooping some soup into a cup for Baruti. "I don't want our baby's father to get ill."

Baruti took the cup from Qamra and kissed her hand. "I'm just grateful I don't have to bury our son."

Qamra and Baruti raised their heads as they heard Imani's voice raised in anger. A series of intelligible screams filled the air. "Nassar!"

Qamra and Baruti ran out of the slave home towards the Al-Sakhir household. Nakia's loud, angry protests echoed through the air. Baruti saw a tall, muscular man hovering over Nakia and another figure.

"Kaemwaset, where did you find him?" Imani asked.

"This little insect thought he could escape from me!"

Baruti and Qamra ran to Nakia and gasped when they saw Nakia's twin laying unconscious in his brother's arms. "Nassar? Where have you been?"

"Take both of them to the stake," Kaemwaset growled. "They will learn a lesson!"

"You will not chain those boys, Kaemwaset! If I were you, I'd be more worried about your son!"

Kaemwaset glared at Imani. "I told you our son is dead!"

Qamra's eyes widened as she covered her mouth. "Master Amsi is dead?"

"Master Am-no, he can't be dead! I should have gone with him!" Nakia sobbed as he held onto his brother protectively.

"Kaemwaset, you shed no tears. Why?" Imani asked sorrowfully. "Why do you not shed tears for your son, your flesh and blood, whom you shall never see again?"

Kaemwaset took a deep breath. "My son has brought pain to my heart, but I did not kill him, Imani!"

Ini-Herit grabbed Nakia's arm. "I'll drag you first!"

Baruti lunged for Ini-Herit and punched the large man in the face. The slave brought his fist down upon the back of Ini-Herit's head, making the thief fall to the ground.

"Keep your hands off them!" Baruti growled.

"Baruti, take the twins to your home. Kaemwaset, we shall see Ipa-witu in the morning. I cannot live with a man who shows no remorse at his son's death."

Kaemwaset narrowed his eyes at Imani. "We are not going to Ipa-witu! You will not separate from our bond!   If you separate from me, your name will be soiled in the Nobility and you will receive nothing. Ipa-witu will see that you would not be able to provide for yourself let alone the slaves you wish to take with you."

"You are behind Master Amsi's death, aren't you, you jackal?" Baruti asked angrily.

Imani turned her back on her husband. "You are right, Kaemwaset."

Kaemwaset turned to Baruti. "Get everyone in the slave home, Baruti."

Baruti glared at Kaemwaset as the Nobleman stepped into his home. "Lecherous old fool," Baruti growled as he kneeled beside Nakia. "Let me carry him."

"Master Amsi, I should have went with him, Baruti. I failed."

"No, you didn't fail, Kelile. Master Amsi saved you from dying with him. Let's return to the home."

Baruti gathered Nassar in his arms and looked down at Ini-Herit. He carried Nassar into the home and set him on Nakia's mat. Nakia sat beside his brother.

"I tried to stop Kaemwaset from seeing him," Nakia said sadly.

"He'll be alright, Nakia."

Qamra caressed Nassar's cheek. She checked his skin for red patches and lesions. Baruti sat beside the burning fire, keeping a diligent eye on the cloth covering the entrance to the home.

XXVIII

Beloved of Seth

Aneksi eyes gazed into the fire solemnly. The hut echoed with a heavy silence as Osiris Clan members gathered. Darwishi crossed his arms as he stood beside the door. The large sentinel clenched his fists angrily. His teeth clenched together as a low growl rumbled in his throat. Carim sat before the fire sharpening his scimitar.

Qeb leaned against the wall with his bow resting against his chest. Giladi sniffled as he cuddled beside the archer. Qeb put his arm around the orphan protectively. The eleven-year-old put his head against Qeb's chest and cried. "Why, Qeb?"

"Our duty is not to ask why," Qeb whispered. "It is to continue living and honor the blessed dead."

A desperate knock sounded on the door. Darwishi opened the small sliding window and opened the door. Sekani ran into the hut and bowed his head. "Aneksi, I need your help. My little brothers are missing and I can't find them!"

"Perhaps they have wandered away to look for you," Carim said as he turned his blade to sharpen the edge.

"I left them with Nassar and when I returned to the alley, Nassar was gone!"

Qeb raised his head. "Nassar probably went with them. Maybe your brothers ran away again and Nassar pursued them to keep them out of trouble."

"Qeb, please help me find them! Carim, please help me!"

Another desperate knocking at the door made Darwishi check the window. When he opened the door, Halimah gripped her scythe in her hand. "The Seth Clan has been spotted in *Iunu*! They have broke into Nen-Re's bakery and are setting fire to any shop they see!"

Qeb grabbed his bow and narrowed his eyes. "Those sons of pigs dare destroy *Iunu*?"

Carim jumped to his feet and gripped his scimitar. "No doubt they are celebrating Azizi's death."

Aneksi rose to her feet and grabbed her club. "We cannot allow *Iunu* to fall into the hands of the Seth Clan. We must protect our territory."

Giladi rose to his feet and gripped onto Qeb's cape. "Take me with you!"

"Little one, you are safer here."

"Jamila is out there somewhere! We have to find her!"

Sekani took another club from Aneksi's corner. "I have to find my little brothers."

Darwishi unsheathed his two swords as he heard *Iunu* residents screaming. The bitter smell of smoke crept along the road. "For Azizi and *Iunu*!"

Darwishi lead the Osiris Clan into the streets. Giladi's nose wrinkled as he smelled burning wood. "Jamila! Where are you?"

"Saqr! Khalil!" Sekani called as he looked around in alarm.

Qeb watched as smoke bellowed into the air with flames reaching towards the stars. "Sweet Osiris!" Qeb exclaimed as he saw people scattering through the streets seeking shelter.

Halimah saw Amari raise his spear into the air and strike down a fleeing man.

"*Iunu* is now the land of Seth!" Amari exclaimed.

Darwishi raced down the street, raising his weapons high. Qeb turned towards an alley and climbed onto the roof of a home. He readied his weapon as he saw Kaphiri and other Seth Clan members slicing through the fleeing crowd.

Giladi huddled beneath a street cart as people raced through the streets. "Jamila! Saqr! Khalil!" Giladi jumped as he saw a woman fall beside him. He watched wide-eyed as people ran over the woman in panic. Giladi's heart beat wildly as he heard the woman scream and reach for him. The boy shifted away from her as metal clashed nearby.

Giladi gasped as a cracking bone silenced the woman.

The boy ran from the cart and pushed through the crowd to the alley he called home with Jamila. Giladi turned the corner and saw Marid chasing a woman down the alley.

Marid grabbed the fleeing woman's hair as Giladi raced towards him.

Giladi kicked Marid in the leg, making the woman's assailant release his grip.   Marid looked down at the child and growled at him. "Prepare to die, boy!"

Giladi slowly backed away from the man as the woman turned towards her assailant. Marid grabbed Giladi and brought him close to his face. "You have made a very deadly mistake, Osiris Clan member."

Marid grabbed the rope as Giladi kicked his attacker.   Marid slammed Giladi against a smoking wall and tied the rope around the child's neck. Giladi punched the man as the rope tightened around his throat. The wall began to glow with fire.

"You will either die by fire or strangulation, boy!"

The woman behind Marid grabbed a piece of fallen timber and smacked Marid's back. Marid dropped Giladi, who punched him between the legs.

"Let's go, Giladi!" the woman said, taking the boy's hand.

Giladi grabbed the end of his rope and ran away with the woman.
When they raced out of the alley, Giladi looked into Lakia's eyes.
Giladi smiled and threw himself at the woman. "Thank you!"

Lakia quickly removed the rope from the boy's neck and kissed him on
the cheek. "You shouldn't be here, Giladi! There are Seth Clan
members in *Iunu*."

"I can't find Jamila! She's my friend and I have to find her!"

"Giladi, you cannot be here!"

Lakia and Giladi raised their heads as thunder raced towards them.
Mounted soldiers raced down the street. Lakia grabbed Giladi and
raced down the street. Giladi breathed heavily as they turned the corner.
The fire in the quarter singed his throat as he breathed in hot air.

Giladi heard an angry man's growl followed by a shrill scream.
"Ini-Herit!"

Giladi raced down the alley as he saw Jamila on the ground. Giladi
raced towards Jamila and glared up at Ini-Herit. "You monster!"

Ini-Herit punched his open fist. "Good. A new punching bag has
arrived."

"What have you done to Jamila?"

"The same I will do to you, boy!"

"Giladi! Run!" Lakia called.

Ini-Herit swung his fist towards Giladi, but the boy jumped backward. Giladi punched Ini-Herit in the face as his body lowered to the ground. Giladi struck the man again and jumped on the man's back. He wrapped the rope around Ini-Herit's neck as the man reached behind him. Giladi held onto Ini-Herit tightly as he slipped the rope through the hole at the end. Giladi tightened the noose and pulled.

Ini-Herit stood and quickly twisted his body side-to-side to throw the child from his shoulders. Giladi yanked tightly on the rope as Ini-Herit's fists flew wildly around him.

"Lakia, get Jamila away from here!" Giladi yelled as he tugged on the rope.

Lakia gathered the girl in her arms and carried her away from the alley.

Giladi heard women screaming down the road as he tightened his grip on the rope. His victim's struggle became less vigorous. Choking sounds from his victim increased as Giladi wrapped his legs around Ini-Herit's neck. Ini-Herit's arms fell to his sides as the large man crumbled to his knees. Giladi heard Ini-Herit gagging through his constricted windpipe. His victim fell to the ground as Giladi rolled onto the ground.

The eleven-year-old laid on the ground breathing heavily and trembling as he held the end of his rope. "May...Osiris....welcome you." Giladi staggered to his feet as he grabbed his rope.

The boy ran down the alley as he heard the women screaming at Mbizi's. Tabora and Thana raced out of the bordello as Hairdar grabbed them. Giladi watched in horror as Hairdar's dagger sliced through Tabora. Tabora fell to the ground as Hairdar grabbed the little girl.

"Seth welcomes you," Hairdar grinned.

Giladi saw Aneksi racing towards Hairdar with her club raised. Hairdar dropped the little girl as Giladi raced towards her.

"Where are Saqr and Khalil?" Aneksi asked as she battled Hairdar.

Hairdar chuckled. "They belong to us now!"

Giladi heard women screaming on the top level of the bordello.

"Giladi, take the little girl and run!" Aneksi growled as she gripped her club angrily.

Giladi took Thana's hand and raced her away from the bordello.

"Help! Somebody!" Kahla and Maysun screamed above.

"*Iunu* belongs to the Seth Clan! All worship Seth for he is mighty!" Kaphiri screamed from the top floor.

Egyptian soldiers ran towards Aneksi and Hairdar. Aneksi dashed out of the way as the soldiers grabbed Hairdar. Giladi threw himself at Aneksi and held onto her tightly.

"Aneksi!" Giladi sobbed as the woman's arms wrapped around him. "We have to rescue Saqr and Khalil!" Giladi froze as a woman's blood-curdling scream resonated from the top floor of the bordello. The eleven-year-old startled as a building crashed to the ground beside them.

"We'll get them back, Giladi. Let's go, children," Aneksi said, taking Giladi and Thana's hands.

*   *   *

Pharaoh Runihura glared at the merchant quarter below. Thick, black smoke dissipated into the air, giving it a bitter scent that stung his nose. The pharaoh's lip curled in a grin. *I need not raise a finger to destroy those miserable wretches. They will simply destroy themselves! How convenient!*

Neka and Janani flanked the pharaoh on the balcony as a chorus of panicked and pain-filled screams rose into the night sky. Neka folded his hands against his chest and bowed his head. "This is terrible, Janani."

Runihura chuckled. "How do you suppose this is terrible, Neka? Their screams are like the songs of birds, beautiful and melodious. Musicians could not make better melody."

Janani turned her head in disgust. "Those people are dying, my lord! It is terrifying!"

Neka's eyes focused at the orange-red flames rising above the city. The sixteen-year-old's eyes struggled to peer through the heavy smoke towards the home of his family.

"This can't be happening," Neka said as his voice cracked with sorrow.

"This will be the perfect catalyst for my plan," Runihura said as he put his arm around Neka's shoulder. "These little pests will destroy themselves. Besides, Neka, why should you mourn for them?" Runihura turned his head and kissed Neka's ear. "Your family sold you to me for nothing more than the price of a stale loaf of bread. You should be enjoying the entertainment these rats have created."

A chill of repulsion crawled up Neka's spine as the pharaoh chuckled in his ear. "Listen to their screams, Neka. Smell the scent of burning wood, savor the aroma of scorched earth, and indulge in the hymn of their plea to Rā for deliverance."

Janani watched as Neka tried to step away from the pharaoh, but the pharaoh tightened his grip on Neka's arm. Runihura chuckled as his vice grip on Neka intensified.

Janani looked towards the gate where two soldiers were dragging a man behind their horses. "My lord, the soldiers have captured a man!"

The pharaoh's attention diverted from the shaken slave, much to Neka's relief. "Bring him to me!"

Runihura heard a roar in the distance as several buildings collapsed from the spread of the fire. "Tomorrow, you and Neka will ride with me through the quarter and see what is left. I'd like to see the devastation for myself."

Runihura continued to watch the chaos below until two soldiers dragged the captive into the pharaoh's presence. Runihura turned as he watched the captive be thrown to the ground. "What is your name?"

The captive tried to rise to his feet as the soldiers pushed him onto the ground again.

"My name is Hairdar Seti."

Runihura slowly approached the red-caped captive. "Have you caused mayhem within the boarder of my territory?"

Hairdar grinned and chuckled low in his throat. "I owe no allegiance to a follower of Sekhmet. Seth is mightier than thou."

The two soldiers kicked the bound Hairdar onto the ground. "Hold your tongue before your god-king!"

Runihura chuckled. "So, you worship the god of chaos, do you? Well, Hairdar, tell me why you have decided to send so many to the Underworld this night?"

Hairdar rose to his knees and chuckled. "Azizi Keket is dead. My clan brothers found a perfect opportunity to take what is rightfully ours.

How could we pass up this opportunity to strike at our enemies and expand our territory?"

"So you are a member of the Seth Thief Clan, are you? Well, I have heard of the battle you wage with the other thief clans within the boarders of *Iunu*. Forever do you battle with them like Seth with his brother, Osiris."

"They are our sworn enemy and we will never relinquish our territory to a bunch of death-worshippers!"

Runihura tapped his chin with deep thought. "In which quarter does your clan reside?"

"*Khasekhemwy* is where our territory lies. Skilled artisans and craftsman reside in our quarter, lining our pockets with much coin."

"Tell me, Hairdar, what spoils have you gained thus far from your siege before my soldiers dragged you into my magnificent presence?"

Janani and Neka exchanged disgusted glances. Neka's nose wrinkled with repulsion and shivered, still feeling the pharaoh's hand on him from a distance.

Hairdar laughed. "We have two young captives from the Osiris Thief Clan. They are very good boys."

"I would be willing to help your clan destroy your rivals," Runihura said as he turned his back on Hairdar and watched the flames lick the night sky. "However, you must accept my conditions."

Hairdar narrowed his eyes at the pharaoh. "Why would we want to accept your help?"

"Isn't it obvious, you dumb mule? I can provide you with soldiers and arms."

"What if I refuse?"

Runihura turned his head to look at Hairdar with one golden eye. "I kill you instantly."

Runihura turned to Hairdar, his golden eyes glowing brightly. "You will accept my terms without question."

Hairdar's eyes widened as he felt a powerful force grip his mind. His world around him evaporated into mist, his will quickly disappearing into one goal-to please the pharaoh-god. "Yes, my lord, I will accept your demands."

"You will take me to see the ones you have captured."

Hairdar bowed his head. "Yes, my lord."

"Take him to the dungeon for the night. For he and I will travel together in the morning."

Runihura turned toward the burning city. A grin crossed the pharaoh's lips as he put his arm around Janani. "Could this night become any more perfect?"

Neka watched the pharaoh kiss Janani's lips from the corner of his eye and shuddered in revulsion.

XXIX

The King of Thieves Returns

Amsi watched as Tunis came into view beside the boat.   Amsi kept his face wrapped in white material to hide his identity from the fishermen casting their nets into the Nile.   Fishermen bowed their heads toward the Noble passing by their boats. Minoru rowed the boat by himself against the Nile's current.

I have to keep my return a secret should anyone warn my father of my return. So far, everyone is falling for my plan.

"Amsi?"

Amsi turned and disappeared into the shelter.   The Noble teen unwrapped the material covering his mouth.

Azizi looked up at his friend, his face dripping with perspiration. "Where am I?"

"We are almost home," Amsi said, drying Azizi's face with a soft cloth. "How do you feel, Aziz?"

"Home?" Azizi asked tiredly. The teen's head turned listlessly to the side. "I thought we were at the Temple of Isis."

Amsi nodded. "You have had a terrible fever for days from your infected wound, Azizi. Minoru and I have been applying medicine to your wounds and feeding you. Do you not remember?"

Azizi slowly turned his head to Amsi. "You? You fed me?"

Amsi nodded. "I couldn't let you starve."

"Why did you not toss me overboard?"

"Why would I want to do that? I told you that I would not let you die. I promised I would not leave your side."

Azizi reached toward Amsi's chest and placed his sweaty hand lightly on Amsi's skin. "Thank you. You are a true friend."

Amsi smiled and placed his hand on Azizi's forehead. "You would have done no less for me. Let me help you up."

Amsi grabbed Azizi's hand and helped the thief to his feet. Azizi held onto Amsi's shoulders as his legs trembled beneath him. Amsi felt his friend's fingernails dig into his skin as he struggled to keep his balance.

Azizi looked at his bandaged chest and wrinkled his nose at the stench. "Couldn't you put one of your sweet-smelling perfumes on there to keep it from smelling like death?"

"I did. There's nothing more I can add to the linen that will make it smell less repulsive. Your wound had become infected and diseased. The physician made enough unguent if we needed more on our journey."

Azizi sighed. "I owe you my life, my friend. I could never repay you enough."

Amsi hugged Azizi and smiled. "Your fever has broken and Rā has answered my prayers for your recovery. That is all the reward I need." Amsi reached to the ground and wrapped Azizi's black cape around his neck. He tied the rope around Azizi's neck and nodded. "Let's return home and stop Runihura."

Azizi watched Amsi wrap his face with the white linen and return behind Minoru. *I owe Amsi my life. Does he know what he has done? If befriending a thief is punishable by death, saving one from death's cold clutches could be eternal damnation. Who else would aspire to commit such an act of mercy?* Azizi lowered his head. *Kaemwaset is blind to the caring person his son has become. Would Kaemwaset still condemn his son to death knowing he has saved another human being? Yes. Kaemwaset would only see that his son has saved a thief...an enemy of the pharaoh.*

Azizi placed his black hood over his head and stepped from the shelter. As he stood beside Amsi, his nose wrinkled from a bitter scent in the air. He watched Minoru shake his head as he continued to row the boat.

"The air is most foul," Minoru said.

Azizi raised his hood to see light smoke wafting into the air from Heliopolis. "Blessed Osiris, what has happened?"

Amsi swallowed nervously. "I don't know, but it doesn't look promising."

The teens watched as the boat slowly came to port.   Qamra was kneeling beside the Nile with the twins beside her.   A pile of laundry laid beside Nassar. Amsi watched Nakia and Nassar rise to their feet quickly.

Amsi made a noose for the dock and tied the rope around the post. Qamra stood and watched in disbelief as Amsi stepped off the boat.

"Master Amsi!" Nakia squealed excitedly as he ran to embrace his long-absent owner.

"Worg A-ee-ee!" Nassar smiled as he rushed to Azizi. "Where haff you beem?"

Azizi pat Nassar on the arm. "How is the clan?"

Qamra stepped forward toward Azizi. "There was smoke rising into the night.   We don't know how your clan has fared."

"What happened?" Amsi asked.

"Maffer Kaemwa-et cap-kure me an bing me back to hif wand."

Azizi raised a curious eyebrow. "What?"

"Master Kaemwaset captured Nassar about a week ago and brought him back to the Al-Sakhir lands."

Azizi saw a bandage around Nassar's right arm. "What did he do to you?"

Nassar lowered his head. "He burmed off my mark."

Azizi narrowed his eyes and growled. "That man will pay for this!"

Nakia released Amsi and kneeled before him. Amsi watched his slave bow his head and begin to cry. The slave's ribs stuck more prominently from his sides. "Master Amsi, we thought you were dead," Nakia sobbed into his hands. "I mourned you as I mourned my brother. I have not eaten. I have not slept. I have only prayed for your spirit."

Amsi kneeled in front of Nakia and hugged his servant. "I missed you, Nakia. Don't cry for me. Be cheerful, for I have returned."

Nakia wrapped his arms around Amsi and sobbed into his friend's shoulder. "Master Amsi, welcome home, my glorious Lord."

Azizi turned to Qamra. "I'm taking Nassar with me."

"No, you can't, Azizi!" Qamra exclaimed.

Azizi narrowed his eyes at Qamra. "You can't tell me what to do! Nassar belongs with my clan."

"Master Azizi, if Nassar does not return with us, Kaemwaset will do something horrible!"

"That beast does not frighten me!" Azizi snarled at the slave. "What can he do to me?"

Nakia shook his head. "It's not about what he would do to you, but to everyone."

Amsi rose to his feet. "What do you mean?"

Nakia looked up at his master. "Master Kaemwaset has gone mad, Master Amsi! He and your mother have given into vicious quarreling. They have gone to see Ipa-witu."

Amsi looked at his servant. "The man of law?"

Nakia nodded as he lowered his head. "I'm sorry, Master Amsi."

"Azizi, Nassar has to return with me."

Azizi folded his arms against his chest defiantly. "You would send your own servant into the hell from whence he escaped?"

"My father is capable of great cruelty!"

"Exactly why Nassar should return with me to the Osiris Clan!"

Amsi turned to Azizi. "My father has already tried to arrange my murder. I cannot allow my mother and my friends to suffer under his fist. I promise that Nassar will be alright."

"Nassar, do you wish to return with me to the clan?"

Nassar looked at his twin and Amsi. "My bruffer nee me."

Azizi snorted with derision. "Very well. Amsi, we have to get to the Temple of Hapi to retrieve the Circlet of Isis."

Minoru stepped off the boat and stood before Amsi. "Lord Al-Sakhir, I offer you my unending gratitude for saving my life. Come see us again and you will be rewarded for your bravery."

Amsi watched Minoru run towards the desert. "Qamra, please inform my mother of my return. Make certain my father does not know."

"Have you found a cure for the Red Fever, my lord?"

Amsi nodded. "Azizi and I must break the Circlet of Isis to beat the plague."

"The *Bedu* have helped Khentimentiu, who has fallen ill with the sickness."

Amsi gasped. "How is the boy?"

"Khenti has begun to eat again, but is still weak. Your father has burst into the home yelling at the boy to return to work. How can the boy work when he cannot eat and soils his blankets by the hour?"

Amsi watched as Azizi wavered on his feet. Qamra grabbed the thief before he could fall onto the ground.

"We cannot waste any more time," Azizi said. "We must make haste to the Temple of Hapi before it's too late."

Azizi and Amsi covered their heads as carts of corpses were carried towards them. Azizi turned his head as he and Amsi made their way towards the city. Amsi's nose wrinkled with the stench of death as they saw charred bodies placed along the banks of the Nile.

"What horror has happened in our absence, Azizi?" Amsi whispered.

"Something terrible. Kahla, I pray that you are safe."

Azizi and Amsi crossed the archway between the two Runihura colossi and watched with disbelief as crumbled buildings smoldered. Old women were mourning the dead and throwing dirt over their heads. Men were removing debris from the streets as children wandered aimlessly among the ruins of their homes.

Azizi walked towards Mbizi's bordello and saw Kahla standing outside, much to his relief. Azizi grabbed Amsi's wrist and weaved through the crowd toward her.

Kahla saw the two caped figures approach her and pull her into the bordello. Kahla struggled with the two men until Azizi removed his hood.

"Kahla, it's me!"

Kahla's tears fell down her cheek as she threw herself at Azizi and sobbed wildly. "Azizi, we all thought you were dead."

Azizi caressed Kahla's black hair and tried to soothe her with a kiss. "No, Kahla. I'm here now."

Kahla gripped onto Azizi's cape and trembled with fear. "Kaphiri's clan rampaged through *Iunu*. They set fires! They plundered! They killed Maysun and Tabora!"

Azizi narrowed his eyes and grit his teeth with fury. He clenched his fists in rage. "So Kaphiri is behind this madness! I'll kill him for this!"

Amsi saw a woman sitting on a chair quietly nearby. "Are you alright?"

The woman started to sob. "Maysun, how could you be dead?"

Amsi walked toward the woman and put a supportive hand on her shoulder.

Azizi turned his head. "Oraida, Kaphiri will pay for their deaths with his blood!"

"Thana is missing, Azizi," Kahla whimpered. "We can't find her. I pray Kaphiri's clan didn't kill the girl as she fled."

Azizi looked into Kahla's green eyes and caressed her cheek tenderly. "I will find her, beautiful."

Kahla's bottom lip trembled. "I've missed you so much, Azizi. Praise the gods you have come back."

Amsi watched Azizi press his lips against Kahla and kiss her gently. Kahla wrapped her arms around Azizi and cried softly into the kiss. Azizi's hands caressed her back and her cheek as they reunited. Azizi slowly and reluctantly pulled from the kiss.

"I must go, Kahla."

Kahla shook her head and held Azizi tightly against her. "Don't leave me, please!"

"I must. We still must obtain the Circlet of Isis before the pharaoh."

"Please come back tonight. I don't want to be alone."

Azizi nodded. "I will return tonight."

Kahla hesitantly withdrew from Azizi's embrace and wiped her eyes free of tears. "I love you."

Amsi's eyes widened at Kahla's profession.

"I love you, too, beautiful. Stay safe," Azizi said, caressing her cheek. "Time to go, Amsi."

Amsi and Azizi replaced their facial coverings and returned to the streets. Azizi watched women crying at the devastation around them. Some feral dogs were sniffing around Nen-Re's bakery for some salvageable scraps of food. The King of Thieves shook his head despondently. "These people had nothing before the fire. Now look at them, Amsi."

Amsi watched with pity as a young woman cried over the smoldering ashes of her house. "They have their lives. Human life cannot be replaced."

"I know Mbizi is trying to replace Tabora and Maysun." Azizi lowered his head. "Maysun shall be avenged, Amsi."

Amsi looked down at Azizi. "Didn't Maysun take care of you while your mother worked?"

Azizi nodded slowly. "Yes, Amsi. I shall miss her. I must do what I can for the people who have lost everything in the destruction. However, we have a job at the Temple of Hapi."

Amsi nodded. "Yes. I must return home before my mother comes looking for me."

"I'm worried about the children," Azizi said as he broke into a run for the temple. "They are easy prey for Kaphiri's talons."

Amsi followed his friend down the road. When they turned the corner towards the temple, the pharaoh's chariot raced through the street. Azizi darted into an alley and pulled Amsi behind a pile of rubble.

The teens hid behind the pile of wood and ash. The boys held their breaths as the pharaoh's chariot stalled.

Amsi swallowed nervously as the horses stomped their hooves impatiently.   Azizi felt a bead of sweat creep down his neck as a wave of dizziness threatened to overcome him.   A wave of fatigue made his body relax against his will.   Azizi gripped his hair tightly. *What is happening to me?* Azizi looked at the blisters on his skin. *It's the illness. The scorpion's venom must have speeded the disease.* "Amsi, I don't have much time."

Amsi put his arm around Azizi and raised his head, ready to react should the pharaoh charge towards them.   Azizi and Amsi tensed as they heard the pharaoh step from his chariot.

"My lord, what is it?" a timid voice asked.

"Stay there, Neka. I thought I saw a rat."

Azizi and Amsi tensed as they reached for their weapons. Amsi looked at his white cape in horror. *I gave us away!*   Azizi gripped the hilt of his dagger as his breath came in sharp gasps. Amsi kept his eyes focused beside the pile of ash. *Glorious Rā, protect us.*

The sharp sound of steel drawing from a metal sheath made both teens tense.

"I thought you were dead, Amsi Al-Sakhir. Stand up from behind that rubble."

Amsi nodded to Azizi and stood up slowly with his sword drawn. "What do you want?"

"I will be the one asking the questions here, traitor!" Runihura snarled. "You have nerves of steel to show your face around Heliopolis. Your father is rather anxious to see your corpse."

Amsi narrowed his eyes at Runihura. "You have corrupted my father's mind with your bigotry! Your magic has wooed him into believing all of your sick, demented lies!" Amsi barked angrily at the pharaoh. "My father would never want me killed! What did you tell him for him to command my death?"

"It's his disappointment in you and your actions that have condemned you to death, Amsi. It was not I who had introduced you to that street thief. It was not I who caused you not to live up to your father's expectations." Runihura grinned. "You have just become one, never-ending disappointment to your father and to your station. You are better than to consort with filth."

Azizi gripped the hilt of his dagger and stood beside Amsi. He pointed the dagger in front of him. "You are one to speak of filth, pharaoh! You yourself give the word 'filth'a bad name."

Runihura's golden eyes widened. "Azizi Keket? No! You were supposed to be dead! Gahiji slaughtered you!"

Azizi chuckled. "I am very much alive, Great Pharaoh. I have sworn on Osiris'name that I would defeat you and end your tyranny."

"We shall both die together, Azizi, for I will be taking you with me into the Hall of Judgment! Neka! Guards! Come!"

Azizi grabbed Amsi's arm and pulled him away from the pharaoh's sword. "Quick! The temple!"

"The scroll at Kadesh said we had to 'tame the lion-goddess.'"

"Kill them both! I command you!"

Azizi turned his head to see soldiers chasing them with their swords drawn. "He doesn't look so tame to me!"

Amsi blocked a soldier's sword from slicing toward Azizi's head as they emerged from the alley. Azizi stabbed into the man's thigh and pulled him off the horse. Azizi mounted the white horse and pulled Amsi behind him.

"Kill them! Don't let them get away!" Runihura growled.

Amsi wrapped one arm around Azizi and struck at the guards with his weapon. The Noble teen sliced through a mounted guard who had intercepted them at the end of another street.

A group of soldiers raced towards them, firing their arrows and trying to throw daggers towards them. Azizi nudged the horse into a full gallop to the Temple of Hapi. Amsi jumped from the horse's back as Azizi climbed off the saddle. The teens raced up the steps and into the temple.

Amsi grabbed the wooden bar and sealed the temple door shut. Amsi panted heavily as he leaned against the door. "That was close."

Azizi kneeled on the floor as the light from above glowed upon him. "Amsi, we have to break that circlet." The thief fell forward on his hands, struggling for air.

Amsi rushed to Azizi's side and helped his friend to his feet. "Just a little longer, Aziz. Come with me."

Amsi lead Azizi into the main hall of the temple. A statue of Hapi, the Nile God, stood within his shrine. Torches beside the altar flickered. Amsi's eyes scanned the murals of Isis painted on the wall.

"Quick, look for evidence of the Circlet!"

"The priests of Horus kept the Eye locked in a box."

Amsi looked at the sanctuary of Hapi. "Wooden box."

Azizi slowly walked to the altar and leaned on it. His palm rested against the sanctuary. "It's sycamore wood, favored by Isis."

Amsi raised his sword. "Stand back, my friend!"

Azizi leaned against a nearby pillar, his face covered in a thick veil of sweat. "Amsi."

"Hold on, Aziz! I'll cure you!"

Amsi closed his eyes. *Please forgive me, Mother Isis. I must save Azizi.* Amsi's sword sliced through the wood as a golden circle with red, blue, and green jewels fell from the box. The Circlet of Isis rolled off the altar and tapped against Azizi's bare foot.

The thief fell to his knees and reached for the artifact with trembling hands. Azizi held the Circlet of Isis in his hands. A winged Isis stretched her wings across the front of the circlet.

Azizi quietly chuckled as he looked at the glittering, golden object in his hands. "Amsi, we can save the lives of everyone affected by the Red Fever! Quick, recite the chant!"

Amsi grabbed the scroll from his hide bag.

Divine Mother Isis, who gives the gift of Breath

Shall save her children from Osiris'Grip of Death

The Circlet of Isis resides in city divine

City of the Sun, Temple of Water, Cut in twine

Break the Circle and Illness fight

Beware the sting of Sekhmet's bite.

The Circlet of Isis shimmered brightly in the torch light. "Now we have to break it," Amsi said, holding his two swords in his hands.

A large blast from the reception hall echoed through the Temple as Pharaoh Runihura burst through the wood.

"I think we have company, my friend," Azizi said as his right hand began to convulse.

Runihura stood in the doorway to the main hall and glared at the teens. "You are both trapped. There is no escape."

"It's two against one, pharaoh," Azizi said, holding his dagger in front of him. "I would say the odds are not in your favor."

Amsi held his sword in front of him. "Do you wish to risk your life fighting us?"

Pharaoh Runihura chuckled low in his throat. "You would once again desecrate this holiest of sanctuaries for a taste of revenge? If you wish to shed my blood, Amsi Al-Sakhir, son of Kaemwaset, then be my guest."

Amsi raised his swords slowly above his head, his eyes glaring angrily at the pharaoh. "You corrupted my father's mind against me!" Amsi growled as his hands began to shake.

Pharaoh Runihura grinned as the golden Eyes of Horus glittered in the dim torch light. "I am yours to kill, Amsi."

Amsi's eyes widened as he heard the pharaoh's voice within his mind. *I am not your enemy, Amsi. Your father who stands beside you is your enemy. He has signed your death warrant.* Amsi lowered his head and gasped as he felt his willpower slipping. Amsi dropped one of his swords as his body trembled.

Azizi watched Amsi lower his sword and cover his forehead in pain. "Amsi?"

You think you could escape my powers? *Your loyalty to your friend may be strong, but the anger you bear for your father is a far easier manner of controlling your mind.* Amsi winced as he heard the pharaoh's voice echo through his mind.

"Azizi….run."

The pharaoh's voice continued. *You are nothing more than a puppet to be manipulated by your father.* *Your father has caused the death of so many close to you.* *Remember Issâm, the old priest of Thoth? You watched your father beat him.*

"Issâm, why?" Amsi whispered as he felt a tear crawl down his cheek. Azizi watched Amsi raise his head and scream into the air.

"You leave him alone, you coward!" Azizi lunged towards the pharaoh.

Amsi held out his sword and blocked Azizi's strike.   The teen turned his head towards Azizi and growled viciously. Amsi's eyes and his mouth glowed with a bright, yellow light.

The teen thief stared with surprise and horror into the eye-less holes of his friend's face.   "Amsi! It's me!"

Amsi raised his sword and struck towards Azizi's side. "You murderer!"

Azizi grabbed Amsi's wrist and held onto it tightly. "Snap out of it!"

"You killed Jinan! You hurt Issâm! I won't let you tell me how to live my life anymore!"

Amsi snapped a punch towards Azizi's chest, but the thief's grip remained on his wrist. "Now you want me dead, too? I'm your son!"

Azizi winced at the pain in his chest. "I'm not your father!"

Amsi spit into Azizi's face. "You're not worthy to be my father!"

Amsi grabbed Azizi's wrist and threw Azizi into a nearby pillar.

Runihura crossed his arms casually. "I do not need to lay a finger on you to kill you, Azizi Keket. I'll let you die by the hand of the Anointed Companion of Rā."

Azizi watched as Amsi chuckled in front of him. "That just shows what a true coward you really are, Great Pharaoh."

"Finish him, Al-Sakhir."

I can't control myself! Amsi lunged toward Azizi and grabbed his friend's cloak as he dodged. Azizi kicked behind him, hitting Amsi in the stomach. Amsi leaned forward as Azizi brought his fist down upon Amsi's back. The Noble teen fell to the ground.

Azizi turned toward Runihura and grabbed Amsi's sword. "Now we fight like men."

"You are nothing more than a boy, Azizi," Runihura said, grabbing his club.

Azizi slowly approached Runihura with his dagger and sword in front of him. "I will avenge my parents."

Runihura grabbed a shield behind his back and grinned. "Prepare to die, child."

Azizi and Runihura's weapons clashed within the sanctuary. Sparks flew as Amsi's sword struck hard against Runihura's shield.

"Only a coward hides behind a shield," Azizi said as he raised his arm to block the club.

"Tough talk for one who is about to die." Runihura's club struck Azizi's shoulder, making the thief yelp.

Azizi narrowed his eyes and punched the pharaoh. The thief seized the opportunity to tackle the pharaoh onto his back. Runihura's shield and club flew across the floor and crashed against the pillar. Azizi grabbed the pharaoh's wrists and pinned them to the floor.

"This is for my parents!" Azizi raised his hand and punched the pharaoh viciously in the face. "You are a butcher!" Amsi punched the pharaoh across the jaw again, making the king's head snap to the side.

Runihura kicked his leg upwards and forced Azizi to lose his balance. Runihura tossed Azizi off him and crawled towards his lost weapon.

Amsi rose to his feet and saw Azizi pursuing Runihura. The Noble teen raced to Azizi's side and kicked Azizi in the ribs. Azizi fell to his side with a grunt of pain and wrapped his arms around his sides as Amsi smashed his foot against Azizi's ribcage. *Azizi, I'm sorry. I can't control myself!*

The thief winced in pain as Amsi grabbed his hair and kicked Azizi in the throat. Amsi watched with a grin as Azizi grabbed his throat and laid on the ground coughing up blood and gasping for air.

Runihura rose to his feet and looked down at Azizi with a grin. "Nice job, Amsi. Perhaps you are loyal to your people. There is one way to convince them of your allegiance."

Azizi felt tears creeping down his cheek as the pharaoh stepped over him and grabbed the sword on the ground. "Amsi, listen to me," Azizi gasped for air. "You are not like him.   You are not cruel of heart. Look inside yourself to see who you truly are."

The pharaoh's foot struck Azizi's back as the thief laid on the ground. "You are wasting your final breath, Azizi."

Azizi looked into Amsi's glowing eye-sockets. "Amsi is not a waste."

Runihura stepped over Azizi again and handed the sword to Amsi. "Kill your friend."

Amsi looked at the sword and reached for it with trembling hands. *No, I don't want to kill him!*

Amsi took the sword slowly from the pharaoh. He looked down at the thief holding his ribs and coughing. Azizi laid his head weakly upon the ground.

The plague and his wound from the temple is overwhelming him. He *needs medicine.*

Amsi kneeled before the pharaoh and leaned on his right knee. "My pharaoh, may I please-." Azizi watched as Amsi closed his eyes tightly. His friend's grip on the hilt of the sword intensified.

"Fight him, Amsi," Azizi groaned as he rolled onto his back. "I know you can fight him. I have faith in you!"

You can't fight me. You cannot win, Runihura said within Amsi's mind. Runihura watched as the thief coughed and began to struggle for breath. *You cannot fight the grip I have upon your mind, Noble Amsi.*

"I can't…hurt…Azizi," Amsi growled as he kneeled before the pharaoh.

"Kill him, Al-Sakhir. Kill your friend and prove your loyalty to your people and your motherland."

Azizi rolled over on his stomach and pushed himself to his knees. With quivering legs, he rose to his feet.

Runihura's attention was stolen from the Noble teen. "You must enjoy pain, thief. Why else would you stand before me ready to battle? You are hardly in a condition to challenge me again."

Azizi held his side as he staggered toward the Circlet. Runihura narrowed his eyes and quickly kicked the staggering thief to the ground. Amsi saw the pharaoh return before him. Azizi laid face-down on the temple sanctuary floor. His sides burned from Amsi and Runihura's attack. His face glittered with sweat from the illness.

"Al-Sakhir, you will obey me! Kill that insolent boy!"

"No! I won't kill him!" Amsi exclaimed.

Azizi and Runihura looked at Amsi, who stabbed his sword through his right foot. Amsi screamed loudly in pain as his foot began to bleed. The Noble teen trembled with agony as the blade pierced through his flesh and bone.

Runihura growled at Amsi and slapped the sword away from Amsi. Runihura gripped Amsi's cape and shook him angrily. "You fool! Look at what you did!"

Amsi glared at Runihura with his furious eyes. The bright lights had disappeared from his mouth and eyes. "I will fight you with every ounce of strength I have, pharaoh!" Amsi punched the pharaoh in the face.

Runihura released Amsi and staggered back. "You ignorant fool!"

Amsi grabbed the sword and rushed toward Azizi. He kneeled beside his friend and put his hand on Azizi's back. "I'm sorry, my friend."

"We must break….the Circlet of Isis, Amsi," Azizi struggled to say as he crawled toward the circlet laying on the ground.

Amsi raised his eyes to see the pharaoh hovering above them and striking his sword to behead the thief. Amsi's sword blocked the pharaoh's strike as he rose to his feet.

"This will be a test of all that Gahiji has taught you."

Amsi kicked the pharaoh in the stomach and brought his sword down upon the pharaoh's head. Runihura dodged backward and returned the strike towards his foe. The sword sparked against the pillar. The Noble's foot burned as it trickled blood onto the temple floor.

Azizi watched as Amsi and Runihura's swords clashed. Runihura swung at Amsi's head, but the Noble ducked. *I must break the Circlet of Isis.* Azizi crawled toward the golden circlet and gasped for breath. With trembling hand, the thief reached for the circlet on the ground. The thief coughed onto the ground, forming a tiny pool of blood beneath him. *I'm running out of time.*

Amsi kicked the pharaoh's leg, making him lose his balance. "Time to send you to Osiris!" When Amsi's sword struck towards Runihura's right eye, the blade shattered into pieces.

Amsi's eyes widened in surprise as he looked at the hilt of his sword. *What kind of magic is this?*

Runihura chuckled as he gripped his sword. "I am impervious to your weapons by the grace of Horus."

"No, this can't be!"

Runihura grabbed Amsi's white cape and placed the tip of the sword near Amsi's left eye. "Let us see if Horus protects your eyes."

"Pharaoh!" Azizi called from across the room.

Runihura and Amsi looked at the thief standing over the Circlet of Isis. Azizi gasped for breath as he gripped Amsi's second sword in his hand.

Runihura laughed. "So, Azizi, you're going to waste your last moment of life trying to die a Noble death?"

"I won't let you win!" Azizi growled. "This ends now!"

Amsi watched as Azizi struck the Circlet of Isis on the ground. A bright, hot light filled the room as Amsi's sword struck the holy relic.

Runihura dropped his sword and released Amsi. His scream raised and echoed through the sanctuary walls.   Fire-hot air licked his eyes as scalding heat surrounded him.

Amsi covered his eyes with his cape and hands as the temperature in the room spiked. Through the pharaoh's nearby screams, he heard the clanging of metal near the circlet.

Amsi's nose winkled at the bitter smell of smoking flesh. The Noble teen fell to his knees as his white cape protected him from the light and heat.

"Azizi!"

The bright light faded within the room and the air had cooled. Amsi peeked from under his cape and found the pharaoh had fled.   He saw Azizi's legs from behind a pillar. "Azizi!"

Amsi limped towards his friend and saw the circlet broken in half at his feet.   The Noble teen kneeled beside his friend and touched Azizi's neck.   "Azizi, wake up," Amsi said as he brought Azizi's upper body into his arms. Amsi moved Azizi's cape aside and saw the red patches and boils gone.   "Praise be to the Great Mother!" Amsi took Azizi's hand and saw the pus-filled blisters had dried.   "The power of the gods is great!"

Azizi took a deep, sharp breath and opened his eyes. His chest rose and fell rapidly as he caught his breath. "Amsi?"

Amsi smiled and hugged Azizi tightly. "You're alive!"

"Is the Circlet of Isis broken?"

Amsi reached for the broken item and showed Azizi. "The pharaoh cannot wear it now. Look, my friend, your skin no longer riddles with disease!"

Azizi looked at the back of his hands with wonder and amazement. "I can't believe it!"

Amsi winced at the pain in his foot and released Azizi. The thief saw the Noble teen sit on the floor and wince at the pain. Azizi tore a piece of material from his skirt and wrapped Amsi's foot.

"I will take you to Aneksi. She will help dull the pain," Azizi said standing beside Amsi.

Amsi shook his head sadly. "I almost killed you."

"You didn't succeed, did you? I'm sure she will be surprised to see both of us, my brother," Azizi offered his hand to Amsi with a smile.

Amsi slowly took Azizi's hand and rose to his feet. Azizi grabbed the Circlet of Isis and supported Amsi toward the temple entrance. Their eyes winced at the sunlight surrounding them. People were cheering and raising their hands towards the sun in praise.

"Our wounds have been cured!" the people chanted. "The pharaoh's intervention with Hapi has cured our wounds!"

"What? The pharaoh didn't cure them!" Amsi exclaimed.

Azizi's eyes scanned the crowd. "Where did the pharaoh run?"

"He ran like a coward," Amsi groaned.

"We'll chase him until there's nowhere left to hide," Azizi said as the teens descended the temple steps.

Carim spotted from his hiding space beside the temple. "He's alive! My king!"

Azizi and Amsi turned to see Carim stepping from the shadows. Carim placed his hands on Azizi's shoulders. "My lord, you have returned! Everyone thought you had died!"

Azizi raised a curious eyebrow. "Who said I was dead?"

"The pharaoh held your body to the assembled crowd and proceeded to stab your corpse!" Carim kneeled before Azizi. "Osiris has blessed you with a second life."

"I was never dead, Carim," Azizi said.

"You came close to death, though," Amsi quickly interjected.

Azizi looked around the cheering crowd. "This is not the best place for a reunion. My friend needs help for his wound."

Carim nodded and rose to his feet. "I will escort you to Aneksi. Seth Clan members have been taking liberty to raid our quarter in your absence."

Amsi limped beside Carim and kept a vigilant eye on the crowd. "How did your clan fare in our absence?"

Carim sighed as he gripped the hilt of his scimitar. "Poorly."

Azizi grit his teeth as he thought of Kahla, Maysun, and Tabora. "They won't get away with this."

"Kaphiri knew Azizi had gone and they seized their opportunity to strike at the weakest members of our clan."

Carim, Azizi, and Amsi turned the corner where Halimah stood guard. A momentary smile on the woman's face expressed her elation that Azizi had survived his journey.

Carim knocked on the door as Darwishi opened the little window. "Our king has returned, Darwishi."

Darwishi quickly opened the door and stared at Azizi as if he were a ghost. "You-you are dead!"

"Do I look dead to you?" Azizi asked casually as he stepped past the guard.

Amsi followed Azizi through the threshold and found Aneksi weeping beside the fire. Aneksi raised her head slowly to see Azizi supporting Amsi on his uninjured foot. The woman's bottom lip quivered as her eyes widened in shock and surprise.

"Azizi!" Jamila exclaimed as she threw herself at the other teenager. Jamila's arms tightly wrapped around Azizi's body as she sobbed. "You're not dead!"

Azizi put his arm around her and pat her back. "No, I'm not dead."

Aneksi rose to her feet slowly as she walked around the fire to the two teens. "I cannot believe my eyes. You have returned!"

Jamila released Azizi as Aneksi approached the King of Thieves. Aneksi cupped Azizi's face in her hands and caressed his cheek with her thumb. "My precious boy has returned," Aneksi whispered as she leaned forward and kissed Azizi's forehead tenderly. "My heart rejoices."

"It's good to be home, Aneksi, but Amsi needs his foot mended."

Aneksi looked at Amsi's foot which was bleeding through the material. "Sit him down. We need to sterilize the wound."

Azizi helped Amsi to sit on the ground and turned to Jamila sitting beside Giladi. Giladi's arms were wrapped around himself as he rocked himself in Jamila's arms. The boy pulled at his side-lock of youth and stared wide-eyed into an invisible horrific scene before him.

Azizi kneeled beside Giladi and placed his hand on the boy's shoulder. Giladi jumped and snuggled closer into Jamila's arms. Giladi buried his face into Jamila's breast and shook his head, shivering.

"Giladi, it is I, Azizi. Look at me."

"He saw a woman trampled to death by people fleeing Kaphiri's raid, Azizi," Jamila said, holding her friend. "He has not spoken one word since that night."

Azizi slowly reached for Giladi's head and caressed the boy's scalp comfortingly. Giladi screamed in terror into Jamila's chest. "Tell me what happened, Jamila."

"Hold him still, Darwishi," Aneksi said as she placed a poker in the fire.

"What are you going to do with that?" Amsi asked as Darwishi grabbed his arms.

Jamila held Giladi tightly. "Kaphiri's clan came and they raided shops, stealing bread and setting the buildings ablaze when they had taken their fill. They ran through the streets, cutting people down and proclaiming the glory of Seth."

"I think my foot feels better already, Aneksi!"

"The pain will be temporary," Aneksi said softly.

Azizi heard Amsi scream and smelled flesh burn as Aneksi burned Amsi's foot to staunch the wound and kill infection.

"Pharaoh's soldiers flocked through the quarter. It was nothing but chaos," Jamila said. "Giladi tried to protect me from Ini-Herit that night."

Aneksi turned to Azizi. "Giladi killed Ini-Herit."

Amsi winced at the pain in his foot. "How?"

"Giladi strangled him," Jamila said.

"I've never seen Giladi so distraught," Azizi said. "What about the others?"

Aneksi sat beside the fire. "Saqr and Khalil have been captured by Kaphiri's clan."

Azizi jumped to his feet and clenched his fists. "What?"

"Saqr and Khalil are being held for ransom by Kaphiri."

Amsi gasped. "What are their demands?"

"The surrender and diffusion of the Thief Clan Osiris."

Azizi narrowed his eyes. "I'm not giving up our territory without a fight!"

"Aziz, they are children!" Amsi exclaimed. "Give them what they want!"

"Those children are as good as dead as long as they remain in the grip of the Seth Clan," Azizi said. "We must get them back."

Amsi struggled to his feet after Aneksi dressed his wound. "I will offer them any amount of money to save them."

"Leave the Seth Clan to me. You have your own battle to fight, Amsi."

Darwishi bowed before Aneksi. "Allow me to take Master Amsi to his home."

Amsi raised his eyebrows in surprise. *What did he just call me?*

Azizi placed his hands on Amsi's shoulders. "My clan needs me now, Amsi. Darwishi will take you home."

"Will you be alright?"

Azizi nodded. "My family requires my attention. Your family requires your presence." Azizi kissed Amsi's cheeks. "You have done well."

Amsi returned the friendly gesture. "You will always be my brother, Azizi. May Rā bless you."

Azizi held the broken circlet in his hands. "I will ensure the pharaoh never finds this." Azizi watched Amsi leave the hut. He looked into the fire, his eyes and blood burning with similar flames of fury. "Vengeance shall be mine!"

*   *   *

Darwishi helped Amsi off his horse. "You have returned our king safely to us. You have my gratitude."

Amsi crossed his arms. "Does this mean you will begin to treat me as an equal?"

"It means that I need not sneak into your bedroom while you sleep and slit your throat. You live another day."

"It's nice to see you again, too, Darwishi."

The tall, muscular man mounted his horse and rode away.

I wonder if my father will give me a similar greeting. Amsi walked onto the family lands and heard Baruti singing in the fields with Laila and Meskhenet.

Meskhenet raised her head when she heard footsteps along the path. "Master Amsi! Father! Our Lord has returned!"

Baruti and Laila raised their heads and dropped their tools. "Master Amsi!"

Amsi watched his slaves bow before him. Laila threw her arms around Amsi and held him tightly. Amsi returned the embrace. "It's nice to see all of you!"

"Your father told us you were dead!"

Amsi sighed. "That's what Azizi and I were told by his clan."

"Your mother will be very happy to see you," Baruti said. "Nassar and Nakia will welcome you with open arms."

"How is my mother?"

"Go to her, Amsi," Baruti said. "Joy will return to her heart when she sees you."

Amsi tried to walk on his injured foot, but winced in pain as he did so. *Mother must have been saddened to hear that I was dead. I can only imagine the lies my father had told her about my death. I hope my father has not mistreated her in my absence.*

Amsi opened the front door and encountered an eerie silence. Hairs on the back of his neck stood on end as he could feel tension in the air.

Amsi slowly walked down the hallway towards his mother's quarters. His eyes wandered to the murals on the walls exhibiting cracking. A piece of plaster was missing from one of his ancestor's arms as if someone's head collided with the wall. Similar cracks lined the other murals along hallway giving evidence of bodily impacts.

Amsi heard muffled crying from behind his mother's door. Amsi turned the handle on the door and slowly opened it. His mother sat beside the window, crying into her hands.

"Mother?"

Imani raised her head and covered her mouth in surprise. "Amsi? Is that you, my child?"

Imani jumped to her feet and raced towards Amsi. Amsi held his crying mother tightly as she hugged him. "My son! My boy is alive! Praise be to Rā for answering my prayers!"

"Mother, I was worried about you!"

"I never thought I would see you again!"

Imani kissed Amsi's cheek and caressed his bald head. "Rā has given me back my baby," Imani whimpered as she kissed his cheek again.

"Where is father?"

Imani slowly pulled back from Amsi and wiped a tear from her eye. "Kaemwaset is at the home of Ipa-witu."

"Is he trying to buy more land?"

"No, my son. Your father and I-."

"You!"

Amsi and Imani turned towards the doorway where Kaemwaset seethed in fury. "What are you doing here, traitor?"

Amsi narrowed his eyes. "I am your son!"

"You are a disgrace to my family!"

Amsi pointed an accusatory finger at Kaemwaset. "Gahiji told me all about you! How did it feel to sign the death warrant for your own son?"

Imani gasped. "Kaemwaset Al-Sakhir! Is this true?"

Kaemwaset narrowed his eyes at his son. "You are upsetting your mother, boy!"

"It's about time she finds out what a snake she married," Amsi growled.

Kaemwaset flew towards Amsi and grabbed his son by the throat. Amsi punched his father's stomach angrily as Amsi crashed against the wall. He winced as his foot burned with pain.

Imani rushed toward Amsi and grabbed Kaemwaset's arm. "You leave our son alone, Kaemwaset!"

Kaemwaset narrowed his eyes at Imani and pulled his right hand from Amsi's throat.   With a swift motion, he slapped his wife across the face, sending her to the floor.

"Mother!"

Kaemwaset raised his hand and punched his son across the face angrily. Amsi fell to the ground beside his mother. Amsi closed his eyes as his cheek burned.   His arm was draped over his mother's legs as his father hovered over them.

"You will keep your lips silent about this, both of you," Kaemwaset growled.

Amsi crawled to his mother nearby and held her in his arms.

"You are no longer my wife, Imani. Amsi, you and your mother are my property. I consider it an act of mercy keeping you under my roof for you would starve to death without my compassion!"

Amsi held his mother in his arms and glared at the heavy-set man standing over him. "You don't know the meaning of compassion," Amsi winced in pain. "You beat your own son and your wife. How is that showing compassion?"

"Hold your tongue, boy, before I remove it," Kaemwaset growled. "You both belong to me and don't you forget it!" Kaemwaset left the room, slamming the door behind him.

Amsi looked sadly down at his mother and wiped away a trickle of blood coming from her mouth. His body trembled as he held his unconscious mother in his arms.

From the hallway, he could hear Kaemwaset yelling at Qamra to bring him his jug of wine.

Why would he strike my mother and I? My father is full of rage and hatred. I want to take my mother far from here. If only we could grow wings like Isis and fly far away from here where we are free from my father's rage, my father's hate, and my father's wine flask.

Where would we go, my mother and I? I could strike my father down now and we would live happily. If mother and I left, the slaves would be at the mercy of my father. I want to free them, but legally, I cannot because I am not their legal owner yet.

Azizi's clan, his family, was happy to celebrate his return. My mother welcomed me home with welcome arms. Unfortunately, now I know the reason for the cracking on the murals. My father's use of his wine flask is becoming more frequent.

How could he strike my mother? How could he sign my death warrant? My mother and I are not property! Where would we go? I want to visit Zahra's camp, but I cannot leave my mother.

Amsi held his mother against him as tears crept down his cheeks. Amsi began to cry as he kissed his mother's forehead. *Mother, I'm sorry I couldn't protect you.*

XXX

The War Begins

Azizi sipped from the lake waters with his hand. The oasis'spring was cool, a distinct change from the heat of the blazing fire nearby. As he scooped more water into his right hand, it began to tremble again, spilling all the water back into the lake. The thief sighed with frustration. *I wonder how long it will take for the scorpion's toxin to leave my body. Maybe it's a small price to pay for surviving the creature's attack.*

The thief sat up and warmed his hands beside the fire. His dark eyes looked up into the starry night above. *Osiris couldn't have given me a better night.*

Azizi's hands went to the box that Aneksi had given him to hold the two new treasures. One of those treasures was for Kahla. The other was meant to be for his own.

The Circlet of Isis had melted with much resistance in the jeweler's kiln. Belen was the Clan's appraiser of stolen jewels, necklaces, and other accessory items. He told Azizi the metal had taken ten hours to melt in the fire. To access the powers of the Circlet of Isis, the pharaoh would need both rings. Belen told him changing the metal would not change the powers granted to the Item.

Azizi heard two horses approaching in the night. The thief grabbed his sword and shifted towards the brush to surprise his assailants.

Aneksi and Kahla emerged from the brush cautiously. "Azizi Keket?"

Azizi breathed a sigh of relief and shifted closer to the fire. "Thank you for bringing Kahla here, Aneksi."

Aneksi bowed her head. "I brought you more medicine and unguents for your chest. How are you feeling, my king?"

"I'm worried about Saqr and Khalil."

"Sekani is continuing his search with Qeb."

Kahla approached Azizi and sat beside him. "Thank you, Aneksi, for bringing me to him."

"I will be here to pick you up in the morning, Kahla. Goodnight, my boy."

Azizi smiled and bowed his head to his clanswoman. Azizi put his left arm around Kahla. "Do you think Mbizi will miss you tonight?"

Kahla shook her head. "No, we buried our friends this morning and now we have to replace them. Mbizi is too busy with that to oversee what we are doing. I think it's our first night off in ages."

"How fortunate for me!" Azizi turned his head and kissed Kahla on the lips. The teen and the woman closed their eyes as they moaned into the kiss.

Kahla raised her hands and caressed Azizi's curly black hair. A tear fell down her cheek as they kissed softly. Kahla opened her eyes and pulled from the kiss reluctantly. "I was so heartbroken to hear that you had died, my love. I didn't want to believe it was real."

Azizi raised his right hand and caressed her cheek lightly. "I would have died if it weren't for Amsi's diligent care. He could have left me behind in the crumbling catacombs." Azizi paused. "Amsi risked death to save my life. He bit into the tail of a scorpion, Kahla. How many people would do that to save another?"

Kahla looked at the wound in Azizi's chest. "I must tell him how I appreciate his sacrifice."

"I kept calling your name," Azizi said as he looked into the crackling fire. "Did you hear me?"

"I think I heard you in my heart. I asked everyone if they had heard news of your return."

Azizi removed his arm from Kahla and reached into his hide bag. He removed a small black pouch tied by a thin rope. "I found something that I thought you would like."

Kahla smiled as she timidly took the pouch from Azizi's hand. She slowly opened the pouch to remove a necklace with a gold chain. A green emerald was set in the middle of a silver sun. Kahla smiled. "Azizi, you shouldn't have! It's beautiful!"

"That's not all," Azizi said, taking the small box in his hand. The thief opened the box and revealed two gold rings.   He graciously took Kahla's right hand with his left. He slipped the ring onto her finger with a shaking hand.   "I love you." Azizi kissed the top of her hand. "That's also for you, Kahla, my future wife."

Kahla smiled as she hugged Azizi tightly. Another tear coursed down her cheek. "Thank you so much, Azizi. Your safe return is all I needed." She slipped the other golden ring onto his finger. Kahla kissed his hand. "I love you, Azizi Keket."

Azizi leaned forward and kissed his lover again. Kahla wrapped her arms around Azizi and laid on the ground. The thief smiled down at her and slowly lowered his head to kiss her again.

*   *   *

Kaphiri paced before the blazing fire with his arms behind his back. Curtains blocked much of the sunlight from entering the sparsely decorated room. A table surrounded by six elegantly decorated chairs stood near the corner of the room.

Marid poked his dagger through the chicken cage, making the blind-folded, gagged captive squeak in fear. A playful chuckle was quickly followed by the dagger poking the prisoner's rib again with the tip of the blade.

Kaphiri looked at the prey bound with its hands tied behind its back. The child breathed heavily as it felt the blade poke against his arm. Saqr bounced in the cage, hitting his head against the metal bars. "Careful, Marid. We don't want our little prisoner to die of fear."

Kaphiri stepped towards the pair of chicken cages holding their two Osiris Clan prisoners. "We do not want their hearts to stop before we've had our fun."

Kaphiri kneeled before the panting, trembling child's cage. He reached between the bars and caressed the child's cheek. Tiny whimpers of fear escaped the quivering boy's throat as a tear slipped from under the blindfold.

"Now, calm yourself, child," Kaphiri whispered gently. "Be a good boy and do everything we say. Otherwise, we may give you a slower death than what we plan."

Saqr nodded quickly as he curled up into a fetal position within the cage.

Kaphiri smiled at caged prisoners and stood. "Make certain to feed them today, Marid. Pig fat will be good enough for them tonight."

Hairdar and Chakir entered the home and bowed before Kaphiri. "Great One, Azizi Keket is not dead! He has returned!"

"I thought he was dead!" Kaphiri growled and kicked Khalil's cage, making the bound child gasp through his gag. "No! *Iunu* was ours for the taking!" Kaphiri growled angrily.

"He may be alive, but we have one advantage over him and the Osiris Clan," Hairdar said. "The pharaoh wants to see our little prisoners and says he has an offer we can't refuse."

Kaphiri narrowed his eyes at Chakir. "Who told you he has returned?"

"Qasim was patrolling *Iunu* and he saw the pharaoh flee from the Temple of Hapi. Runihura was supposed to come here to see our little captives."

486

Chakir stepped near the fire. "The Great Pharaoh retreated toward his palace with burns across his body. Azizi and his friend emerged moments later."

Kaphiri kicked Khalil's cage again and stomped his foot angrily on the ground. "This will not stop us! If Azizi and his clan ever want to see these two boys alive, they will give in to our demands."

Chakir shook his head. "Azizi will not negotiate with us. He is determined to keep control of *Iunu*'s territory."

Kaphiri chuckled low in his throat as he stepped near the chicken cages. "Let his clan celebrate Azizi's return."

Saqr whimpered from his cage and begin to weep quietly. Khalil trembled in his cage as he struggled with the rope binding his wrists.

"We will not relent, my comrades," Kaphiri said as he grabbed his twin swords strapped to his belt. Kaphiri crossed the swords above his head. "Let the war between the Seth Clan and Osiris Clan begin!"

References for <u>The Circlet of Isis</u>

Budge, E.A Wallis, <u>The Egyptian Book of the Dead</u>, Dover Publications Inc: NY, 1967.

Lichtheim, Miriam, <u>Ancient Egyptian Literature Vol. 2: The New Kingdom</u>, Univ. of California Press: CA, 2006.

Lichtheim, Miriam, <u>Ancient Egyptian Literature Vol. 1: The Old and Middle Kingdoms</u>, Univ. of California Press: CA, 2006.

Spence, Lewis. <u>Ancient Egyptian Myths and Legends</u>, Dover Publications Inc: NY, 1990.

Additional Works

<u>Egyptian God Series</u>

#1 :<u>The Rise of Sekhmet</u>

#2: <u>The Circlet of Isis</u>

#3: <u>The Scepter of Osiris</u> (Coming Dec. 2013)